COUNTING FLOWERS

BETH ANDREWS

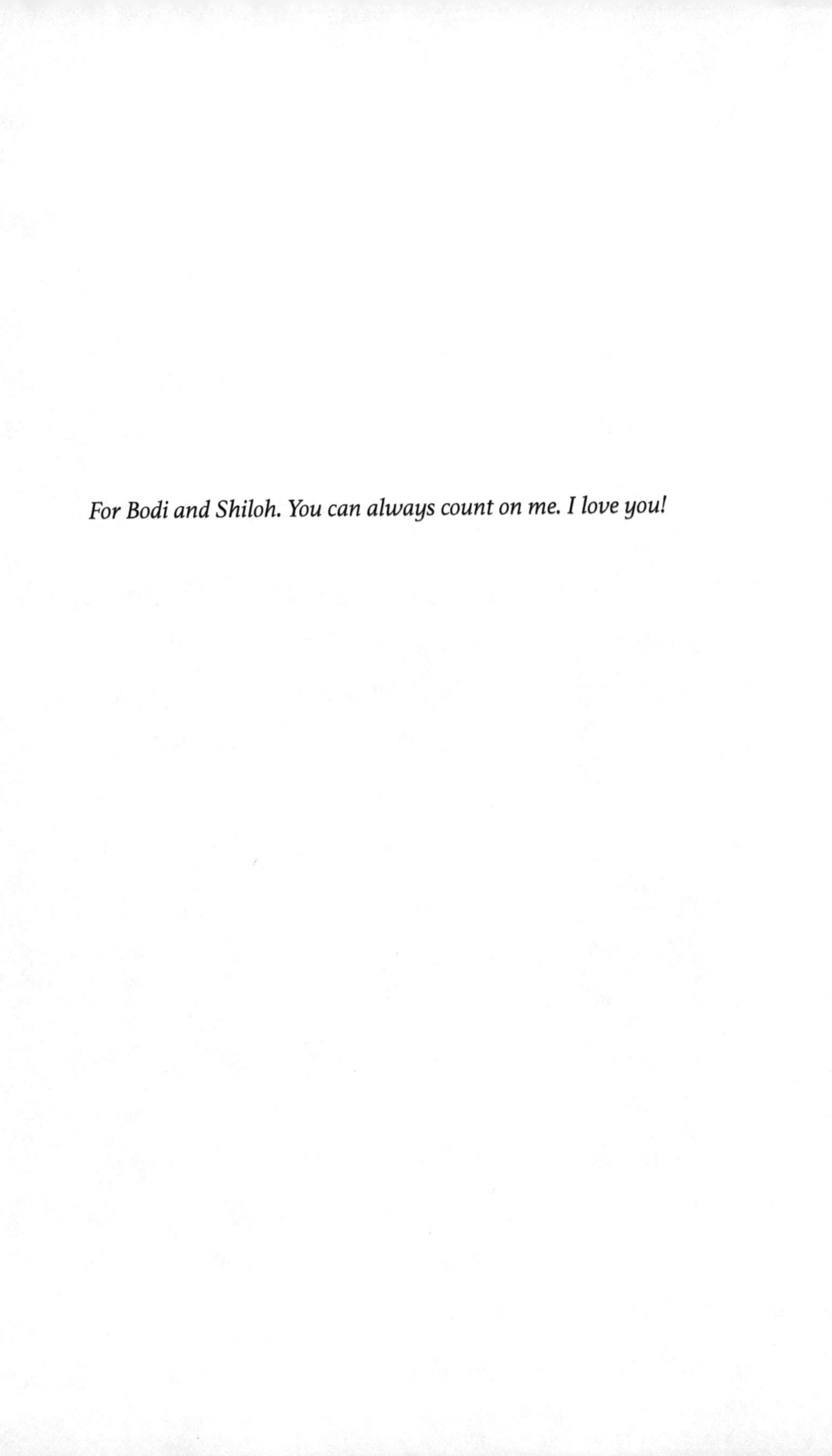

For Bodi and Shiloh. You can always count on me. I love you!

There are eighty-three flowers on my bedroom wall.

Not real flowers. They're in the mural my mom painted for me when I was twelve. It's a wild garden scene bursting with bright, vivid colors. It's the first thing I see when I wake up. The last thing I look at each night.

Eighty-three flowers.

I like to count them.

It started over three years ago when my family was going through a tough time. One night, unable to sleep and feeling anxious, I turned on the light and started counting. When I was done, I felt better. Calmer.

Comforted.

So I kept doing it. Counting them. It's soothing. The flowers are always there. I don't have to worry about them disappearing or withering and fading away. They won't drift apart from each other, or suddenly go from blue to orange, or shrink or grow without explanation.

They don't change. Ever.

Plus, I just like to count things. The flowers on my wall. The number of windows and doors and rooms in my house. How many songs play during the drive to school. Anything. Everything. I count, and I make lists. Written to-do lists broken down by month, week and day. Mental lists of silly things like everyone I know whose name starts with the letter M, or how many fruits and vegetables I can think of, or my class schedule each year of middle school.

I know it's unusual, but the counting, the lists, they're harmless habits. We all have them. We all have secrets.

This is mine.

I count, and I make lists.

It's no big deal. Some people hum incessantly. Others bite their nails. Or smoke. I'm hardly the first person to develop a few odd quirks. At least mine aren't annoying, unsanitary or unhealthy.

They're unique. Different.

And completely under control.

1

I WAKE UP FIVE MINUTES BEFORE MY ALARM, LIKE I DO EVERY DAY.

Rolling onto my side, I turn on the bedside lamp then grab my phone, unplug it and shut off the alarm before putting in my earbuds and selecting a Beyoncé song.

Like I do every day.

I prefer my mornings to proceed in a specific, organized way. And that specific, organized way starts with my listening to Beyoncé.

And no, Destiny's Child doesn't count. Neither do movie soundtracks or anything where she's the featured artist.

It has to be one of her songs from one of her albums. Period.

It's good luck, starting my day with Queen Bey.

Today's song is "Drunk in Love" and I turn up the volume before sitting up. Leaning back against the headboard, I stretch my arms overhead, yawn, then focus on the wall opposite me.

And I count the flowers there.

Like I do every morning.

I start at the light blue tulip in the top left corner—like I always do—then scan the wall, left to right, like reading a book. But when I get to the orange coneflower at the bottom right corner, I frown.

Eighty-two.

I've missed one.

Now I have to start again.

Crap.

There are eighty-three flowers in the mural on my wall, that is a given. I know this, I've counted them hundreds...thousands...of times. But I can't *not* count them again. Not because I want to.

I have to.

There's a knot in my chest, and a fluttering, unsettled feeling in my stomach. And neither will go away until I count the flowers and get eighty-three.

The song switches to "Goner" by Twenty-One Pilots and I kick off the covers and crawl to the bottom of my bed, then settle on my knees on the mattress.

And I count the flowers again, slower, more carefully, this time saying each number under my breath.

Eighty-three.

The knot loosens. The fluttering eases. But I'm not done. I repeat the process, this time in reverse order, starting at the orange cone-flower and ending with the light blue tulip, right to left, bottom to top. Up and up, side to side until finally, eighty-three.

Then I start again, this time counting color by color. Blue first (19), then purple (17), red and pink (14 and 14), yellow (11) and orange (8).

Eighty-three.

Once again, I reverse the order. Orange, yellow, pink and red, purple then blue. The blues aren't just blue, of course, they're aqua-marine and cobalt, navy and sapphire. The purples are violet, plum and mauve. Reds as bright as fresh blood and as dark and deep as a rose. Pinks both soft and neon. Sunflower yellows and golden oranges or a combination of the two, like the burst of colors in a sunrise. Melding like the warm glow of a sunset.

I keep it as simple as possible, though God knows I could make this even more complicated. But I fight the urge to break the colors down even further, consider it a personal victory that I'm able to do so.

Besides, it's not so much the counting or grouping that's important. It's the familiarity. The repetitiveness. The order to it.

Each time I reach eighty-three I'm able to breathe a bit easier.

But honestly, I hate that number. Eighty-three. Not only does counting and recounting that many flowers take up a good chunk of my time, the number itself makes me uneasy. You can't divide anything into eighty-three evenly. It drives me crazy.

Something I'm trying like to mad to avoid at all costs.

I could always ask Mom to paint another flower, but then I'd have to explain why I want the flower added. And while my mom gets me better than anyone else, and I hate keeping things from her, I can't tell her. It's embarrassing how often I perform this particular habit. How I can't start my day without it. That I can't fall asleep at night until it's done.

If Mom knew that, she might get the wrong idea. She might think it's a problem. Or worse, that there's something wrong with me.

So, nope. Not going to ask for another flower. Yes, eighty-four is a much stronger number and can be divided by so many other numbers evenly (2, 3, 4, 6 and 7) but if there were eighty-four flowers, I'd probably think of even more ways to drag out my flower counting. It might go from being a quirky, slightly OCD-ish habit into a full-blown obsession.

It's a shame, though. A new flower wouldn't take long to add, and it would make the entire mural better. I even have the perfect spot for it; on the left, about halfway up the wall between a pink rose and purple aster. Of course, the new flower would have to be blue because the number of colors increase by three—except between purple and blue.

And the fact that I'm thinking of this, that I've contemplated it, oh...once or twice or one hundred times before...makes me think I'm not doing all that well with the whole *avoid going crazy at all costs* thing.

Luckily, right now, my flower counting is still just a quirky, slightly unusual habit. One I can manage just fine, thanks all the same.

For the most part, at least.

To prove it, I get to my feet, determined not to start the entire process all over again. Afraid if I do, I'll be here all day, counting and recounting flowers, until my secret is revealed to the world.

Counting and recounting until I lose my ever-loving mind.

I'm not sure which would be worse.

Either one of them would put a damper on my senior year and I have too many plans, have set too many goals to let anything get in my way now.

I head toward my adjoining bathroom, a woman with places to go, things to do, and worlds to conquer. A woman in control of her thoughts. Her mind.

But not, it seems, in control of her body. Because as I walk past the mural, I can't help but trail my fingertips along the wall, tracing the edge of a butterfly. And imagine that perfect blue, eighty-fourth flower filling that tiny, empty space.

2

———————

After getting dressed, I call my brother Chase.

It rings about a hundred times then goes to voicemail.

Older brothers. Seriously, they are the bane of a girl's existence.

At least, mine is.

He's ignoring me. Has been for the past three days.

It's very annoying.

Yes, yes, he's got his hands—and time—full studying for his B.S. in Biochemistry and Molecular Biology at Penn State, but come on. He posted on Instagram last night, a picture of him with his arm slung around the shoulders of one of his look-alike frat buddies, identical, wide, toothy grins on their stupid handsome faces.

Red plastic cups in their hands.

He's obviously eked out a minute or two in his pursuit of a higher education for things like drinking with his pals—the last thing he should be doing. You'd think he could've found the time to answer one of the six calls I've made to him since Friday or responded to one of my texts. He knows we have plans to discuss and schedules to synchronize for Mom and Dad's twenty-fifth anniversary celebration next month.

Okay, so maybe all the planning has been taken care of. But that's only because I couldn't wait around for his input, which if I had to guess, would have been along the lines of him telling me whatever I decide is fine.

So I decided. Everything. I made reservations for all of us at their favorite restaurant in the city. Came up with the idea for their present, made that idea into reality, paid for and wrapped it. I bought a new dress and ordered him a new shirt and tie to be delivered to his apartment in State College because, even though there's plenty of time for him to do that himself, he won't. I even planned a brunch menu for the next day, just like the family brunches we used to have on Sunday mornings.

And it's not so much a celebration as a nice, quiet, intimate family dinner. Just Mom, Dad, Chase and Leah, his girlfriend, and me and Philip, my boyfriend.

But there are still a few things we need to go over, the biggest one being what time, exactly, he plans on getting into Pittsburgh. He needs to be at the restaurant at least twenty minutes early so he's there waiting to surprise Mom and Dad when we arrive.

With a sigh, I disconnect the call without leaving a message. God. You'd think I'd asked for one of his kidneys. After all the work I've done to make sure Mom and Dad's anniversary is special, the least Chase could do is give me just the tiniest bit of cooperation.

Since he hasn't and doesn't seem interested in doing so, I text Leah.

Hey! Trying to get a hold of Chase. Can you please tell him to call me? Thanks! Have a great day! Heart emoji. Blowing kiss emoji. Thumbs up emoji.

If anyone can get Chase to do something, it's Leah.

Actually, she's the only person who can get him to do things.

Must be nice. Having that much influence over someone.

Having someone love you that much.

I put my phone in my bag and go downstairs. When I step into the foyer, I see my parents in the kitchen. Dad at the far end of our large, farm table, hidden behind the morning paper, a light gray suit coat hanging on the back of the chair next to him. I don't need X-ray vision to know that he's wearing a crisp, white, dress shirt, a perfectly knotted tie in either blue or black, that his dark golden hair with its subtle threads of gray is purposefully rumpled, and his face clean-shaven. Not a nick, stray whisker or imperfection in sight.

Or allowed.

Mom sits next to him reading something on her phone, an open notebook at her elbow. Her hair, two shades lighter than my own blond thanks to monthly appointments with her hair stylist, is pulled back into a ponytail. Her face is free of makeup, which somehow makes her look even younger than usual—and people honestly mistake us for sisters as it is. She's in yoga pants and a loose, gray, long-sleeved top.

All is right in our world.

As usual.

The thing is, it's way too easy to forget how quickly *as usual* can turn into *as far from normal as possible*. But I haven't forgotten. It's always there, at the back of my mind, pushing and pushing at me to remember. To worry it'll happen again.

And that, unlike the last time, it'll be something that tears us apart for good. Something that changes all of us. Forever.

Which is why I'm so vigilante about doing anything and every-thing within my power to make sure that doesn't happen. Like lightly tapping the door frame.

Knocking on wood might not be a scientifically proven method for staving off a future disaster, but it can't hurt.

And at this point, I'll take all the help I can get.

Especially since I can't stop thinking about that red cup in Chase's hand.

"Good morning," I say as I step into the room, a bright, sunny smile on my face, my tone all sing-songy and chipper.

Hey, I know my role.

And I play it well.

Plus, playing the part of Little Miss Sunshine suits me. I *like* being happy and sweet and kind.

Like having people think of me that way.

"Good morning, Natalie," Mom says.

I bend to kiss her cheek but her phone buzzes and she turns away so I end up smooching air.

"Hello?" she says into the phone. "Yes, this is Kristin Hewitt." Standing, she shoots me a small, apologetic smile then crosses the kitchen to the hall, ponytail swinging, sneakered feet padding softly, her voice drifting away with her. "Thank you so much for returning my call, Ms. Fowler. I'm very interested in your art work..."

The art work is for Kaleidoscope, the store/art gallery she's opening downtown to sell and show local art and crafts. She came up with the idea the beginning of the year and has devoted pretty much every waking hour since to bringing what she calls her exciting new business venture to life.

Dad calls it her little hobby.

He's joking of course.

And smart enough to never say it in front of her.

Dad lowers the corner of his paper and gives me a smile. "Morning, princess."

"Good morning." I lean down and this time make contact with my parent's cheek, but something's not right. It takes me a good ten seconds to realize what is and when I do, my nose wrinkles. "You smell different."

"New cologne," he says.

"What was wrong with your old cologne?"

He raises his eyebrows. Either because I sound like an idiot, blurting out that question, or at how accusing I'd come across.

But really, a man can't just change his cologne like that. Especially when he's worn it for as long as I can remember.

"Nothing was wrong with it," he says. "But your mother thought it was time for a change." He tips his chin up to me, a clear invitation to take another whiff. "What do you think?"

What I think is that I like his regular cologne. Any time I smell it, I'm reminded of him.

Time for a change.

Ugh. That is such a dumb saying. Like there's a limit to how long someone can be a certain way.

I much prefer the old, reliable adage *if it isn't broke, don't fix it.*

Or mess with it in any way, shape or form.

I'm not big on change. I prefer things to be a certain way.

The way they've always been.

Life is easier when there's a plan to follow and a schedule to adhere to. Calmer when there's a place for everything and all those things are in their places. More comfortable when everyone acts how they've always acted.

Safer when you know what to expect.

Change one thing and you get a domino effect and suddenly, everything is different—and out of your control.

Talk about a nightmare.

I lean down again and sniff. It's not bad, exactly. It's just different. Not him.

"It's okay," I say. "But I like your old one better."

"Me, too. But your mother is worried I'm getting stuck in my ways."

"And new cologne is going to help you get unstuck?"

"I've long ago given up trying to figure out your mother's logic." He winks at me then lifts his coffee cup only to take a drink and grimace.

Dad hates lukewarm coffee.

"Here," I say, taking the half-empty cup, "let me get you some more."

I walk over to the coffee pot near the stove and fill his mug. When I set it in front of him, I notice the table is empty. No plate or bowl or silverware or food in sight. I check the time on the microwave. 7:03.

Dad always leaves for the hospital at 7:35 on Mondays.

"Did you eat?" I hear myself ask, like I'm his mother, making sure he has a healthy breakfast before sending him off to tackle his busy day.

He shakes his head. "I thought I'd grab something on my way into the city."

"I'll make you something," I tell him.

He frowns. Checks his watch. "Are you sure you have time?"

Not really, but if I eat my own breakfast on the drive to school, I should have time to fix his. "It's fine."

"You don't have to wait on me, kiddo."

"I know. I want to."

He pats my hand. "You're my good girl."

I flush pleasantly. It's the same thing he's said to me my entire life and I still love hearing it. So often being kind and polite and going that extra mile for others goes unnoticed. It's just expected. Especially from me.

It's nice being appreciated.

Turns out we're out of eggs, oatmeal, fruit and anything else resembling a healthy breakfast. Telling myself it's the thought that counts, I pop a bagel into the toaster. At least it's whole wheat so the man will get some fiber. When it's done toasting, I let it cool before spreading it with the last of the cream cheese.

Used to be, before Mom became obsessed with taking the small business world by storm, we never ran out of anything. There was always milk, coffee creamer, bread and bananas. She fixed Dad's breakfast every morning, cooked gourmet dinners every night and stocked up on necessities like she was preparing us for The End of Days.

Now we're lucky if she feeds us canned tomato soup and grilled cheese and if there's one lone roll of toilet paper in the house between the five bathrooms.

I'm setting the bagel in front of Dad when Mom comes in, no longer on the phone. She sighs the sigh of mother's everywhere— long, low and filled with disappointment. "Ben, you are perfectly capable of making your own breakfast."

"She insisted," he tells her with a wide-eyed, innocent expression.

"I'm toasting one for myself," I say, "and it's just as easy to do two as one."

"You're sweet to take care of your daddy that way. But don't let him fool you. He's not helpless." She slides Dad a raised-eyebrow look. "With some practice, he could probably learn how to operate the toaster and use a butter knife."

"Operate," Dad repeats with what can only be described as a guffaw. "She said *operate*," he explains to me when I don't fall on the floor, convulsed with laughter. "And I'm a surgeon."

I scratch the side of my nose. "Yeah. I got it."

Still chuckling, Dad wipes a tear of laughter from his eye. "Operate. Surgeon."

Mom and I exchange a look then both roll our eyes. But we're both grinning.

Dad's and their jokes. So dorky.

Mom takes a sip of her coffee then rinses her cup in the sink. "I'm meeting with my contractor at six so I might be late getting home tonight." She puts the cup into the dishwasher. "I'll pick up pizza on my way home."

"Can we do Mexican instead?" I ask as my bagel pops up in the toaster. I slather peanut butter on it right away so it gets all melty. "We had pizza twice last week."

"Sure." She gives me a quick hug. "Have a good day."

I lick peanut butter off the side of my thumb. "You, too."

On her way to the door, Mom stops by Dad's chair and the way he looks up at her, like she's his own personal bright, shining star... well...let's just say the peanut butter isn't the only thing getting all melty.

She lays her hand on his shoulder and leans down. He wraps his arm around her waist, his hand settled on her hip and says something only she can hear. With a nod she straightens and trails her fingertips along his jaw before giving him a soft kiss.

It's a relief, seeing them act the way they've always acted.

Gives me hope that at least one thing will never, ever change.

3

———————

HALF AN HOUR LATER, I'M SITTING IN MY JEEP IN THE PANOSES' driveway checking my reflection in the visor mirror while waiting for my best friend Astrid. My hair is driving me nuts. I straightened it but there's a wave on the right side, barely a ripple, really, but I can't leave it alone. I know it's there and I can't relax until it's fixed. Until it's perfect.

Except I keep smoothing it and smoothing it and smoothing it, but it refuses to flatten.

In fact, I'm making it worse. I keep going, though, determined to conquer that wave with nothing but the heat from my palms and the power of my will.

Astrid jumps into the Jeep and shuts her door. "Hey," she says, her dark brown, shoulder-length hair damp and air-drying. By mid-day it'll be huge, curly and starting to frizz.

And she'll own it like a freaking queen.

I smooth, smooth, smooth again.

She reaches over and flips my visor closed.

I open it.

Smooth, smooth, smooth...

"My mom says perfection is self-abuse of the highest order,"

Astrid informs me as she shuts the visor again. "You look great, so let's go." She snaps her fingers in quick concession—snap, snap, snap—like I'm a dog she's training to obey. "I want to talk to Coach Sherman before homeroom and if we don't leave, like, now, I'm not going to have time."

"You know how I feel about being snapped at."

She grins, wide and pleased and just a little bit evil. "Yep. Why do you think I do it?"

Rolling my eyes, I put the Jeep into Reverse and slowly back out of her driveway. "If you want to get to school earlier, you should consider riding the bus. I hear it's very punctual."

"Don't tempt me."

"Yes," I say, dry as sand. "Because riding on the school bus is so very, very tempting." I wait a beat. "Especially when it picks you up at...what time is it? Seven?"

"Six-fifty," she grumbles.

"I'm sorry. I didn't catch that."

She sighs. "I said the bus comes 'round this way at the ungodly hour of ten to seven."

"Ten to seven," I squeal, like it's some grand prize she's won. "Imagine! You'd never be late for school again."

Her mouth twitches but she fights a smile for all she's worth.

She's stubborn that way.

"You win," she says. "No more snapping."

"You know, what they say is so true. Victory really is sweet."

"Nice of you not to gloat."

I nod, all solemn and sincere. "That's because I'm a good friend."

Not that I want her to ride the bus. Even though her house is out of the way, I like having her ride with me to school. We don't have any classes together this year, or the same lunch period. And with me playing tennis, having dance lessons three nights a week and helping with the younger students at the studio after class Saturday morning, and her running cross country and working at her family's restaurant, we don't have a lot of time together.

I stop at the end of the driveway to let a car go by and tip my head toward the backseat. "I brought the shirt you wanted."

"Ooh, thank you." She turns and grabs my deep purple, peplum shirt. It looks great with her olive skin-tone and brings out her green eyes.

As I'm pulling forward down the street, Astrid unbuckles her seatbelt and strips down to her bra, flashing me, God and her elderly neighbor. She waves at him.

I stop at the stop sign. "Nice of you to give Mr. Lewis a thrill this morning."

"I do what I can," she says, tugging the shirt on then fastening her seatbelt once again. She doesn't check to make sure she didn't mess up her hair or smudge her mascara.

Must be nice.

Her phone buzzes and she checks the message, reads it with a huge smile then responds.

"Sean?"

"Uh huh."

She started talking to Sean Cambridge a few weeks ago when he came into her family's diner, The Fat Greek, for lunch. He graduated from our school last year and commutes to Robert Morris University.

I turn onto Winter Street. "How'd you do at yesterday's meet?"

Astrid is the cross-country team's number one runner and currently has offers from six colleges who want her to run for them next year.

She's typing on her phone. "Good."

"How's your grandma doing?" I ask. Her mom's mom has breast cancer and just started chemotherapy.

More typing. "Better."

"Are you joining the homecoming dance committee?"

No typing. But only because she's reading what must be Sean's response. "Hmm."

There's no sense me saying anything else. Though Astrid is sitting right next to me, she's gone. I've lost her.

Truth is, she started drifting away a year and a half ago when I started dating her twin brother.

I drum my fingers on the wheel. One...two...three...four...five. Five...four...three...two...one. One...two...three...four...five.

The longer I drive, the quieter it gets. It's like silence is pressing in on me, filling my head with pressure. I force myself to concentrate on the sound of the engine rumbling quietly, of the cars passing by. Of Astrid tap, tap, tapping on her phone.

We used to talk the entire drive from her house to school. We never even played music because we couldn't get through a song without one of us turning it down to say something, trying to fit a day's worth of conversation into one ten-minute car ride.

Now we don't.

Which is okay. I mean, I'm glad Astrid is talking to Sean. He seems like a nice guy and she deserves the best. Especially since she's never really had a serious boyfriend before—which is nuts as she's pretty, smart and fun.

So I don't call her out for the way she's ignoring me. If I say something, she might get the wrong idea. Like I'm jealous or something. I'm not. I want her to be happy. It's just that right now, I want her to be, you know...present. To answer my questions with actual responses instead of grunts and offer up her own topics of conversation. I want her to ask me about what's going on in my life.

Mostly, though, I want *us*, to stay the same.

Even if sometimes I'm afraid it's too late for that.

* * *

"Come on," Astrid says over her shoulder to me as we walk across The Fat Greek's parking lot. "And no dilly dallying once we're inside. I mean it. We're getting our coffee and bam—" she claps her hands. "—right back to the Jeep."

I pick up my pace. "It's not easy to jog in heels, you know."

Not to mention a rather snug mini-skirt.

She waits for me at the diner's front door, one hand on the

handle, the other on her hip. "Please, I've seen you run in heels twice that height."

"Once," I say, reaching her. "And that was an emergency."

A party we'd been at had gotten busted by the police.

Run? I'd done a full-on sprint for four blocks.

Opening the door, Astrid waits for me to go first, but I do a little wiggle/tug combination first, putting my skirt back to rights. I step inside to the scents of bacon, fried potatoes and toasted bread. Half the tables and booths are filled, and I stand next to the display case filled with homemade bread, muffins, scones and cinnamon rolls and search for Philip.

Astrid finds him first.

It's their twin-sense. They always know where the other is.

"Back there," she says, inclining her head toward the rear of the building. "Corner booth with his fan club. Five minutes," she warns me. "I mean it."

And she takes off toward the kitchen to see her dad.

I rise onto my toes to see the back corner and, sure enough, Philip is sitting in a booth surrounded by not one, not two, but five underclassman girls (three across from him, two on the same side), all brunettes, all pretty and all crushing hard on my boyfriend.

Fan club, indeed.

Philip catches my eye as I approach. I raise my eyebrows and he gives me a small shrug and an aw-shucks-what's-a-gorgeous-guy-to-do? embarrassed grin.

Yes, the poor boy. All the girls love Philip Panos.

Including me.

I try not to get upset when I find him, as I often do, surrounded by a bevy of flirting girls. It's not his fault they flock to him.

He's all sorts of pretty with dark, wavy hair, brown, soulful eyes and a soccer player's leanly muscled body.

I even cut the girls some slack. I understand, more than most, where they're coming from. Philip is hard to resist. Handsome and charming, he's a true prince among the other boys in our school. I can't blame them for hoping that one day, he'll leave me for one of them.

It'll never happen, of course, but who am I to take away their dreams?

And fighting about is a waste of time. Been there, done that—many, many times. Philip doesn't understand why it bugs me to see a bunch of pretty, hopeful girls flirt with him.

I don't get how he can be so freaking clueless.

For the most part, Philip and my relationship has been a smooth, steady ride—one going on two years now. Yes, we have our disagreements, but we always work through them. We're not in the constant break up/make up cycle so many other high school couples go through. We're solid and steady.

In part, because I've learned to choose my battles carefully.

"Hey," I say when I reach the booth.

Three of the five girls turn my way, two of them looking guilty, the third—Jessica Rettig, a junior whose greatest dream, it seems, is for me to somehow choke on my own spit and die—lifts her nose then turns away to gaze adoringly at my boyfriend.

"Hey, babe," Philip says with a swoon-worthy grin.

"Done working?"

"Just waiting for you."

"Hmm." I am a few minutes behind my usual schedule. "Sorry if I'm late."

"No problem," he says, his voice dropping to downright husky as he holds my gaze and adds, "You're worth waiting for."

Jessica practically melts and two of the girls across from him sigh and nudge each other. It's a sweet thing to say, if not, entirely sincere. He hates when I'm late. Hates waiting.

I find myself wondering if he said it as a soundbite. Something his adoring fans can take with them, to prove he's worthy of their devotion.

And not something meant just for me.

"Thanks for keeping me company," he says to the group at large.

Three of them get the hint and stand, which makes the remaining two follow suit and they all, eventually, make their way out of the booth. They'd like to stay, I'm sure, if only to stare at my boyfriend's face a little longer.

"Excuse me," I say brightly to Jessica. She grudgingly moves aside, and I slide onto the seat next to Philip.

I set my phone on the table next to the mocha latte Philip made for me, then lean over and kiss his cheek. He's already shaved this morning, his skin smooth and smelling of the cologne I bought him for Christmas last year. I let my lips linger there for one moment, then two, before slowly pulling back.

"Hi," I say softly, combing my fingers through the soft, wavy hair above his ear then settling my hand on his thigh.

"Hi," he says, a knowing, satisfied grin on his face.

Knowing because it's clear I'm marking my territory here.

Satisfied because I'm not usually big on PDAs and he likes that I've made an exception.

Someone makes a rather loud gagging sound and we both look at Jessica. "Sorry," she says with a mean smile. "I just threw up in my mouth a little."

Philip and Astrid both think I should tell Jessica off when she makes one of her passive/aggressive or just aggressive/aggressive comments, but I refuse to stoop to her level.

"So nice to see you, Jess," I say, all smiles and good cheer. "I love that shirt."

She doesn't thank me. Or smile back. She just walks away, the We (heart) Philip Panos brigade following.

"Good luck at your volleyball match!" I call.

She flips me off behind her back and keeps walking.

"I think I'm growing on her," I say to Philip. He laughs, and I grab my cup as Astrid comes out of the kitchen, a tall, iced coffee in her hand. She gives us a pointed look and heads straight for the door. "I mean it," I continue as we slide out of the booth. "Before the end of this school year Jessica and I will be the very best of friends, share our every secret and braid each other's hair during our weekly sleepovers."

"Don't even joke about that," Philip says, opening the door for me. "You should never sleep when Jessica is around. Now that I think about it, you shouldn't even blink. She seems like the kind of person to strike when people are at their most vulnerable."

"You're probably right." I sip my drink. "Mmm. Thanks for the latte."

"You're welcome. I have a few ideas of ways you could repay me for it," he says in a voice way too casual to actually be casual. "In case you feel indebted to me."

His tone is so suggestive, his expression so wicked, I'd have to be an idiot not to realize he's talking sexual favors.

And I'm no idiot.

"A few ideas, huh?"

"One or two or twelve. To be honest, I stopped counting after eight." He grins. "Eight's a really, really good one."

Boys. Such simple creatures.

He winks to let me know he's joking.

At least partly.

I mean, Philip and I do have sex, but it's not all we do. We're not animals.

"Very thoughtful of you," I say. "Thinking of me that way."

He trips over his own feet then catches his balance. "Uh, not the best time for me to be remembering the ways I was thinking about you. All respectfully, of course."

I keep my expression serious. Nod. "Of course."

Okay, so *I'm* not an animal. My boyfriend, on the other hand, is at times a walking, talking hormone.

"I gave you extra whipped cream," he tells me. "Thought you could use a pick me up before Calc. class."

I smile. Last night I'd mentioned that we're getting Friday's quiz back today in A.P. Calc. and he remembered. He remembered, and he gave me an extra one hundred calories to cheer me on. He really is the sweetest, most thoughtful, most perfect boyfriend ever.

If the We (heart) Philip Panos club ever needs a new president, I'm their girl.

I throw my arms around Philip's neck. "Thank you."

Then, smack dab in the middle of the parking lot, I kiss him—a long, warm kiss on the mouth that's just for me, just for us, and not to prove anything to anyone.

When I lean back, he laughs. "Wow. If I'd known you'd react this way to a little whipped cream..." He trails off, his eyes glazing. I nudge him, and he shakes his head. "Sorry. Just had an idea for that thirteenth way you can repay me."

Laughing, I slap his arm playfully. He grabs my hand and, eyes on mine, lifts it to his mouth and kisses my palm. "Love you, babe."

My life really is perfect.

And I don't ever want it to change.

I squeeze his hand, this boy who has my heart. Who'll always have it. "I love you, too."

4

———

B-.

I squeeze my eyes shut so hard that when I open them again, it takes me a moment to focus. But when I do the bright red B (and let's not forget the minus part) is still at the top of my Calc quiz, right next to my name.

Two things that definitely don't go together.

I rub my thumb over the B again and again and again, trying to erase it from existence.

I don't understand. I pay attention in class. I ask questions. I take copious, in-depth notes. And I studied. I studied for hours. What did it get me?

A freaking B-.

Unacceptable.

The bell signaling the end of the period rings and I realize I've missed the last few minutes of class. Including the homework assignment.

I flip my test over then gather my things, taking as long as possible, my head ducked so I don't have to talk to anyone. When everyone else has left, I head toward the front of the room.

Mr. Langworthy is behind his desk, erasing today's lesson from the white board, his skinny back to me. I clear my throat. He keeps erasing.

Mr. Langworthy is okay—though his comb-over and that porn-star mustache give him a decidedly creepy vibe—but he's not exactly the best teacher I've ever had.

If he was, I wouldn't have gotten a B-.

I clear my throat again and he turns, raising his eyebrows as if shocked to find me at his desk when I should be frolicking with my friends in the hall. "Yes, Miss Hewitt?"

I hold out my test. "You graded my test incorrectly."

He glances at the paper. "No, I didn't."

Kids start filing in for his next class and I step closer. Lower my voice. "Would you at least check?"

With a sigh, as if his job is just so darn difficult, he takes the paper from me. I wait, expecting him to sit down and go over it, thoroughly and carefully, but he just skims it.

And hands it back. "This is the correct grade."

"It can't be." Glancing behind me to make sure no one is close enough to hear, I lean over the desk. "I've never gotten a B before."

"There's a first time for everything."

Uh, maybe, but I've always gotten *As*. Straight *As*. And I'd very much like that streak to continue.

I'm taking two other AP classes besides this one along with my regular scholar courses. It's a heavy workload, as heavy as last year, but while Dad says junior year is the most important when it comes to what colleges are looking for, Chase told me I need to continue to push myself my senior year.

"I'd like to retake the test," I say.

"That's not an option."

"At the beginning of the semester you said that if we did poorly on a quiz or test, we'd have the chance to retake it."

"You did not do poorly. You passed. With an above average grade."

The noise level in the room has risen as more and more kids arrive, their voices filling the space, chairs scraping against the floor as they sit. "I can do better."

A *B* will bring down my entire Calc. grade and my GPA, which won't exactly wow the admissions office at Penn—Dad's Ivy League alma mater and my dream school.

It could also mean giving Conor Miller (of the single N, the second highest GPA in our class and my scholarly nemesis) the opportunity to finally move up to first in the class.

My position.

My chest gets tight. Like there's a rubber band around it, squeezing the air from my lungs. My mind goes fuzzy. Mr. Langworthy's lips are moving so he must be talking, but his words are all mushing together, until he sounds like some cartoon adult—*mwah, mwah, mwah.*

It's like I'm suffocating but I must be breathing, right? Because I'm still upright. Still standing on my own two feet and not passed out, blue-faced, on the floor.

Mr. Langworthy is frowning at me.

"I'm sorry," I say, with an apologetic smile. "What did you say?"

He sighs again. The trials and tribulations of a high school teacher. So much stress! So much angst!

"I said, I'm sure you'll bring your grade up with the next quiz."

Well, of course I will. But that doesn't change *this* grade. "Is there extra credit I can do?"

His mouth all but disappears under his bushy mustache. Yes, I'm just *sooo* hard to deal with, what with my high expectations, strong work ethic and give-it-my-all attitude. "Happiness, Miss Hewitt, can only exist with acceptance. Specifically, acceptance of oneself and your limitations."

I give an inner eye roll. Outwardly, though, I nod, seemingly enthralled by his deep insight and wisdom. "Oh, I understand, Mr. Langworthy. And I want to assure you, I'm perfectly happy."

I'll just be happier when I have an A and my spot as first in the class is once again secure. When I graduate as Valedictorian of West Brook Academy. When I get into Penn.

"I'll have an extra credit assignment ready for you after school Thursday," Mr. Langworthy finally agrees.

Thursday? That's three whole days away. Plus, I have a match after school Thursday.

Still, I know better than to push my luck.

Even though I want to.

"Thank you so much, Mr. Langworthy," I say.

When I step into the hall, it's empty. Our school has a strict no loitering policy and we're only allowed to go to our lockers before homeroom, after lunch and at the end of the day. I'm not supposed to be out here without a hall pass, but my next class is Phys Ed and if I tell Miss Ashby I was talking to another teacher, she'll let my tardiness slide.

I head toward the gym, gaze on the floor tiles—white alternating with either red or black, school colors—staying three rows in from the wall to my right, stepping directly into the center of each one, not touching the lines.

One...two...three...

White...black...white...

Four...five...six...

Red...white...black...

Rounding the corner, I look up to find Owen Radlowski approaching me. Now, normally, that wouldn't be a problem.

Except he's walking three rows in from the wall on my right.

My row.

My steps slow. We're getting closer. And closer. He's looking at me so he can clearly see that I'm walking here, that this is *my* row. But does he smile at me and politely scoot the heck out of my way?

No. Blond, broad-shouldered Owen Radlowski with the grim mouth, flat gaze and unfriendly attitude heads right toward me, until we're both forced to stop.

With one tile between us, he gives me a quick up-and-down look that I'm pretty sure is just a habit for him and does not mean he's interested in me in any way, shape or form.

Owen doesn't like me.

Maybe he and Jessica could form a *Down with Natalie Hewitt Club,* complete with T-shirts and meetings where they try to out-scowl each other and throw darts at a picture of me.

But while Jessica's feelings toward me are super clear, Owen's are more implied.

I mean, it's not like he's ever come out and said, *I think you're a spoiled brat.* He actually hasn't said more than a few words to me, ever. Not last year when we had a study hall together. Not when he's at my house doing yardwork for the landscaping company he works for. Not when we bump into each other socially, which, come to think about it, is pretty much never.

He's all badass and silent, no matter how friendly, sweet and chatty I am.

And I am. All of those things.

Even when I don't feel like being any of those things.

"Owen," I say, smiling and chipper as all get out. "Hi!"

He nods.

Owen Radlowski, boy of few words.

I shift my books to my other arm. "Funny how, out of all the space in this hallway, we're both occupying this same, straight line."

He doesn't respond. He doesn't move, either, which was my hope.

I should step aside. Should wave him past and send him off with a *have a nice day!*

And I totally would. But I can't move. I can't get off this tile. I have to stay in this row.

If I stay in this row, in the center of each tile and don't touch the lines, I'll bring my Calc. grade back up to an A. If I stay in this row, in the center of each tile and don't touch the lines, nothing else will go wrong today.

Silly, I know, and not exactly a guarantee of good luck or better grades but still...

I believe it.

I believe it so much, that I clear my throat and say, "Uh, Owen, do you think you could...move?"

He tips his head, the better to assess me through his narrowed, blue-eyed gaze, I guess. "What?"

I swallow. My face is so hot, I'm surprised steam isn't wafting from my forehead but I'm no quitter and I forge ahead. "I really need you to move."

"You want me to move?" he asks, his voice rusty sounding—probably because he doesn't use it often.

Maybe his lack of verbal skills has affected his ability to understand simple English because I'm pretty sure my request was super clear.

"Yes, please." I almost add *if you don't mind*, but honestly, I don't want to give him an option. I need him out of my row.

Which he does, after giving an irritated shake of his head but, whatever.

"Thanks so much!" I chirp then stand there while he walks away. When I'm sure he's long gone, I start to take a step except after our little interlude, I've lost count.

I'm late for my next class, breaking the school's rules by being in the hallway between periods without a pass, and have just had a humiliating run-in with a fellow student. But none of that matters.

I have to start over.

I hurry to the corner and peer around it. Empty. I go to the tile directly in front of Mr. Langworthy's room, spin around and head back the way I'd just come.

One...two...three...on and on and on.

White...black...white...always in the center.

Four...five...six...never touching the lines.

Red...white...black...on and on and on.

5

———————

I had my Thursday all planned out.

I worked up a schedule this morning, wrote it in my planner and put it into my phone. I checked and rechecked it throughout the day, adding homework assignments, adjusting it where needed. Then during my study hall last period (which I spend in the library working as an English tutor Tuesdays and Thursdays), I memorized what I still had to do.

3:05 – Get extra credit assignment from Mr. Langworthy.

3:15 – Change into tennis uniform.

3:30 – 6:00 – Tennis matches (I play both singles and doubles).

6:10 – Home. Change into leotard, pack bag for dance class, put by door.

6:15 – 6:30 – Grab something to eat, Spanish homework (review for test on Friday).

6:30 – 9:30 – Dance classes.

9:40 – Home again. Shower.

10:00 – 10:30 – US History (read chapter six in textbook, make notes for quiz).

10:30 – 11:00 – AP Language homework (read next chapter of *The Things They Carried*).

11:00 – 11:30 – AP Chemistry (study elements for quiz on Friday).

11:30 – 12:00 – Sociology (write first draft of paper on group conditioning).

12:00 – 12:30 – AP Calculus (worksheet).

12:30 – 1:00 – Calculus (extra credit assignment).

It's mostly reading and reviewing, a little bit of writing and that extra Calc. Nothing I can't handle and it shouldn't take all that long, but I've found it's less stressful to give myself at least thirty minutes for each assignment even though I'm hoping most will only take twenty.

All I have to do is follow my well-thought-out, extremely organized, super *strict* schedule for the rest of the afternoon and evening and I'll be able to get everything done.

There's only one problem.

I'm not even home yet. Am well over three miles away.

And it's already 6:24.

Six. Twenty. Four.

That's fourteen minutes behind my well-thought-out, extremely organized, super *strict* schedule.

And it's all Mr. Langworthy's fault.

The bastard.

Though he said he'd have my extra credit assignment ready after school today, he, in fact, did not. He'd actually seemed surprised to see me in his room two minutes after the day's final bell (and a full three minutes ahead of schedule, I might add). As if he'd forgotten all about our discussion Monday.

And me reminding him just yesterday.

He'd muttered about the lessons he had to teach, assignments to hand out and tests to grade. The man had spouted plenty of excuses as to why he hadn't done what he'd said he'd do. What he hadn't offered?

An apology.

If a student had blown off one of his assignments, the only acceptable excuse would be death—the student's. Even then Mr. Langworthy would probably demand a note from the kid's mother.

I had to wait while he wrote out my assignment.

My afternoon went downhill from there.

And my schedule was shot to pieces.

It was all cause and effect, really.

Mr. Langworthy didn't have my assignment ready which made me late to my tennis match. Coach Jordan laid into me in front of both teams which was completely humiliating. We started late, and I was so flustered it took me five very long sets to beat my singles opponent. The doubles match was even tougher and went even longer and we didn't even end up with the win.

Now, here I am, late, stressed, sweaty, and irritated with the whole situation, the world in general and Mr. Langworthy specifically.

I turn onto Tucker Avenue, driving five miles below the posted limit, my gaze darting from the road in front of me to my rearview mirror to one side mirror then the other and back to the road.

Driving is extremely stressful.

Yet, here I am, fully licensed by the great Keystone State, legally able to operate a four-thousand-pound vehicle capable of obtaining speeds of well over one hundred miles per hour (the thought of which makes me break out in actual hives) and sharing the road with other cars, trucks and—the worst of all—pedestrians.

I drive because I have to. To prove I can. Because I am a strong, intelligent, independent, almost-eighteen-year-old who is NOT afraid to get behind the wheel and tool down city streets, country roads or even the highway.

But I really, really hate it.

Especially driving alone.

Don't get me wrong. I'm a good driver. I aced the written portion of the driver's exam and passed the road test on the first try. I can parallel park, do a perfect three-point-turn, and know all the rules of the road.

And I don't have a phobia about driving (of which there is no official name—I looked) like certain people (Chase) think. There's just so much to do and remember—speed limits and keeping a good distance between you and the car ahead of you and figuring out when to start braking so you actually stop at the intersection and not six feet before or three feet past it. How hard to turn the steering wheel going around a curve, checking your blind spot again and again and again before passing on the highway without drifting prematurely into the left lane, and figuring out how much space you have on narrow streets where cars are parked on both sides and another car is heading straight toward you.

It's a lot to take in.

But I can handle all that. What I can't handle? The many, many things that are out of my control. Like other drivers. Who knows what those people are going to do? Also motorcycles. Pennsylvania doesn't require motorcyclists to wear helmets (who thought that was a good idea?) so even a slight tap of my bumper and that biker is going flying. And landing face-first on the pavement.

There are also bicyclists, weaving in and out traffic (though, unlike the motorcycle riders, the majority of them *do* wear helmets—figure that one out), animals of all shapes and sizes from baby raccoons scampering around after dark to huge deer leaping onto the road then staring you down until you have no choice but to either hit them or veer off the road, ending your day with a fiery crash into a tree.

But the worst are kids. Little kids playing in the yard. Middle-schoolers pushing and shoving each other playfully on the sidewalk. Even babies and toddlers in strollers or holding their parents' hand on their way to the park.

They scare the crap out of me.

And it's all Morgan French's fault.

Morgan is the six-year-old girl who lives down the road from us. Two months after I got my license, I was on my way home after ballet class one Saturday morning when I spotted her and another little girl playing in the Frenches' front yard. They were laughing and chasing each other around, the sunlight highlighting their hair, their round cheeks pink. It was cute. Sweet.

Until Morgan ran out into the road.

Right in front of me.

I'll never forget that sick feeling in my stomach, the way everything seemed to be in slow motion.

The horrible sensation that I wasn't going to be able to stop.

I did, of course, slamming on the brakes so hard my entire body pitched forward then was yanked back painfully by the seatbelt. And while I sat there shaking and sweating and trying not to puke, Morgan grinned and waved cheerily then skipped (*skipped*, for the love of God) back into her yard.

Now when I'm driving and see someone under the age of fifteen, I slow to a crawl, break out in a cold sweat and hold my breath until I'm safely past them.

The breath-holding thing? It totally works. It's also useful for driving over one of Pittsburgh's many bridges or through one of the numerous tunnels.

So, yes, I'm a cautious driver. Cautious, not scared. I have good reason.

It's hardly the worst thing I could be.

But it is sort of a pain, especially when two tween boys burst out of a house to my right. I tap the brakes, inhale deeply and hold it. I don't exhale until I'm three houses past them.

My phone rings through the speakers—Chase finally calling me back after six days.

I press the button on the steering wheel to answer. "Hello?"

"Hey," Chase says. "What's up?"

"What's up? I've called you, like, a hundred times! What if there was an emergency?"

"Is there?" he asks, totally unconcerned.

Almost makes me wish there was one.

"No," I grumble. "But there could have been."

We have a really good connection. His sigh comes through loud and clear. "Nat, what do you want?"

What do I want? I want to know why it took him almost a week to return my calls. I want to know why Leah didn't text me back until Tuesday night and why all she wrote was *K*. I want to know what was in that red plastic cup in his Instagram post. I want to know if he's been drinking.

I want to know if he's using again.

But I'm afraid to ask so I do what the Hewitts do best:

Pretend everything is just fine.

"We need to go over our plans for Mom and Dad's anniversary," I tell him.

"We've gone over it a dozen times already."

I'm pretty sure that's an exaggeration—but not by much. "I just want everything to be perfect."

Another sigh. But then, because deep down, he's a decent guy and good brother, he gives in. "I'm leaving here at four—"

"Four? Don't you think you should leave earlier? And don't you mean we? Leah's still coming, right?"

"My last class doesn't end until 3:30 and before you ask, no, I'm not skipping it."

"I wasn't going to ask you to," I say, which is such a lie, I touch my nose to make sure it's not doing the whole Pinocchio thing. "But what if there's traffic?"

"I'm not skipping class," Chase repeats in a stern, *I will brook no argument on this* tone that reminds me of Dad. "If there's traffic, we'll all somehow survive it."

"Fine," I mutter.

"We'll be at the restaurant at six-thirty waiting for you, Mom and Dad to arrive at seven at which point there will be much joy, frivolity and celebration of twenty-five-years of happily wedded bliss."

He probably thinks he's teasing me, quoting what I'd texted him three weeks ago when I put this whole plan into motion.

I'm just glad he actually read it.

"You should tell Mom and Dad you have plans for that weekend," I say. "So they don't suspect anything."

"What's the big deal if they find out I'm coming home?"

"The big deal is we want to surprise them. Hey," I continue before he can tell me I worry too much or worse, to relax. No one relaxes when they're told to relax. It's impossible. "Have you talked to Mom lately?"

"Why?"

Guess I'm not the only one he hasn't been calling.

"I think she's having some sort of midlife crisis."

"She's not having a midlife crisis," he says, like that's the dumbest thing he's ever heard. "She's starting a business."

"This isn't about her opening Kaleidoscope," I insist, signaling my turn onto our street. "She's never home anymore, and when she is, she's in a hurry to leave again. She quit her book club, hasn't attended a PTA meeting all year and resigned as Board Member of the library."

And she's missed my last three tennis matches, including today's, despite her telling me just this morning that she'd be there.

My scalp prickles. I get hot all over.

Wait...she told me that *after* I'd offered to pick up a few groceries on my way home. I thought if I helped her out, she'd be able to spare an hour or so for me.

And last night I promised Dad I'd get his dry cleaning.

I totally forgot both. Didn't put either of them into my well-thought-out, extremely organized, super strict schedule.

Ca-rap.

My eyes sting with tears but I blink them away. Tighten my grip on the steering wheel. Crying is hardly a viable solution to this problem. No. The only solution is driving back into town.

Even though I'm only half a mile from my house, but whatever.

It has to be done.

I do an expertly executed three-point-turn and head the way I came.

"This is important to Mom," Chase is saying. "You should be proud of her for working so hard."

"As much as I'd love to go on your little guilt trip, I'm afraid I don't have any free time until Christmas."

"It's not a guilt trip. I just think you should cut Mom some slack."

"I'll definitely take that bit of wisdom under advisement. Thanks so much. Gotta go."

I slow when I'm three houses away from the driveway with the boys playing basketball. There's no sense talking to Chase about this. He doesn't get it.

He's too far away to understand. Too far removed from our lives.

"Nat—"

"*Bye*," I stress. "Love you."

"Love you, too," he mutters after a moment.

I hang up. Creep along, getting closer and closer to the boys.

And hold my breath until my lungs burn.

6

———

It's after seven when I finally get home, all of my carefully laid plans just...whoosh!...gone with the wind.

I hate when that happens.

There's no sense trying to make ballet class so I decide to skip it, do the makeup class on Saturday and just go to Modern Class tonight at eight. But I haven't eaten since lunch so as soon as I park in my driveway, I order a pizza to be delivered within the next twenty minutes.

Despite needing to start doing something, anything, that will help me tick things off my list, I'm still sitting in my Jeep. I need to plan. Planning gives me a roadmap. Helps me figure out the best way to tackle my messed-up schedule and makes me feel in control. As if I can still manage to get everything done.

I keep this new list as simple as possible, no easily messed up timelines assigned to it, just the bare basics.

Put away groceries.

Hang up Dad's suits.

Pack bag for dance, put by door.

AP Language homework (read next chapter of The Things They Carried *while eating).*

Spanish homework (review for test on Friday).
Change into dance leotard.
Dance class.
Home again.
US History (read chapter six in textbook, make notes for quiz).
AP Chemistry (study elements for quiz on Friday).
Sociology (write first draft of paper on group conditioning).
AP Calculus (worksheet).
AP Calculus (extra credit assignment).

I go over it again and again and again but I'm still anxious.

So I focus on three items at a time. After I've completed the first task, I'll add another.

Groceries.

Suits.

Dance bag.

Groceries…suits…dance bag…

Groceries…suits…dance bag…

Much better.

I've totally got this.

Oh, me and my pesky optimism!

I sip the iced caramel macchiato I bought on my second trip home, toss my phone into my purse and sling the strap over my body crosswise then I put my backpack strap over my shoulder and palm my keys. Reaching into the back seat, I slide the handles of all three grocery bags over my right wrist, stretch farther to reach Dad's plastic covered suits then open the door with my left hand. I press the lock button before picking up my coffee, grabbing the gallon of milk from the front seat and getting out and shutting the door with my hip.

There will come a day when I'll have to make two trips from the car to the house after errands, but that is not this day.

The warm air smells of freshly cut grass and I take a moment to shut my eyes and breathe in that scent. Hold it in my lungs for as long as possible.

But instead of momentary calmness and peace, I feel restless.

I exhale and turn, but I don't walk toward my house. I can't.

Because even though I remember pressing the lock button, and even though I can clearly see through the window that the button is, indeed, down, I still have to pull on the door handle. I have to make sure.

I set the milk on the driveway then tug on the handle, the grocery bags on my arm swinging. I pull on it a second time.

And a thi—

"Need help?"

I jump and coffee squirts out of the straw and splatters the back of my hand. I hadn't realized anyone was behind me. Was close enough to notice my quirky, harmless habit of checking the car door three times.

I turn to find Owen standing in the middle of my driveway, big as life, face glistening with sweat, his Radnor Landscaping T-shirt clinging to his wide chest.

It throws me for a loop, this second close encounter of the Owen kind in three short days. "What are you doing here?"

He lifts his eyebrows as if I've suddenly gone braindead. "Working."

My gaze shifts to the front yard. The thick grass is a deep green and still has the neat rows marking it freshly mowed.

Plus, there's a riding lawn mower near the huge elm tree.

Of course. I laugh nervously then wince at the grating, high-pitched sound.

I clear my throat. "Sorry. I didn't notice your truck."

"It's at the other house."

The other house being the guest house on the other side of the wooded area at the edge of our back yard. It's hidden from view, but you can get to it on foot by following a worn path through the trees, or circumvent our house entirely and follow the long, gravel road off the main street.

"Sorry," I say. Again.

"Do you need help?"

My mind blanks. Just...empty slate. What does he mean? Mental help? "Excuse me?"

He tips his head toward my hand. "Do you need help with your groceries?"

That's when I remember I'm holding them. Actually, the bags are weighing me down and I'm leaning to the side to keep my balance, Dad's suits and my coffee in my hand, my back hunched trying to keep my backpack from sliding off.

A blond, ponytailed Quasimodo in tennis whites and sneakers.

"I've got them," I say, "but thanks."

I give a confident smile and bend to pick up the milk then straighten as best I can—which isn't much—to prove I'm a strong, capable woman who needs no man.

Or something like that.

Which is when my coffee, the plastic cup slick with condensation, starts to slip from my grasp. I instinctively try to catch it with my other hand—my other hand that's holding a gallon of milk and has three grocery bags hanging from my wrist.

Before everything can come crashing down—my coffee, the milk and groceries, my ego and self-respect—Owen steps forward and plucks the cup from my hand.

I lift my head to thank him, but we're even closer now than we were at school the other day and I find myself speechless. Breathless.

And completely unsettled.

It's an odd sensation and I stare at him, realize that though he's always seemed big to me, wide shouldered and broad and thickly muscled, he's not that much taller than I am.

He's not as tall as Philip.

And for some reason, I do not like thinking about my boyfriend while standing this close to another boy. To *this* particular boy.

I step back and hold out my hand for my coffee. "Thank you."

"Give me the milk."

My hand tightens on the handle. "I told you, I can carry the groceries."

He tips his head to the side, the better to consider me and what is obviously a whopping lie. "You're stubborn," he says, as if this is a surprising development.

"Determined," I correct. "And more than capable of carrying my own groceries." I wiggle my fingers in the universal symbol of *gimme*. "But thanks for the offer."

"Determined," he repeats under his breath sounding, if I'm not mistaken, amused. So glad I can give him a giggle. "See, the thing is, I'm stubborn. When you give me the milk, I'll give you back your coffee."

I blink. "Are you blackmailing me?"

His mouth twitches and I try to remember if I've ever seen him smile.

Nope. Can't say as I have.

"It's a trade," he says. "Not extortion."

"I'll just keep the milk and take my coffee back."

Frowning thoughtfully, he seems to ponder that one over.

Then shakes his head once. "That doesn't work for me."

And, his eyes on mine, he lifts the cup and takes a long, deep sip through the straw.

My straw.

I wrinkle my nose. "That is so unsanitary. You have no idea where my mouth has been."

He gives a short, sharp laugh and I realize what I've said. I blush so hard, my eyes water.

When his gaze flicks to my lips, that warmth lowers, seeps into my neck and chest. My stomach. "I'll chance it."

He raises my coffee again.

I should let him drink it, I'm wasting time standing here arguing with him, but then, I wasted eight precious minutes sitting in the drive-through line at Greens and Beans ordering the stupid drink in the first place.

Plus, the longer this goes on, the more it seems he's, well, it seems as if Owen is flirting with me.

And that I'm flirting back.

I'm not. I have a boyfriend. And Owen doesn't exactly seem enamored with me.

Most of the time it's like he can't even stand me.

I shrug—no easy task, weighed down as I am. "Enjoy the coffee."

My grand exit consists of one whole step before his voice stops me.

"You have a problem letting someone help you out?" he asks. "Or maybe you just don't want *me* helping you?"

He probably thinks I'm some snob who considers herself way above him because he's at West Brook on scholarship. Or because he mows my lawn.

He probably thinks I'm some snob, period.

And that bugs me way more than it should.

"It's not *you*," I say. "I just...I like to do things for myself."

"Because you're determined."

Huh. Who knew Owen Radlowski had a sense of humor? Or at least a sense of the absurd. "That's part of it."

Owen watches me, patient and serene, in no hurry to do anything other than wait me out.

"I like to do things for myself," I admit, my arms aching, "because people don't expect me to. They see where I live, who my parents are and what I look like and discount me. They think I'm spoiled and lazy and stuck-up and stupid. But I'm not." For some reason, my throat is tight. My voice shaking. For some reason I want him to understand. "I'm none of those things."

"So you prove them wrong."

"Yes," I say, relieved. "I prove them wrong."

I have to prove myself. Constantly.

I have to be perfect. Always.

"You don't have to prove anything to me, Natalie," he says quietly. "No one has to know if you let me help you out. It'll be our secret."

The sound of him saying my name makes my mouth dry. Or maybe it's sharing a secret with him, a boy I barely know.

A boy who is not my boyfriend.

Flustered, hot and viciously nervous, I shove the milk at him. "Here."

"Thank you," he says, a solemn and gracious winner. He sets the milk down and holds out his hand. "And the bags."

I don't bother arguing, just hand over the groceries.

I know when I've been beat. And I don't want to do anything to prolong the defeat.

When things don't go my way, I prefer to get them over with as quickly as possible.

He inclines his head toward my house. "After you."

I turn on my heel and start walking, stride easy, hips swinging. Owen is behind me like a shadow, silent and unshakable. This is completely surreal, having him there, following me to my house.

We had an honest-to-God conversation. I even told him why I'm always pushing myself to do things on my own.

Today is a day for the record books.

I round the front of the Jeep but as soon as I reach the brick walkway that leads to the patio, I remember I didn't check my door handle a third time. Not fully. And I didn't press the lock button on the key chain.

It's locked. I've already proved that. But I want to check it again. I need to. And I have no idea why. I'm not worried someone is going to break into my car and steal anything or hotwire it and take off, I just... I have to do it. To be sure.

To be safe.

I try to fight it. I force myself to keep moving, making it to the far corner of the house, the edge of the patio. The kitchen door is there —right there. Just a few more steps and I'll be inside. Just a few more steps and maybe the urge will pass.

But then I stop. My stomach turns with unease. My hands shake, rattling the ice in my cup, rustling the plastic on Dad's suits. I can't breathe.

And I know—I have to go back.

7

"PROBLEM?" OWEN ASKS.

"I don't have a key," I lie and curl my fingers around my key chain so he can't see it hanging there. "I'll open the garage door with the remote in the Jeep and we'll go in that way."

I hurry to the Jeep where I open the door, lean inside and push the button on the remote on the visor. The garage door rises with a quiet hum as Owen sets the milk and bags down and brushes at the bits of grass clinging to his jeans.

I shut the door and pull on the handle three times in quick succession. My face is hot and itchy and though I can feel Owen watching me, I still have to push the button on the key.

I have to.

It's not until the horn beeps and the headlights flash that I can finally take a full breath again.

I turn and lock eyes with Owen.

And I know he saw the whole thing. That he noticed my strange quirk.

No one has to know. It'll be our secret.

Somehow that both reassures me and scares me to death.

I lead him through the garage, into the mudroom then the kitchen. "You can set everything—" I wave my hand toward the large island in the center of the room. "—there."

I lay Dad's suits carefully over the back of a chair at the table before shrugging off my backpack and setting it on the floor. Repeat my list in my head.

Groceries...suits...dance bag...

I set my coffee down and take off my purse. Notice a note on the table, written in Mom's loopy script—*Natalie, please give this to Owen.*

This being a fifty-dollar bill.

Mom's a big tipper. I think it's because she worked as a waitress while Dad was in Med School. Chase says it's because she grew up poor and feels guilty about having more than her fair share.

Dad says Chase is full of it and that Mom is just being generous.

I think we're all probably a little bit right.

I pick up the money. Owen's standing next to the island, hands in his front pockets. He's scowling. The semi-pleasant, almost-smiling boy I conversed with in my driveway is back to the brooding, narrowed-eyed, silent guy I'm used to.

I have to say, it's a relief. At least I know what to expect from that Owen.

"Mom left this for you," I say, setting the money on the counter in front of him.

I didn't think it possible, but his mouth goes even flatter and, unbelievably, his cheeks get red.

I didn't even know Owen could blush.

Can't figure out why he's doing so now.

"Thanks," he mutters, not taking the money.

Not meeting my eyes.

Groceries...suits...dance bag...

"I should go," he says after a moment.

"Oh." I cross my arms. Uncross them. "Okay."

Neither one of us moves.

He smells good, like sunshine, fresh air and just mowed grass. His dark blond hair is cut short, the temples and nape damp with sweat. His eyebrows are thick, his nose slightly crooked and I wonder if he broke it playing hockey.

Stop myself from asking.

A bead of sweat forms just under his ear and slides down the line of his neck. He lifts his shoulder, wiping it away and his T-shirt rises, exposing an inch of his ridged stomach.

"Do you want something to drink?" I blurt, jerking my gaze to a point over his shoulder—the only safe space I can think of to look.

But I only bought a few basics and other than the milk (still on the island) all we have is one bottle of sugar-free raspberry iced tea.

"We have water," I continue because there's no way I'm offering him a glass of moo juice. "Or raspberry iced tea. But it's sugar free."

"Tea's good."

I get the tea from the fridge, shake the bottle, twist off the cap and hand it to him, like he's a kid and I'm his mother or something. Ugh.

"Thanks," he says, taking it and drinking deeply.

I pick up my coffee but the idea of drinking after Owen, of putting my lips where his had been on the straw, seems sort of...wrong.

I take the lid off and set it—and the straw—aside. Sip from the rim.

Groceries...suits...dance bag...

I can't run upstairs and put Dad's suits away or go to my room and pack my bag. Not with Owen in my kitchen. When I glance over again, he's watching me. Our gazes lock for one heartbeat. Then two.

I look away. Take another longer, deeper sip of coffee.

"You recycle?" he asks, waving the empty tea bottle.

"Uh, yes." I hold out my hand. "I'll—"

"I've got it." He heads over to the sink, rinses the bottle then gestures to the lower cabinets. "Under here?"

I nod. "On the left."

He opens the door, pulls out the recycling bin and sets the bottle in it.

I take another fortifying drink of caffeine then pick up the milk and carry it to the fridge. When I turn back, Owen is unloading the groceries onto the island. I consider telling him he doesn't have to, but if it saves me a minute or two (after losing several during our driveway standoff) I'm all for it.

We work without speaking; him unloading bags, me putting the food away. Usually, I'd be chatting nonstop. Good girls are always charming and sweet and fill any silence with polite conversation.

But I had a craptastic afternoon and am currently in the midst of a stressful evening. I'm in no mood to play my most famous role right now.

Not when the quiet is so nice. Much nicer and more comfortable than I ever thought it could be.

All good things must come to an end, though. And, really, five minutes without speaking while in someone else's presence is a record for me.

I search my mind for something to say. It's not like Owen and I have anything in common. Sure, we live in the same town and go to the same school but the only things I know about him are that he's at the school on scholarship, plays hockey and is, by all standards, a loner with a capital L.

"So," I say, clearing my throat. "How do you like working for Radnor Landscaping?"

He shrugs.

Okay, I realize my question is all sorts of lame but it's the best I could do. He could try and cooperate.

God.

I glance at the microwave clock. 7:18. Forty-two minutes until dance class. Forty-two minutes I could be getting more items checked off my list, not pulling conversation from some guy's mouth, one word at a time.

"So you don't like it?" I prod.

He stacks the plastic bags on top of each other and folds them in half. Then in half again. Then again. "Some people do things because they have to. Not because they want to."

"Really?" Leaning over, I set my elbow on the counter, rest my chin in my hand and look up at him as if I'm mesmerized by his great insight and wisdom. "Do tell."

He shakes his head, irritated with me. Or life in general. "You wouldn't understand."

I straighten. Wrinkle my nose. "Because I'm an airhead? Us pretty blondes, we just don't have much up here." I tap my head. "Then again, when you look like this—" I circle my face with my finger then sweep my hands down to indicate my body. "—who needs brains, right? But maybe, if you use small words and speak slowly, I can follow along. Oh. Or maybe it's because I'm such a princess, here in my castle, frittering away my days. I mean, what could I possibly know about hard work or responsibility? If it's not fun or easy, I just refuse to do it."

Owen grabs the back of his neck. "I didn't say that. I didn't say any of that."

"No, you didn't say it. But it's what you meant, isn't it?"

His gaze flicks away.

And I have my answer.

Guess I was right. He does think I'm a stuck-up, spoiled princess. I shouldn't be surprised.

I definitely shouldn't be disappointed.

"Well," I say, hands linked at my waist to keep them from shaking —or, you know, strangling him, "I'm sure you're anxious to be on your way."

"You mean you're anxious to get rid of me."

I swipe up the fifty dollars, cross to the door and open it with a flourish. He approaches, all broad and grim.

"Don't forget your tip," I say, waving it at him. "After all, you earned it."

He gets closer. And closer, his jaw tight, gaze intense. I shrink back, my shoulders pressing against the door. Not out of fear, but because nerves are doing weird things to my stomach. Confusing my mind.

"You putting me in my place, Natalie?" he asks softly.

My face heats. Yes, that's exactly what I was trying to do. Put him in his place. Get back at him for being so narrow-minded.

For seeing only what everyone else sees when they look at me.

But I'm the one who ends up feeling small. Stupid.

And as much the spoiled princess as he obviously thinks I am.

"Not at all," I say, but it comes out breathless and shaky. I might as well have a neon sign above my head flashing the word LIAR in giant letters. "I just didn't want you to forget it."

His eyebrows lift. "Thoughtful of you."

"I do my best to be considerate of others."

He snorts softly. "Yeah. I can tell that's important to you."

I wait, money still in my hand. Why doesn't he take it already and go? I have things to do, things I can't do while he's here.

Breathing, it seems, is at the top of that list.

Finally, thankfully, he snags the fifty between his fore and middle fingers.

He opens his mouth. Shuts it. And is back to scowling. "Thanks for the tea."

I'm pretty sure that's not what he was originally going to say, but maybe this is better. A definite end to our strange and disturbing encounter. "You're welcome. Thank you for carrying in the groceries."

"You're welcome," he says, mimicking my own serious tone. He makes it to the end of the garage before turning back. "Did you win?"

"This little standoff?" I ask. "I like to think so."

But I'm not so sure. I'm afraid that as far as things go, I'm 0 and 2 with Owen.

He shakes his head. "Your tennis match."

I frown and, without meaning to, step into the garage. "How did you know I had a match today?"

"Just a guess," he says dryly, and I remember I'm wearing my tennis uniform for God's sake.

"I won my singles match."

"Still undefeated?"

My eyes narrow. "How do you know I'm undefeated?"

He hesitates, his gaze dropping for a moment before lifting again.

"You'd be surprised what I know about you," he says so quietly, I wonder if I imagined it.

Before I can decide, he walks away.

I watch as he crosses the driveway and skirts the patio. I watch him cut through the yard to the trail leading into the woods separating the main house from the guest house. I stand there and watch.

Long after he's disappeared.

8

____

You'd be surprised what I know about you.

Owen had that one right. I am surprised—totally and completely —that he'd notice anything about me, let alone my singles record in tennis.

He doesn't exactly seem like the super observant type. At least when it comes to people he doesn't even like.

After our weird little interlude, I can't stop thinking about him. That whole night I replay our encounter over and over and over in my mind.

That's not unusual. I often worry I've said the wrong thing and recount every word of a conversation again and again and again. Or, in this instance, if I overreacted and what I could have done to make things less awkward between Owen and me at the end.

I wonder if I owe him an apology or if I was right all along and he owes me one.

By the next morning, I've convinced myself I'd blown the whole thing out of proportion and resolve to move on with my life with no more thoughts of Owen. It's a vow I totally would have kept, too, if not for the fact that everywhere I turn (every-freaking-where), there he is. Heading up the stairs as I went down. Passing me in the hallway after

English and again when I'm on my way to the library. Ahead of me in the lunch line.

I have a hard-enough time letting things go once they're in my head without being reminded of them constantly. There was no way I could NOT think about him.

Talk about annoying.

But I thought for sure all of that would be over and done with by Monday.

Nope.

Instead, I've spent the day actively searching for him, looking for a glimpse of him in the hall between classes. Trying to find his light hair in the cafeteria at lunch.

It's not until halfway through Spanish class that I have an epiphany (*epifania*) and realize why this whole Owen thing has gotten to me. It's not because of anything *I* did. It's what he said.

You'd be surprised what I know about you.

That is so not a normal thing to say. It's actually sort of disturbing and stalkerish.

But once I find out why he said it—and what, exactly, he meant by it—I can forget the whole thing ever happened and move on with my life.

And not a moment too soon, either. It's becoming quite the preoccupation—the thinking and searching.

I mean, what kind of guy says something like that to a girl he barely knows? Chances are it was a harmless, offhand comment, but what if it wasn't? What if he's obsessed with me?

And, yes, okay, I get how that sounds seeing as I'm the one currently stalking him but whatever. The simple facts are I have a boyfriend and Owen barely knows me so there's no reason for him to be thinking about me at all.

There are even fewer reasons for me to be thinking about him.

I'm looking forward to those thoughts stopping.

And they will. Once I get some answers.

Which is why after school, I wait by the auditorium doors, full backpack at my feet, Chem book in my arms, pressed against the wall so as not to get run over by the swarm of students heading outside as I search for Owen one last time.

I'm standing on my tiptoes, trying to see over the noisy throng, when someone snakes a tight arm around my waist. I jump and whirl around, the corner of my Chem book jabbing Philip's stomach hard enough to have him grunting and bending over in pain.

"Oh, my God," I cry loud enough to have several heads turning our way. "I'm so sorry! Are you okay?"

Rubbing the spot, he straightens slowly. "I think you knocked out my kidney."

"Your kidneys are in the back."

"Appendix then."

"Other side," I say, gesturing to his right side. I'd hit his left. "And if you don't want any internal organs nudged out of place, you shouldn't sneak up on people."

"Who's sneaking? I walked down the hall along with everyone else. You're the one who was zoned out."

My face heats and I duck my head. Another unpleasant side effect of the past few days—the twinge of guilt I feel every time I think about Owen.

"I really am sorry," I say, and I can't help but wonder if I mean for more than just jabbing him in the stomach. "Will you forgive me?"

He touches my hip, his face close to mine and everything within me settles. All thoughts of Owen disappear. "For anything," Philip assures me.

Relief flows through me and I'm reminded of how good I have it. How much I love him.

"What were you thinking about so hard anyway?" he asks.

"Nothing important," I say, which is true enough.

Philip nods his head in greeting to Stuart Dobson and Josh Kahle as they pass. "I thought you had tennis practice."

"I do." I shift the books to my other arm. "But I wanted to see you. Wish you good luck at your soccer match."

Again, not a lie.

Not entirely.

"You already wished me luck at lunch," he reminds me.

"I wanted to tell you again."

"You're sweet," he says, his voice low, his grin pleased. He gives me a quick kiss on the cheek. "Walk you to your car?"

"Do you have time?"

The varsity team doesn't play until seven but their coach requires them to watch both the freshman team and Junior Varsity games which are at three-thirty and five respectively.

"I've got a few minutes," Philip says, taking my Chem book and picking up my backpack.

He holds the door for me and we step out into the sunlight.

Love, real love, is calm and easy and just...right. It's what my parents have. It's what Chase and Leah have.

It's what I have with Philip.

As we walk hand-in-hand across the parking lot, our hips bumping, I realize how stupid I was to waste even a moment thinking about another boy. No matter how innocent those thoughts were. It doesn't matter why Owen said what he said. He doesn't matter. Not to me.

Mom told me once that the key to a strong, lasting relationship is choosing the other person every day. Choosing to be kind to them. To forgive them. To love them.

Choosing to be with them.

I choose Philip.

And I always will.

9

———————

WHEN PHILIP ASKS IF I WANT TO HANG OUT FOR A LITTLE BIT Wednesday night, I can't say no—even though it's already past eight-thirty and I have at least three hours' worth of homework.

But I don't have modern dance class on Wednesdays and he got home early from his soccer match and we're both busy for the next two nights and he'll be at a tournament out of town this weekend...

And even though I really didn't do anything wrong, the fact that I had fleeting, purely innocent and harmless thoughts about another boy has me wanting to make it up to Philip.

Even if he doesn't realize it.

Philip is at the school, having been bussed there after his game, waiting for me to let him know if he's allowed to come to my house.

And I'm on Main Street knocking on the door of Kaleidoscope, waiting to be let inside.

I try calling Mom—again—but there's no answer. She's in there. All the lights are on and her Lexus is parked across the street and, really, where else would she be? Ever since she came up with the idea for Kaleidoscope and purchased this building, she spends most of her time here.

Using the side of my fist, I pound on the door and even though I know it's locked, I try the handle. You know, in case my knocking has somehow vibrated the lock loose.

It hasn't.

And I can't help but feel like this locked door is less a decision made for safety reasons, and more like one meant to keep me out. As if I'm not allowed entry into Mom's inner sanctum without direct consent and a convoluted password.

I cup my hands around my eyes and press my face close to the glass of the door. The interior is spacious with piles of boxes in the corner, glass-front display cases against the wall and a long, marble-top counter directly across from the door. The wind picks up and I shiver. Once the sun set, the temps dipped a good fifteen degrees. I'm freezing.

I should go. I should get in my Jeep, crank the heat and call Philip and tell him we'll have to postpone hanging out. Then I can go home, shower and maybe, possibly, get my homework done before the wee hours of the morning.

I'm about to do just that when Mom comes out from the back room, completely oblivious to the fact that I'm here. She has her earbuds in and her jeans and sweatshirt are splattered with paint, her hair pulled back in a messy bun. But still, she's beautiful, her hips wiggling to whatever song she's listening to, her cheeks flushed.

She must sense me staring at her, nose pressed against the glass, because her head jerks around. When she realizes it's me, she smiles warmly and hurries to the door.

"Natalie," she says, taking her earbuds out as she steps aside, her face lit with pleasure. "What a nice surprise."

"You're not answering your phone."

Her smile fades at the snap in my tone.

"Did you call me?" She pulls her phone from the front pocket of her jeans. Frowns at it as if it's somehow to blame for this predicament. "I'm sorry. I put it on Silent when I met with our accountant earlier and forgot to switch it back."

She does so now, making a production of it as if that alone makes up for her oversight.

For ignoring me.

"Come on back," she says, already walking away. "I'll show you what I'm working on."

Having no choice, I follow her down a short hallway that leads to a storage room. She has a studio set up there complete with paints, drop cloths, easels and extra lighting. There are various projects in differing stages of completion, but instead of showing me one of her paintings, she leads me to an old-fashioned, wooden dressing table with curved legs and an oval mirror on top. It has a small drawer on either side and a sunken top. She's painted it white then distressed it and added vines that climb the legs, curl around the mirror.

"What do you think?" she asks. "I'm going to use it out front to display jewelry."

"It's pretty," I say because it is. Plus, Chase's words are floating in my mind, his admonishment to cut Mom some slack. To be more supportive. Because I love her. And I really am proud of her for wanting to have a career.

But maybe I'm also trying to be extra nice so she'll let Philip come over.

"You could hang scarves on the mirror," I add, imagining it out in the storefront. "Keep the drawers open and have rings and bracelets in there."

Her smile is back, genuine and relieved that I added my opinion. That I'm interested in what she's doing.

Even if I might have the teeniest, tiniest bit of an ulterior motive.

"I was thinking the same thing." She wraps one arm around me to give me a quick squeeze. "Are you hungry? I could order pizza."

"Astrid and I had Nero's after her meet."

She doesn't ask me how school or tennis practice was. If I had fun at ballet. She used to. She used to be interested in my life. She used to want to be a part of it.

Now it's as if everything not directly involved with Kaleidoscope is a distraction.

And no, I'm not exaggerating (or whining), no matter what Chase says.

She scrolls through her phone. "I'm starving," she murmurs, as if speaking to herself. "You sure you don't want anything? I'm getting a sala—"

"Don't you want to know why I'm here?"

She presses a button and lifts the phone to her ear. "What?"

"I called you, like, three times. Texted you at least six times. Don't you want to know why? I mean, what if something's wrong?"

"Is there?" she asks, looking confused. But not worried. Not the least bit concerned.

"There could have been."

"Hello," she says, holding up a finger to me in the universal sign for *Hold that Thought*, before turning her back to speak into the phone. "Yes. I'd like to place an order..."

The longer I stand there waiting for her to get back to our conversation, to focus on me for just a few minutes, the more self-righteous I feel. What if there *had* been an emergency? What if something had happened to me or Chase or Dad? I could have needed help, could have needed *her*.

But she'd never have known it. Would have continued with her evening, listening to stupid hair bands from the eighties, painting furniture or sweeping the floors here.

"Can Philip come over?" I ask as soon as she ends her call. Because I don't want to give her the chance of saying something first. Of offering up some lame, insincere apology.

Or not offering one up.

"Is your father home?"

"I'm not sure." Though we both know the chances of Dad being home before midnight are pretty slim. "You could come home, though."

Gathering her paint brushes, she shakes her head. "I have at least another hour's worth of work here." She looks around as if gauging how much more she still wants to get done. "Possibly two. You can go to Philip's house if his parents are going to be there."

We could but Astrid is home and I only spend time with Philip at his house when she's not there—and vice versa. Once Philip and I became a couple, it got to be too awkward for me to hang out with both of them at the same time. They'd deny fighting over me but that's exactly what it was. If I was there to hang out with Philip, Astrid's feelings would get hurt and she'd sulk. If I was there with Astrid, Philip would accuse me of not giving him enough attention.

No matter what I did, I just couldn't win.

Don't get me wrong. I love both Astrid and Philip, but sometimes being best friends with your boyfriend's sister is a pain in the butt.

"Mr. and Mrs. Panos go to bed super early. By the time we get there, it'll be time for me to leave. I don't understand why he can't come to our house." And yes, I hear the whine in my tone loud and clear, I just choose to ignore it. "It's not like we're going to *do* anything. We're just going to study."

Probably.

I'm pretty sure Mom knows I'm not a virgin. I'd asked her to take me to get on birth control after Philip and I had been dating for eight months and she'd done it. There'd been no judgement, no harping or lectures. We'd discussed it, had talked over the ramifications, complications and responsibilities—both physical and emotional.

I turned to her and she came through for me in a big way. And while she's never asked directly if Philip and I went through with it, she's not stupid. She has to know we hook up. She knows, and she's never told Dad, mainly because he'd flip out if he thought his princess was no longer a virgin.

So we keep that little bit of truth from him. That's one of the things about me and Mom.

We have our secrets.

"You know the rules," Mom says, scrubbing the brushes clean. "You're not allowed to have your boyfriend over unless your father or I are home."

"I guess he'll never come over again, then, seeing as how neither of you are ever home."

"That's a bit of an exaggeration."

"It's not." I cross my arms. "This isn't fair. Don't you trust me?"

She shakes the brushes, spraying drops of water over both of us. "This has nothing to do with trust. This is about respecting and obeying the rules we've already established. Philip can come over tomorrow night."

"I have ballet and modern tomorrow night," I remind her. "And he's going to a tournament in Virginia this weekend, so he'll be leaving right after school Friday."

"Then he can come over when he gets back."

There's no point arguing more with her—though that's exactly what I'd like to do. I want to discuss and debate this until she's worn down and gives in, but one of the few things about her that hasn't changed recently is her resolve. Once Mom makes a decision, that's it. And the more you fight with her, the harder she digs in.

"Fine. Whatever," I say. "We'll go to Philip's."

Is she grateful I'm giving in? That I'm not yelling and screaming and throwing a major tantrum about not getting my own way like so many other girls would? No. She just nods, certain in her authority. In the outcome of this little disagreement.

In my complete and total obedience.

"Be home by ten," she says almost automatically. It's a habit, reminding me of my school-night curfew. Not an order. She's not the least bit worried I'll be late. Why should she be? I've never missed a curfew yet.

I don't respond, don't say goodbye, just walk through the storefront and out onto Main Street. Climb into my Jeep and blast the warm air. It's not fair. In the past few months so much about our family has changed. So much about *Mom* has changed and I'm supposed to act as if everything's fine and dandy because that's what I do.

I behave. I agree. I keep the peace.

There's no rebelling. No causing trouble. No arguing or backtalk.

I do what's expected of me.

She's changed everything—*everything*—except the "rules"

governing my life and I keep sitting back and taking it because *I* haven't changed. I'm still a good girl.

And good girls always, always do as they're told.

But maybe, just this once, I won't.

10

Even though I told my mom we were going to Philip's house, we don't.

Instead, I ask him to meet me at our guest house.

I wait for him in the dark on the porch steps, still freezing in the sweatpants and T-shirt I put over my leotard. To pass the time, I go over my homework list again and again and again.

Language.

History.

Chem.

Soc.

Calc.

It's almost nine and at this rate, I'll have to stay up most of the night to get everything done. But I don't cancel with Philip. I don't want to disappoint him. Don't want him getting upset with me.

Plus, I owe him this time together. My attention.

Time where I can focus fully on him. On us.

Without thoughts of another boy interfering.

Philip pulls up, headlights off like a thief in the night and it hits me what I'm doing.

I lied to my mom.

I never lie to her.

Not that I tell her everything. Our family has a Don't Ask, Don't Tell policy. That way we can avoid all the little truths we don't really want known. All the imperfections and problems no one wants to acknowledge.

Don't get me wrong, it's not like I've never broken a rule before. But those were small infractions. Nothing like this...this...premeditated act of defiance.

This is big. Huge. At least for me. Ugh. What was I thinking, sneaking down here? I let my emotions get the best of me. Let my anger get out of control, push me to be reckless. Foolish.

Unlike myself.

Oh, God, if Mom finds out, she's going to be so mad.

Worse. She'll tell Dad.

Doubly worse, they'll both be disappointed.

With a groan, I lay my head on my bent knees. Tap it there a few times. This isn't me. I'm not a troublemaker. I'm no rebel. Never wanted to be one.

Not after what happened with Chase.

I don't cause my parents problems.

Never want to do anything to make them worry.

"Hey," Philip says as he walks toward me, his features hidden in the dark. He sits next to me. Our thighs touch. "Everything okay?"

"Yeah." My voice comes out hoarse so I clear my throat. "Fine. Why?"

I feel him shrug, his arm brushing against mine. "You sounded upset when you told me to meet you here. Plus, the fact that if your dad finds out we're here, alone, I'm pretty sure he'll take a scalpel to my throat. And not to perform surgery."

"He probably won't kill you. He takes his Hippocratic Oath very seriously."

"That's a relief." Philip leans back on his elbows. Nudges me with his knee. "What's going on, Nat? Really?"

I want to tell him. I want to tell him everything, about Mom acting so differently and Chase coming home less and less. How my classes are getting harder and as much as I hate to admit it, it's taking more effort for me to keep up. How weird things are between me and Astrid.

How sometimes I feel so overwhelmed and anxious, the only way I can keep calm is to count or make a list.

I want to tell him, but I don't. I can't. The thing with secrets is, once you share yours, they're out of your control forever.

So I keep mine hidden. Safe. If I keep pretending everything is fine, eventually everything will *be* fine.

The breeze picks up and gooseflesh rises on my arms. I'm antsy, need to move to relieve some of the restless energy inside of me so I jiggle the leg not touching his. "Nothing. I just...I miss you. We hardly get to spend any time together anymore."

Sitting up, he puts his arm around me.

And I keep jiggling my leg.

"Things will settle down after tennis and soccer are over," he says.

"That's not for another month." Jiggle, jiggle, jiggle. "And if you guys make the playoffs—which you will—you'll be playing well into November." Jiggle, jiggle, jiggle. "Then we'll be busy with college applications and you'll start basketball..."

He reaches across and sets his hand on my knee, stilling my movement. Gives my knee a gentle squeeze. "We'll do our applications together."

That's not the point, but I don't know what the point is so I keep quiet. All I know is that there's this knot in my chest, strands of worry and guilt and anger looped around and around and around each other, and it won't go away.

"What if we end up at colleges on opposite sides of the state?" I ask, one of the many, many fears taking up residence in my head.

Our plan is for Philip to attend college as close to Philly as possible so we'll be able to see each other on weekends and maybe a few nights during the week.

"No matter where we go," he says, cupping my cheek, voice low, tone insistent, "nothing is going to change between us. Nothing is ever going to change how I feel about you."

"Do you promise?" I whisper.

He kisses me, warm, soft and sincere. "I promise."

I want to believe him. I want to absorb his words into my skin, let them soak into my bones. I want to trust his feelings for me—and mine for him—always. I used to. But right now, I can't. Doubt creeps in, nudges aside that hope. That belief.

Pushes away that trust until I'm empty. Hollow.

And so very, very afraid of losing him.

I lean over and kiss him, pressing my body against his, taking the kiss deeper and deeper until we're both breathing hard. I break the kiss and link my hand with his. "Let's go inside."

"Nat," he says, his husky voice tugging at something deep in my belly. He glances at the woods. My house is just beyond them, hidden by the thick, leafy trees. "Your parents..."

"They won't be home until later. And even if they do come home, they think I'm at your house. We'll leave the lights off. They'll never know we're here."

Philip hesitates. "I don't want you to get into trouble."

It's sweet. And so like him to think about me. But it's obvious he wants to go inside. His hand is tense in mine, his voice just a bit unsteady and so very rough. I slide my free hand behind his neck, comb my fingers into his soft hair. When I press my mouth against his, he groans.

"Are you sure?" he asks against my lips.

In answer, I squeeze his hand, stand, and lead him to the door.

And inside, in the dark, with the taste of Philip's kiss on my tongue, the feel of his touch on my skin, the emptiness inside of me starts to fill.

Inside, in the dark, it's easy to once again believe we'll always be together.

* * *

At 10:05 I hear Mom's footsteps as she comes upstairs and pauses outside of my bedroom. I wait, torn between wanting her to keep right on walking and wanting her to knock on my door.

After a moment, she does knock, and I consider, briefly and with no little amount of brattiness, about ignoring it or pretending I'm asleep. Seeing as how my lights are on, I'm pretty sure she won't buy that. "Come in."

She does, looking tired but in a good way.

A happy way.

I drop my gaze, stare at my History book but don't really see the words. Mom's happy and I'm a complete, selfish brat because I want her to go back to how she used to be. To *who* she used to be. Because it scares me, this newfound confidence and commitment to Kaleidoscope. To herself.

If she's happy now, does that mean she wasn't happy before?

What else will change?

"I'm glad you're still up," Mom says, sitting on the edge of my bed. "Can we talk?"

My heart races but I keep my gaze down. Oh, God. She knows. She knows I snuck Philip into the guest house. Knows what we did there.

Guilt churns in my stomach making me feel sick and hot. *Please, please, please, don't let her know.*

I swallow. "I have a lot of homework..."

"This won't take long." Mom sets her hand on my knee. "Please, Natalie."

I sigh, as if it's a huge inconvenience to give her a few minutes of my time—which, it sort of is, considering all the work I still have to do. Plus, it's not like she's been all that generous with her time and attention lately.

Sitting up, I scoot back against my headboard. "Fine."

"I want to apologize," she says, tucking her legs underneath her. "I'm sorry about tonight, about not answering your calls and texts. I realize that I've been busy getting Kaleidoscope up and running and I'm sorry if you're feeling left out or neglected."

"I'm not." I'm seventeen. It's not like I need my mommy around me every minute. "I just...I miss you. It's like you're never here anymore and when you are, you're preoccupied,"

Her expression softens. "I miss you, too." She crawls up to sit next to me. Puts her arm around me and pulls me close. Kisses the top of my head. "Maybe you could help me out at the store a few times a week? I'd love your input, especially in choosing merchandise. Oh! You could go with me to that trade show in Philadelphia in November."

She doesn't need my help. And she really doesn't need my input on what merchandise to stock. One thing about Kristin Hewitt that hasn't changed—she has excellent taste.

But she's trying. And she looks so nervous and hopeful, as if she's scared I'm going to reject the idea. Reject her. Shame washes over me. She was so excited when I showed up at Kaleidoscope earlier, so eager to show me what she'd been working on despite me not showing any interest in her new business.

"Sure," I say. "That sounds like fun."

Her shoulders relax, and she hugs me again. "Great. We'll stay the weekend." Mom slides off the bed, pulls out her phone. "I'll make a note to check out if there are any shows we want to see. Ask Leah if she'd like to join us for dinner one of the nights." She finishes typing into her phone then bends to give me another hug. "Good night, baby. I love you."

I hold on, longer than necessary but she doesn't seem to mind. "Love you, too."

She straightens and brushes a hand over my hair before walking out and shutting my door quietly behind her. I drag my History book toward me but after reading the same paragraph three times and still not remembering one word, I lean my head back. Exhale heavily.

And count the flowers on my wall.

Again and again and again.

11

—————

Despite Miss Marchand doing her best to spread the word of her new English tutoring program (complete with posters in the hallways, the foyer and cafeteria, handouts given to every kid in all English classes, and several mentions of it over the morning announcements) the response thus far has been slightly underwhelming.

No one—and I mean, not one person—has shown up.

Guess the need for English tutoring isn't as vast as she thought.

Then again, it's only the end of September. I'm sure things will pick up mid-term.

Not that I'm complaining. I'd been worried about the time this tutoring gig was going to cost me but sitting at a corner table in the research section at the back of the school's library every Tuesday and Thursday during last period all by myself has actually been sort of nice. Relaxing.

Plus, I get a good head-start on my homework.

Today I'm working on Calc. (thanks to that extra credit, I brought my grade up to 87.5 and if I ace the next quiz, I'll have a solid A) and am hoping to write another page of my History paper before the final bell.

My earbuds are in, my head down and bopping side to side to Rihanna's "Work" when the nape of my neck prickles with awareness.

I scan the aisle in front of me but it's empty. Glance left, then right, but all I see are floor-to-ceiling shelves of ancient encyclopedias, dictionaries and thesauruses, their thick spines cracked and worn.

I get back to Calc but the sensation of being watched sticks with me, like an itch between my shoulder blades. I shrug, do a little shoulder wiggle but it remains in the middle of my back.

Out of reach.

I turn in my seat, which is stupid as the only thing behind me is a wall. With a shake of my head, I once again face forward.

And leap a good foot out of my seat.

I yank my earbuds out. "Owen!" I say, trying to convey my ire as quietly as possible because we are in a library after all. "You scared me. God! Where did you even come from?" I lean over the desk, lower my voice even more. "Are you some sort of ninja?"

He doesn't look like a ninja. He looks normal in jeans and a long-sleeved, blue Henley that brings out the color of his eyes.

Which I notice because yes, I am female, and his eyes really are a very pretty blue and not for any other reason.

I am one hundred percent devoted to my boyfriend.

Which I proved last night when I was willing to risk getting into trouble just to spend a bit of time with him.

"You sounded just like your mom," Owen says.

I frown. "What does that have to do with you sneaking up on me? And when did you talk to my mom?"

"I didn't sneak up on you, I walked down the aisle. You didn't see me because you weren't paying attention. And I talk to your mom sometimes when I do your yardwork."

Of course. It's no surprise he and my mom have chatted. Mom is super friendly and treats everyone she sees with warmth and respect.

I get a twinge of unease, worried that maybe I haven't always done the same. Not with him. After all, the last time we spoke, things did not go well. Or at least, they didn't end well.

And I realize that's what my sort-of fixation with him this past week has been about! The thinking about him, looking for him, hoping to talk to him again—it was so I could make amends for being rude and bitchy. No other reason.

It's a relief, I'll admit, to have an answer to a question I'd been afraid to ask myself.

Now's my chance to get him to see how wrong he is about me. To prove I'm not some stuck-up, snotty princess, even if I did kind of act like one.

Now's my chance to make him like me.

"Is there something you needed?" I ask, determined to be sweet and friendly no matter what.

His mouth flattens. "You're the English tutor?"

"That's what it says on my desk."

No, really. There's a name plate made of folded red construction paper on my desk that says Natalie Hewitt – English Tutor in colorful script and is decorated with tiny book stickers.

I really think Miss Marchand missed her true calling as an elementary school teacher.

Owen stares at the ceiling, his jaw working as if he's grinding his teeth to dust.

I get to my feet. "Are you okay?" When he doesn't answer, I tip my head back and look up, too. "What are we looking for?"

"Just trying to figure out who up there hates me," he mutters.

I glance at him, surprised and pleased. "You made a joke. I'd sing out a good old-fashioned hallelujah but I don't want to do anything to break this fragile moment so I'll just shut my eyes and have a moment of silence in gratitude."

I do so but when he sighs, I open my eyes again.

"It wasn't a joke," he says.

It's then I notice he's holding something in his hand—a paperback copy of *The Catcher in the Rye*. He's squeezing it so hard, it's nearly folded in half.

I lean across the top of the desk and reach for the book. I must take him by surprise because I'm able to tug it free of his death grip, but the damage is done; curled pages, cracked spine, bent cover.

"You monster," I say, trying my best to smooth the bottom corner of the cover. "And in a library, too."

He sticks his hands in his pockets, but his expression is less severe, almost amused. "It deserved it."

"It's an American classic."

"It's crap. That Holden guy is a whiny douchebag."

"He's not so bad. Mostly he's just clueless." I've done all I can but there's no way that book will ever be the same. I hand it back. "Did you get to the part with the prostitute?"

Owen immediately starts flipping through the book. "What chapter is that?"

"Don't get your hopes up. It's not salacious. It shows a better side of Holden."

Having lost interest, Owen closes the book. Slaps it against his thigh. "I doubt there is a better side."

I lean against the desk. "Are you reading it for American Lit?" I took that class as a sophomore but read *The Catcher in the Rye* the summer after eighth grade. Owen nods. "How far are you?"

He shrugs. Keeps his eyes on the poor, battered book in his hand. "A few chapters."

A few chapters? We've been in school four weeks now. He should be further than that. Unless...

Unless that's why he's here. Because he needs help.

Because he needs me.

"You're smiling," he says, low and gruff and suspicious. "Why are you smiling?"

"It's just something I do when I'm happy. You should try it once in a while."

"Talking about a fictional douchebag makes you happy?"

"No. Well, actually, yes, but mostly I'm happy to have a tutee to tutor." I tap the sign on the desk. "Congratulations, you're my first."

Owen grimaces and shifts the book from one hand to the other. Then back again. "I didn't know you were the tutor."

Something in his tone makes me tense. But then I notice how uncomfortable he looks, how embarrassed, color climbing his neck, suffusing his cheeks, and I soften toward him.

"Is that a problem?" I ask, not sure how it possibly could be.

I've got it all figured out. I'll help him whiz through *The Catcher in the Rye*, give him some pointers on writing a kick-butt essay on it and when our time together is through, we'll be friends.

Stranger things have happened.

Though, at the moment, I can't think of any.

"Yeah," he finally says in answer to my question. "It is."

And once again, I watch Owen Radlowski walk away from me.

12

____

I can't let it go.

I tried to. Really. I didn't chase after Owen demanding to know why my being the tutor was a problem. And when Miss Marchand came in later and asked if anyone showed up for help, I told her no.

But I couldn't stop thinking about it. About him.

Again.

I spent the rest of Thursday and all of yesterday going over our conversation, wondering if I'd offended or upset him. I wondered and worried and wondered some more until last night when I realized this isn't about me. Not really. It's about Owen.

He needs my help.

He's just too stubborn to ask for it.

So I'll just offer it. Save him the embarrassment.

I'm generous that way.

After dance class Saturday morning, I drive across town and park across the street from 77 South 3rd Street.

Owen's house.

I get out, lock and shut the door then pull on the handle three times and hit the lock button on my key so that the horn beeps.

There's no crosswalk but I still walk to the corner, wait for a car and truck to go by then cross.

The closer I get to Owen's house, the slower my steps get. Maybe I should have called.

And I totally would have except I don't exactly have Owen on speed dial. I could have asked Jake Green or Stuart Dobson if either of them have his number—they both play Varsity hockey, too—but Jake and Philip train with the same trainer off-season, and Stuart's been friends with Astrid for longer than I have.

Not that it's a secret or anything, me trying to get a hold of Owen.

I just don't want my boyfriend or best friend to know.

And I couldn't ask any of Owen's friends for his number because I don't know who any of them are. I'm not even sure he has any friends. All the times I can remember seeing Owen at school, he's been alone.

It's sad if you think about it. And even more reason for me to befriend him.

Poor guy's probably lonely.

I head up the sidewalk leading to his house. It's two stories with chipped, brown paint and a sagging porch. The front yard is small but neatly trimmed and scattered with toys—a blue kickball, a plastic whiffle bat, and a faded pink Barbie camper with several Barbies (most of them naked) and one fully dressed Ken lying next to it.

And can I just say that Ken is looking waaayy too pleased with himself.

Must have been one heck of a camping trip.

There's a light blue bicycle in the driveway next to an ancient gray minivan. A smaller bike with training wheels next to the porch steps.

I glance at the surrounding houses but it's barely fifty degrees and no one's out and about to see me climb the crooked, cement stairs, step onto the porch and knock on Owen's front door.

While I wait for my knock to be answered, I shift my weight from my right leg to my left. Wipe my palms down the front of my jeans.

Owen's neighborhood is nothing like mine. My house is on a hill overlooking town, the closest neighbor a good quarter mile away. Here the houses line the river and are so jammed together that if you stood between two of them, you could touch them both at the same time.

It's like I've wandered into an alternate reality.

Or maybe that's just because I'm here, knocking on the door of a boy I barely know. A boy I've had exactly two real conversations with. A boy who needs me.

A boy who won't get out of my head.

But I'm not going to focus on that little fact. Nope. Just going to shove that back into the shadowy recesses of my mind and pretend it doesn't exist.

We Hewitts excel at that.

The door opens and my heart slams in my chest. But it's not Owen staring at me, it's a little boy, maybe four or five, wearing a Hulk T-shirt and Iron Man underwear.

Owen's house must be pants optional.

All those naked Barbies are making much more sense.

"Who are you?" the boy asks. His brown hair is wavy and keeps falling into his eyes so he snaps his head back with enough force to dislodge a few vertebrae. Obviously lifting a hand and brushing that troublesome hair aside is just too darn hard. He has a round face, a small pot belly and skinny legs with scabs on both knees.

"Hi," I say. "I'm Natalie. What's your name?"

"Gus." He gives me a shrewd onceover that's at odds with what really is an angelic face complete with big, blue eyes. "Do you have any candy?"

"Uh...not on me."

"You got any money?"

I raise my eyebrows. What is this kid, a mugger in training?

"Nope." I glance over him into the house but all I can see is a tiny foyer, the floor littered with shoes, boots and coats. I hear a television in the background. "Is Owen home?"

Gus shrugs and steps back and I step forward but he's not letting me in.

He's shutting the door on my face.

It slams shut and I rock back on my high heels. Guess since I'm not out here, randomly knocking on doors to hand out candy or money to little kids, he's lost interest.

Owen's home life is getting curiouser and curiouser.

I knock again. A moment later, the door opens. This time it's a girl—older than Gus and a bit chubbier, her straight brown hair reaching her waist. They're so similar in appearance, they must be brother and sister.

Owen's little brother and sister.

Huh. Who knew?

Before she can say anything, Gus runs up behind her and taps her shoulder at least a dozen times.

"I'm hungry," he says, half-demand, half-whine.

"I'll make you a peanut butter and jelly in a minute," the girl tells him.

His eyes fill with tears. It's like, one moment he's fine, all clear-eyed and bugging his sister, the next...waterworks.

"I don't want a sandwich! There's only crusty pieces of bread left!"

"I'll flip them inside out. You won't even taste the crusts."

"No," he says with a huge sniff. "I want mac and cheese!"

"You had mac and cheese yesterday."

"I want it again."

"We only have one box left."

His face sets in stubborn lines, his shoulders going rigid. "I want it."

She glances at me then turns toward Gus and lowers her voice. "Today's Saturday. If you eat it now, you can't have it again until Wednesday. That's four more sleeps."

He nods. Rubs his knuckles over his eyes. "That's okay."

Sighing the sigh of the world weary—which is nuts as she's maybe nine or ten—she shakes her head in defeat. "Fine. But don't even think about crying to me tomorrow at lunch when you're eating a crusty peanut butter and jelly sandwich."

"I won't," he says, now dry-eyed and grinning.

But I think we all know that when the time comes, this kid is going to pitch a major fit.

"Get the box from the cupboard," she tells him, "I'll make it for you in a minute."

Gus takes off, bare feet slapping against the floor.

Owen's sister faces me again. "Who are you?"

"I'm Natalie," I say. "Is Owen home?"

"No."

And once again, I get a door—this, specific door—shut in my face.

I knock quickly before she can get too far away and almost immediately, it opens again.

"Will Owen be home soon?" I ask.

"Why do you want to know?"

God. Suspicious, much?

"We're...friends." It's not really a lie. We're probably going to be the very best of friends.

As soon as he realizes how much fun I am.

"I need to talk to him," I say.

"Who is it?" a man I assume is Owen's dad growls as he joins us. He's tall and skinny with long, scraggly black hair and a several tattoos including a bulldog on his neck.

"Natalie," the girl says. "She's a friend of Owen's."

Holding a can of Bud Light in one hand (guess he lives by the adage that it's five o'clock somewhere though right here, right now, it's not even 11:00 a.m.), he leans over Owen's sister, putting his free hand on the door above her head. She shrinks back but doesn't leave. For which I'm super grateful, especially when Mr. Radlowski gives me a slow, thorough once-over that is completely inappropriate and extremely creepy.

"Well, Natalie—" he draws my name out then gives me a smarmy grin that makes my skin crawl. "—Owen isn't here right now but we expect him back any minute." He pulls the door open wider. "Why don't you come in and wait? We'll get you a drink."

And he winks at me.

Blech.

I take a step back because...eww. "That's okay. I'll just...I'll talk to him at school on Monday."

Where everyone will see us and wonder what we're chatting about. Philip and Astrid will do more than wonder. They'll demand to know. And it's not my place to share Owen's business, such as him needing help in English.

"You say Owen will be home any minute?" Maybe I can wait on the porch.

Or in my Jeep. With the doors locked.

"He won't," Owen's sister says before her dad can speak. "He won't be home until at least three."

Mr. Radlowski's grin widens. "More time for us to get to know Natalie better. Nothing I like more than entertaining one of Owen's *friends*."

And the way he says *friends* he might as well have said *bondage sex partner*.

I take another step back. "That's okay. I'd hate to disturb your morning."

He shrugs. Sips his beer. "Suit yourself."

Then he tugs the girl out of the way and shuts the door.

I stare at the door. It shouldn't be this difficult to track down one boy, clear the air between us and get him to accept my help. And he does need my help—after meeting his father, that's clearer than ever.

I knock once more.

Please let Owen's sister answer. Please, please, please.

She does.

"Do you know where Owen is?" I ask.

"Yeah." She tips her head to the side and studies me. "Are you a cheerleader?"

"Are we having the same conversation? Because I asked where Owen is."

She shrugs. "You look like a cheerleader."

Not sure how that can be since I'm wearing dark, skinny jeans, an off-the shoulder sweater and high heeled, peep toe booties, and not a short skirt and sneakers and shaking pom-poms. "Well, I'm not. No rah-rah for me, but I do play tennis." She's less than impressed. "And I take ballet." Still nothing. Tough crowd. "And I took gymnastics for a few years."

Her expression lights up and she steps onto the porch, pulling the door shut behind her. "Do you know how to do a cartwheel?"

"Of course."

"Can you teach me how to do one?"

"Maybe," I say, picking up on her game. Information for a few cartwheel lessons. "If I do, will you tell me where Owen is?"

"Maybe," she says with a confident grin, certain she's gotten her way.

She has. And I can't help but admire her for it.

13

———

Almost forty minutes later I'm sitting in my Jeep in the parking lot behind Sanderson's gym which, to be honest, looks more like a warehouse than an actual fitness facility. After our successful cartwheel lesson, Piper—Owen's sister—told me he works Saturday mornings until elven then trains for a few hours.

I would have preferred catching him mowing someone's lawn where I could grab a quick word or two then be on my carefree way. Where it could be just the two of us. But nope, he's inside the very building I've been staring at for the past ten minutes like I'm his stalker. Watching. Waiting.

Ugh.

I force myself to climb out, do my door-lock-triple-handle-check-horn-beep thing, then walk across the lot. I hesitate at the door because...again...it doesn't exactly look like a gym, plus there's the whole I'm-here-for-Owen thing, but I open it and step inside because I am a woman on a mission.

Even if I'm not sure why the mission is so important to me.

I scan the gym. It's huge, almost industrial, very bare bones and basic, a long, open space with racks of dumbbells, weight machines, treadmills, stair-climbers and stationary bikes. There are suspension trainers attached to the far wall, a boxing ring in the center and several sizes of punching bags in the rear, right corner. The high ceiling captures the noise—AC/DC's "Thunderstruck" blaring over some unseen sound system, the hum of the treadmills, the clang of barbells being dropped because guys love nothing more than letting everyone know they've just lifted a weight so incredibly heavy, there's no way they can set it down gently.

There's also grunting, talking, laughing and good-natured shouting.

It's all very...male.

Especially the smell.

"Can I help you with something, miss?"

I turn to find a tall, older, bald guy with a full, red beard, sweatpants and a green Sanderson's Gym T-shirt approaching me.

It occurs to me that this could be Owen's personal trainer.

And that he might not exactly be thrilled to have someone showing up, interrupting his trainee's session.

"Hi," I say with a big, friendly smile. "I actually just came to ask Owen—Owen Radlowski?—a quick question. Real quick, as in two seconds."

He studies me for a moment, but not in the icky way Owen's dad did. "That so?"

I keep smiling. "Yes. That is so."

He inclines his head and starts walking, which I take to mean I should follow him. I do, feeling the eyes of every guy on me as we pass them.

Of which there are many.

I follow Red Beard to the other side of the gym, catch sight of Owen whipping a set of weighted ropes up and down as hard and fast as he can. He's wearing loose, gray running shorts and a black ballcap.

What he is not wearing is a shirt.

He has a tattoo. A huge, black phoenix, its wide, outspread wings tipped in red flames, covers most of his upper back. His feet are planted wide, his knees bent, quads and hamstrings clenched, back muscles bunching and flexing, making the phoenix seem as if it's about to take flight.

I can't look away from him—from the play of those muscles, the smoothness of his tanned skin, the width of his shoulders.

It's all very...disconcerting.

Then Red Beard steps up next to him and says, "Someone here to see you."

And Owen glances over his shoulder and meets my eyes and it's so much worse.

It's terrifying.

Oh, yeah, this was a really, really bad idea on my part.

But it's too late now because Owen has dropped the ropes, turned and is staring at me. "What the hell are you doing here?"

"Waiting for the treadmill," I say, gesturing to them. "Thought I'd work off that third slice of pizza I had last night."

He is not amused.

"I'm really sorry to bother you during your workout—" I say, tossing Red Beard a quick, apologetic smile. "—but I need to ask you something."

"What?"

I tip my head toward the empty back corner of the gym.

Owen stares at me.

God. What is with him? It's like he has some sort of personal force field against my cheery, friendly, charming attitude.

"This—" I repeat the head tip. "—is the universal sign for *let's talk over there*."

"I'm busy," he says, his mouth barely moving. Pretty amazing trick, that.

"Take a break," Red Beard says.

"Now?"

Red Beard checks his watch. "Ten minutes." Then he grins at Owen in that way guys have when they've one-upped the other. "Mandatory."

Glaring at him, Owen mutters *asshole* under his breath then stomps over to the bench lining the wall, swipes up his shirt and heads to the corner I'd indicated.

"Thank you so much," I tell Red Beard. "I won't keep him long, I promise." I catch up to Owen. "I'm pretty sure you shouldn't call your trainer that. It's rude."

"So's interrupting someone else's workout. Gym time isn't free, you know."

I wince. I hadn't thought of that. Of course he's paying Red Beard to train him. And every minute he's with me is costing him. Literally.

My throat gets tight and I swallow. "I'm sorry," I tell him when we reach the corner. "I didn't think."

He takes his hat off and tugs his shirt on. His hair is damp with sweat and sticking up like crazy. He runs his fingers through it then puts his hat back on.

Doesn't seem to notice that his shirt is inside out.

"You didn't think what?" he asks.

"Didn't think this whole idea through."

His eyes narrow. "You seem like the type of person who thinks everything through. A hundred times."

He's right. It's unsettling how right he is. How he seems to see me so clearly.

"I've decided to follow my instincts more often," I say. "Be more...spontaneous."

It's not even a complete lie. Chase is always telling me I overthink, well, everything. Philip says I take way too long making decisions like which ice cream flavor to get or what movie we should watch. Astrid says I need to learn to go with the flow.

No better time to start than the present, right?

Owen leans against the wall and crosses his arms. "Okay, Miss Spontaneity, how did you know I was here?"

"Piper told me."

"Piper?" He straightens slowly, his arms dropping. "My sister Piper?"

"Do you know any other Pipers?" I ask, truly curious. "Because it's a unique name."

He cuts his hand through the air, wiping that question away. "When, exactly, did you talk to my sister?"

"About forty-five minutes ago."

"Where?"

"At your house."

He growls. The boy literally growls at me. Guess if he'd been home, he would have been the one slamming the door on me. "Why the hell would you go to my house?"

"Because I don't have your cell phone number."

He starts pacing, muttering under his breath, which I don't even try to decipher because I'm pretty sure those mutterings are about me.

And not the least bit flattering.

Okay, so he doesn't want me at his house. It's no big deal.

Oh, who am I kidding? It's a very big deal. It's a huge deal.

It's also irritating and insulting. I'm not a leper, for God's sake.

He stops pacing and whirls on me. "How do you even know where I live?"

"My mom has your address."

Mom sends out Christmas cards—with a generous bonus—to the landscapers, her hairstylist, personal trainer and massage therapist every year.

Once I remembered that, it was easy enough to log onto her laptop while she was in the shower and find out where Owen lived.

If possible, his expression hardens even more. "You had no right to go there."

"Why not? You're at my house at least once a week."

"Working," he spits out. "In the yard."

"Uh, not all that long ago you were in my kitchen." But that sound, reasonable argument only seems to tick him off more. "What's the big deal? So, I was at your house. It's not like I was in your room, snooping through your stuff. When your dad invited me in—"

"You went inside?" Owen asks, stepping toward me, all broad and looming and very, very angry.

My heart kicks up a notch and I shake my head quickly. "I stayed on the porch."

He shuts his eyes briefly and it hits me. He's not angry. Or at least, not just angry.

He was worried.

"He's not my dad," Owen mutters.

"What?"

"Ray. The guy at my house. He's not my dad. He's my mom's boyfriend."

"Oh, thank God," I say, the words rushing out of me before I can stop them. My face heats. "No offense or anything. I mean, he seemed very..." Gross. Predatory. "Nice."

"I doubt that." He relaxes a little, watches me carefully. "What do you want, Natalie?"

I shift. Remember how hearing him say my name last week caused the same, fluttery feeling in my stomach I'm experiencing now. "Why is my being the English tutor a problem?"

Why won't you let me help you? Why don't you like me?

"It's not."

My phone buzzes in my front pocket. Probably Philip again. He called twice while I was with Piper but I didn't want to answer. Didn't want to lie him if he asked me what I was doing. Where I was.

I let it go to voicemail.

"You said it was," I remind Owen as the buzzing stops. "Right before you walked out on me."

"I didn't walk out on you. I left."

"*After* you found out I was the tutor. It doesn't take a genius to get the connection."

"Might not take one, but I bet you are one."

I roll my eyes. "Hardly. But I am smart enough to help you with your English assignment."

He's not saying anything and the way he's looking at me, all intense and probing, it makes me itchy. Anxious.

"Did I do something to make you mad?" I ask. "Because I didn't mean to. And if this is about that day at my house, I'm sorry if I was rude—"

"You weren't."

"I kicked you out."

He snorts. "In the most polite way possible."

"Politest way," I correct, because proper grammar is important. "But it was still rude."

"You got pissed. You have the right. Just like you had the right to toss me out on my ass for saying something stupid."

I'm pretty sure that's an apology. Or as close to one as I'm going to get.

I'll take it.

Relieved, I smile. "So there's no reason we can't work together now. We'll start Tuesday. I'll re-read *Catch*—"

"No."

I blink. "Excuse me?"

"I said *no.*"

"I don't understand."

"Not used to hearing that word?"

"What I don't understand is why you're saying it."

"Because I don't want your help."

And he walks away.

I hurry after him. "You may not want my help, but you obviously need it. You wouldn't have come to the library in the first place if you didn't."

"I changed my mind."

"Because of me," I say. "Because...because you don't like me."

He just keeps walking. Doesn't deny my words. Doesn't rush to assure me that he has nothing against me.

I hurry around to stand in front of him.

His mouth flattens. "You're in my way."

"Look, I've gone to the trouble of tracking you down. I even apologized for whatever it is I've done that ticked you off. The least you can do is explain why you won't let me help you."

"You want an explanation?" he asks, and I can see he's frustrated and exasperated and impatient with my inability to let things go.

Welcome to my world, buddy.

"I'm not your personal charity case."

I'm stunned, not just by his words, but by the vehemence in his tone. "I...I don't think you're a charity case at all."

"You want to swoop in," he continues, low and bitter, "and save the day so you can make yourself look good. Then, when it's all said and done, you get to add one more item to your list of accomplishments and give yourself a big old pat on the back for a job well done."

There's a rushing sound in my ears, a tingling sensation in my hands. "Is that...is that what you really think?"

"You going to try and tell me any different?"

"No," I say softly. "I'm not going to tell you any different."

What would be the point? He's already made up his mind about me. Nothing I say is going to convince him otherwise.

Well, at least I still have my pride. It's battered and bruised, but strong enough to get me through this.

"I rescind my offer," I tell him with as much dignity as I can manage. "I'd rather teach Sex Ed to eighth-grade boys than help a judgmental jerk like you."

I move to brush past him but this time, he's the one blocking my way.

"I am not judgmental," he grinds out.

"All you've ever done is look down on me—"

"Look down on *you*? You live in a mansion on top of a hill. You look down on the whole goddamn town."

"—you think I'm a spoiled, selfish bitch. But you don't know me. You know nothing about me. But I now know enough about you to say, with absolute conviction, that you are a complete and utter dick."

With that, I storm off. But good manners won't let me leave—not yet.

Stupid manners.

I change course, cross to the bearded guy. "Thank you," I tell him. "And again, I'm sorry for interrupting your day."

I walk away before he can respond.

I feel Owen watching me, but I don't look back, just push open the door and step out into the bright sunshine.

My eyes sting but I refuse to cry. Owen's opinion shouldn't matter to me. I shouldn't care what he or anyone else thinks of me.

I shouldn't.

But I do.

14

———

I'M SO UPSET AFTER WHAT HAPPENED WITH OWEN THAT I STOP OFF AT Greens and Beans before going home. I need some caffeine and sugar and yeah, okay, a doughnut to get back my equilibrium.

The smoothie/coffee shop is packed, all the tables filled, both lines to place orders long and slow moving. A group of teenagers takes up two tables in front of the large window overlooking the street and I wave at John Miller who's in my History class. I'm all for waiting in line. Gives me time to read the entire menu. Scan the display cases.

Gives me time to make my choices.

I've just decided on the peanut butter cream filled doughnut with chocolate frosting when my phone starts buzzing.

It's Philip. Again.

I let it go to voicemail.

Again.

I assuage any guilt I feel by promising myself I'll text him in a little bit. After I figure out what I'm going to tell him about why I didn't answer his earlier calls. Or the texts he sent. Why I can't talk until later.

I just...I need some time to think things through. To figure out how much I want to tell him about my morning and visit with Owen.

Not that I plan on lying to him. I'm just going to be choosy in what I say.

If I say anything at all.

He's at yet another soccer tournament this weekend—this time in Ohio—and I don't want to burden him with what's going on. He'll want to help, to fix things for me and while that's sweet, this is my problem. One I need to solve on my own.

Anyway, what would I say? Owen was mean to me? That would only cause unnecessary problems. Like Philip confronting him on it. Or Philip wondering why I tracked Owen down in the first place. Why it's so important to me that Owen let me tutor him in English.

No, not going to tell Philip. He'd only get the wrong idea.

He wouldn't understand.

The line moves forward again, and I focus on what drink to get. It's a toss-up between the Heath Bar blended coffee drink or my usual iced caramel macchiato. Well, it used to be my usual. I haven't had one since Owen confiscated it that day at my house, though I usually drink at least three a week.

But no more. I refuse to give up my favorite drink because of Owen Radlowski.

And I'm going to order *two* doughnuts, by God. That should make me feel better.

If it doesn't, I'm in worse shape than I thought.

Someone behind me taps my shoulder. "What are you getting?"

I turn to find Mary Alice Gibson standing behind me. I smile. It's sort of impossible not to smile at her (even if you're in a crap mood), she's just so bright and happy all the time. Literally bright. Her hair, a super short, cute pixie cut, is cotton-candy pink and she always wears neon colors. Today's outfit is a lime green stretchy miniskirt, striped green and white tights, a chunky purple sweater and pink high-top sneakers.

It's like the eighties threw up on her.

"Ice caramel macchiato and a Bavarian cream doughnut," I tell her, changing my mind about the peanut butter one. "And a chocolate-dipped, cake one."

She sighs. "Must be nice. If I even think about eating *one* doughnut, I put on five pounds."

"I'm lucky to have my mom's metabolism," I say lightly, but the truth is, what I really have is five tennis practices, six dance classes and three five-mile runs a week.

But people would rather believe I've been blessed by the good gene fairies, which, I guess, I have been, but it doesn't negate the time and effort I put into keeping in shape.

"So just coffee for you?" I ask.

She nods. "A skinny mocha latte—which will make up for the fact that I'm also getting whipped cream on it."

"Sounds like a solid compromise. If not, technically, mathematically sound reasoning."

She laughs. "Yeah, but it does the trick for me."

I really like Mary Alice. I mean, we're not friends exactly. She goes to Brantford High, our town's public school, but we've been in the same dance classes for the past six years. She's funny and very nice.

"Will you be at class on Monday?" she asks me as an elderly man leaves the counter and the line moves forward again.

My tennis matches next week are on Tuesday and Thursday. "Yes."

"Good. I was thinking we could start working on the kids' program, maybe come up with the song choice at least? Maybe something from a kid-appropriate Broadway show or a movie?"

Mary Alice and I help with the younger classes and this year our teacher, Miss Laurie, is letting us choreograph a dance for them for the end of the year performance.

"That's a great idea," I say, my mind already spinning with possibilities as we step up to the counter. I place my order then turn to her and wave her to go ahead. "My treat."

"Thanks."

I wait until she's ordered her drink to slide my credit card into the reader. "What about a medley of songs?" I ask. "From, like, *Frozen* and *Coco* and *Beauty and the Beast*..."

She claps her hands—that's the thing about Mary Alice. If she's happy, you know it. "I love that idea!" She pulls out her phone and types a note into it. "How about we each bring a list of...I don't know...a dozen songs we think will work? Then we'll whittle it down after class."

The reader beeps and I take my card out. "Or we could do it now," I say as casual as possible because I don't want her to think I'm some loser who has nothing else to do today.

Although, with Philip out of town and Astrid hanging out with Sean after her cross-country meet, that's exactly what I am.

Surprise crosses Mary Alice's face before she offers me an apologetic look. "I can't. I'm meeting my friends." She inclines her head toward the two tables in front of the window. "If you don't want to do it during class, we could meet beforehand? Say six-fifteen?"

She doesn't offer to introduce me to her group. Doesn't invite me to join them.

She doesn't want to hang out with me. Doesn't want to be my friend.

"Sure," I say weakly. "That'll work."

There's a sick feeling in my stomach—embarrassment, I'm sure, from having my pride and ego shredded twice in less than an hour. Luckily, our order is ready so I turn, and take my doughnuts and coffee.

Pasting on a bright, toothy grin, I face her again. "I'll see you Monday then."

But the smile must not be some of my better work because she frowns. Looks concerned. About me.

Oh, God, she feels sorry for me.

What is up with this horrible, rotten, crappy morning?

Mary Alice gives the barista a smile as she accepts her coffee then turns to me. "Listen, Nata—"

"See you," I repeat then hurry out of there before she can ask me if I'm okay. Or invite me to join them out of guilt.

Or worse, pity.

* * *

I'm pulling out of the parking lot when it hits me.

Astrid is my only friend.

It never really occurred to me before but, oh, man, it's occurring to me now.

It never bothered me before. Certainly never worried me.

Wish I could go back to that time.

Maybe then I wouldn't feel so completely pathetic. So...lonely.

I mean, I know plenty of people. Like most of them. And plenty of people know and like me, too. We chat during classes or in the cafeteria at lunch. Hang out at parties. I always sit with Claudia, my doubles' partner, on the bus for away matches. Talk to Mary Alice and a couple other girls at dance class.

But we're not friends.

We don't text or call each other. Don't spend any time together outside of school or tennis practice or dance class.

They're more like...friendly acquaintances. Any relationship we have is based totally on convenience. It's all very casual.

I just hadn't realized until now that it was also very superficial.

And super depressing.

My hands tighten on the wheel. What if...oh, my God...what if the whole reason I tracked Owen down this morning, why I was so desperate to get him to like me wasn't because he needs a friend?

But because *I* do?

But it's fine, my very small, insular world. It's good. I mean, there's no point trying to expand it. I'm going to graduate in eight months. Will be living on the other side of the state this time next year so really, trying to build friendships now would be a waste of time.

They wouldn't last.

Besides, I'm not really alone. Not really lonely. I have my parents and brother. My best friend and boyfriend.

I don't need anything else.

Don't need anyone else.

It's my new mantra, one I repeat all the way home.

One that gets harder and harder to believe as the day progresses.

Especially since Mom's in D.C. at an art show and won't be back until late tonight and Dad's at the hospital and I doubt I'll see him before the end of the weekend.

I try calling Chase, but he doesn't answer so I leave a fake cheery message, telling him I was just calling to say *Hi* and he doesn't need to get back to me.

Even if I hope he will.

Okay, so I'm technically alone for the day but it's no big deal. It's not like I don't have things to keep me busy. And really, everyone needs a day or two of solitude, right? To focus on their own emotional health and well-being.

Solitude. It's good for the soul.

I text Philip and make plans to talk to him later then send Astrid a message, asking how she did at her race. I eat my doughnuts.

And an hour later I scarf down a huge bowl of mint, chocolate-chip ice cream with chocolate syrup and crushed up Oreos and call it lunch.

I do two loads of laundry and clean the bathrooms—all in the name of trying to be more helpful to Mom. I finish my homework and make a list of song suggestions for the kids' performance piece.

Later in the afternoon I go downstairs to the studio my parents had built for me and work on the solo I'm choreographing for my Modern Dance class. After I shower, I order Chinese takeout and curl up on the couch with my cashew chicken, spicy vegetables and egg roll to watch reruns of *Friends*.

And at the end of the night, exhausted from all of my very busy activities and inner reflection, I go to my room, shut the door and turn on a Beyoncé song.

Then I count the flowers on my wall.

And for a little while, I'm not sad. I'm not lonely.

For a little while, I'm not sad at all.

15

———

Monday night after my last dance class, I'm texting Philip while waiting in the alcove of the studio for the rain to let up so I can make a mad dash to my Jeep when Mary Alice joins me.

I don't even look up.

"It's really pouring," she says, shifting aside to let a group of giggling middle schoolers out the door.

"Uh-huh," I say, scrolling through my Instagram feed, which is so incredibly bad-mannered I get all itchy, as if I'm breaking out in hives.

That's me. Allergic to rudeness.

Mary Alice jingles her keys. "Do you want to go to Greens and Beans? My treat this time."

My fingers still, my jaw tightens. If that's not an invitation born out of pity because of how I ran out of the coffee shop the other day, I don't know what is.

"No. But thanks," I add after a moment, proud that I leave it at that. That I don't offer any excuses or explanations or trip all over myself trying to make sure she's not mad at me.

She wrinkles her nose. "Yeah, we probably wouldn't make it anyway." The coffee shop closes at 10:00 and it's already 9:45. "We can grab a slice of pizza instead. Or we can plan something for later—"

"You don't have to pay me back."

She blinks. Tonight her hair is all spiky, like neon flames sticking up from her head, her cheeks still pink from class. She has a bright yellow sweatshirt on over her black leotard and matching yellow legwarmers. "What?"

"You don't owe me anything for buying your coffee Saturday," I explain.

Mary Alice frowns, looking like a very confused, mildly irritated pixie. "This isn't about me paying you back. I thought it would be fun for us to hang out."

"You don't have to say that." I mean to sound kind. Patient and understanding. But my tone is too sharp and more than a bit petulant. "You don't really mean it."

Now she raises her eyebrows. Forget mildly irritated. Huh. I didn't even know Mary Alice could get angry.

"I think I know what I mean more than you do."

I just shrug and glance through the doors. In the glow of the streetlight I see the rain has slowed but is still steady. Taking my keys out, I decide to make a run for it, but when I reach for the door handle, Mary Alice touches my arm, stopping me.

"Is everything okay with you?" she asks. "You're acting very...un-Natalie-ish."

"Because I'm not being super sweet and accommodating?"

Her eyes widen in surprise, either at my dry tone or because I know, fully well, what people expect of me. How they expect me to constantly act.

"Uh...yeah," she says. "That pretty much covers it."

"Everything's fine. I just...I don't need you feeling sorry for me," I blurt then snap my lips together before any other annoying, embarrassing truths come out. "You don't have to pretend you want to be friends. I mean, friends outside of dance class. It's fine."

And I smile and pat her arm, letting her off the hook with my generous spirit and forgiving nature.

At least, that's what I'm shooting for.

But instead of going on her way, absolved of her sins, her spirit redeemed, she stands her ground. Who knew someone so little would be so hard to budge?

"Is this because I couldn't do something with you the other day? Because it was sort of short notice."

Can't argue with that.

I mean, I will. But I probably shouldn't, seeing as how she's right and all.

But I'm feeling defensive, which I hate. It's not like I can admit how hard it was for me to ask her to hang out, to put myself out there when I wasn't sure I'd get the result I wanted. How terrified I am of rejection. Any rejection.

Talk about lame.

"You didn't invite me to join you," I say. When she just shakes her head in confusion, I clarify, "You and your friends at the coffee shop. You could have invited me to join you, to hang out with you all, but you didn't."

Now she gapes at me—jaw slack, eyes wide, the whole bit. "Is that what this about? How was I to know you'd even want to hang out with us? We're not exactly your usual crowd."

I don't have a usual crowd. Just Philip and Astrid.

"How do you know what my usual crowd is?" I ask. "We don't even go to the same school."

"Penny Richter."

"Excuse me?"

"Penny Richter. She's Brantford High's version of you. Tall, gorgeous, smart and good at everything. And though she's nice to everyone from the lowliest freshman to the principal, she wouldn't be caught dead hanging out with anyone I'm friends with."

"I'm not sure whether to be flattered you think I'm good at everything or insulted you seem to think I'm some snob like Penny Richter. Hey," I continue before Mary Alice can say anything, "maybe I should call Penny. We could become BFFs and spend our time looking down our noses at you peons and practice acting condescending together."

Crossing her arms, Mary Alice gives an eye roll so epic, I wouldn't be surprised if she sees her own brain.

"I'm not saying either of you is a snob, so don't put words into my mouth," she says in this authoritative way—like she's talking to one of the little girls in our dance class, schooling them on proper etiquette—that I want to obey just become I'm conditioned to. "What I'm saying is that in society, people tend to group together—like with like. Not everyone mixes well. And I never thought you wanted to mix with us at all."

I'm feeling chastened and I have no idea why. Not sure I want to know. "Well, you thought wrong."

She nods. Smiles at Kerri Sumpter and Riley Case as they brush past us and leave. "I realize that now," Mary Alice says quietly when we're alone again. "And I'm sorry I hurt your feelings. Truly. But—"

"My best friend's mom says when someone adds *but* to the end of an apology or explanation, what they're really saying is *forget everything I just said.*"

Mary Alice sighs. "Look, I was surprised you wanted to do something with me. We've known each other...what? Six years? And you've never, not once, wanted to spend time with me—or any of us—outside of dance class. Anytime we asked, you always made excuses."

"That's not true," I insist, even though part of me wonders if it is.

She gives me an *oh, really?* look. And begins ticking items off on her fingers. "Last year we invited you to go Christmas shopping in Pittsburgh with us. For three months straight freshman year we asked you to get lunch with us on Saturdays after class. You've been invited to hang out at our houses, to help with choreography after class and to meet up for brunch on Sundays. You always decline—politely, of course. But a no is a no. Now, you tell me, how was I supposed to know that suddenly, after all these years, you've changed your mind?"

My face is hot with embarrassment. My throat tight with shame and regret.

She's right. She's totally right.

I knew I shouldn't have argued with her.

Now I have to face the truth. I was hurt and offended by what I felt was Mary Alice's unfair judgment of me. Her rejection of me. So furious at Owen for the same reason, thinking they both viewed me as a stuck-up bitch. I laid the blame at their feet, righteous in my indignation, confident I was the victim. And maybe they were partly to blame—especially Owen. But there's one common denominator in both situations.

Me.

"You couldn't have known I changed my mind," I tell her. "But I have."

"Why?"

"I just...I guess I realized what I've been missing."

"Oh, you've been missing a lot. We're awesome." She grins. "Me, especially."

I smile. "Awesome enough to still want to get pizza?"

Her hesitation makes me nervous. Maybe it's too late. Maybe I've blown it.

Maybe I don't deserve a second chance.

"I would," she finally says, but she's not looking at me, she's looking at something outside, "but you'll have to give me a raincheck. No pun intended."

"Sure," I say, as if it's no big deal. "Of course."

But I must not be as good at hiding my hurt as I'd like to think because she gives me another eye roll. "I want to, but you seem to already have plans."

"No, I don't." Other than the four hours of homework waiting for me, that is.

"Yeah," she says, with a nod outside. "You do."

Frowning, I follow her gaze.

And lock eyes with Owen.

16

I take an automatic step forward but stop myself before I can do something completely idiotic like press my nose against the glass to make sure I'm not seeing things.

Owen is on the sidewalk, shoulders hunched against the rain, hands in his pockets, blond hair dark and wet, rivulets of water running down his unsmiling face.

"You see him, too, right?" I murmur to Mary Alice.

"Hard to miss Owen Radlowski," she says way more cheerfully, in my opinion, than the situation calls for.

I'm not surprised she knows him. They probably went to school together up until Owen started at West Brook sophomore year.

"What do you think he's doing here?" I ask because I haven't the slightest clue. Does his sister take classes here? If so, why haven't I seen her before?

"If the way he's staring at you is anything to go by, he's here for you."

"He doesn't want me." But that doesn't sound right so I try again. "I mean, he's not here for me." I think about it for a minute. "Unless he's here to kill me. But he doesn't really strike me as a murderer. Just a tool."

"Well, there's only one way to find out what he wants," Mary Alice says, and before I can evade, she grabs my hand and tugs me outside. Owen straightens and takes his hands out of his pockets.

"Owen, hi," she calls as we step onto the sidewalk.

"Hey, Mary Alice." He flicks an unreadable glance at me then gives Mary Alice what I'm guessing by the slightly upturned corners of his mouth is supposed to be a smile. "How's it going?"

"Good, thanks. Are you waiting for someone?" she asks, the rain glistening on the ends of her hair.

But as curious as I was a moment ago to find out what he's doing here, I suddenly don't want to know.

Tell myself I don't care to know.

"We're just leaving," I say before he can answer her question, then give myself a mental forehead slap because...duh. What else would we be doing? I consider giving Owen one of my bright, sunny smiles but then I remember I'm mad at him so I don't. Ha. Take that you jerk. "See you later."

It's my turn to tug Mary Alice along but before I can go two steps, Owen touches my shoulder. "Do you have a minute?"

Because I am still mad, I make a show of looking around. Touch my chest and widen my eyes. "Me?"

Once again, he's not amused.

Too bad.

Mary Alice gives my hand a reassuring squeeze before tugging free. "I'll see you Wednesday, Nat."

She leaves, jogging off toward the parking lot before I can stop her. Or beg her to stay.

You know, just in case he really is here to kill me.

Chin lifted, I do my best to look down my nose at Owen—I'm pretty successful, too, if I do say so myself. It helps that he's not that much taller than me. "Yes?"

He opens his mouth. Shuts it then wipes his palm down his wet face. "Let's sit in my truck," he says, nodding at a pickup parked in the lot next to the studio, two rows behind my Jeep.

I don't move. "Sorry. My mom told me never to get into a stranger's vehicle."

"You want to stand in the rain? Fine. I'm going to my truck."

"Okay." I almost wish him a good night (those stupid manners again, they really are deeply ingrained—maybe I need a twelve-step program) but I clamp my lips shut without so much as a polite *goodbye*.

He falls into step beside me as I head toward the parking lot. I press the unlock button on my key and my Jeep's headlights flash.

"You won't leave," Owen says as if this is some foregone conclusion.

I open the driver's side door and toss my bag inside. "Pretty sure that's exactly what I'm doing."

"You won't leave," he repeats. "You're too curious about why I'm here."

And he walks away.

Well, I'll show him. I get into my Jeep and slam the door shut. He thinks he knows me? Double ha.

But I don't turn on the ignition. I don't even put the key in, just hold it in my hand and run the pad of my thumb along the ridges, up and down. Up and down. Driving away seems like the wrong choice, like I'm running from him and I refuse to give him that satisfaction.

I'll wait him out.

I mentally recite all my homework assignments three times, then count the number of street lights I can see then I list everyone in my modern dance class and all the kids in ballet one.

When I check my rearview mirror, his truck is still there.

I groan and let my chin drop to my chest.

Then I get out of the car and stomp the two rows to his truck. He reaches across the seat and pushes the door open and I climb in, settle on the passenger side of the bench seat and yank the door shut. I stare out the rain-spotted windshield and don't so much as glance his way.

I really don't want to see him gloat.

"Curiosity," I say in a snotty tone, "is a sign of high intelligence."

"It is."

My eyes narrow at his agreement. Was that smugness in his voice? Hard to tell without looking at him.

Which I refuse to do.

"And for the record, I'm not curious about what you're doing here," I say. "I'm simply wondering how you knew I'd be here in the first place."

"Same way you knew where I was Saturday. Piper."

That's right. I had mentioned to his sister that I took dance classes three times a week and on Saturday mornings. She asked a lot of questions. Now I know why.

She was digging for personal info.

"She's pretty free with information that's not hers to share," I say.

"Not free. I had to pay her ten bucks."

"I'm thinking I should ask her for half."

"Good luck with that."

I shiver. I shouldn't have sat so long in my Jeep without running the heater. Especially since I'm wet. "What did you want to talk about?"

"Here," he says, handing me a T-shirt. I'm so surprised, I just stare at it. But he must think I'm being prissy because his voice goes hard when he says, "It's clean."

I take it. It's incredibly soft, like he's worn it often. "Thanks."

He fiddles with the heating vents and a moment later, warm air blows. "Okay?"

I nod and use the shirt to blot the water from my face. It smells good, like laundry detergent and fresh air and I wonder if his mom dried it on a clothesline.

I hand it back to him, not bothering with my hair. It's still in a bun, the front and back completely smooth.

If I so much as brush my hand against it, it'll probably explode in a mass of frizz so huge, we'll both be knocked right out of the truck.

He twists the shirt in his hands...twist, twist, twist.

Silence fills the cab and it's so unnerving, it and this entire situation, I start babbling like a fool. "This is a surprise. You being here, I mean. At my dance class. A surprise and the last thing I ever, ever, *ever* expected."

He faces me. Lets the shirt drop to his lap. "I doubt that."

There's something hard and angry and just, well, accusing in his tone. Can't say as I like it much.

Don't ask, I warn myself. *Whatever you do, do not ask...*

"What's that supposed to mean?"

I sigh, my words echoing in the truck. Why do I even bother? I never listen to my own good sense.

"You knew I'd show up. That you'd get your way eventually. Don't you always?"

Yep. I was right. I shouldn't have asked.

"First of all," I say, my tone stiff, my shoulders rigid, "I had no idea you'd show up here tonight, or anywhere at any time. Why would I? And as far as me always getting my way, the answer to that is a big fat no." I reach for the door handle. "So if you dropped by to insult me I think I'll just skip it and be on my way."

"You taught my sister how to do a cartwheel," he spits out as if I'd taught her how to pole dance.

I freeze, the door partway open, my eyebrows raised. "Yes," I say slowly. Why on earth would *that* make him mad? "Don't tell me, you find cartwheels morally reprehensible." I pause. "Reprehensible means—"

"I know what it means." His mouth flattens. "You took off your shoes."

I glance at my feet.

"Not now," he says, but his tone is exasperated. Or maybe amused. "Piper said you took off your shoes and did some fancy flip."

"Is that illegal? Because I'd like to see you try doing a round off backhand spring in three-inch heels."

"She's been practicing constantly," he continues as if I haven't spoken. "I had to watch her for a half an hour when I got home Saturday before I could even get inside the house. She's broken a lamp, knocked over the same plant five times and kicked Gus in the face. Twice."

"I told her to practice outside only. And you'd think Gus would figure out after the first time to give her a wide berth."

"Yeah. That's what I told him."

"Wait..." I shake my head. "Did we just...did we agree on something?" Pressing one palm to my chest, I tip my head back and shut my eyes. "No, no," I say when I sense he's about to speak. "Don't. I'm having a moment and you'll just ruin it."

He sighs so hard, I feel his breath, warm and soft, against my cheek. "It was nice. What you did for Piper."

I open my eyes. "Well, in case you haven't heard, I'm an extremely nice person."

"You called me a dick."

I blush. Oops. I forgot about that.

Boys. Such delicate, sensitive creatures.

"Do you want me to apologize?" I ask.

"That depends."

"On what?"

"On whether or not you'd mean it."

I open my mouth to assure him that, of course, I'd mean it. Nice girl, remember? Always sweet and good and kind.

With the very rare exception of calling people dicks, of course.

But even though apologizing is the right thing to do, I can't.

Or maybe I won't.

Doesn't matter. My stubborn—I mean, my determined—silence is enough for him to get the point.

I don't do what's expected. And I like it.

He follows suit, doing the last thing I expect of him (other than showing up at my dance class, that is).

He smiles.

It's quick, just a flash really, but I catch it.

And go warm all over.

Because the heat's on full blast, I assure myself. But just to be on the safe side, I avert my gaze. Play with the string of my hoodie.

Actually, it's Philip's hoodie, one of his soccer ones, with his last name on the back.

Philip who is probably, at this moment, texting or calling me. Who will get worried when I don't answer.

Who'd be very, very unhappy to find out I'm sitting in a dark, empty parking lot with another boy.

"Anyway," I say, reaching for the handle again, needing to get out of Owen's truck and in my Jeep, needing to get home and talk to my boyfriend, "you're welcome."

"For what?"

"For teaching Piper how to do a cartwheel. Isn't that why you're here? To thank me?"

"No."

I wait but that seems to be the extent of that explanation.

"Well you should," I say, crossing my arms and yes, pouting just a little. "It'd be the polite thing to do."

"Piper didn't thank you?" he asks, and I get the feeling he'd be very upset if his little sister had as few manners as he does.

And how that makes sense in his strange little world, I have no idea.

"She did." Piper had been effusive in her gratitude, giving me hugs and thanking me again and again. "She's a very sweet, very *polite*, little girl."

A white lie, but he doesn't need to know she slammed the door on me and basically blackmailed me into teaching her how to do a cartwheel.

Then again, he'd probably commend her. At least for the door slamming part.

"She's a good kid," he says, his hands are on the steering wheel, his thumbs stroking back and forth. Back and forth. "And I do appreciate you teaching her how to do a cartwheel so...thanks."

I feel like I've won a prize—Owen's gratitude. A hard trophy to get.

I swallow. "You're welcome."

The rain is a steady thrum against the truck. It should be soothing, but it's getting too warm in Owen's truck. It's too cozy, sitting this close to him, breathing in the scents of his laundry detergent and the underlying smell of grass and dirt from his job.

Way too intimate.

"I'd better go." I push the door open, bringing in the misty rain and cool air. The interior light flicks on. "Goodni—"

"Will you be at the library?" He clears his throat. "Tomorrow during last period."

I pause, one foot out the door and swinging above the pavement, my right hand on the door handle. So that's what this is all about.

He does want my help.

He's just too stubborn and proud to admit it. To admit he was wrong.

I can relate. Being wrong sucks.

"Yes," I say, careful to keep my tone mild, as if I couldn't care less about why he's asking. "I'll be there."

He nods and...well...and nothing. Just that nod which I guess is left to me interpret.

I climb out but before I shut the door, I lean back into the truck. "Hey, Owen?" I wait until he meets my gaze then say softly, "I'll see you then."

17

———

THE NEXT MORNING, ASTRID YANKS THE PASSENGER SIDE DOOR OF MY Jeep open but doesn't get in, just stands there, damp hair blowing in the cool breeze, messenger bag worn crosswise, backpack on. She braces both hands against the Jeep's frame and leans into the interior. "What's this about you and Owen Radlowski? Were you with him last night? Does Philip know?"

It's a lot to take in—Astrid's rapid-fire questions and accompanying suspicious tone and astonished expression. Especially when I only got four hours of sleep last night. After doing my homework, I stayed up to skim through *The Catcher in the Rye* just in case Owen really does show up at tutoring today.

"Good morning to you, too," I say. "Would you like to actually get into the Jeep before you start grilling me? Or maybe you'd prefer running alongside while I drive? You can bark questions at me through the open window."

She rears back but continues holding onto the Jeep so that she looks like a sheet that's been caught in the wind. "This isn't a joke, Nat." Now she sweeps forward, sticking her entire upper body into the Jeep as she lowers her voice. "Grant told Sean he saw you with

Owen last night. In Owen's truck. In the dance studio parking lot. What happened?"

Ah, small towns, where everyone knows everyone else and their business.

You either love them, or you hate them. Small towns, that is, though I suppose that covers the gossips, too.

"If you get in," I say, "I'll tell you."

She does so, jumping in, slamming the door and clicking her seatbelt all in quick succession. "Well," she demands before I can even put the Jeep into Reverse. "Is it true?"

I start backing out of her driveway. "Yes."

Out of my peripheral vision I see her shake her head. "What? But...*why*?"

I glance at her then pull to a stop at the corner. "What do you mean?"

"I mean, why were you with Owen Radlowski last night, in a dark parking lot in his truck? Did he kidnap you or something?"

"Yes, he abducted me outside of dance class and demanded a million dollars for my ransom. But all Mom had on her that late was fifty bucks so he took it and we called it even."

"No need for sarcasm," Astrid says, which is hilarious as she lives and breathes sarcasm. It's her coping mechanism for...well...everything. Sadness. Disappointment. Anger. Happiness. "Excuse me for being curious," she continues. "I hadn't realized you and Owen were such good buddies. The kind that hang out in trucks in dark parking lots late at night."

"Okay, first of all, you keep saying *dark parking lot* like most people say pay-by-the-hour-cheap-motel. Secondly, we weren't hanging out, we were talking about school work."

Sort of.

"Uh-huh. And does my brother—you know, your *boyfriend*— know about this little gabfest?"

I hesitate before admitting, "Not yet."

I can feel her surprise.

And her disapproval.

"How could you not tell him?" she asks, her voice just shy of a shriek but shrill enough to have the hair on the back of my neck standing on end. "Why would you keep something like that from him? Unless..."

Stopping at the intersection, I glance at her. "Unless what?"

"Unless there's a reason you don't want Philip to find out."

I pull forward, my hands clenched tight around the wheel— better that than my best friend's throat, right? "There's not. I haven't told Philip yet, because, as you've mentioned, it happened late last night and I knew he'd already be in bed." It starts raining softly and I turn on the windshield wipers. "I planned on telling him today."

In person. A decision I made last night while driving home.

I don't keep things from Philip.

Well, not important things, anyway.

"I don't get why you're so upset," I tell Astrid.

"I just...I hate hearing things about you from other sources."

"Let me get this straight; you're mad I didn't tell Philip but you're also mad I didn't tell you? I'm confused as to the amount of information I'm required to give you in a day and in what order. You first then Philip? Him first?"

"This isn't you telling me you washed your hair and decided to go for a braid today, it's you spending quality time with Owen Radlowksi."

"For the love of God stop saying both his names. It's weird. And I didn't tell you because it's not a big deal."

"Not a big deal?" she repeats, turning in her seat to gape at me. "Not a big deal?"

"Say it one more time," I grind out from between clenched teeth, "and I'm making you walk the rest of the way."

"The fact that my best friend was in a dark parking lot with *Owen Radlowksi* is very much a big deal. I had no idea you even talked to him on a regular basis—or at all—let alone that you know him well enough to hang out with him." She pauses. "In a dark parking lot."

"I don't talk to a lot of people on a regular basis," I point out, something that became clear to me over the long, lonely weekend. "Does that mean I can never talk to them?"

Because that's just too depressing to even consider.

"I'm just wondering what's changed in this particular situation."

"He wanted to talk to me about tutoring him in English."

"Why did he go to your dance class? Why didn't he just talk to you about it at school?"

For a moment, I consider telling her everything, from Owen helping me carry in groceries to him stopping by my tutoring station to me going to his house and tracking him down at the gym. She is my best friend after all.

But she's my best friend second.

She's Philip's sister first.

And she's already freaking out about an innocent chat that yes, just happened to occur in a dark parking lot. I shudder to think what her reaction would be to the fact that last night wasn't the only time Owen and I have spent together.

She wouldn't understand.

I stop for a pedestrian crossing the street. "He probably went there because he doesn't have my phone number. As for why he didn't just talk to me about it at school, who knows what goes on in the minds of teenage boys?"

"They are a strange and mysterious breed of humans," she agrees, albeit begrudgingly. "But I'm not surprised Owen needs help in English. He's not exactly a scholar."

I frown. "That's mean. You have no idea what his grades are."

"Please, it's a small school. We all hear things and it's common knowledge he's no brainiac."

When I stop at a red light, she unbuckles and shifts forward to take off her backpack—must have been an uncomfortable ride with that thing on.

Good.

"I just think you need to be careful," she continues, buckling back up.

"Owen isn't a serial killer. We've gone to school with him for three years."

"Yeah, but what do we really know about him?"

I know he has a younger sister and brother, his house needs painted, and his mom's boyfriend is a creep. I know he has a tattoo, that he works and trains hard, that he keeps the inside of his truck clean and he's a slow reader.

I know that he's stubborn and judgmental and that he put his pride aside to find me last night.

None of which I'm sharing with Astrid.

"I don't get what your problem is with him," I say.

"I don't have a problem with Owen. I have a problem being put in the middle of you and Philip."

"No one is putting you anywhere."

That's a space she jumped into all on her own the minute I told her I liked her brother.

"Maybe not on purpose, but I'm there anyway. Because I know something about you that Philip should know but doesn't. So now I'm faced with either keeping quiet and betraying my brother or telling him and betraying my best friend."

"There's no betrayal involved. I always planned on telling Philip so you can stop worrying I'm sneaking around, hooking up with random guys in *dark parking lots*."

She has the grace to look abashed. "I don't think you're sneaking around on Philip. Or hooking up with other guys."

I snort. "Could have fooled me."

"Whatever," she mutters. "Believe what you want."

"Fine. I will."

I give an inner roll at my lame comeback.

I'll come up with something better, something witty and scathing —a truly spectacular response that will put Astrid in her place.

Of course, that won't happen until later (more than likely in the middle of the night, that perfect putdown waking me from a sound sleep), after I've relived this conversation a dozen or so times.

Too bad. At least once I'd love to be able to conclude an argument with Astrid in a way that lets me know, for certain, I've won.

What can I say? I'm competitive. And I do so love to be proven right.

Just ask my brother.

Until that happy day arrives, Astrid and I will do what we always do after a fight.

She'll get quiet and sulk until she gets over it at which point, she'll pretend it never even happened. Me? I'd prefer to hash it out until it's resolved. That way I'll know for sure the argument is over. I won't have to wonder and worry if she's still mad at me. Won't have to feel guilty for being upset with her, questioning myself on whether or not I really am to blame.

I won't have to be scared that she's going to stay mad at me forever.

But I could talk my head off, trying to get the matter settled here and now, but she'll just ignore me.

Astrid is very good at ignoring things she doesn't want to deal with or acknowledge.

Like how she was way out of line to attack me that way. How she insinuated that I'm cheating on Philip and that I'd be crazy, selfish and evil to expect her to take my side.

She used to. There was a time when she had my back. Always.

Then I changed things by hooking up with her brother.

And the price I paid for falling in love with Philip was losing Astrid's unwavering, unquestioning support.

I learned early on not to complain about Philip to Astrid, no matter what he's done. Don't get me wrong. I'd like to. There have been times when I would have loved nothing more than to go on a rant to my best friend about some dumb thing my boyfriend did or said. As wrong as it is, I'd like her to get mad at him, too, on my behalf.

Even if just on principle.

But their whole twins thing puts me at a distinct disadvantage.

Sharing a womb with someone for nine months forms an unbreakable bond.

And there's no point complaining about Astrid to Philip. He'd just tell me whatever the issue is it's not that big of a deal or that I shouldn't let her get to me or, my least favorite, that I just need to get over it.

If I wanted that kind of useless advice, I'd go to Chase with my problems.

So now when I get mad or upset with either of them, I keep it to myself.

When I want to push Astrid to talk to me, to clear the air, I keep quiet.

When I need someone to turn to, I handle it myself.

It's easier. Keeps things smooth and comfortable and safe between the three of us.

Like always.

18

———————

Astrid and I drive the rest of the way to The Fat Greek without speaking.

Good. Great. All the better for me to alternate between fuming silently in righteous indignation, worry she'll never talk to me again and, oh, yeah, wonder if my boyfriend is going to break up with me because I sat in another boy's truck unchaperoned.

That last one didn't even occur to me until I turned onto Main Street a few minutes ago. Why would it? I didn't do anything wrong. While it did cross my mind last night when I was in Owen's truck that Philip wouldn't exactly be thrilled by the situation, I wasn't overly concerned. Philip's not some Neanderthal who forbids me to talk to other guys. And once he hears how innocent it was—and that it was because of school work—he'll understand.

He trusts me.

By the time I follow a silent Astrid into the restaurant, I'm feeling much better about the whole thing.

Until she stops suddenly inside the doorway and I plow into her back.

"I was afraid of this," she mumbles over her shoulder at me.

I don't like the sound of that. Or her pinched expression. Something is not right.

My stomach jumps with nerves. "Afraid of what?"

She ever-so-slightly inclines her head to the right and I follow her gaze. Philip is standing next to the take-out window by the cash register, but he's not alone. Jessica is with him, her hand on his arm, a sympathetic expression on her face. His head is down, his mouth a thin line.

He must sense me watching him because he lifts his head. Meets my eyes.

I swallow. Crap. Crap, crap, crappity, crap, crap.

He knows.

And I didn't get a chance to tell him.

"Come on," Astrid says, taking my hand—much the same way Mary Alice did last night...no...nope, not going to think about last night or another boy when my boyfriend is right here, looking so unhappy.

Not when Jessica notices us approaching and smiles meanly.

Leaving her hand on my boyfriend's arm.

Mainly because he hasn't stepped away from her.

What is up with that?

"Hi," I say, giving Philip a big smile, but if possible, his expression grows even darker. My heart sinks. But I keep smiling, amping it up a few notches, even. "You ready to go?"

"What's this?" Jessica asks, shifting into my line of sight which means shifting closer to MY BOYFRIEND whose arm she's still touching. "No cheery good morning for me? And here I thought the great Natalie Hewitt was always sweet, always polite."

"You're looking a little haggard, Jess," Astrid says with a sneer, linking her arm with mine. She wrinkles her nose as if she smells something nasty. "Just roll out of bed? And what's with that skirt? Couldn't find it in your size?"

Jess smooths a hand down the side of her very tight, very short skirt which, of course, draws more attention to it.

Draws Philip's attention to it, however briefly.

I narrow my eyes. Seriously? Put a lock on those hormones for two seconds, would you? God.

"Actually," Jessica says, "I've been up for hours."

"I imagine you'd have to be," Astrid agrees with a fake smile. "Just to trowel on that makeup."

Under a considerable amount of foundation, blush and bronzer —good Lord, but the girl loves her bronzer—Jessica's cheeks fill with color.

I'd feel bad for her if not for the fact that she's basically Satan.

And she wants my boyfriend.

Satan...I mean, Jessica...lifts her nose and turns to me. "You look exhausted. But then, that only makes sense considering what I heard. You know, about you and Owen Radlowski."

Why does everyone keep saying his last name? As far as I know, he's the only Owen in our school. At least in the upper grades.

"Really?" I ask. "And what did you hear?"

Jessica shrugs languidly. "Oh, just that you and Owen looked quite cozy sitting in his truck last night."

She says *cozy* in a way that's filled with innuendo and suspicion. I glance at Philip who's still doing the whole ticked-off-silent routine.

"Are you actually buying any of this?" I ask Philip. "Because if you are, there's really no point in me wasting my time here."

"Is it true?" he asks. Ah, the man speaks! "Were you with Radlowski last night?"

"I wasn't *with him*, with him. We had a conversation—"

Philip snorts and it takes all I have inside of me not to kick him in the shin. Hard. "A conversation you didn't tell me about. One I had to hear about from someone else."

Now he's shooting daggers at Astrid who shakes her head and holds up her hand in surrender. "Nuh-uh. Don't look at me. I didn't know."

I look from Philip to Astrid and back again. Though Astrid's arm is still linked with mine, she's not on my side. Not really. And neither, it seems, is Philip. They're two of the most important people in my life, two people who know me better than anyone else and they're treating me like a criminal. Like I'm guilty.

They don't trust me.

They don't believe me.

It hurts, the realization that my boyfriend and my best friend both believe I hooked up with some other guy in a public parking lot where anybody could—and did—see.

Part of me is terrified I'll lose them both. The same part that wants to beg Philip to listen to my explanation. To forgive me. The part that wants me to promise Astrid I'll never keep anything from her again, to take the full blame for our earlier fight.

To grovel and plead and debase myself smack dab in the middle of The Fat Greek in front of dozens of people and Jessica Retting.

But the other part? That part is saying, *oh, hell, no.*

Yeah. That's the part I'm going with.

Because they should have more faith in me. Because they should know me better than that.

But mostly because, while I have no problem wallowing in guilt when I've done something wrong, this isn't one of those times.

"You know what?" I say, shaking Astrid's arm off as something inside of me just snaps. "Since it's so easy for both of you to believe the worst in me, why don't you find another ride to school?"

I turn and leave without, I might add, a backward glance to see their reactions. My fury carries me all the way to my Jeep but my hands are shaking so hard, it takes me three times to actually get my door unlocked. By the time I do, Astrid has caught up with me.

Astrid. Not Philip.

I tell myself I'm not disappointed my boyfriend's not the first one to come chasing after me.

"What was that all about?" she asks, hands on hips, hair flying in the breeze.

"You were there," I say, yanking open the door. "You know what it was about."

She steps between me and the Jeep. "Look, just because you're pissed at Philip, doesn't mean you have to take it out on me. I didn't do anything."

I hold up my pointer finger. "You attacked me the moment I picked you up." I lift another finger. "You accused me of purposely keeping something from your brother." A third finger joins the first two. "And you accused me of cheating on Philip." I wiggle my fingers. "Any of this sound familiar?"

She flushes but I can't tell if it's with embarrassment (as it should be!) or anger (which is more likely). "I told you I don't think you're cheating on Philip. Now, let's go back inside and get Philip so you two can resolve this and I can move on with my life."

"I'm not going back in there. If he wants to resolve this, he can come out."

To prove I mean what I say, I brush past her and climb behind the wheel. After a moment, she opens the rear door and gets in, too—sitting in the back as if it's a foregone conclusion Philip will be joining us any second.

I shut my door and turn on the ignition. Pretend to check my phone.

Any second now...

I adjust my rearview mirror. Take my time buckling up.

Any second...

But when I glance at the restaurant door, it remains shut. I hear Astrid typing on her phone and I know she's texting Philip. Probably asking where he's at. If he's coming out.

And though it galls me to no end, I wait. One minute. Two. Then three.

I tap my fingers against my thigh again and again and again.

One two three four five. Five four three two one.

One two three four five. Five four three two one.

One two three four five. Five four three two one.

I count the windows of the restaurant, try to remember how many are on the side and the back but honestly, the building is huge with a banquet hall on the second floor and apartments on floors three and four, and there are so many, many windows, I realize I'll never get them all. Not without getting out and walking around the entire building.

I give up. I can't keep going when I know I won't get a correct count.

So with nothing to count and the minutes tick, tick ticking away, I have no choice but to face the truth.

Philip isn't coming out.

He isn't coming after me.

I put the Jeep into Drive and pull forward slowly, glancing at the shut door again and again and again.

"Don't go," Astrid says, leaning between the front seats. "He's coming."

I brake and turn to face her. "Did he tell you that?"

"No," she admits. "But I'm sure he will. Just...let's wait a few more minutes."

I could. I absolutely could sit out here like an idiot, waiting for my boyfriend to tear himself away from another girl, a girl who is probably at this moment filling his head with lies, her stupid hand on his stupid arm.

Yeah, I could wait. I could give him more time to make the right decision.

But I don't. I gently press the gas pedal and I drive away.

19

For the rest of the drive to school, Astrid gives me a myriad of excuses for why her brother didn't come out. *He got stuck dealing with a customer. Our dad probably wanted to talk to him. His replacement was late, and he had to stay until she showed.*

All very good, very valid reasons for why the seat next to me is empty as I pull into the school parking lot. For why Philip hasn't texted or called me.

Good, valid reasons that I don't buy for a minute.

I doubt Astrid believes them either. No matter how badly she's trying to get me to.

Astrid and I get out of the Jeep. I'm reaching inside for my bag when I hear her mutter, "That dumbass."

And I know what I'm going to see when I straighten so I take my time, gathering my things as slowly as possible, but then realize I'm being a complete ninny, afraid to face the truth.

Afraid to get even more upset with Philip because feeling this way, being this angry with him scares me. Makes me worry I won't be able to get over it. That this will change things between us.

Which is ridiculous. Couples argue sometimes. Being perfect for each other doesn't mean you always agree. Even the strongest relationships take work. Compromise. Listening to the other's point-of-view calmly and rationally.

Forgiving each other when one of you makes a mistake.

Yanking my bag and purse out of the Jeep, I straighten and immediately look toward the red Toyota that pulled into an empty spot a few spaces over.

The red Toyota with my boyfriend in the passenger seat and a smug-looking Jessica behind the wheel.

Yep. I was right. I don't like what I see.

"Don't be mad at him," Astrid says quickly, stepping in front of me so I'm stuck standing inside the open door. "He's a guy. They're idiots. We know this."

"Don't be mad?" I repeat. "Seriously? Should I be happy he's in Jessica's car?"

"I'm just saying give him a chance to explain before you get too upset."

"Like he gave me a chance to explain what happened with Owen?" I shake my head. "You know, sometimes I really wish you two weren't related. It'd be nice to have my best friend actually be on my side for once."

Her mouth thins, her face goes white, but I don't apologize. Don't take my words back.

Not when they're the truth.

Astrid hikes her backpack onto her shoulder, chin lifted, frizzy hair blowing in the breeze. "Yeah? Well, there are times when I wish *my* best friend wasn't in love with my brother. But then, you never ask how I feel about that, do you?"

And she turns and stalks off like some Amazon queen.

Like she's the one who has a right to be mad.

Like she's the one who is right, period.

I take a step forward, ready to chase her down and demand to know what the heck she's even talking about. I mean, yes, Astrid and I were friends first, but it's not like I fell for Philip to spite her.

And I did ask her what she thought about Philip and I getting together before it happened. If it would bother her. Of course I worried about how my falling for Philip would affect Astrid or our friendship.

Didn't I?

I'm no longer sure and I quickly sling my purse over my head crosswise, lock the door and shut it. But I can't chase after Astrid the way I want to. Not until I've done the rest of my quirky little habit and press the lock on the key then tug the handle three times. When I turn, Philip is standing in front of me, arms crossed, jaw tight, eyes narrowed.

Stupid quirky habit.

"Excuse me," I say, quite clearly, too, despite my teeth being clenched.

He doesn't move. "We need to talk."

I glance over his shoulder, but Astrid is already at the track entrance and moving fast. There's no way I'll catch her now.

I want to. I want to choose Astrid. I want to put her first.

Am afraid I haven't done enough of that. Not in a long time.

But I can't just walk away from my boyfriend. He has to be the most important person in my life. He *is* the most important person.

That's what a good relationship is. Choosing the other person. Always.

"You want to talk now?" I ask because while I may put him first, that doesn't mean I'm letting him off the hook that easy. "Homeroom starts in five minutes."

And I hate being late. Which Philip knows.

"Yeah," he says, all stubborn and immovable and grouchy. "Now."

Cocking my hip, I look pointedly at Jessica who is standing next to her car, typing on her phone. Probably pretending to text someone so she can try to overhear our conversation. I lower my voice. "Seems to me, if you wanted to talk so badly, you would have ridden to school with me instead of Jessica."

With that, I head toward the school because there is no way I'm getting a tardy slip. I've gone my entire school career without one and I refuse to break my perfect record now because my boyfriend is being a doofus.

"You left!" Philip says, catching up to me easily despite my going at what I thought was a very fast clip. "It was either hitch a ride with Jessica or ask my dad to take me."

"And you thought going with her was your best option?"

"You know how pissed my dad gets when he has to leave the restaurant during peak times. And I wouldn't have had to get a ride with Jessica if you hadn't left without me."

I roll my eyes which doesn't have the same effect since I still refuse to look at him, but whatever. "Please. I sat out in the parking lot for like, five minutes. You never came out."

"Because I had to finish clearing a table and punch out," he says, throwing his hands in the air as if I'm the one being so unreasonable. "By the time I got outside, you were gone and Jess was there. It's not like I wanted to be with her."

I snort. "Could have fooled me."

Before we reach the entrance, Philip tugs me around the corner of the building.

"We're going to be late," I say, but he doesn't stop until we're next to the band room door.

He bends his knees so we're eye to eye and waits until I (grudgingly) meet his gaze. "I didn't want to be with her," he repeats, sounding sincere, looking all forthright and honest and completely trustworthy. "I don't want to be with her or any other girl. You know that."

He's right. I do know that. I do. It's just... "She was touching your arm."

"What?"

"At the restaurant. She was all..." Grabbing a hold of his forearm, I press against him and bat my eyelashes. "Oh, Philip, did you hear? Your mean old slut of a girlfriend cheated on you last night. You poor baby. Here, let me go down on you in the ladies' room and make it all better."

"First of all, I didn't even realize she was touching my arm. And to be fair, she never said you cheated on me."

"Oh, by all means," I say, dry as a bone, "let's be fair to Jessica. She may not have said I was unfaithful, but she sure implied it. An implication you jumped on, by the way. How do you think that makes me feel?"

"Probably as shitty as I felt when I heard you'd been with Owen Radlowski last night."

"I told you, I wasn't *with* him. Not like you're thinking, anyway. We had a conversation."

"In his truck."

"It was raining so we sat in his truck—him on his side, me on mine—in a public parking lot. We didn't touch. Didn't hook up or bond emotionally or anything like that. We had our conversation and went our separate ways. God. It's not like I was chatting with the boy in his bedroom."

Although in this moment I am very, very glad I didn't tell anyone about my little trip to Owen's house and gym Saturday morning.

I'm thinking that's one of those little details best kept to myself.

"If it was so innocent," Philip asks, "why didn't you tell me?"

"I didn't want to wake you." After I left Owen's truck, the first thing I did was check my phone. Philip's last text said he was going to bed. "I'd always planned on telling you this morning. I didn't think someone else would beat me to it. Or that you'd believe the worst about the situation. That you'd believe the worst about me."

"I don't believe the worst and I don't think you hooked up with him. I was upset, yeah. How would you feel if someone told you they'd seen me in another girl's car?"

"Uh, I did just see you in another girl's car."

"Come on, Nat. You know what I mean."

I sigh. Yeah, I know what he means. "I wouldn't like it."

He nods and edges closer. "And I wouldn't like it if you jumped to the wrong conclusion about it." He takes my hand. Squeezes it. "I'm sorry."

I link my fingers through his. "I'm sorry, too. If anything like that ever happens again—which it won't—I'll tell you right away."

"Thank you." He leans down and kisses me then lets go of my

hand to brush his fingers over my hair. He twirls a strand of it around and around his finger. "Are we okay?"

I kiss him again. Smile. "Always."

He nods, relieved. "What did Radlowski want to talk to you about?"

"Can we discuss this later?" I ask, as two sophomore girls heading toward the school glance our way. "Or at the least walk while we talk? The bell—"

"If we're late I'll just tell Mrs. Patchett it was my fault. She'll give you a pass."

Mrs. Patchett, the school secretary, has a soft spot for Philip.

It's that *all the girls love Philip Panos* thing. Even women old enough to be his mother.

"It's no big deal," I say. "Owen just wanted to talk to me about tutoring him in English."

Philip jerks, tugging on my hair.

"Ow," I say, eyes watering from the sting.

"Sorry," he says, immediately contrite as he loosens the hair from his finger. "I'm sorry."

"It's okay. Maybe you shouldn't tell anyone about the tutoring thing, though," I say. "I'm not sure I'm supposed to discuss it with anyone. Do you think there's some sort of student/tutor confidentiality agreement? Like doctor/patient privilege?"

I'll have to ask Miss Marchand. I don't want to break any rules— even unknowingly.

"Do you..." Philip clears his throat, his gaze down. "Maybe you should ask Miss Marchand if she can find someone else to tutor him."

"Why?"

"Radlowski...he's bad news. I don't like the idea of you being around him."

"First of all, I'm not going to *be around him*, I'm going to tutor him, in broad daylight in the library during school hours. And what do you mean *bad news*?"

Yes, Owen is quiet and keeps to himself, but I've never heard of him getting into trouble. If he did, he'd lose his scholarship.

Philip's answer is an irritated shrug, mouth set in a stubborn line. "I want you to talk to Miss Marchand about it, anyway."

"I'm not going to do that," I say slowly because obviously my boyfriend is having a hard time understanding simple concepts this morning. "I'm the only tutor she has."

Besides, Owen needs me.

"Hey, guys," Gage Burlingham, one of Philip's soccer teammates, says as he rushes past.

I smile and wave. Philip gives him one of those *what's up?* nods males like to use in place of an actual greeting.

"I don't get why this is a big deal," I say. "Would it bother you if I tutored Gage?"

"Not exactly the best comparison."

"Why not?"

"Because Gage is a skinny freshman with zits, a few strands of facial hair and a love for online gaming. His voice hasn't even changed yet. He's like a talking chipmunk."

"So you're threatened by Owen because his voice has changed?"

Philip bristles, all affronted male ego and raging testosterone. "I'm not threatened by Radlowski. I just don't like him."

"You don't have to. *I* don't even have to. I just have to help him with English. Think of it like my job."

He snorts. "Sure. I'll think of it like it's your job. A job you don't actually have to do."

"Ha-ha. You know what I mean." The bell rings and I twitch, as if I'm having an actual physical withdrawal from not being where I'm supposed to be—namely sitting at my desk in homeroom, a check next to my name on Mr. Pattison's daily attendance sheet. "Do you really have a problem with this?"

If he does, I don't know what I'll do. I don't want to back out of tutoring Owen, not even for Philip. Not after I practically begged Owen to let me help him.

Not after he set aside his pride last night.

Why can't life be simple?

It's so annoying.

Finally, thankfully, Philip sighs and shakes his head. "Nah. It's fine." He takes my hand and pulls me away from the building. "Like you said, it's sort of your job to help him. And you'll be in the library, right?"

"Right. And I don't know, exactly, what he needs help with," I say as we walk around the front of the school. Since we're late, we'll have to be buzzed in. "It might be something simple and only take a session or two to fix."

"It's weird, though. That he went to your dance class to talk to you about it."

"I guess. But it's not like he has my phone number."

"Yeah, but how did he even know you were there?"

This is my chance to come clean, to tell Philip everything, but I can't. He's not exactly thrilled with the situation—no matter what he says about it being fine. No way am I making things worse by telling him the truth.

It'd only upset him and what good would that do?

"Maybe he asked around?" I suggest. It's not even a lie. Owen did ask around. Sort of.

He asked his sister.

"Maybe..." Philip stops and, as he's holding my hand, I'm forced to stop right along with him.

I glance at the school. We're next to the science wing and through the windows I can see Mrs. Gable's homeroom standing for the Pledge. Ack. At this rate, we're not only going to miss homeroom completely, but we'll also be late for first period.

I break out in a cold sweat just thinking about it.

"Phil—a"

"I love you, Nat."

I blink at the intensity in his tone. The seriousness.

"I love you, too."

"You'll always tell me everything, right?" he asks, fingers tight on mine, a thread of something I can't quite define—worry or suspicion —in his tone.

I cup his face in my free hand, rub my fingertips against the soft stubble of his whiskers. "Of course."

"Promise," he whispers urgently, his dark gaze intense. "Promise me, Nat."

I look into the eyes of the boy I love, the only boy who's ever had my heart, and tell him what he wants to hear. What he needs to hear.

"I promise."

It's a vow I totally intend to keep.

Starting now.

20

Philip was right. He talked Mrs. Patchett out of giving us tardy slips and even charmed her into writing us hall passes so we wouldn't get in trouble being late for our first classes.

That boy is magic, I tell you.

Magic and sweet. So sweet that as I walk down the hall toward the library at the start of eighth period, my phone buzzes with a text from him.

Hey, just thinking about you. Love you.

Smiling, I text him back, relieved he's no longer upset about the whole tutoring thing. Makes it a lot easier for me to help Owen if I don't have to worry that spending fifty-five minutes in the library with another boy is going to send my boyfriend over the edge.

Things with Astrid are still chilly, but I'm going to resolve that situation as soon as possible. I've already made an overture: I texted her after lunch and invited her to spend the night this Saturday. I'm sure we'll work through our issues. We always do. Just like Philip and I always do.

Stepping into the library I wave at Mr. Ames, the librarian, and head toward my tutoring station, surprised to see Owen is already here.

He must sense my presence because his shoulders stiffen. He lifts his head and slowly turns and when his eyes meet mine, this swooping sensation comes over me. Like I'm dizzy, the ground shifting beneath me.

Shaking it off, I close the distance between us. "Hi," I say cheerily, hugging my books to my chest. "You came."

His expression darkens. For some reason, it makes me want to smile. "You knew I would."

I nod. "Sure did. And I do so love being proven right."

"I bet."

"I knew you'd come," I repeat, scooting around him to the other side of the desk, "but I figured you'd show up twenty minutes from now, feet dragging. I had no idea you'd be all eager-beaver ready and waiting at the start of the period."

"Eager beaver," he mutters to the ceiling. "Jesus."

"It's fine. It's good. I'm glad you're excited about learning and that you're on time. I admire punctuality. It's one of the traits I regard highly in myself. Hey," I say, eyes widening, "look at that! We have something in common. I mean, other than the facts that we go to the same school, live in the same town and probably know quite a few of the same people."

"We don't have anything in common."

"Not true," I say simply as I set my books on the desk and open a new notebook. "*You* like being on time. *I* like being on time. Who knows what else we share? Tell me, do you have a deep and abiding love for peanut butter on graham crackers? Have you watched every single episode of *Friends* on Netflix—three times? Is it your greatest wish that Drake and Rihanna get married and produce at least four gorgeous, rapping/singing babies?"

When he doesn't answer, I stop setting out my supplies and give him an expectant look.

"You're being serious?" he asks.

"It's called having a conversation. Back and forth," I say, gesturing between us. "Give and take. Since we're going to be working together, we should get to know each other."

"And you knowing my view about peanut butter on graham crackers is going to do that?"

"Definitely. You can tell a lot from a person by how they like their graham crackers."

He sighs—either at my solemn tone or that he's come, once again, face-to-face with my adorable determination. "I don't like anything on my graham crackers."

"Really? Not even a square of chocolate and a toasty marshmallow? Because I'm pretty sure that's un-American."

"I like them plain." He switches his copy of *The Catcher in the Rye* from one hand to the other. He clears his throat. "With milk."

I blink, then stare at him. "Do you mean...are you...a dunker?" He gives an infinitesimal shrug I take as a yes. "Huh."

"You're not talking," he says after a moment. "You're always talking. Have you blacked out?"

I shake my head. "Sorry. I just never would have pegged you as a dunker. It's like a whole new side of you is being revealed. I'm guessing you're also a Ross-and-Rachel-shipper, then. All dunkers are."

"I've never seen *Friends*. And before you can ask, no my greatest wish isn't for Rihanna to marry Drake. My greatest wish is that she marry me."

"It's good to dream big, I always say."

He gives me this look—part exasperated, part irritated—you know, his normal expression around me. "Yeah. You would say that."

I'm not sure that's a compliment, but I decide to take it as one. "Thank you."

I set out everything we'll need for our session: pencils, an eraser, a red pen, several highlighters and my own copy of *The Catcher in the Rye*. When I look up, the strangest, most bizarre thing is happening.

Owen is almost smiling.

At me.

So I, of course, smile back.

Which makes him, in turn, go all stony faced.

Such a strange, contrary boy.

"Shall we get started?" I ask.

"You might want to straighten your notebook, first. It's a little crooked."

I look down at my desk. I've piled my books neatly in the front, left corner, out of our way, set the notebook in the middle and lined up, like little, educational soldiers, my eraser, mechanical pencil, red pen and three highlighters—yellow then blue then green (because yellow and blue make green)—next to it.

He's teasing me. I get that. I'm not an idiot. Plus, my brother is always giving me a hard time about stuff like this which is how I know I shouldn't let it bother me. And I definitely shouldn't touch the notebook. But it *is* a tad off...

I straighten it, making sure it's lined up perfectly with the edge of the desk.

Making Owen smile for real.

"Yes, I'm very amusing," I say, fighting the urge to return his grin because...been there, done that, didn't go over so well. "My organizational skills and penchant for symmetry and order are hilarious."

"A few books on that shelf behind you aren't perfectly lined up with the other books. You want fix them?"

I don't look because if I see it, then yes, I will want to straighten them. "I like things a certain way. I'm not sure why that's so horrible."

He's still smiling, which I'm pretty sure must be a record for him. "It's not horrible," he says. "It's cute."

I drop my gaze to the desk as a wave of heat just...*whoosh*...rises from my toes to my head.

Owen thinks I'm cute.

No. No, that's not right. He thinks one of my quirks is cute and that is not the same as him thinking I'm cute.

Not at all.

I'm not sure what to do with this information, where to go with this part of the conversation. "I wish everyone thought so." I move the green highlighter up a centimeter, but it doesn't look right so I move it back. "It drives my brother and boyfriend crazy. I mean, you get bored one afternoon and organize someone's extensive CD collection by artist in alphabetical order and suddenly you're a freak. Who even has CDs anymore?"

"Panos got pissed you did that?"

I'm not surprised Owen knows Philip is my boyfriend. But it's still weird, hearing him say Philip's name. Well, his last name.

Just as weird as it was when Philip said Owen's.

"It wasn't Philip. It was my brother, Chase. One minute I'm anal retentive—" I make air quotes around the last two words. "—but when he can find his copy of Guns 'n' Roses' *Appetite for Destruction* in under thirty seconds, I'm suddenly a genius. An assessment I'm sure you'll agree with once I show you my foolproof method for writing a well-organized, well-thought-out English paper."

I sit.

He doesn't.

"We could do this standing," I say, "but in case you haven't noticed, one of us is wearing heels."

"If your shoes aren't comfortable, you shouldn't wear them."

"They're extremely comfortable for walking to and from class. Not for standing for the next—" I check my phone. "—forty-eight minutes."

He hesitates, like he's having an internal debate about sticking around or not. Swear to God if he takes off, I am not chasing after him.

I just don't have it in me today.

Finally, he turns the chair around and straddles it.

"Why do guys sit like that?" I ask. "It can't be comfortable."

"We have to. It's in the guy handbook."

"Oh, so you read the handbook but not *The Catcher in the Rye*?"

He tosses his poor, abused copy of the book on the desk. "It was easier. There aren't all that many lessons. Just how to swear and spit and grab ourselves."

I laugh. "You know, you're actually not so scary."

He flinches. "You afraid of me, Natalie?"

"Not me. But the whole strong, silent, unfriendly thing you've got going on makes people nervous."

"People," he repeats, watching me intently, his voice low. "But not you."

"Guess I'm just not easily intimidated. Now," I continue, holding up my copy of *The Catcher in the Rye*, "I re-read this—"

"When?"

"Excuse me?"

"When did you re-read it? You didn't know we'd be doing this until last night."

Knowing he's having trouble getting through it, I don't want to make him feel bad by admitting I read it cover to cover last night. "I skimmed through it, really. Just to familiarize myself with it again so I don't miss anything. And I made some notes."

I slide the notebook toward him and he flips through it—page after page after page. "Some?"

"Once I get started on something, I have a tendency to get carried away. But we can get back to those." I take the notebook and close it. "Let's start with your thoughts on the story. You said you were a few chapters in?"

He stares at his book—his poor, tattered, abused book. "I'm up to the part where he arrives in New York."

I keep my expression neutral, though that's not very far along at all. Maybe he has a reading disability? "Okay. Good. While you're reading, try to see if you can come up with some ideas as to what you think the theme of the book is. That'll help when you write your paper."

"Theme, you mean like, spoiled, rich brat gets expelled for being an idiot?"

"That's more of a plot point. A theme is the bigger message, I guess you could say. Like for Spiderman it's *with great power comes great responsibility*. For Harry Potter it could be *the power of friendship* or just *good triumphs over evil*."

"Yeah. Okay."

"Do you find it's the writing style you're not connecting with or the story in general?"

"Both, I guess." I didn't expect him to answer me and am glad he did, that he's trying. "The story sucks and douchebag Holden sucks."

"Why don't you try and find something in common with him? That's what I do when I'm reading something I have a hard time relating to."

"I doubt you ever have a hard time understanding something."

I raise my eyebrows. "Yes, well, my life is mainly roses and cupcakes and sunshine and rainbows but even a princess has to deal with the occasional irritant. Unruly peasants. Fire-breathing dragons. Trying to choose which knight in shining armor to ride off with."

"There you go again," he murmurs, "putting me in my place."

"Just reminding you not to be so quick with the judgements. At least, not until we get to know each other better."

"So how do you do it? Find something to relate to?"

"Well, right now in one of my classes we're reading *The Things They Carried*. Now, I don't have anything in common with a group of men fighting in the Vietnam War. I can't comprehend how scared they must have been or how brave they were to go on patrol or even sleep in that jungle. But I can relate to other aspects of the story, like how much they care about each other and the friendships they made. It's sort of like high school. They were forced together and, in that situation, they formed relationships, the same way we do here."

"That's different," Owen insists. "I can't relate to douchebag Holden. He's a spoiled rich kid who makes idiotic decisions without caring or worrying about the consequences."

"And you've never done anything without thinking through the consequences first?"

"No," he insists, but he drops his gaze and I get the feeling, he's lying.

I don't like it. Not one bit.

But we're not friends—not yet—so I don't have the right to call him on it.

"We'll just find something else for you to relate to in Holden."

Leaning forward, Owen crosses his arms over the back of the chair. "Not possible."

"Oh, ye of little faith. Have I ever steered you wrong?"

"This is only the fourth time we've actually ever talked to each other."

"So I haven't. Give me a little bit of time and I'll figure something out. In the meantime," I say, handing him his book. "Let's see what crazy shenanigans douchebag Holden gets up to in New York City."

21

———

"WHAT ARE YOU DOING?" OWEN ASKS AFTER SCHOOL WHEN HE SEES ME standing by his locker.

"Waiting for you." It's something I'm perfectly comfortable doing since Philip (and most of his friends) left for an away soccer match over an hour ago and Astrid is on the other side of the building getting ready for her own home meet.

Oh, yeah, and because I'm helping a fellow classmate and absolutely not doing anything wrong.

Owen's gaze narrows. "Why?"

"Hmm?"

"Why are you waiting for me?"

I bat my eyes at him. "Isn't it obvious? I can't get enough of your charming nature."

He grunts and I'm not sure if that's a step up or down from one of his shrugs. "Charm is Panos's gig," he says, opening his locker. "Not mine."

"Charm isn't Philip's *gig*. It's who he is naturally."

"Right," Owen mutters.

I'm about to ask what he means by that remark when he opens his locker.

136

"When are you taking the SATs?" I ask, spying an SAT prep book on the shelf.

He shrugs, and it seriously takes all I have in me not to smack him.

"That isn't actually answerable with a shrug," I say. "It's one of those questions that requires a verbal response."

"I don't know if I'm taking them or not."

"You should. Most people raise their scores by an average of, like, forty points the second time they take them. It's definitely worth it."

"Not for me." He takes out a few books—the prep book is not among them—and tucks them under his arm. "I haven't taken them a first time."

"Oh." Everyone I know took them for the first time either spring of junior year or, at the very least, early summer after finishing 11th grade. "Well your PSAT score will give you an idea of where you're at so you can work to improve on that."

"I didn't take that, either."

"So you didn't take the PSATs and are sort-of-maybe thinking about taking the SATs for the first time a few months before college applications are due?" It gives me a stomach ache just thinking about it—the risks, the lack of planning, the high chance of failure. "Your guidance counselor should be ashamed of herself."

"Him," Owen says, shutting his locker door and spinning the lock. "Mr. Long. It's not his fault."

"It's his job to guide you! He should have at least suggested you take the SATs over the summer in case your score was lower than what you wanted. Though I suppose you can still take them twice, but it won't give you much time to study in between test dates."

"He did suggest it," Owen says. "Signed me up and everything. I didn't show."

Then he starts off down the hall as if we're not in the middle of a conversation here.

As if he doesn't want to talk to me about this anymore.

I hurry to catch up with him, my backpack bouncing against my back, the grocery bag in my hands swinging. "Why not?"

His face is set. "Because I'm not going to college. I don't...do well in school. I can't even get through a fucking book without help. What school is going to accept me?"

He's not exactly a scholar.

I hadn't liked it when Astrid said that and I like it even less now, hearing something similar coming from Owen's mouth.

"I'll help you," I offer as we walk toward the side entrance that leads to the school's ice rink. "We can go over a few things Thurs—"

"We barely got through one chapter today. We won't have time for anything else."

He's right. Fifty-five minutes twice a week isn't long enough to go over his English assignment and help him study for the SATs. "Okay, so we'll set something up for a few days a week outside of school."

And won't Philip love that?

I push the thought, the worry, aside. This isn't about Philip. It's about Owen. About helping him. About doing what's right.

Owen holds the door open and I step outside. Walk next to him across the small, back parking lot.

"Bring your SAT prep book with you Thursday," I tell him, "and we'll go over some vocabulary."

"Just vocabulary? Don't tell me you suck at math."

"I don't suck at math." Although I'm still trying to raise my stupid AP Calc grade to where it should be. "I don't suck at anything."

"Except maybe humility?"

"Ha ha. I meant, I don't suck at any school subject." The wind blows my hair in my face. I brush it back. "But there's no need for jealousy—which is a useless emotion. I'm smart—"

"And humble."

"But a big part of the reason I'm smart is genetics. Just as it's the reason I look the way I do—"

"Your modesty," he says, digging his keys out of his jeans pocket, "is truly inspiring."

I give an epic eye roll. "I look like my mother—what am I supposed to think? I had nothing to do with that or with the amount of intelligence I was born with. But my work ethic? My sparkling personality and the choices I make? Those are all mine. I own them and I'm proud of them. Yes, I'm naturally smart. I could just get by and I don't. I put in the time and the effort to excel. It's like you with hockey."

"What do you know about hockey?"

"Not a thing," I say brightly as we stop next to his truck, "and that's more than I ever want to know. But I'm assuming all the natural ability in the world isn't enough to make a hockey player successful. You have to put in the time and effort, just like I do. Except I put it toward my school work."

"Why?"

More wind. More hair in my face. "Can you hold this, please?" I ask, shoving my bag at him so that he's forced to stop and take it.

Using the hairband around my wrist, I scoop my hair into a messy bun.

"Thanks," I say. "You were saying?"

He doesn't respond. Doesn't seem to notice I'm reaching for my bag, either. He's staring at me, his expression unreadable.

"You okay?" I ask.

Shaking his head, he takes a step back, hand fisted around the handles of my bag. "You're smart," he says, his voice gruff. "Getting good grades probably comes easy for you. Why put in the time and effort?"

"It does come easy, but that doesn't mean I take it for granted. I take a great amount of pride in doing my best. At everything."

"But that's not the only reason."

A car drives by, honking as it leaves the lot, but I don't look to see who it was.

I can't look away from Owen, from the understanding I see in his gaze. "No?"

"No." He lowers his voice. "You want to prove your worth."

My mouth drops open and it takes me a moment before I remember my confession to him that day in my driveway. How I always feel like I have to prove myself. How I have to be perfect.

He gets it. He gets *me*.

It's unsettling, that thought. Exciting.

Terrifying.

"Is that why you play hockey?" I ask, because it's only fair that he gives me something in return. A small piece of himself after I've given him my secret. Some part of him I can know. "To prove yourself?"

"No."

"No?" He remains silent and I raise my eyebrows. "And we were making such good progress with the full sentences."

"It's not about proving anything," he finally says. "It's my way out."

It's my way out.

I think about his house with its peeling paint and sagging porch. About his mom's creepy, tattooed boyfriend. About Piper and Gus and that last box of macaroni and cheese.

He wants to escape his life.

I get it.

There are times I want to escape mine.

He opens his truck door. Throws—literally throws his books— inside. He leans in, grabs a large duffel bag then straightens and shuts the door. "I have to get to practice."

"Oh. Okay." But he doesn't move. "Do you need directions? Or just my permission?"

"Neither."

"Yet, still you remain," I point out when he does just that. Remains in front of me, big and brooding and now, it seems, amused.

"Did you want something?" he asks.

"From the ice rink? Like what, my very own Zamboni?"

A reluctant grin tugs on his mouth. "You wanted me."

My scalp prickles, those three words causing some sort of short-circuit in my brain for some reason.

"You were waiting for me at my locker..." he prods.

I exhale heavily and only then realize I'd been holding my breath.

"Oh, right." I go for a carefree, light-hearted, tinkling laugh but what comes out is a croaky, nervous, *heh, heh, heh*. "I...uh...actually came to give you that," I say, nodding at the bag still in his hand.

Frowning, he sets down his duffel then opens the grocery bag to peer inside.

And gets even frownier.

"Not sure this'll fit me," he says, pulling out a sparkly, purple gymnastics leotard which looks extra dainty and feminine in his big, scarred, masculine hand.

There's a strange tickle in my throat and I clear it away. "Won't know until you try it on. It's actually very stretchy."

Hooking the leotard's strap over his thumb, he digs into the bag again, this time pulling out a multi-pack box of macaroni and cheese. "Why are you giving me these?"

"I'm not giving them to *you*, exactly. The leotard is for Piper and the mac and cheese is for Gus."

His eyes narrow to slits. "How do you know Gus likes mac and cheese?"

"What kid doesn't like mac and cheese?"

"Natalie…"

My back is starting to ache so I slip off my backpack. Set it on the ground at my feet. "He asked Piper to make him some that day I stopped by your house."

"And?" he asks, watching me in a way that makes me hot and itchy, as if he's trying to see inside my head.

See all my secrets, as if he has a right to them just because I let one or two slip out to him before.

"And Piper mentioned it was the last box so I bought him that so he'll have a surplus."

As I speak, Owen's expression gets darker and darker, a flush in his cheeks, his fingers denting the box.

Good thing I didn't mention how I figured out that they couldn't buy more mac and cheese until tomorrow.

"Because…uh…there's nothing worse than running out of mac and cheese," I finish lamely.

Owen throws the mac and cheese and leotard into the bag then shoves it toward me. "I don't need your goddamn charity."

I tuck my hands behind my back. "It's not charity. One is a used leotard that no longer fits me. The other is a box of cheese powder and SpongeBob-shaped pasta. And, as I already mentioned, neither of them is for you. They're for Piper and Gus."

He shakes the bag, as if trying to entice me to take it from him and all those little SpongeBobs rattle and roll. "We don't want them."

"*You* don't want them. I'm almost positive your sister and brother will feel differently."

He doesn't relent, just continues holding out the bag.

His pride at work again.

At least, I'm guessing it's his pride and not that he thinks I'm trying to...I don't know...lord my family's financial situation over Owen or make him feel bad.

But if there's one thing I understand, it's having too much pride.

God knows mine bites me in the butt all the time.

"I thought Piper would get a kick out of wearing her leotard while practicing her cartwheels," I tell him quietly. "No pun intended. And I couldn't give her something without giving something to Gus, too. I'm not trying to make you feel...less than...in any way."

He lowers his head. Starts slapping the bag against the side of his thigh and it sounds like a tambourine, all that shaking pasta, the rustling of the plastic bag. His shoulders rise and fall with a deep breath, then he turns and unlocks his truck door.

And tosses the bag inside.

It's a win for me. Not because I got my way or because Owen gave into me.

But because it means he believes I'm telling the truth.

He trusts me.

I go warm and fuzzy and am no doubt glowing with joy and happiness when Owen turns, grabs his duffel bag from the ground and leaves. Just walks away without so much as a goodbye or a see you later.

Or a thank you.

Ah, the thrill of victory.

Never lasts as long as you'd like it to.

I pick up my backpack and hugging it to my chest, chase after Owen. For the second time today. I can't stop myself. It's like one of my quirks. I *have* to do it.

Even though I know I shouldn't.

"Did it help?" I ask when I catch up to him a few cars away.

"What?"

"Our tutoring session. Did it help at all or make things even a little clearer?"

He glances at me. "Fishing for compliments?"

"No." Maybe. And a little appreciation wouldn't be amiss. "I just... want to be sure I'm doing it right. I mean, that I'm explaining things in a way that makes sense and that's..."

"Helpful?"

"Yes. Because if it wasn't, I need to know so I can fix it."

He sighs, as if I'm so demanding with my need for feedback, constructive criticism and desire to do the best job I can. "It helped."

I wait but that seems to be all he's saying on the subject. "No, no," I say. "Please, don't go on. Flattery will just go to my head."

"That's what I'm afraid of. If your ego gets any bigger, there won't be any room left for the rest of us."

I want to grin but I keep it in check and, as we've reached the sidewalk leading up the ice rink, I stop. A couple of his teammates give us curious looks as they pass.

Owen just keeps walking.

And again, I know I should let him go. That I shouldn't call any more attention to myself—to us—than I already have.

"Will I see you Thursday?" I ask in a rush.

It's a fair question. Harmless. As his tutor, I need to plan our schedule. Work on coming up with more notes that'll help him. Do some research into when he can take the SATs.

He faces me, the wind lifting the ends of his hair, the sun bringing out the lighter strands and I'm once again hit by how pretty his eyes are. How broad he is, the material of his shirt stretched over his chest.

The tickling sensation is back, this time settling deep in my chest, nerves and anxiety twisting and turning together. Taking up all the space. Using up all my oxygen.

But then Owen nods, his decision made. And he finally says, "Yeah. You'll see me Thursday."

I can breathe again.

22

———

"DO YOUR PARENTS KNOW CHASE IS DOING SO MUCH PARTYING?"

I'm sitting on the floor in my bedroom painting my toenails when Astrid asks that out-of-nowhere, loaded question.

"He's not partying," I say, but my hands are suddenly unsteady and I get bright blue nail polish all over the top of my big toe.

So far, my Saturday night is not going the way I'd planned or wanted.

I hate when that happens.

From her spot on my bed, Astrid rolls her eyes. But keeps her attention on whatever super important text she's sending to, or receiving from, Sean. "He's a Frat Boy. That's, like, the definition of partying."

Teeth gritted, I carefully put the tiny brush back into the nail polish bottle and twist it closed. "My dad was in a fraternity."

"Dr. Ben is the exception, of course."

I'm only partially mollified.

I climb to my feet. Walking on my heels, I cross the room and open the door to check that Mom and/or Dad aren't lurking in the hallway, ears pressed to the wood, trying to hear whatever scintillating conversation their daughter and her best friend are having.

They're not missing much.

Then again, ever since Astrid got here over two hours ago—an hour and a half later than she'd originally said she'd be here—she's spent the majority of her time and focus on her phone.

Which is fine. I'm not trying to get between her and her brand-spanking-new boyfriend. I mean, yeah, she and Sean have only been together a few weeks while she and I have been friends since we were eight, but whatever. I understand how it is when you first fall for a guy.

And I have a feeling I owe her for that. For getting too caught up in my romance with Philip at the beginning. For not giving her the time and attention a good friend should.

For going out with her brother in the first place.

I shut the door and turn to head back to my spot next to my bookshelf when I'm seized by a familiar fluttering sensation in my stomach and I shut my eyes on a silent groan.

Not now. Please, not now...

But the need takes hold and the harder I fight it, the longer I resist, the more urgent it becomes, until I'm struggling for each breath. And like that afternoon in my driveway with Owen, like the other day when Philip and I were fighting, I have to open the door and shut it again.

I have to.

And since I have to, I turn and do so as quickly and quietly as possible. Open and shut.

Open and shut.

Inhaling, I hold it and count to five then let it go.

Better. That's much, much better.

Even if the fluttering remains, soft but insistent.

A reminder that my little quirks are always there.

A warning that if I'm not careful, they might just take control.

With that jolly thought, I brace myself and turn back to Astrid.

But there's no curiosity on her face. No confusion. No disgust. And there are no questions—probing or teasing or otherwise.

She didn't even notice.

Which is good. Great, even. This sleepover is tense enough with all the awkward pauses and superficial conversation and both of us trying too hard.

Or neither of us trying hard enough.

Who's to say? I'm obviously not the best judge as I'm having the strongest, strangest urge to go to the door and do the whole open/shut, open/shut, open/shut thing all over again.

If only so she'll notice.

I force myself to take one step toward the bed. Then another. Ha. Take that quirks! I am still in charge of my own destiny. Or at least my body.

For now.

"Fraternities aren't all bad," I say as I climb onto the foot of the bed. "Members usually have higher GPAs and are less likely to drop out of school, plus being in a fraternity fosters a sense of community and belonging, and it's great for networking."

"Someone's done her research," Astrid says lightly, a grin on her face.

For the first time since she got here, I start to relax. "I may have looked up the pros and cons of fraternities and sororities when Chase first told us he was thinking of pledging."

Actually, it was Dad that suggested it. Chase had a such a hard time when he first started school, always coming home on weekends, not making any new friends, his grades subpar. Dad had such a great fraternity experience and is still close to a lot of his Frat Brothers and wanted that for Chase.

I just wanted him to get back to how he used to be. Confident. Ambitious. Happy.

At first I'd had the same views about fraternities as Astrid. I thought they were all Dens of Excessive Drinking, Depravity and Douchebaggery.

Then Chase got accepted into one and I finally had my brother back.

Everything that had been so messed up for so long was finally fixed. Everything was finally back to normal.

That's what I'm hanging on to so tightly. That normalcy.

"Look," Astrid says, "I'm not trying to be a jerk. I'm just not sure someone with Chase's issues should be drinking as much as he is. Or at least, as much as he's portraying on social media."

Chase's *issues*.

That's one way to put it.

And she's not wrong. For the past six months, Chase's Instagram account has been an ongoing record of him at bars and parties or just sitting on his couch, beer bottle in hand.

"I'm keeping an eye on it," I tell her. "If it seems like he's getting out of control, I'll tell my parents."

She opens her mouth as if to speak but then her phone buzzes and she glances at it. Gives me a shrug. "Sure. Okay."

And reads her text message.

On one hand, I'm relieved she's distracted. At least from the subject of Chase, his current level of partying and his past *issues*.

Seems like I've thought about my brother constantly for the past four years. My entire family's focus on getting him healthy. On getting him sober. On keeping him that way.

It's exhausting. The constant worry and fear.

I just want a break.

Which is where that other hand comes in, the one where Astrid's preoccupation with her phone/Sean is annoying as all get out.

I invited her over because I thought we could use a little BFF time. We've both been so busy since school started, I wanted to catch up. Reconnect.

Get past all that unpleasantness from Tuesday morning when Astrid didn't have my back with the whole Owen's truck situation.

When I started to think that maybe I didn't have hers when I started liking Philip.

Tonight was supposed to be about us getting back to how we used to be.

It's not. It's nothing like how we used to be.

I'm not sure if it's Astrid's fault or mine. Probably a combination of both.

I also don't know how to fix it.

Though I'm guessing me nagging her to get off her phone isn't it.

Too bad. It's the only idea I've come up with.

"So," I say, dragging the word out until it's at least three syllables long. "I take it things are going well with you and Sean?"

Typing a reply to the text, Astrid nods.

"That's great," I say, all happiness and light. "He seems like a really good guy."

Okay, so that part isn't exactly true. I mean, for all I know it could be true. Fact is, I've only spoken to Sean a few times and that was when he was a senior and I was a sophomore so I have no idea what he's like.

But if Astrid likes him, he must be nice.

Astrid doesn't suffer fools lightly and she doesn't put up with anyone's crap.

It's because she has three brothers—she and Philip have an older brother, Nick, who's serving in the Marines, and a younger brother, Alexander, who's in eighth grade. She's learned not to let any boy walk over her.

Since she hasn't bothered to respond to my really good guy comment, I keep going.

I will not be deterred.

"Maybe we could go out sometime. The four of us."

Astrid shoots me a glance. "Sure. Maybe."

Wow. The only way she could give me a less enthusiastic answer is if she was in a coma.

God.

Okay, I lied. I will be deterred. A woman can only bang her head against a brick wall so many times before she either gives up—or knocks herself unconscious.

Flopping onto my stomach, I reach for my phone from the floor. But if I want that break from thinking/worrying about Chase, I can't scroll through Instagram. I could text Philip but he's at yet another soccer tournament and has to get up early and I don't want to keep him up.

And that's the extent of the list of people I text on a regular basis.

Yeah, I really need to expand my social circle.

I tap my fingers on my phone.

One, two, three, four, five. Five, four, three, two, one.

Except I have expanded it.

One, two, three, four, five. Five, four, three, two, one.

I'm sort of friends with Mary Alice. I could text her.

One, two, three, four, five. Five, four, three, two, one.

Or Owen.

My fingers twitch, my face heats. I glance at Astrid.

Who is still busy ignoring me and can't possibly know I considered, even for the briefest of seconds, texting the boy I'm tutoring.

Which is the only reason I even thought about it. To check if he's made any progress on *The Catcher in the Rye* since our session Thursday—which he showed up for, just like he said he would. To ask if he's written anything on his paper he wants me to look over. To see if I can change his mind about taking the SATs.

Not that I'm going to do any of that. There's no reason to.

Plus, I don't have Owen's number.

"Can you take me to Pittsburgh next Saturday?" Astrid asks, suddenly remembering I'm alive and sitting right next to her.

Friday is Mom and Dad's anniversary and Chase will be here all weekend, but he usually hangs out with his high school friends for a few hours whenever he's home. "You want to go shopping for our Homecoming dresses?"

"I doubt we'll have time. I have a meet in the morning and my appointment at the clinic's at two and I promised Sean we'd hang out after."

"The clinic?" And it hits me what she's talking about and I sit up. "Wait...are you...are you and Sean having sex?"

She goes crimson but her lips are in a thin line. "Not yet. But we've come close and I want to be prepared for when we do."

"Oh."

Yeah, that's all I've got. *Oh.*

My best friend is talking about losing her virginity—when, not if —to some guy she's only known a few weeks, like it's no big deal.

Don't get me wrong. Astrid is smart and perfectly capable of making up her own mind about when and with whom to have sex.

This all just seems really, really sudden.

And unlike the Astrid I know.

Seeing as how I routinely have sex with her brother, though, I'm in no position to question her decisions. Or her motives.

"So?" she asks and, miracle of miracles, she actually looks at me instead of her phone. "Can you take me?"

I force a smile. "Sure."

But she still looks worried. "Promise you won't tell Philip."

"Astrid…"

"Please, Nat," she says, gripping my hand. "You know he'll tell my parents and they. Will. Freak. Out. I'll be grounded until I'm thirty." Her eyes widen and she squeezes my hand harder. "Oh, God, they'll make me stop seeing Sean."

Okay, that much is true. Astrid's parents are super strict, and I'd never want her to get into trouble. I also don't want to do anything to cause problems with her and Sean if she really likes him that much.

And I honestly can't imagine a conversation with Philip where I'd bring up his sister's sex life but promising to keep something from him just seems wrong. Like she's putting me in an unfair situation. Making me choose her trust over Philip's.

All of which she accused me of doing the other day after she found out I'd been in Owen's truck.

"Promise me, Nat," Astrid says, and I know this is it. Make or break for our friendship.

Even if that friendship has changed.

"I promise," I tell her, turning my hand over in hers so I can return her squeeze. "I promise I won't tell Philip. Or anyone."

She smiles. "Thanks."

For a moment, we sit there, hands linked, smiling at each other.

For a moment, we're back to how we used to be. To who we used to be.

Then her phone buzzes and she lets go of my hand to pick it up. The moment is over. I'm dismissed once more.

But it doesn't matter. No matter what happens to our friendship, no matter how much it changes, I'll always keep my promise. I'll keep her secret.

Because she's kept mine.

23

———————

There were no signs.

Or maybe there were and we just missed them.

More than likely, we just didn't want to see them. Because acknowledging them would mean admitting something was wrong.

It would mean facing the truth: Our family wasn't perfect.

Worse than that, scarier than that, was the realization that our family wasn't as strong as we thought. Not nearly as solid.

And the smallest, slightest crack could tear everything apart.

It started after Chase blew out his left knee playing soccer his junior year. We thought everything was fine. That everything was returning to normal after his two surgeries and rehab and physical therapy sessions. And, for the most part, it had. Chase no longer needed crutches and had progressed so far that his doctor told him he'd be able to try out for the Varsity Baseball team that spring.

When he was surly, grumpy or rude, we blamed it on the pain. When he spent hours alone in his room, door locked, headphones on so he couldn't hear us knocking, we told ourselves he just needed some time and space. When he fell asleep on the sofa after school every day, we blamed it on his grueling schedule and sudden bout with insomnia. When money disappeared from Mom's purse or Dad's wallet or my nightstand, we blamed ourselves for misplacing it.

And when Chase came out of his room, giddy and smiling and full of energy, we were so relieved, we didn't question it.

Didn't want to question it.

His friends still came over. There were pickup games in the drive-way, impromptu pool parties with a dozen teenage boys yelling and running around. He and Leah were strong as always, spending most of their free time together, laughing and as in love as ever.

We didn't know. Didn't see.

And in the end, Chase had to save himself.

He'd gotten hooked on the pain medicine his doctor had prescribed after his first surgery. Dad had made sure that first 'script was only for enough pills to get him through the worst of the pain, but Chase had gotten more from a guy he met at the rehab center.

And he kept getting more and more. But it was never enough so he started drinking and smoking pot, trying to find that same high. He tried to quit, but the withdrawal was so bad, so painful, he kept going back, each time telling himself it was the last time.

Finally, he told Mom and Dad what was going on. They spent the whole night talking, the three of them.

I sat on the stairs listening.

The next morning, Mom and Dad took Chase to an addiction treatment center outside Denver. He spent the entire summer there.

We told everyone he was doing a summer STEM program then was traveling.

Everyone, that is, but Astrid. Midway through the summer, I told her the truth. Because I hated lying to my best friend. Because I was tired of pretending and acting as if nothing was wrong.

Because I couldn't keep it inside any longer.

She swore she'd never tell a soul.

When Chase came home a week before school started, he was happy and healthy. He and Leah were stronger than ever and he resumed his friendships and refocused on his studies. It was almost like none of it had ever happened. Everything returned to normal.

Everything, except for me.

* * *

"Natalie!" Mom yells up the stairs Sunday morning. "You have a visitor."

Astrid must have forgotten something. Not surprising, given the way she took off an hour ago, shooting out of here like a rocket, her new boyfriend laying on his car horn in our driveway.

Classy.

I'm not going to lie. I was relieved when she left.

Which, of course, was immediately followed by a huge dose of guilt because that is not how someone should feel about her best friend.

Even if that best friend ignored her all night.

All. Night.

And yet, I kept my mouth shut. Partly to keep the fragile peace between us. Partly because I know this thing with her and Sean is new and exciting and she's caught up in the moment.

Partly because, as much as I'd like to think otherwise, I can't guarantee that I didn't do the exact same thing to her when Philip and I first got together.

Hard to take the moral high ground when you're not sure you deserve to be breathing that mountain air.

"Coming!" I call down to Mom then roll off my bed and pad across my room to the door.

I'm halfway down the stairs when I wonder why Astrid didn't just come up. Then I wonder why she rang the doorbell—Astrid and I have been letting ourselves into each other's houses for ten years.

And that's when I hear the low rumble of a male voice. A familiar male voice.

Goosebumps cover my arms and I freeze. Just...stop moving, right there on the staircase, my hand on the railing, one bare foot suspended in mid-air, breath held.

It's Owen.

Owen is here.

At my house. At ten-fifteen on a Sunday morning.

I glance down at myself.

And I'm in my pajamas.

I whirl around and race back upstairs.

"Natalie!" Mom calls. Again.

In case I've lost what's left of my mind and forgotten she's yelled up to me once already.

God.

"One minute!" I say before tearing down the hallway and into my room. I grab Philip's sweatshirt and yank it on over my tank top as I hurry into my bathroom. Swish mouthwash and tug my brush through my hair then spit the mouthwash into the sink.

I catch sight of my reflection in the mirror. My hair is crazy, big and frizzy, but my cheeks are flushed a pretty pink, my eyes bright.

From the adrenaline of rushing around.

No other reason.

But I'm practically running back out into the hall.

And plow into my dad at the top of the stairs.

"Oof!" He catches me by the shoulders so I don't take a header down the staircase. "Where's the fire?" he asks, which is such a Dad thing to say I roll my eyes.

What do they do? Give out handbooks of the worst puns, jokes and sayings to every male alive and don't let them procreate until it's memorized?

"No fire," I say, but I'm already rushing down the stairs. "A...uh... friend from school dropped by. That's all."

Yep. That's all. Just a friend from school. Nothing to worry about. Nothing to read into.

Nothing to feel guilty about.

Ah, guilt. The theme of my day so far. Let's hope that trend doesn't continue.

I force my steps to slow as I hit the bottom step. Take a deep breath and smooth a hand over my hair before turning and heading toward the foyer.

"There you are," Mom says as if I've been wandering the desert for forty days and forty nights and not taken three whole minutes to answer her summons. "Owen's here."

Yes, he certainly is.

He's here, somehow managing to look nervous and ticked off at the same time, and I'm jittery with my own onslaught of nerves. Stunned to have him here, blond, blue-eyed and big as life in faded jeans and a gray hoodie, hands in his pockets.

Stunned. And sort of glad.

"Owen," I say, shooting for a super casual tone but I seem to have developed a squeak sometime in the past sixty seconds. I clear my throat. "Hi."

And then, because I need to take control of this situation—and, yeah, partly because I know it'll bug him—I give him a big, toothy, welcoming grin.

His mouth goes grim but he nods.

As always, he's *thrilled* to see me.

You'd think someone forced him to come here at gunpoint. Jeez.

"I'm heading down to Kaleidoscope," Mom says, getting her jacket and purse from the closet. "Why don't you stop by around noon?" she asks me as she puts on her jacket. "We'll get some lunch."

She's been doing that a lot lately, making more time for me ever since we had our argument over Philip not being allowed to come over. Making sure both she and Dad were at my last home match. Coming into my room at night so we can talk and catch each other up on our day.

She's trying. The least I can do is try, too. "Sure. I can stay for a few hours, if you want. Help paint or sort inventory."

"That would be great." She kisses my cheek then turns to Owen. "Nice seeing you, Owen."

He gives her one of his almost grins. "You, too, Mrs. Hewitt."

We both watch her disappear into the kitchen. A moment later, I hear the door leading to the garage open and shut.

"So," I say, turning to my unexpected visitor. "What's up?"

He shifts. Drops his gaze to my bare legs before jerking it up above my head. "You busy?"

"Nope."

He shifts again. Inclines his head toward the porch. "You got a minute?"

"Sure," I say and step outside.

The wooden floor of the porch is damp and cold under my bare feet, the air cool, but I'm too curious to find out why he's here to go inside for a coat or shoes.

If guilt is the theme of the day then curiosity is the running theme when it comes to me and Owen.

Mainly that I have too much where he's concerned.

He shuts the door then walks past me. His truck is parked in the driveway behind my Jeep and he waves at it. The passenger side door opens and Piper climbs out, followed by Gus.

"You left your brother and sister in the truck?" I ask Owen as they run toward us.

Piper's faster than she looks, her legs scissoring in her pink yoga pants, her hair flying behind her like a banner. Gus is trying to keep up but failing miserably.

Too much mini potbelly for those skinny legs, I guess.

I'm just glad he's wearing pants.

Owen's hands are back in his pockets. "I wasn't sure you were home."

"You parked behind my Jeep."

He shrugs. "You could've been with Panos."

At the mention of Philip, there's a pressure in my lower back, like someone's poking a raw nerve. Reaching behind me, I rub at the spot until it goes away.

I hold out my hand to Owen. "Give me your phone."

Owen pulls his phone from his front pocket and lays it in my palm. I open it, add my name and number to his contacts then send myself a text so I'll have his.

I hand it back. "Now you can just text me and ask if I'm home or not."

"Watch me!" Piper calls from the edge of the yard, arms raised, leg straight at an angle, toe pointed. "Natalie, watch!"

"She's watching," Owen grumbles. "Just do it."

I give him an admonishing look but as he's staring straight ahead and not at me, it has no affect.

"Go ahead," I tell Piper. "I'm watching."

She does a cartwheel. Then another. Then a third.

And sticks the landing with an arms-raised, face-flushed, grinning, "Ta da!"

I clap, impressed. "Great job. You must be practicing."

She shrugs—shades of her big brother. "Yeah. Plus, I'm just really good."

As if to prove it, she does another one.

"Ah," I say, giving Owen's arm a nudge. "A girl after my own heart."

"Big-headed?" he asks dry as sand, still staring out at the yard.

"Confident," I correct. "Nothing wrong with a girl knowing her power."

Now he looks at me and it's...it's intense. Serious. As is his tone when he says softly, "I don't think you know half of yours."

And I'm the one who has to look away.

Suddenly, I no longer need a jacket or shoes or even socks. My entire body is on fire, heat starting out as a blush in my cheeks then seeping into my throat and chest, spreading down my arms and torso. I gather my hair with one hand and fan the back of my neck with my free hand.

"Are you a princess?"

Gus has arrived, a little sweaty and a lot out of breath.

"What?" I shake my head. Let go of my hair. "I mean...excuse me?"

"Are you a princess?" he asks, tone exasperated, expression mulish. Like a little Owen-in-training.

"Uh...no."

"Then why do you live in a castle?"

I look behind me. You know, just in case the house I've lived in my entire life has suddenly morphed into Buckingham Palace or something.

"It's not a castle," I tell him. "It's just a house."

Owen snorts at the same time Piper calls out, "It's a mansion."

"It's not a—"

"What's a man-shon?" Gus asks her.

"It's where rich people live."

Gus whirls on me, eyes narrowed in contemplation. Or accusation. Or maybe he's just trying to figure out how to shake me down for a few bucks. "Are you rich?"

I don't answer right away, thinking Owen is, at some point, going to tell this kid not to ask such impolite questions.

Yeah. That doesn't happen.

"I'm not rich. I don't even have a job."

Another snort from Owen.

Setting my hands on my hips, I glare at him. "What?"

"Nothing," he mutters, shoulders hunched. "Gus, tell Natalie thank you for the SpongeBob mac and cheese."

"Thank you for the SpongeBob mac and cheese," Gus dutifully repeats. He wipes his nose with the back of his hand. Ugh. "You got any more?"

Owen descends the porch steps, turns Gus by his shoulders and gives him a gentle nudge. "Back in the truck." As Gus walks away, Owen calls to his sister. "Piper, come on."

She does one more cartwheel before skipping over to join her brother on the sidewalk.

He sends Piper a meaningful look then jerks his head in my direction.

Fortunately, Piper is fluent in Owen-speak.

"Thank you for the leotard," she tells me. "And for teaching me how to do a cartwheel."

"You're welcome."

She glances at Owen then eyes me shrewdly. "If you teach me how to do a backflip, I'll tell you a secret about Owen."

Before I can agree—because, let's be honest, that's a deal I can't pass up—Owen steps between us and looks down at his sister. "I'll give you twenty bucks if you don't say another word until we get home."

Piper turns to me as if waiting for my counter-offer.

"Sorry. I can't outbid him. I don't have any cash."

It's a lie but it's for a good cause:

We all have the right to keep our secrets.

"Fine," Piper tells Owen on a sigh, as if she didn't just become twenty bucks richer. She mimes locking her mouth and throwing away the key then heads down the sidewalk.

Owen puts his hands into his pockets yet again. Takes them out. "Guess I'll see you Tuesday."

I step onto the first stair. "You're leaving?"

He nods. "We just came over so they could thank you."

"Oh." I move down to the next step. "You could stay. Piper could use some tips on her cartwheeling technique," I add quickly.

I'm blushing once again. Good God, I might as well turn red permanently.

"You said she did great," Owen points out.

"There's always room for improvement."

Always a way to get better. Always more we can do.

"What's the matter?" I tease when he hesitates. "Afraid I'll try and wheedle your secret out of her?"

I'm expecting him to deny it, complete with a growl and a scowl. Instead, he takes a careful breath.

And simply says, "Yes."

I move down another step. "You do realize you're only making me want to find out what it is even more."

This time his soft snort is more of a short, humorless laugh. "Yeah, well, even a princess can't always get what she wants."

I drop my gaze, hurt and confused as to how we got back to him thinking so little of me. Wondering why I bother trying to be his friend.

Why I still want to.

I don't look up until I hear the sound of his truck door closing.

Then I watch as he backs out of the driveway. Piper waves at me. Owen doesn't even look my way.

I wave back then turn and climb the stairs.

Even a princess can't always get what she wants.

No kidding.

But I didn't really want his secret.

I just wanted him to stay.

24

During the following four days, it's clear the budding friendship between me and Owen has hit a major snag. One he doesn't seem the least bit interested in unraveling.

Which is why I don't even look at him Friday afternoon during the school-wide assembly. Nope. Not even going to send a quick glance near where he's sitting in the auditorium—three rows back and five seats over from me. No smiling or waving or acknowledging him in any way, shape or form.

I keep my gaze on the stage as Dean Walters explains, as she does every year, how West Brook Academy chooses its Homecoming Court. The teachers pick a boy and girl from each lower grade to be representatives of their class then choose twelve seniors to run for Homecoming King and Queen. The students then vote for their favorite couple next Friday morning with the official "crowning" taking place during half-time at Friday night's home football game.

Dean Walters announces the freshman representatives and I let go of Philip's hand to clap as they make their way from the back of the auditorium to the stage.

I look over my shoulder for no other reason than to check their progress when I—fully and completely by accident—meet Owen's eyes.

I send him the teeniest, tiniest smile imaginable—because it's the polite thing to do and no other reason—and he looks away.

I slump back in my seat.

Yep. We've definitely hit a snag.

He was so weird at my house Sunday—all that snorting and frowning, muttering and grumbling—like he didn't even want to be there when he was the one who showed up unannounced. And the way he took off...it was as if he couldn't wait to get away from me.

The second person that morning to act that way.

It's enough to give a girl a complex.

Good thing I don't have any self-esteem issues.

But if I hang out with Owen or Astrid much more, I might develop some.

Not that I have to worry about that. Astrid's been too busy with Sean all week to even give me the time of day—even when we're in the car together in the morning. Though she has asked me, four times, if I'm still taking her to Pittsburgh tomorrow afternoon.

As for Owen, he seems more than happy to keep our relationship strictly professional.

Something he made very clear when he showed up late for our tutoring sessions both Tuesday and Thursday, and barely said more than a dozen words both days combined.

Okay, so Owen being stingy with his thoughts and words isn't that unusual. It's just...I thought we'd gotten past all that. Past his reticence. His bad attitude.

Past his dislike of me.

Being wrong sucks.

The sophomore reps are announced and I clap again.

But it's fine that Owen doesn't want to be my friend or even be friendly the two times a week we're together. It gives me more time to focus on my new friendship with Mary Alice. We got pizza before dance class Wednesday and have plans to go to Greens and Beans after class Saturday—before I chauffeur for Astrid to the clinic.

Plus, having Owen as a friend, probably wouldn't go over too well with certain people in my world. Like Astrid.

And Philip.

I slide Philip a glance. He's reading a text, a smile on his face. When he feels me watching him, he looks up. Winks at me.

No, he hasn't said anything else about me quitting as Owen's tutor, but it's pretty clear he doesn't like me spending time with another boy. Before each tutoring session, Philip sends me a *Love you, babe!* text. Texts again about twenty minutes later even though he has AP Bio last period and should be paying attention to Mrs. Swanson and not texting me how much he misses me or that he can't wait to hang out later or telling me how pretty I look.

All things, I'd like to point out, he could just as easily text or even say to me in person earlier in the day.

It's like he's reminding me he still exists.

He doesn't have to. I'm well aware he's my boyfriend. That he comes first in my life.

In my heart.

We clap for the junior class reps and I take Philip's hand in my once again. Squeeze.

He lifts our joined hands to his mouth. Kisses the knuckle of my ring finger.

I don't look back at Owen. Not when Philip and I are the fifth couple announced and he pulls me to my feet and gives me an enthusiastic hug.

Not when Philip hams it up, acting shocked, imitating a beauty contestant who's just been crowned, even though he's been telling me for the past two weeks that we're shoo-ins.

Not when we make our way to the stage, Philip doing a Royal wave that has the crowd roaring.

Not when we take our spot next to Tristan Jarvis and Hope Miller and wait for the final couple to be announced.

I don't look at Owen.

But I want to.

* * *

I decide to tell my family about the Homecoming nomination at Mom and Dad's anniversary dinner that night. Might as well celebrate two good things, right?

At six-fifteen, I step into the foyer.

"Is that what you're wearing?" Dad asks me.

And so the evening begins with what I'm assuming is to be an unsolicited fashion critique by my middle-aged father who wears scrubs the majority of the time.

Hooray.

I glance down at myself then at Mom who gives a little *men-are-clueless* shrug.

"Yes," I say. "Why? What's wrong with it?"

"Don't answer that," Mom sort of sing-song-whispers to Dad. "Be smart here, Ben."

He ignores her. For someone so brilliant, sometimes he can be really dim.

"It's a little..." He gestures at my dress—my bordering on modest, perfectly appropriate for a family dinner, dress. His frown deepens. "Mature. Don't you think?"

This is one of those times when I really, really wish I could do that whole one-eyebrow-raised trick Mom does so well. "I think it's pretty. Which is why I bought it for this joyous, special occasion."

"Kristin," Dad says, giving Mom a help-me-out-here look. "What do you think? Isn't it...mature?"

Mom, applying lipstick in the mirror near the door glances at him in the reflection. "You'd toss your own wife in the middle of this? And on our anniversary? Have you no morals? No sense of decency?"

Dad shifts, looking completely uncomfortable. As he should.

Or else he'd just irritated his partner in parenting is sitting this one out.

"It's just so...revealing," he finally says.

I gape at him. "Are you serious?" I turn to Mom. "Is he serious?" She holds her hands up as if in surrender so I whirl back to Dad.

"This dress is not revealing." I circle my own chest which is completely covered by the high, wide neckline. "No cleavage. None. The only part of me this dress reveals are my clavicle bones and a little of my back." I hold my arms out. "It's even long-sleeved!"

"Maybe *revealing* is the wrong word," he mutters.

"You think?"

"Maybe a better word is...short."

Seriously? The hem reaches halfway down my thighs.

Give or take an inch or two.

"I'm seventeen," I say. "My dresses are supposed to be this short. If I wear one that's longer than this, I'd be laughed right out of the local soda fountain! Then the cool kids would never invite me to the weekend sock hop!"

"I'm not being old-fashioned," Dad says. He looks at Mom. "I'm not."

She pats his arm. "Of course you're not. You're no fuddy-duddy. You're hip. And cool."

I cover my ears with my hands. "Ugh. Please, stop. He might actually believe you."

He gestures at me again. "That dress is so tight—"

"Tight?" I ask, my voice cracking in disbelief. "*Tight*?"

"Have you lost your mind?" Mom asks him. "Fathers have been killed for less than that. And their teenage daughters have gotten away with it, too. It's justifiable homicide."

"What do you mean *tight*?" I slam my hands on my hips. "Are you saying I'm fat?"

"Run," Mom tells him in a dark undertone. "For God's sake, run for your life."

He nods and starts backing away slowly, eyes on me as if I'm a wild animal who could pounce at any moment. "I'll just...uh...warm up the car," he says, still walking backwards.

I narrow my eyes. "It's, like, fifty degrees outside. And your car is in the garage. The *heated* garage."

"Right, but I don't want your mother to catch a chill," he insists then turns and takes off.

"All you're doing," I call after him, "is pumping more exhaust into the environment. You're ruining what's left of the ozone layer!"

He lifts a hand as if to say, *No problem! Just doing my small part to contribute to climate change!*

Once he's gone, I turn to Mom. "I know children aren't supposed to have a favorite parent but right now, you're my pick. Congrats."

"Well, my competition wasn't very stiff."

"Hey, a win's a win."

"True. And I have to say you playing the *do you think I'm fat?* card was a nice touch. Put the fear of God into him."

"He deserved it."

She wrinkles his nose. "He sort of did, huh?"

"There's no sort of about it." Thanks to him, I now have fashion anxiety. "Should I change?"

"Absolutely not. You look gorgeous."

I twist and turn, trying to see myself from all angles in the mirror but even if I could rotate my head a full 360 degrees, it wouldn't help. I can only see myself from the waist up. "It's not really tight, is it?"

Mom links her arm with mine and steers us toward the garage, united in our resolve against the tyranny of men and their stupid, old-fashioned rules for what women should—or shouldn't—wear.

"It's not too tight," she says, "and it's not too short. Your father just doesn't like being reminded that his little girl is a young woman now. But you are growing up which is why I think it's time I tell you one of life's hard truths." She stops in front of the door to the garage, turns me to face her and lays both hands on my shoulders. "Males are... well...there's no easy way to put this. They're idiots."

"No!" I say with a fake gasp.

She nods. "I'm pretty sure it's biologically ingrained in each and every one of them. Not all the time mind you, but every once in a while, even the best of them have a weak moment and that idiocy slips out."

I open the door and we step into the garage. We're taking separate cars because Dad wants to check on a patient at the hospital before dinner so I'll pick up Philip and we'll meet them at the restaurant at seven.

Chase texted me an hour ago when he stopped to get gas to let me know he'll be there by six-forty-five.

Everything is going according to plan.

Dad has backed the car out and left it running. When he sees us coming, he gets out and walks around to open her door for Mom.

He makes it really tough to stay mad at him.

"So we're just supposed to take it because it's some sort of instinctive response they can't help?" I ask.

"That's the question and totally up to you. But my advice is if the male in question's idiocy only comes out rarely, it's best to cut him some slack."

"Because we're females and biologically ingrained to be nurturers, forgivers and accepters?"

She laughs. At the sound, Dad smiles and watches her, as if he can't take his eyes off her.

Yeah, not staying mad at him tonight.

"Not at all," Mom says. "But if you cut him some slack for being an idiot, maybe he'll do the same when you're one."

25

Cut him some slack. Cut him some slack. Cut him some slack.

Nope, not working. No matter how many times I repeat Mom's advice to myself.

"What do you mean you can't come?" I ask Philip.

We're in his driveway, me sitting behind the wheel of my Jeep, my window down. Philip is standing next to my door, both hands on the lower edge of the window frame.

"I'm sorry, babe," Philip says and though he's doing his best to look contrite, all sad puppy eyes and turned down mouth, he's not sorry. He's not sorry at all. He's only saying it so I don't get mad at him.

Too late. Way, way too late.

"Becca dumped Travis," he continues. "He needs someone to hang out with tonight. He's totally messed up right now."

The front door to the Panoses' huge Victorian house opens and Travis Rowe steps out, talking on his phone, laughing at something the other person said.

I raise my eyebrows at Philip. "He looks really broken-hearted."

Philip waves that off but he does, I notice, shift to the side to try and block my view of his best friend lounging on the porch swing. "He's talking to Evie Maestrano. Trying to make Becca jealous."

"If he hooks up with Evie," I point out, "there's no way Becca will take him back."

"Hey, I told him it was a bad idea. This is why he can't be left alone tonight. He'll screw things up with Becca for good if someone doesn't keep him on a short leash."

I sigh. Crap. I should have known something was up the moment I pulled into Philip's driveway and saw him racing out to meet me in jeans, an old soccer T-shirt and bare feet—not exactly dressed for a semi-fancy dinner with my parents, brother and my brother's girlfriend.

"Okay, so he can't be left to his own devices tonight," I say. "I get that. But why do you have to babysit him? Can't someone else hang out with him? Just until we're done with dinner. I promise, I'll have you back here by ten at the latest. You could ask Stuart or Wes--"

"I'm not just going to ditch him, Nat," Philip says, giving me this look, like I should be ashamed for wanting my boyfriend to do what he said he'd do—go to dinner with me and my family. "You know he's been having a really rough time since his folks split up."

I'm not going to win this one. I'm not even sure I should want to because Travis *has* been having a rough time lately. And while I do feel bad for him and don't want him to be alone, I don't necessarily want my boyfriend to be the one to be there for him.

At least until after dinner.

"So you can't ditch Travis," I say, "but you can ditch me?"

"Come on," Philip says softly, giving me one of his lopsided grins —the one he pulls out when he's trying to charm his way out of trouble. "You know it's not like that. Don't be mad. You won't even miss me, you'll be too busy catching up with your brother and Leah. Besides, your family should celebrate your parents' anniversary with just you guys. I'd feel out of place, like a fifth wheel."

"It would have been nice if you'd told me this before—like a month ago when I first asked you to go, or any of the other times I've brought it up since then—and not wait until the last minute, literally, and come up with some excuse as to why you can't go."

"I did want to go," he says but it's sort of hard for me to believe that right now. "I still do. It's just—"

"Yo, Panos!" Travis calls, his voice slurred. "You coming?"

Philip holds up his hand as if to indicate he'll just be another teeny, tiny minute pacifying his silly, irrational girlfriend.

"Is he drunk?" I ask, incredulously.

Philip's parents both work at the restaurant on Friday nights but they'll notice if someone's been dipping into their liquor cabinet.

"Not yet," Philip admits, "but he's getting there. Which is another reason I can't leave him alone. What kind of friend would I be if I turned my back on him?"

And now I'm the bad guy. Because he's right. He's totally, completely right. He would be a horrible, terrible friend if he went to dinner with me.

A good boyfriend, but a crappy best friend.

"I wish you would have told me sooner," I grumble. "Like before I left to come here to pick you up."

He nods, all solemn and agreeable and I can't help but wonder if it's all an act. One to shut me up and get me on my way. "You're right. I should have and I'm sorry. He showed up with a bottle of his dad's vodka, already buzzed and flipping out, and it took me a while to talk him down. Then I lost track of time." He reaches through the open window and trails a finger down my cheek. "I'm really sorry, Nat. Forgive me?"

What choice do I have? I don't want to stay mad at him—I don't want to be mad at him period. Especially after our last fight. Things are just getting back to normal between us.

"Yeah." I sigh. "I forgive you."

He grins. "How about a hug before you go?"

I almost refuse. It's late and I don't want to miss seeing Mom and Dad's surprise when they arrive and see Chase and Leah there. But refusing Philip now would only seem like I'm holding a grudge, like I don't really forgive him.

This being the better person thing is tough on a girl.

I open the door and get out, leaving the Jeep running in case he gets any ideas about us sneaking up to his room for a few minutes since his parents aren't home, but I guess I don't have to worry about that because when I step forward, he frowns and steps back.

"Is that what you're wearing?"

Lowering my arms, I do a slow scan of the area. "Am I in a time loop? Or have you been possessed by the over-protective spirit of my father?"

"What?"

"He asked me the same exact thing," I say, narrowing my eyes. "Did he call you?"

"No." Philip scratches his chin, his irritated gaze trained on my legs. "It's short."

It takes everything I have inside of me not to tug at the hem. "You think?"

He nods, somehow missing the iciness of my tone. "And tight."

My right eyelid twitches. "That's what I hear."

Leaning over the porch railing, Travis gives me a long, low whistle. "Hey, Natalie," he says, drawing my name out, "looking hot tonight!"

"Rowe," Philip snaps, "shut the fuck up."

Travis stumbles back, hands lifted—and almost takes a header into a basket of yellow mums. "Just giving your girl a compliment."

"Don't compliment her," Philip tells him, jabbing a finger in his best friend's direction. "Don't even think about her. And stop looking at her!"

Travis immediately shuts his eyes, weaves like a tree in strong wind then burps so hard he almost topples over.

Idiots.

"I'm leaving," I say, giving Philip a quick kiss on the cheek. "Bye."

I turn to my Jeep and Philip grumbles, "Jesus Christ, Nat. There's not even a back to it."

Not true. The dress has a back. It just happens to be cut wide and low—just above my bra strap.

But Philip, unlike my dad, isn't being a prude. He isn't even being protective.

He's jealous.

And I'm a horrible, horrible person, because I'm glad.

I smile, wide and bright and pretty. "Have fun with Travis."

Then I get in my Jeep, buckle up for safety and slowly back out of the driveway.

Leaving my boyfriend to eat his stupid heart out.

* * *

Turns out Philip wasn't the only no-show tonight. Leah didn't come to dinner, either. Chase said she had some sorority thing Saturday afternoon and it was easier for her to stay in Philly, that way Chase could spend the weekend at home.

Other than my brother and I both being stood up by our significant others, everything else went exactly as I'd envisioned. Mom and Dad were thrilled and very surprised to see Chase there, and they loved our gift to them (a picture of me and Chase in the backyard, the pose copied from a photo taken when we were little—my idea). All my planning and worrying and scheduling and numerous texts and calls to Chase were worth it.

Which he refuses to admit, but whatever.

I'd hoped that after dinner we'd all hang out, maybe go home and watch a movie, but Dad got paged by the hospital as we were finishing dessert and left early. Mom is meeting with her contractor first thing in the morning so she had Chase take her home so she could go to bed. After dropping her and his stuff off, Chase is meeting friends at a local bar.

Leaving me to drive home. Alone. At night.

I'd been too angry at Philip to be worried about driving into the city by myself, and I figured I could talk someone into riding home with me, but when Mom said she'd ride home with Chase, I couldn't say anything. After all, she hasn't seen him for weeks.

And I don't want her to think there's something wrong with me.

But I am in a hurry to get home. So much so, that I take the back way into town instead of the highway, cutting a good ten minutes off my drive.

Which is why I'm now fifteen miles outside of town, alone, in the dark, in the woods, on a winding, hilly, foggy road.

All by myself.

Just me, myself and I.

Did I mention the alone part?

But it's fine. Really. I mean, I dislike driving alone in the dark even more than I do driving alone in daylight, but I do it several times a week.

I do it.

I just prefer not to.

Another reason to hold onto my anger toward Philip. If he'd come with me, he could be the one behind the wheel. Instead, I'm in the driver's seat, leaning forward, shoulders tight, neck aching with tension as I drive ten miles under the speed limit, my eyes dry from the fact that I'm pretty much terrified to blink, lest I veer off the road or hit a deer or cross the center line and run into an oncoming vehicle.

Not that there are any. Other vehicles, that is. Seems everyone else is smart enough to stick to the brightly lit, straight and spacious highway.

Except highways give me even more anxiety, what with people speeding and passing and all those huge semis. It's nerve-wracking. Especially at night.

No matter which route I choose, it's a losing situation.

At least this way I can take my time without worrying someone is going to fly by me or worse, that I'll actually have to pass someone else.

While this is better, it's far from ideal what with the fog and the inability to see more than a dozen or so feet in front of me. I squeeze the steering wheel, imagine it's Philip's head. Yeah, I'm definitely holding on to some of that anger toward him. At least until I get home.

Then I'll think about forgiving him.

But only if he takes back what he said about my dress.

Approaching a sharp curve, I slow even more and round the corner. My headlights reflect on something in the road and it takes me a second to realize what it is. Eyes. There's a raccoon in the middle of my lane and though I keep heading right for him, he doesn't move.

Mouth dry, heart pounding, I jerk the wheel hard to the right. There's a definite thump and I brake too fast. The back end swerves. The front end drops off the side of the road onto the berm. I overcorrect, yanking the wheel to the left and end up in a spin. There's a loud pop, another harder thump and then, finally, I'm stopped.

Horizontal. In the middle of the road.

Shaking, gulping in breath, I press the gas gently but as the Jeep moves forward, it's clear something's not right. I pull off the road, put my four-way blinkers on and notice the low tire indicator light is lit on the dashboard.

Crap.

I rock—back and forth, back and forth—in my seat. My eyes sting, my throat hurts. I sniff mightily. Okay. Okay, okay, okay. There's nothing to cry about. It's no big deal. It's just a flat. I'm fine. I'll call Philip, have him get me and tomorrow, in the daylight, Dad can send a mechanic out to change the tire.

I pull out my phone and dial Philip's number. It rings. And rings. And rings. When his voicemail picks up, I hang up and text him.

Call me.

He doesn't. I text him again. Try calling a second time.

Nothing.

It's just after ten so I doubt he's in bed already. Especially if Travis is spending the night...

I scroll through my contacts. Call Travis.

"Yeah?" he says in greeting, but it's so loud where he's at—people laughing and shouting, music playing—I can barely hear him.

Travis, it seems, is at a party.

And if my boyfriend is with him, he can forget about any forgiveness coming from me anytime soon.

"Is Philip with you?" I ask, hoping he's not. Praying he's at home, in his bed, sound asleep or maybe watching TV with his parents. Exactly where he should be on a Friday night after ditching the plans we made.

"What?" Travis yells.

But even though I have hope, a bigger, more pragmatic part of me—the part that knows my boyfriend as well as I know myself—recognizes that hope is pretty much useless. "Get Philip!"

"Yo, Panos!" Travis shouts, about piercing my eardrum. "Your warden wants you."

Warden. As if I constantly call and check up on Philip when he's out with his friends because I have nothing better to do. It's no wonder Becca dumped Travis.

He's such a dumbass.

It's a good thirty seconds before Philip gets on and when he does, it's noticeably quieter. Like he went outside or into another room.

"Hey, babe," he says. "What's up?"

"Where are you?"

He hesitates, and I get the sense that he's trying to decide what to tell me. Which is crazy. Philip doesn't lie. He's one of the good guys.

Usually.

Tonight, it seems, is the exception.

"Carlson's. But only for a few minutes," he adds.

I can't believe it. "You went to Justin's party? Is that why you ditched me? So you could go there?"

"No! I told you, Travis needed me. Look, it wasn't even my idea," Philip says. "Travis heard Becca was here and I couldn't let him come alone. He was already drunk, and I knew he'd make things worse with her."

"Yes, you're a great friend." If the grunt of frustration coming from Philip is any indication, my sarcasm is not lost on him. "It's so awesome of you to sacrifice your evening for your good buddy. I suppose if I check Instagram or Snapchat I'm going to see that you were only there a few minutes?"

"We didn't plan on staying this long. And we're leaving soon."

"Uh-huh. How soon?"

"Soon," he says in this low, impatient tone, as if I'm the one who's in the wrong here!

God.

"Soon. Right." And then it hits me, why he sounds so weird, his words coming out slowly, as if he's choosing them carefully. Why he's acting this way, all defensive and belligerent. "Are you drinking?"

"I had a couple of beers. Don't tell me," he mutters, "I'm not allowed to have any fun unless you're by my side approving it."

"You're the one who wanted us to both promise we wouldn't drink unless we were together! But I guess what you really meant was that you didn't want me drinking if you weren't there. You obviously have different rules for yourself than you do for me."

He sighs. "Aw, come on, babe. You know it's not like that."

But I don't. I don't know what it's like. And I can't help but wonder if he's acting this way, if he went with Travis instead of going to dinner with me, as a way to punish me for not telling him immediately about Owen and my conversation in Owen's truck last week.

"Just forget it," I say.

"Forget what?"

"Forget I called. Forget the promise you made me." My voice thickens with tears. "Forget you were supposed to be with me tonight, not getting wasted with your friends. Forget everything."

"Nata—"

I hang up, my hands shaking, my breath coming out in short, choppy gasps.

He calls back—three times—and texts me twice. I let the calls go to voicemail. Ignore the texts. I can't even deal with him right now, mainly because dealing with just trying to breathe is taking up all my time and concentration.

My chest is tight, my mind fuzzy and there's this weird tingling in my hands. I'm completely alone, in the dark, in the woods. Not one car has passed the whole time I've been sitting here. Not one. And even if someone does come, it's not like I can just flag them down and ask a stranger for help. It's like a scene in every slasher movie ever made.

Although getting my head chopped off by some psychopath with a limp and sad backstory would serve Philip right.

Of course, there's the teeny, tiny little problem that I'd be decapitated—oh, and super dead—but it would almost be worth it.

The four ways blink, blink, blink and tick, tick, tick. I focus on that, the flashing light on the dash indicating they're on, the sound filling the interior of the Jeep. I try to match my breaths to the ticks but they're so fast, I have to double up or else risk hyperventilating.

Tick...inhale...tick. Tick...exhale...tick. Tick...inhale...tick.

On and on and on until I'm no longer lightheaded. Until feeling returns to the tips of my fingers. Until my mind clears.

I pick up my phone. I should do the responsible thing and call Mom and Chase, try to catch them before they get home. I should do the mature thing and call the auto club, have them send a tow or a mechanic or whoever they send when one of their motorists is stranded on the side of the road.

But I don't. I don't do the responsible thing. I don't do the mature thing.

I do the irresponsible, immature, worst thing I can do. I follow my instincts.

And I call Owen.

26

I COUNT THE RINGS.

One...

Two...

Three...

Four...

Fi—

"Yeah?" Owen says, his voice husky and deep. Like he'd been sleeping.

I open my mouth, but nothing comes out. I freeze, everything inside of me screaming at me to hang up. To get out of this before it's too late. But I can't move. I can't fix this.

I'm not so sure I want to.

"Natalie?" Owen asks, my name a whisper in the dark. He sounds so close, if I shut my eyes it's almost as if he's right here with me. As if I'm not so alone.

"I'm sorry to bother you," I blurt. "Or wake you. Or...or interrupt your eve—"

"Slow down," he says, still in that soft, soothing tone. "Take a breath."

I do, inhaling so fast, so hard, I wheeze with the effort.

"Again," he says. "Slower. Deeper."

There's something about the quiet command that makes me automatically obey. That calms me. I inhale slowly, hold it for the count of ten then exhale.

"Better?" he asks.

I nod then roll my eyes because the boy can't see me, for God's sake. "Yes. Thanks."

"You okay?"

Tears form again and this time, when I open my mouth, everything comes rushing out. "No. I mean, yes, I'm fine but I got into an accident and I think I killed a raccoon and I popped a tire and my brother is out with his friends and I don't want to upset my parents and I just want to go home."

That last bit was said with a bit of a whine, if I'm being completely honest.

Honesty is so overrated.

"Where are you?" Owen asks, and I hear I hear a sound, like sheets rustling and I wonder if he's in bed. Imagine him sitting up, his back against the headboard, his hair sticking up on the side.

I squeeze my eyes closed to erase the image. God. The last thing I need to be doing is imaging Owen in bed!

Tucking the phone between my ear and my shoulder, I reach over and open the glove box. Grab a napkin and wipe my nose. Sniff. "Route 44. About five minutes past the turnoff to the lake on the way into town."

"You're alone?"

"Yes."

"Do you want me to stay on the phone with you?"

I do, but I'm about two seconds away from completely losing it so I sniff again and say, "No. Thanks. Just...could you hurry? Please?"

"I'll be there in twenty minutes. Stay in the car, keep the doors locked and your phone in your hands."

He hangs up before I can thank him again.

Seventeen minutes later, headlights appear coming toward me and I duck down in my seat. Another vehicle passed by about ten minutes ago and knowing it was way too soon to be Owen, I'd practically crawled onto the floor, visions of that previously desired decapitation going through my mind. Luckily, they'd flown past, not even slowing despite my blinking hazard lights and obvious flat tire.

So not a serial killer on the prowl for his latest victim.

Or a good Samaritan looking for someone to save.

The headlights come steadily closer and the vehicle pulls over, facing me. Squinting against the glare, I peer through the windshield, my entire body sagging with relief when the lights go out and I see it's Owen's truck.

Thank God. Another few minutes alone in this Jeep and I was going to go crazy. I'd spent part of the time counting the blinks and ticks of my four ways but when I realized that was an effort in futility, I decided to list all fifty states in alphabetical order.

Except I kept getting forty-nine and I refuse to pick up my phone to Google which one I'm missing since I might be tempted to answer one of Philip's texts.

Owen gets out of his truck and walks toward me, seemingly at ease with being dragged away from whatever he was doing to play hero to my damsel in distress.

I'm not sure whether to be grateful he plays his part so well or irritated that I'm reduced to playing mine.

He doesn't look like a hero. He's in dark sweatpants and a gray hoodie—zipper zipped, hood up, hands in the front pockets. He looks dark and dangerous.

And ready to save me.

He taps on the window and I realize I'm staring at him like a brainless idiot. For a moment, sense returns and I consider keeping the window rolled up, maybe giving him a shooing motion to send him on his way.

But I can't.

And it's not because he drove all the way out here or because I don't want to bother my brother or parents.

It's because I don't want him to leave.

I roll down the window.

"You hurt?" he asks.

"No." I wipe my damp palms down the skirt of my dress. "You know, now that you're here, I'm pretty sure this is possibly the worst idea I've ever had."

"You just figured that out?"

"Well, I'd actually figured it out earlier but you were on your way..." I swallow. "I'm really sorry for bothering you. Were you...were you sleeping?"

"I work at six-thirty on Saturdays."

I groan inwardly. And I woke him up, had him drive twenty miles out of town to help me. "I'm sorry," I repeat lamely.

"Which tire?" he asks.

"Right front. I think."

"You didn't check?"

"You told me to stay in the Jeep. Never let it be said I don't listen to sage advice."

"What about after the accident? Did you check then?" I shake my head and his eyes narrow. "So you don't even know for sure you have a flat?"

What if I don't? What if I've been sitting here all this time, what if I called him to come help me when I could have driven off, merry and free and on four fully inflated tires, no rescue required?

That would sooo suck.

"The tire gauge thingy is lit on the dashboard," I tell him. "The one that says when a tire is low? And it felt flat when I pulled off the side of the road. Plus, there was a pop. A really loud one. I'm sure it's flat." It has to be. "And I didn't check because it's dark and I didn't want to end up some wild animal's midnight snack."

His expression lightens. Great. Now he's amused. Why is it he only finds me funny when I'm not trying to be? "It's ten-forty-five."

"A ten-forty-five snack then. Point is, I didn't want to be on the menu."

"Deer don't eat people."

"Maybe not, but bears do. I saw *The Revenant*. I know." I didn't want to see it—what girl wants to watch Leo DiCaprio get mauled by a grizzly? But Philip was all gung-ho about it. I still have nightmares about the atrocities Leo suffered. "And don't tell me grizzlies and black bears—" which is what we have here in good old Southwestern Pennsylvania. "—are different. They're both bears. They're both bigger than me and they both have sharp teeth and claws."

He scratches his cheek. "There's no sense trying to reason with you, is there?"

"Nope."

"I'll check the tire."

Before he can leave, I lean out the window and grab his forearm. "Wait! The raccoon...could you...that is, would you mind..." He's looking at me that way he does—all patient and willing to wait me out. "Could you check on it? Please?"

"You want me to check on the raccoon you ran over?"

"I'm not one hundred percent sure I ran it over. That's what needs checked."

"Are you serious right now?"

"Please," I say again, letting go of his arm. "I need to know whether or not I should feel guilty about—possibly—squishing one of God's amazing creatures."

"Why don't you check yourself? I'll go with you. Protect you from all those wild, hungry grizzlies."

I wrinkle my nose. "And see it—possibly—all flat and bloody and gross? Ew. No."

He gives me the patented Owen Radlowski stare down. I blink at him innocently. Hopefully.

He sighs and grumbles, "You're a real pain in the ass, you know that?"

And he walks toward his truck.

He's leaving and it's all my fault.

I asked for too much.

I pushed him away.

27

———

"Wait!" I call and I'm in such a hurry to go after Owen, to stop him, to beg him not to leave me, that I forget I'm still wearing my seatbelt and about strangle myself when I try to bolt out of the Jeep. Gah! My hands are so unsteady it takes me three tries before I'm able to unclick the belt. I open the door and leap out, ready to run after his truck if need be but it's not.

Needed, that is.

He's walking toward me.

I blink at him, my heart racing, my palms sweaty. "You weren't... you aren't leaving?"

A beam of light appears and I realize he's holding a flashlight. That he went to his truck to get it.

"I came out here to help you," he points out.

"I know, it's just...you said I was a pain in the ass and I thought..."

I thought that was enough to make him walk away.

"You are a pain in the ass. But I'm not leaving you."

It's not quite a declaration of undying loyalty and friendship, but it's enough to leave me speechless. "Oh."

He edges closer. Reaches out and touches the back of my hand,

185

just two fingers brushing against my knuckles, but it's nice. Comforting. "Bad night?"

"Not completely. It's just...I had it all planned out, you know?"

"And you don't like when things don't go according to your plans."

"Who does?" Chase says it's because I'm a control freak. Philip says I'm too wrapped up in trying to make everything perfect. "I like knowing what's going to happen and when it's going to happen. I don't like surprises or changes. But other than the accident, tonight wasn't horrible or anything. It just..."

"Wasn't how you wanted it to be."

A lump forms in my throat. "Right."

"I'm going to check on the raccoon."

"You really don't have—"

"And then I'm going to get your spare and jack out," he continues as if I haven't spoken. "So I can change your tire."

It takes me a moment, but I realize what he's doing.

He's giving me a plan.

"Okay," I whisper. "Thanks."

He walks down the road to see if my furry little friend made it or not, the beam of his flashlight seeming to bounce right off the fog. I shut the door, hugging my arms around myself against the damp chill in the air.

"No raccoon," he calls as he walks toward me.

But there's something in his tone and somehow, someway, I know he's lying.

To protect me.

"That's great," I say, playing along. "Thanks. Again."

He gets closer. And closer and suddenly, I'm terrified of what I've done. Calling him, having him help me.

Being alone with him.

The beam of the flashlight hits the ground in front of me, then my high heeled booties, then my legs. I barely breathe as that light travels up, up, up—climbing my calves then my thighs, skimming over my hips and waist and flashing against my chest and shoulders before being aimed, once again, at my feet.

"You can wait in the truck," he says, his tone sharp and suddenly angry, his face averted. As if he doesn't want to look at me.

As if he's mad at me.

Then again, I did wake him up, have him drive twenty miles, find a dead raccoon and change a flat tire.

I'd be mad at me, too.

"I should learn how to do this," I say. "So the next time it happens I can fix it myself."

"You won't be able to get the lug nuts off. Mechanics put them on using a power tool. They'll be too tight for you."

"I want to learn," I repeat, stepping closer. He steps back. "And the least I can do after you came all this way out here is help you."

He shrugs and walks around the front of the Jeep. I hold the flashlight as he examines the tire and declares it shredded. And while he gets the spare and jack from the back of the Jeep, I turn on his truck's headlights and meet him at the flat.

Obviously I am a huge help. I'm not sure what he would have done without me.

But though he told me I wouldn't be able to change a flat on my own, he explains everything he's doing; checking the spare to make sure it's properly inflated, how to set up the jack and where to put it (under something called the axel housing which he has me crouch down to see underneath the Jeep).

"Before raising the vehicle," he says, "you need to loosen the lug nuts."

"I'll do it," I say because I feel stupid and useless just standing here nodding and making agreeable sounds.

And, okay, yes, because he told me I couldn't do it.

"You don't have to prove anything to me," he says when I hold out my hand for the bent, lug-nut-unscrewer bar thingy.

I never should have admitted my incessant need to prove myself to him that day in my driveway.

He knows way too much about me.

"I can do it," I repeat and to my surprise, he hands over the bar and steps aside.

I attach the bar to the lug nut on the bottom left and turn it except, it doesn't actually move. Straining with the effort, I put all my weight behind it.

Nothing.

"Other way," Owen says.

I glare at him over my shoulder. "You couldn't have told me that before I dislocated my shoulder?"

"I thought you'd figure it out."

"I would have," I mutter, shifting my body weight to the left and pulling with all my might. "Eventually. How do you know so much about changing tires?" I ask, hoping a bit of conversation will hide the fact that all I'm doing is giving myself a hernia and not loosening the stupid lug nut one centimeter.

"One of my mom's ex-boyfriends is a mechanic."

I wait for him to expound on that, to give me a little more information as I'm curious about him. Interested in his life. But Owen, it seems, can't watch me work and talk at the same time because he goes silent.

Leaving my grunts and heavy breathing to fill the air.

I'm sweating, my arms and back aching and still, it's not working. It's like a personal defeat, the last straw to an incredibly disappointing night. Frustration rolls through me and the tears I held back earlier return with a vengeance, spilling over to roll down my cheeks and plop onto my hands.

"Hey," Owen says softly but I shake my head. Keep my face averted.

"You were right," I say hoarsely. "They're too tight."

"Try one on top."

I wipe my cheek on my shoulder. Sniff. "It won't mat—"

"Try it."

With another sniff, I move the bar to a higher lug nut and give it a half-hearted pull. "I can't do it."

"Come on," he says, stepping up behind me and reaching around to place his right hand on the bar next to mine. "Try again."

But I can't move. I can barely breathe, he's so close, as close as he can get without actually touching me and I find myself wanting to lean back. Wanting to close that little bit of distance between us.

Instead I do the smart thing, the right thing, and ease forward.

"On three," he says, his mouth close to my ear and I glance over but he's not looking at me, his gaze is down, his jaw set. "One, two, three..."

We pull together and the bar turns.

Owen lets go and steps back. "Do the next one. Push and use your leg if you have to."

I set the bar at an angle, press my knee against it and push for all I'm worth.

It moves.

I turn to Owen, caught between the end of my tears and the beginning of a self-satisfied grin. "I did it!"

There are no congratulations from my mentor, no *good job*. Only a short nod of acknowledgement and a rough, "Give me the bar. I'll do the rest."

"But—"

"Look, some of us don't get to sleep in until noon on weekends," he says, once again angry with me—and they say teenage girls are moody. "I'd like to be back in my bed before midnight if that's all right with you."

I don't bother telling him I have ballet at eight on Saturday mornings, or that I never sleep past seven, not even during summer vacation. Just give him the bar and move off to the side so I'm not blocking his light.

It's seriously cold out and it doesn't take long for the warmth from my lug-nut-loosening exertion to fade and I'm freezing. I shift my weight from my left leg to my right. Then back again. Bounce in my booties as I watch Owen finish taking off the lug nuts.

To keep my mind off the fact that my nose is stinging with the cold, my toes going numb, and I'm basically being ignored by my so-called hero, I go back to my previous list, counting the U.S. states on my fingers, determined to figure out which one I'm missing.

Alabama, Alaska, Arizona, Arkansas, California, Colorado,

Connecticut, Delaware, Florida, Georgia, Hawaii, Idaho, Illinois, Indiana, Kansas, Kentuck—

"You and Panos have a big date?"

The question, gruff and sudden, startles me.

"What?"

"You're dressed up," Owen says, but he doesn't look at me. Has barely looked at me since he shined the flashlight on me.

"It's my parents' anniversary. My brother and I took them out to dinner to celebrate."

Pulling the flat off, he pauses. Stares at the tire. "Panos didn't go?"

Shivering, I hug my arms around myself. "It was more of a family thing."

Now he turns and studies me and I get the sense he's trying to read me, as if he knows there's more to my statement than I'm willing to let on.

As if he's trying to see the truth.

But it doesn't feel right, sharing the story of my fight with Philip with Owen. Doesn't seem fair.

To either of them.

Finally, Owen leans the tire against the Jeep and stands. He unzips his sweatshirt, takes it off and hands it to me. "Put this on."

I take an automatic step back. "That's okay. I don't need it."

But he obviously notices my chattering teeth because he steps closer and wraps the sweatshirt around my shoulders. "You can lie to yourself. But don't lie to me."

I have no response to that because, once again, Owen is standing close to me. Very, very close. Head down, I keep quiet and focus on putting my arms in the sleeves then lifting the hood. The sweatshirt is warm from his body and it smells of him, clean and a little spicy and just...good.

So good I want to turn my head and breathe it in.

I try to zip the sweatshirt, to hold on that warmth, to surround myself in that scent, but my hands are too unsteady, my fingers trembling.

Owen gently brushes my hands aside and, eyes down, pulls the material away from my body and puts the end into the pull tab. One hand holding the bottom, he tugs the zipper up slowly, the sound loud in the night.

He's not touching me but I swear every inch that his hand passes over heats. My lower stomach then my waist. My ribs and between my breasts.

He reaches the top but he doesn't let go.

"My mom told me to bring a coat," I say, my words coming out in a rush, "but I didn't think I'd be out this late. Or outside at all. So I didn't. Bring a coat, that is. I should have. That would have made my dad happy, especially if the coat was baggy and covered me from head to toe and I wore it during dinner so no one could see me in this dress. He doesn't like it. My dress," I hurry on to explain when Owen lifts his gaze to mine, his eyes unreadable in the darkness which is a shame.

I want to know what he's thinking.

I want to know more than anything.

The realization unsettles me even more than his nearness. More than his silence and that steady, searching gaze.

Maybe it's that need to know, that desire to hear him speak, or maybe it's the nerves tickling the back of my throat that make me feel antsy and wound up and just a little bit reckless.

That push me into asking, "Do you?"

"Do I what?" he asks, his tone gravely. Hesitant.

"Do you like my dress?"

The words are little more than a whisper. A question I have no right to ask.

One I have no right to know the answer to.

"Fuck," he says under his breath, his fingers tightening, fisting the sweatshirt in his hands, drawing me closer.

Only to suddenly let go.

I sway, off-balance. As I'd been leaning toward him.

Owen steps back. "Wait. In. The. Truck."

This time I don't argue.

This time, I turn and run.

28

Owen insisted on following me home.

I should have told him no. Would have except I'd lost the power of speech right after I asked him if he liked my dress.

I wish I'd lost it before I asked that inane, leading, flirtatious, question.

When he told me—after putting the spare on (by himself) and setting the flat and jack in the back of the Jeep (again, without any assistance from me)—he wanted to make sure I got home safely, I didn't argue. Didn't tell him he'd done enough already and that I was completely fine and not freaking out in the least.

I didn't even thank him.

I just took off, so anxious to get away, to get home, that I exceeded the speed limit several times and didn't even hyperventilate.

All I wanted was to put as much time and distance between me and what had happened on that dark stretch of road as possible.

Except having his headlights behind me, a solid, steady presence, only reminded me again and again and again of how I'd acted. Of what I'd done.

And that he hadn't answered my question.

God. Why did I ask him that in the first place? I have a boyfriend.

It doesn't matter what some other guy thinks of what I wear. Doesn't matter what some other guy thinks of me period.

By the time I get home, I'm sick with a combination of embarrassment, guilt and shame. But not enough of any one of them to pull into the garage until *after* I watch Owen do a three-point-turn in the road and drive away.

There is something definitely wrong with me.

Upstairs in the safety of my room, the door shut and locked, I pace—back and forth. Back and forth. My phone buzzes. Philip texting me again. I can't answer, can't even bring myself to pick it up and read what he said.

Don't trust myself not to call him and blurt out a rambling, heartfelt confession.

But what good would that do? It would only upset him, make our current fight that much worse. He'll think I called Owen just to get back at him for ditching me tonight and going to that party, but that's not me. I don't play those games.

At least, I don't think I do.

I collapse onto the end of my bed, elbows on my knees, face in my hands. I wish I could call Astrid but she's hardly unbiased—and as much as I love her, I don't trust her. Not with this.

I could always go to Mom but she's already sleeping and besides, she'll just tell me I should have called her about the flat, not some boy who isn't my boyfriend.

Which leaves no one. I suppose I could turn to Chase for advice but who knows what time he'll be home. Plus, he's a guy and I'm pretty sure I already know what he'll say.

The same thing Philip would say. That I never, ever, should have called Owen.

Sighing, I fall back onto my bed. I really, really need to get more friends.

As that's not happening tonight, I do the only thing I can do.

I count the flowers on my wall.

Right to left, top corner to bottom, then bottom right corner to left, bottom to top, then by color: blue, purple, red and pink, yellow and orange. And reverse: orange, yellow, pink and red, purple and blue.

I count them, again and again and again, and each time I reach eighty-three, I feel a little bit better.

By the time I go through the process twice, my stomach is no longer churning, and I realize I made what happened with Owen into a big deal when it's not.

Not really.

Yes, I called another boy to help me but only because Philip was out partying with his friends. Really, this is partly Philip's fault, too. If he'd gone out to dinner with my family—like he'd promised—none of this would have happened. I wouldn't have been on that stupid, winding road, wouldn't have murdered an innocent raccoon and wouldn't have gotten a flat tire.

I wouldn't have needed Owen.

I made a few mistakes. And maybe I did ask Owen for help to...well...to punish Philip. But I didn't really want to hurt him. I was upset and let my anger and disappointment get the best of me.

And, yes, asking Owen if he liked my dress could definitely be construed as flirting on my part, but it wasn't intentional. The question just...slipped out. I was feeling a bit self-conscious all evening because of what Dad and then Philip said. Because of how nervous I'd been with Owen so close.

But I blew the whole thing way, way out of proportion, let my wild imagination get the best of me. God, for a moment when we'd been standing there, Owen's bent head close to mine, his hands fisted in his sweatshirt, I'd thought...well, it seems so stupid now, but...I thought he was going to kiss me.

I thought I wanted him to.

Which I don't. If he tried, I would definitely stop him.

And I would not, not ever, kiss him back.

Not that I have to worry about that happening. The boy can barely stand me. He told me just tonight he thinks I'm a pain in the ass. I'm sure the last thing on his mind is kissing me.

Except, maybe he does like me. At least a little. I mean, he did drive all the way out to help me. He wouldn't do that if he hated me.

Maybe...maybe Owen and I really are becoming friends.

And there's absolutely nothing wrong with that.

I just have to be careful. The next time we're alone—as friends—there will be no more touching of any sort, no matter how innocent and platonic. No more standing close and definitely no more remarks that could be taken out of context.

Problem. Solved.

Next to me on the bed, my phone buzzes. I glance at it. Another text from Philip.

I pick it up but I don't respond—I don't even read it. Everything inside of me is still too wound up, my emotions jumbled, my thoughts not quite settled and I'm afraid if I talk to him now, I'll say something I'll regret.

Something I won't be able to take back.

And part of me wants him to suffer, just a little bit, for causing the fight in the first place.

Hey, I'm not proud of it. Just honest with my feelings.

So instead of having a conversation with my boyfriend that could either solve our issues or cause a huge rift between us, I send a text to Owen. I'm embarrassed by how I acted after he changed my tire and I don't want him to read anything into it.

Besides, I didn't thank him and I'd hate for him to think I'm ungrateful. As if I'm so entitled, the princess on the hill he claimed me to be, that I snap my fingers and expect people to do my bidding.

It takes me a good five minutes but I finally come up with a text that's friendly but not too friendly—or flirtatious in any way.

Thank you for your help tonight—I really appreciate it! And thanks to your lesson in Tire Changing 101, I'll be able to take care of myself the next time it happens. (Thumbs up emoji). Good night and thanks again! (Smiley face emoji)

I'm taking off my booties when my phone buzzes.

Owen is texting me back.

Your welcome.

I kick off my shoes and slide back against the headboard.

I thought you'd be sleeping.

Send.

And it's actually you're (you are) welcome. Not your (which would indicate a sense of ownership) welcome which would be like saying the welcome belongs to me, which I guess technically it does, but in the context of your meaning it's incorrect.

He doesn't text back.

He calls.

"Hello?"

"If you thought I was sleeping," he says, his voice as quiet as mine, "why did you text me?"

"I thought you'd look at it in the morning. And I texted because I didn't thank you so..." I prop a pillow on my lap, snuggle down onto my bed. "Thank you."

"Why did you call me?"

I frown. "We literally just talked about this. I didn't call you. I texted you. You, on the other hand, called me. Does any of this sound familiar?"

"Not now. Why did you call me earlier?"

My breath catches and I'm not sure I can answer.

Know I don't want to.

"Didn't I tell you?" I ask, forcing a note of lightness in my voice I am so not feeling at the moment. "It's my parents' anniversary and I didn't want to bother them. I would have called my brother, but he's out with friends and honestly, it wouldn't have done me any good. Chase isn't exactly what you'd call mechanically inclined. Anyway," I rush on, "I really appreciate you coming to my rescue."

"No. I mean...why me?"

I think about telling him he was my last choice, the desperate choice, after going through my entire list of contacts and trying every other person I know, but I can't.

"I don't know," I whisper, running my hand over the pillow—back and forth. Back and forth. "You were the first person I thought of."

I sense his surprise. "Me? Not Panos?"

"Yes. No." I stop. Take a slow, deep breath. "I called Philip. But you were the first person I thought of after that."

"He refused to help you?"

"He didn't know I had a flat. Our, uh...our conversation didn't get that far." I toss the pillow aside then switch the phone to my other ear. "But I really, really appreciate you helping me. You're a good friend."

"Is that what you think we are?" he asks after a moment. "Friends?"

"Don't try to deny it," I say, injecting a teasing note into my tone. "You drove twenty minutes outside of town and changed a flat tire in the dark and cold. You wouldn't do that for someone who wasn't a friend."

"What does Panos think about our...friendship?"

"He's fine with it." It's such a huge lie I duck my head, expecting a lightning bolt to come down from the sky and fry me. When it doesn't, I feel pretty safe in adding another fib on top of it. "Philip isn't the jealous type. Although..." I clear my throat. "Maybe, it would be best if neither of us mentions what happened tonight. To anyone."

Owen is silent for a beat. Then two. Three.

I hold the phone away from my ear but it says the call is still connected. "Are you still there?"

"You embarrassed by me, Natalie?" he asks so quietly, it takes a moment for the words to register. For their meaning to become clear.

"What? No! It's not that. At all. It's just Philip might get the wrong idea..."

"Wouldn't want that."

I'm pretty sure he's being sarcastic.

"No. We wouldn't. Please," I add when he doesn't rush to assure me that he'll never, ever, tell anyone what transpired between us. "Please, Owen."

"Yeah," he grumbles. "Whatever."

But I need more. I can't move on with my life, can't go to sleep or even hang up until I know for sure my secret is safe. "Promise?"

He sighs as I live up to that pain-in-ass moniker he gave me earlier. "Jesus. I promise, okay?"

I shut my eyes in relief. "Okay."

"You sure you don't want me to sign a solemn oath in my own in blood or swear it on my mother's grave?"

"First of all, that's disgusting—not to mention unhygienic. Secondly, your mother's not dead." I pause. Frown. "Oh, my God...is she?"

"Alive and kicking and watching reruns of *Real Housewives* as we speak."

"Then how could you swear on her grave?"

"I was making a point."

"Not very well," I tell him. "Because I still have no idea what it is."

"I was asking," he says slowly, as if my inability to comprehend his meaning is somehow the problem here, "if it's really that easy for you to believe I'll keep my promise."

"Oh. Why didn't you just say so? And yes. Of course it's that easy. We may not know each other well but I know that when you give me your word, you'll keep it." I hesitate, unsure whether or not to say the rest but I want to. I want him to know what I think of him. "I trust you, Owen."

He makes a sound, like a cross between a groan of frustration and a growl of anger. "Don't be putting me up on a pedestal," he snaps. "I'm not some fucking Boy Scout. I'm not Panos."

"Well, you did have a flashlight in your truck," I point out, ignoring his comment about Philip. No way am I going there because he's right. He's not Philip.

I don't want him to be.

"So you've got the always-prepared thing down," I continue. "But don't worry, I'm not putting you on a pedestal. I just..." I hesitate and smooth a wrinkle in my bedspread—smooth, smooth, smooth—and think of what everyone says about him. How he's got a bad attitude. That he's unfriendly and doesn't fit in. That he's not that smart and has a chip on his shoulder. They judge him. But they're wrong. "I'm not putting you in a box, either."

He's silent again but I don't ask if he's still there. I can hear his breathing, can sense him.

He's with me.

"You're killing me," he says softly. "You know that, right?"

A thrill shoots through me but it's immediately followed by panic. Oh, God, what did I say? What am I doing?

"Sorry," I blurt. "I—"

I didn't mean it. I shouldn't have said it. I shouldn't be doing this. Shouldn't be having this conversation with you.

I shouldn't be having these feelings.

All true.

Except for the part about not meaning it.

"I'm keeping you up," I say, desperate to get out of this before it gets worse. Before I do or say something else that's going to get me into trouble. That's going to expose too much. "You're tired and I already dragged you from your bed once tonight and you have to get up early..." I trail off on an inner groan. I need to just say goodbye and hang up already, instead I'm babbling on and on, telling him things he already freaking knows. "Thank you," I say, my tone sharp and clear, "for helping me and for agreeing not to tell anyone about it. Good night."

There. Succinct and to the point.

"'Night," he says but he doesn't hang up.

Neither do I.

I sit there, the phone pressed against my ear, my heart racing, for the count of ten. Then twenty. At thirty I promise myself I'm pushing the end call button, but just as I move the phone away from ear, he speaks.

"Natalie?"

It's stupid. It's just my name, but there's a note in his tone that makes me shiver and I instinctively know I don't want to hear whatever it is he's going to say. That the best thing, the smart thing—the right thing—to do is hang up before he can say anything else.

But I don't exactly have a track record of being smart where Owen is concerned.

And I've never been very good at leaving well enough alone.

I swallow. Curl my fingers into my palm so hard, my nails dig into my flesh. "Yes?"

"I liked your dress," Owen says, the words a soft secret, one more between us. His voice deepens, goes husky. "I liked it a lot."

I inhale sharply and disconnect the call. It buzzes with a text and I toss it aside without looking at it.

Oh, God, oh, God, oh, God.

I should have left well enough alone.

With my pulse drumming in my ears, I stare at the flowers on my wall until they blur, the colors blending together, the outlines of each one fading until all I see are swirls of blues and reds, shapeless bursts of yellows and purples.

I push my hair from my face and realize my hands are trembling. That I'm rocking, back and forth, back and forth, on my bed like an insane person.

And that I'm still wearing Owen's sweatshirt.

29

I'M IN THE KITCHEN SITTING AT THE TABLE STARING OFF INTO SPACE when Chase finally rolls in at 2:20.

"About time," I whisper as harshly as possible—Dad didn't get home until after midnight and I don't want to wake him and Mom. I hurry over to the door, meeting Chase as he comes in so I can snatch the pizza box from his hands. "I'm starving."

"You're welcome," he says, tossing his keys onto the counter— which drives Mom nuts as there are hooks on the wall next to the door specifically for that purpose. He checks his phone as he continues, "No, no. Really. Don't be so effusive with your gratitude."

I set the box on the table and give him an epic eye roll. "Thanks."

"Nice. Very genuine. Even the delivery guy would have gotten a thank you and a ten percent tip."

Walking to get plates from the cupboard, I frown at him over my shoulder. "Ten percent? What do you think I am? The cheapest person alive?"

"Ten percent for takeout and deliveries, fifteen for a buffet style meal where the servers bring your drinks and clear your plates, and twenty for a sit-down meal. It's standard."

"You have thought way too much about this." I lift a slice of pizza from the box and put it on a plate. Slide the second plate toward him. "But thank you for picking up the pizza from the pizzeria you drove past on your way home. The pizza I ordered and paid for over the phone and even added an extra tip so they'd take it out to your car when you arrived, so all you had to do was pull into the parking lot, roll down your window, accept the pizza and leave again." I lift my slice in a mock salute. "Truly. You're a prince among brothers. A god among common, mortal men. Blah, blah, blah..." I wave my free hand. "You get the point."

And I sit and take a huge, cheesy bite of my late-night snack.

"Better," Chase says, crossing to the fridge where he pulls out a bottle of beer. "But your sincerity could still use some work."

He twists off the top and takes a drink.

My bite of pizza seems to stick in my throat. I swallow mightily. "Didn't you just spend, like, six hours drinking at a bar?"

"I spent the past three hours at a bar where I had two beers, spaced evenly apart and early enough in the evening so I could drive home safely."

"So this is your third one?" I ask, just to clarify, though I have no idea if three drinks are too many and if so, by how much. "Tonight?"

He grins, as if he can charm me with his blond good lucks and baby blue eyes. Please.

"I'm of legal drinking age, little sister," he says. "No need to worry. I have everything under control."

He calls me *little sister* when he thinks I'm being bossy. It's his oh-so-clever way of reminding me he was here first. As if the four years he has on me make him more mature, more responsible and smarter.

They don't. They just make him older.

"Uh, of course I'm going to worry," I tell him, forcing myself to take another bite even though I'm quickly losing my appetite. "Do you think it's wise, someone with a drinking problem hanging out bars? Going to so many parties?"

"I don't have a drinking problem," he says, calm as you please. Sitting across from me, he slides a piece of pizza onto his plate and starts eating. "I used to party. Now I don't."

Riiight.

As if it was all normal, teenage shenanigans and getting drunk, stoned and using opioids hadn't been his main hobby for almost an entire year of high school. A habit we would probably never have known about if he hadn't admitted he needed help.

Chase has always been very, very good at keeping secrets.

He's also an excellent liar. He had all of us fooled, that's for sure. All the while he *partied*, he maintained a perfect GPA, rehabbed his knee and worked part-time at the country club. The only reason he even admitted he might, possibly have a problem is because Leah gave him a choice: It was either getting drunk and high or her.

He chose her.

He's been sober ever since.

I watch him sip his beer.

Mostly sober ever since.

He's not angry, defensive or even insulted I subtly suggested he might be better off avoiding alcohol. He's just matter-of-fact.

Chase believes that whatever he thinks is right, whatever he says is truth and whatever he does is the best decision.

I guess healthy—and fairly large—egos run in our family.

Which only reminds me of Owen teasing me about mine except part of the reason I'm down here in the middle of the night, stuffing my face is to NOT think about Owen. Or Philip. At all.

Hey, I can avoid a problem (or in this case, two problems) just as well as my brother.

"*Used to party*?" I repeat, preferring to focus on Chase and his delusions rather than my own issues. "Is that what your counselor calls it?"

"Nat. I'm fine. I know my limits," he says, all serious and sincere. "I've got too many plans, too much to lose, to let myself backslide."

I nod, but I can't relax. Not completely. Can't stop worrying.

Don't get me wrong. I totally believe him. I believe him because once he sets his mind to something—like getting clean—he does it.

I believe him because he's too smart, too disciplined to let anything have that much power over him again.

Too determined to stay clean to do otherwise.

But mostly I believe him because I want to.

Because NOT believing him would mean admitting that something are just out of our control.

"Besides," Chase continues, "you're the one who's inhaled two slices before I've even finished one. What's going on?"

"Nothing," I grumble around a mouthful. "And you should never point out how much a girl is eating. Were you raised by wolves?"

"Ah," he says, steepling his fingers and, I swear, if he wore glasses, he'd be peering at me over the top of them. "Defensiveness. Changing the subject. Feeding your feelings. Classic avoidance techniques."

"You took one psych class. One. You're hardly Freud—you're not even Dr. Phil. So don't even think about analyzing me."

He pushes his plate aside after his one measly piece and leans forward. "Come on. Tell me. What's got you awake in the middle of the night?"

"Oh, you know, just contemplating life and all its amazing wonders, intriguing mysteries and confusing curiosities." Such as why I turned off my phone instead of responding to any of Philip's texts. Why I asked Owen to keep what happened tonight between the two of us.

Why I'm breaking my promise to always tell Philip everything.

"I just..." I toss the crust of my third slice onto my plate. Wipe my fingers on my pajama pants. "I have a lot on my mind."

"High school problems," he says with a tsk. "So serious."

"Forget it," I say, hating how my voice breaks. How tears once more sting my eyes. I stand and start cleaning up. "God. I hate when you do this."

He holds his hands up in surrender. "Do what? What did I do?"

"When you act so above it all. So removed from the life you led *four years ago*. As if anything that happens to anyone under the age of nineteen is a joke." I slam the pizza lid down. "And maybe, when I'm at the advanced, mature age of twenty-one, I'll look back on this and realize that it really wasn't all that big of a deal but right now..." My voice breaks and I have to stop. Clear my throat, but I can't stop the tears from overflowing. "Right now, it's a very big deal. At least to me."

"Jesus, Nat," Chase says, staring at me like I've lost it. Like I'm two seconds away from stabbing him in the eye with my pizza crust—which isn't a bad idea. "I'm sorry. It was just a joke." He stands and hands me a paper napkin. Gentles his voice. "What's going on?"

I wipe my eyes then blow my nose. "I'm just..." Scared. Afraid of how different everything seems to be lately. How out of control my life feels and nothing I do can pull it together. Terrified my own feelings are changing the most. "You were right. It's stupid."

"You sure about that? Because I can't help but notice that you seem a bit...off. As in you want to rip *off* my head and shove it down my throat."

"It's not you. Well, I mean, it was you—that was a really stupid thing to say to me at this delicate time—but it's not *all* you. Some of it is Philip." I start tearing the napkin into tiny pieces. "We're fighting —" or we probably would be if I ever responded to his texts and calls. "—and I guess it has me a little bit on edge."

"I thought so." When I frown at him, he continues, "He didn't show up to dinner. I figured something was going on."

"Leah didn't come either," I point out. "Are you guys fighting?"

"Not at the moment, but I'm sure that'll change soon enough. Couples argue. They disagree. It doesn't mean you're going to break up."

My head snaps back. Break up? Where did that come from? Just thinking about it, about not being with Philip, not having him in my life makes all that pizza churn in my stomach.

"Of course we're not breaking up," I say more harshly than intended. "Philip and I will be fine. It's just a fight. I'm sure we'll make up tomorrow." Chase gives me a self-satisfied grin. I narrow my eyes. "Wait. Did you...did you just use reverse psychology on me?"

"Like a master. And you disparaged Psych 101."

"This night is like a nightmare," I mutter. First Philip, then that whole confusing scene and subsequent phone call with Owen, and now Chase getting the better of me. "I'm going to bed. Before anything else horrible happens."

Chase straightens and pats my shoulder. "Next time you need help, don't hesitate to call Dr. Chase."

"Ew. No. Just...no. *Dr. Chase* sounds like a soap opera doctor. Or a male stripper." But I only make it as far as the doorway before I stop. Turn back. Chase is typing on his phone. "Chase?"

"Hmm?"

"How did you know, for sure, that you and Leah were going to make it? Past high school, I mean."

Something flashes across his expression, a darkness that's so at odds with his usual charming, cheerful demeanor, it sets me back. But when he looks up at me, it's gone. "You thinking about cutting Phil loose?"

"No. It's just...what if Philip stays here, goes to school in Pittsburgh and I'm in Philadelphia?"

"One thing I've learned at the advanced age of twenty-one," he says, tossing my words back at me, "is that we all have choices. If you and Philip choose to stay together, you'll stay together—no matter what schools you go to. If you want you and Philip together, forever, choose it. And make it happen."

It's actually not bad advice.

I mean, it's pretty much what my mom says, too, so it's not exactly *new* advice, but hearing it from Chase, knowing it works for him and Leah, makes me feel better.

Chase's words play through my head as I climb the stairs.

We all have choices. If you want you and Philip together, forever, choose it. And make it happen.

That's what Chase did. He chose Leah over partying. They choose to make it work, despite going to different schools.

I do want a future with Philip.

I'm just now realizing that getting that future might be harder than I thought.

No, not harder. Just more work. But that's fine. I'm not afraid of putting in the time and effort needed to achieve a goal. When I want something, I go after it. I make it happen.

I want Philip.

We're just experiencing a few minor bumps in the road, right now, that's all. Every couple goes through times when things aren't all roses and chocolates and kisses and sweet words. It's completely normal.

And absolutely nothing to be worried about.

Philip and I are meant to be together. When it's right, it's right.

I know how that sounds; like some romantic, fantastical tale spun by a starry-eyed teenager. But I'm not a dreamer. I'm a doer. A planner.

And being with Philip has been my plan for almost two years. That hasn't changed.

I won't let it.

30

———

First thing I do the next morning is take my Jeep to the garage to get a new tire put on. Luckily, no one noticed the spare was on and the mechanic at the garage told me he'd have it ready for me by eleven.

For a little while, all is well in my world.

Until Astrid texts me while I'm at Greens and Beans with Mary Alice after dance class.

Sean got the afternoon off work so I don't need you to take me to Pittsburgh.

I read it then read it again. Wait for another line or two expressing how sorry she is for bailing on me. How she'll call me when she gets back so we can hang out. How she appreciates the fact that I was going to give up a huge chunk of my Saturday afternoon AND the only opportunity I'd have to shop for a Homecoming dress to drive her into Pittsburgh so she can have sexy times with her boyfriend.

I wait but there's nothing. No blinking dots indicating she's typing. No buzz indicating an incoming text or call.

In less than twenty-four hours I've officially been ditched by both Panos twins.

It's a freaking record.

"Here you go," Mary Alice says, setting my iced caramel macchiato in front of me. She insisted I wait at a table while she ordered our drinks and when she slides a plate onto the table, I know why.

"Congrats!" she says.

I blink at the plate. She ordered me doughnuts. I wasn't going to get any because she also insisted on treating this week and she always only gets coffee so I didn't feel right asking her to pay for my sweet tooth.

And because I do NOT feed my feelings like Chase said last night.

I just...give them a snack every once in a while.

There are two doughnuts on the plate: a glazed, pumpkin cake doughnut and a raspberry filled one with vanilla icing. But it's not just her thoughtfulness that has me all choked up.

It's the tiny, sparkling pink plastic tiara stuck in the middle of the raspberry doughnut.

I look up at her, amazed and grateful and for some reason, completely humbled that she'd do something so nice for me. "Did you ask them to do this?"

Taking the seat across from me, she nods. "I told them you were up for Homecoming Queen and asked if they could pipe a crown onto a doughnut, but the barista remembered they had those tiaras left over from some bachelorette party they catered and thought it'd be cuter."

"Thank you," I say, but my throat is tight so it comes out a whisper. I take a sip of my coffee. "How did you even know?"

"That I'm having coffee with the future Homecoming Queen of West Brook Academy?" she asks with a grin and I can't help but smile back. "Social media. Where else?"

Where else, indeed? I haven't seen any posts about the Homecoming court. Probably because I haven't checked Instagram or SnapChat.

Mainly because if there are pictures of Philip having fun at Justin's last night, I don't want to see them.

"Thank you," I say again, this time clearly. "This is really sweet of you."

She waves my gratitude away. "It's not every day a girl gets promoted to royalty. Seems like something that should be celebrated." She sips her coffee then leans forward. "What does your dress look like?" She nods at my phone. "Have any pictures of it?"

I break off a piece of the pumpkin doughnut but don't bring it to my mouth. "I...uh...don't have it yet."

"Oh. Are you ordering it online?"

"No." That is way too risky for something like this. What if doesn't get here in time? What if doesn't fit? What if it doesn't look as good in person as it does in a picture?

Nope. No ordering important dresses online. There are too many unknowns.

It's too much to even contemplate.

"I usually get my semi and formal dresses at Julia's Boutique," I tell her. "But you have to make an appointment at least a week in advance."

She raises her eyebrows. Her hair is purple now—she changed it last week—and I have to admit, it really brings out her green eyes. "And you didn't make an appointment?" she asks as if this is out of the realm of possibility.

She's starting to know me so well.

"I was going to—" had planned on making an appointment last weekend for this afternoon "—but I thought I had plans today and..." I shake my head. "It didn't work out."

I shove the doughnut piece into my mouth before I say anything more.

Like how those plans had been with Astrid only to have her ditch me not five minutes ago. How Philip had done the same thing last night and after repeated texts up until mid-morning, hadn't texted or called me once today.

But I refuse to badmouth my best friend or my boyfriend. Can't complain about them to Mary Alice or anyone. Can't look for sympathy or understanding for how upset I am. How sad. How angry.

No matter how much I'd like to.

I wipe my fingers on a paper napkin. "Where did you get your Homecoming dress?"

Her school had their Homecoming last weekend. Mary Alice showed me pictures of her and her boyfriend Trent and their friends at dance class the next day. Her dress was adorable and perfect for her. The silky fuchsia top was strapless and had a heart-shaped neckline and the skirt was short and puffy with embroidered pink and white flowers. A thin, sparkly belt pulled it all together.

"Formalities," she tells me, pulling out her phone and typing something in. "It's in Bellefonte."

She hands me the phone. I take it and scroll through Formalities' website. It looks perfect, tons of selection and now that my afternoon has opened up, I could go there after I shower.

But Mom's at Kaleidoscope and, as previously mentioned, Astrid is out. And Philip? I wouldn't ask him to go even if I wasn't mad at him.

He's not good with shopping.

I glance at Mary Alice. She's sipping her coffee, humming "Let it Go" under her breath—one of the songs we chose to use for the kids' program. That tune burrows right into your head, I tell you.

"Are you doing anything today?" I ask her then bite my lower lip.

"Not really. Why?"

I shrug. Pick up the raspberry doughnut. Set it down. God. Why is this so hard? The worst she can do is say no.

Which will leave me no choice but to accept that my boyfriend and my best friend ditched me not because they're rude or selfish.

But because they don't want to spend time with me.

"Do you want to go dress shopping?" I ask in such a rush, I'm surprised the force of the words doesn't blow her bangs back.

"Sure," she says. "Today?"

I'm so busy preparing myself to take a major hit to my ego, that it takes me a moment to process that answer.

I nod. "We could plan on leaving in an hour or so. That'll give us time to go home and shower first?"

"Sounds good. Just let me ask my mom." She types a text. "Hey, do you mind if I ask Hailey? She mentioned something about hanging out today."

Hailey is one of Mary Alice's friends.

One of Mary Alice's many, many, many friends.

She's also in our modern dance class.

"No. I don't mind."

I take another sip of my coffee.

"My mom says it's fine," Mary Alice tells me, "but first I have to clean my bedroom. And Hailey's in so we're good to go. She'll come over to my house so you can pick us both up there. In an hour, right?"

"Right."

She stands. "I'm going to go, get my cleaning done." She leans over and gives me a hug. I'm so surprised, I just sit there, stunned, like I'm unused to human contact and physical affection. By the time I think to return it, she's already straightened and reaching for her coffee. But she's smiling, not the least bit put out by my being a complete idiot. Thank God. "See you in an hour!"

It's not until she's gone that I realize I'm smiling.

Okay, so what started out as a fairly sucky morning is turning into a pretty good day. I have plans with not one, but two possible new friends. Girls who want to spend time with me.

Take that, Panos twins.

And then, after removing the plastic tiara, I pick up the raspberry doughnut and take a huge bite.

Feeding my feelings after all.

Happy feelings.

31

SUNDAY MORNING, TWO THINGS ARE ABUNDANTLY CLEAR:

Chase is hungover.

And I'm the only one worried about it.

Or maybe Mom and Dad are just clueless. But it's sort of obvious Chase had more than a few drinks when he went out, again, with his old high school buddies last night. His eyes are bloodshot, his complexion sickly and...well...how do I put this delicately?

He's smelled better.

Much, much better.

He's like the walking dead stumbling into the kitchen looking for a few brains for brunch, grunting in response to Mom's cheery *good morning*, collapsing into a chair at the table, his head in his hands.

"Coffee," he groans. "Coffee."

"Would you like some coffee?" I ask. Loudly.

He flinches and gives me his best shot at a narrow-eyed glare. It's not very effective.

Mom, always the softy, pours a cup and brings it to him. Chase takes a grateful, slurping sip.

"We're just about ready to eat," she says, brushing back his messy hair but even that must hurt because he groans again. "Hope you're hungry."

He drinks more coffee. "I'll just stick with this for now, Mom. Thanks."

"Oh, but look at all the food we have," I say, close to a shout because he's made it too easy for me to torment him. "Bacon and waffles and toast and scrambled eggs with plenty of melted cheese. Yum, yum!"

Chase blanches and slides farther down in his chair.

I pour the last of the batter into the waffle maker. "I didn't know people could turn that particular shade of green. I'm not sure it's your color."

Chase rubs his middle finger against his forehead. A not-so-covert way of flipping me off in front of our impressionable parents.

I look at Dad who's manning the toaster (because, yes, he can work it just fine, especially when his wife tells him he has to or he doesn't get any bacon). "Daddy, Chase flipped me off. Your own son! What kind of human did you raise?"

"Chase, don't flip off your sister."

"Tattletale," Chase mutters.

"I think the word you're looking for is *favorite*. As in, my sister is my parents' favorite child."

"I'm not allowed to say the word I'm looking for," Chase says, obviously coming back to life thanks to mainlining his coffee, "or I'll get my mouth washed out with soap."

"Don't be ridiculous," Mom tells him as she sets the platter of bacon in the middle of the table. "I would never wash your mouth out with soap." She pats his shoulder. "I'd use hot sauce. It's nontoxic."

"What's the number for child protection services?" Chase asks me.

"I have it programmed into my phone," I tell him as I carry the waffles to the table. "But I don't think you're covered anymore now that you're legally an adult."

"The system is corrupt," he says. Dad brings the toast and we all sit and start passing our food when Chase pipes up with, "Shouldn't we wait for Philip?"

In the act of sliding eggs onto my plate, I stop and glare at him. He smirks and mouths, *payback's a bitch.*

Mom's already on her feet. "Of course we should wait. I'll set another place."

"Don't bother," I say, setting the bowl of eggs on Chase's empty plate—scrambled eggs make him want to puke even when he's not hungover (he says they look like brains—guess neurosurgeon isn't on his list of possible career choices)—because he's right, payback is a bitch. "He's not coming."

She sits as Chase shoves the bowl of eggs her way. "Oh? Why not?"

"He's working. And he has practice later."

Plus, I didn't invite him.

That's due to the fact that currently, I'm not speaking to him.

I would be speaking to him if he wasn't acting like such a complete and total ass. But he is. So I'm not.

Yesterday, as I was getting ready to leave my house to pick up Mary Alice and Hailey, Philip texted me. Being in a much better mood, and willing to accept that Friday night I may have made one or two missteps myself, I'd opened it, ready and willing to forgive him for ditching me and my family and going to that party. More than ready to move on past our argument and get back to normal where our relationship is concerned.

Only to open the message and see this:

Going into the 'Burgh to watch the Pitt game with Travis and his dad. I'll call you after.

Which was fine...okay, so maybe it wasn't quite fine...but it wasn't a big deal. I'd made plans with Mary Alice and Becca for the afternoon, anyway. I figured Philip and I would hang out last night.

Except, he didn't call me after the game. Just sent another text around 8:00 p.m. informing me they were getting something to eat and wouldn't be home until late.

Yes, that's right. Instead of spending time with me last night, working through our issues and being together, my boyfriend chose to spend the first free Saturday night he's had in two months with his best friend and his best friend's father.

So, no. I didn't invite him to brunch.

It's his fault I didn't have anything to do last night. Because I thought I'd be with Philip, when Mary Alice invited me to spend the night, I told her I already had plans. I ended up watching a movie with my parents and going to bed early.

And counted the flowers on my wall until I fell asleep.

Eventually, Chase perks up enough to nibble on a piece of toast and join the conversation. For the most part, I stay quiet and just absorb it all. The four of us together, the sunshine lighting the room, the scents of bacon and melty cheese filling the air, the sweetness of the maple syrup Mom buys at the specialty store downtown. Mom's laugh after one of Dad's corny jokes, Dad's look of pride as if making her happy is the best thing he's ever done. Chase telling stories about his professors and fraternity brothers.

I absorb it because it's everything I wanted it to be. Sunday family brunch, just like it used to be.

I absorb it because this, at least, is one thing this weekend that's gone exactly according to plan.

* * *

The music blasts through the speakers, the bass reverberating through the floor. I rise onto the toes of my pointe shoes, extended arms trembling with fatigue, sweat dripping down my face. I leap then pirouette, once...twice...three times before ending in grand plié as the last chord plays. I hold it for a moment...

Then collapse to the ground.

Holy crap.

I lay on the floor and stare at the ceiling, arms outstretched, legs splayed as I catch my breath. I've gone through my solo six times already and each time, I get a little bit better.

But it's still not enough. Luckily, I have until the end of the school year before my dance studio's performance. Plenty of time to perfect it. Because that's exactly what it has to be.

Perfect.

It's what I have to be.

I roll over onto all fours and push myself to my feet with a groan then walk over to the stereo. I pick up my phone to replay the song again and notice I have two missed calls.

From Owen.

Biting my lower lip, I frown at the phone—as if it holds the answer to the question, the dilemma going through my head.

Should I call him back?

I almost don't. He didn't leave a message so whatever he wants, why he called, can't be that important.

Plus, there's the whole, he's not my boyfriend and I decided after our late-night chat-fest two nights ago we shouldn't be having phone conversations—even if they do take place on a sunny, Sunday after-noon and are wholly and completely innocent.

Which I'm sure it is. Innocent. His reason for calling me, I mean.

So there's no reason I can't call him back.

Other the aforementioned one, that is. Which in this instance probably doesn't even count.

And with that logic, I press his number.

"Hey," he says when he answers. "How's it going?"

"Oh, I'm sorry. I must have the wrong number. I thought I was calling Owen Radlowski. Maybe you know him? Only speaks when he has to and doesn't ask silly, leading questions such as how someone is doing. That might lead to an actual conversation and then where would we be? But," I say over his resigned sigh, "since you're so interested, I'll tell you. Everything hurts and I'm dying. Thanks so much for asking."

"You okay?"

I laugh. "I'm working out. It's not as hardcore as whatever you do with Red Beard the trainer, but it hurts almost as much." I take another drink than switch my water for a towel. Pat the sweat from my face and neck. "Did you call just to see what I'm up to? I knew it was only a matter of time before I grew on you. We'll have those matching BFF necklaces by Christmas."

Another sigh. This one telling me we're still a ways off from exchanging gifts or declaring our friendship to the world through jewelry. "You busy?"

"Uh...yes. Haven't you been paying attention? Breathing hard. Dying. Working out. Any of that sound familiar?"

"I mean later," he says. "After your workout."

I hesitate because this is a very strange turn of events. "No," I say slowly. "Why?"

"I signed up for the SATs."

"You did? That's great."

He makes a sound—a cross between a hum of agreement and a snort of disagreement so really, who's to know which one he means? "It's the first weekend in December."

I wait but that seems to be all he's going to give me. Stubborn, stubborn, stubborn.

"And you want to take me up on my generous offer to help you study." When he remains quiet, I tease, "Now, now. Don't beg. It's beneath you and totally not necessary. Of course I'll help."

"Tonight?"

"What?"

"I can come over," he says. "Around six."

"You want to come to my house?"

"Unless you're busy."

"I'm not." My hopes for a leisurely Sunday family dinner were dashed when Chase headed back to school after brunch and Dad had an emergency at the hospital. There's no reason Owen can't come over. "Sure. Six will be fine."

"Okay," he says sounding relieved and I wonder if he was nervous about asking me. "See you then."

"Bye."

I check the time then start the song and go through my dance one more time.

32

———

"I don't know," Mom says later when I tell her I'm conducting a private tutoring session here tonight. Walking out of the master bathroom into her bedroom, she smooths her hands down the front of her form-fitting black dress. She's taking a sculptor and her manager/husband out to dinner to try to convince them to show her work exclusively at Kaleidoscope. "Do you really think you should be taking on any more extracurricular activities? You have a full plate as it is with tennis and dance and your own studies to consider. Not to mention upcoming college applications."

Sitting on her and Dad's bed, I wave that away as if hearing it all broken down like that doesn't make my stomach start twitching. My breathing quicken.

I tap my fingers on my knee. *One two three four five. Five four three two one.*

"I've got everything under control," I say, sounding like Chase did the other night when I asked him about his drinking. I tap faster. *One two three four five. Five four three two one.* "But thanks for reminding me of everything I have going on." And faster. *One two three four five. Five four three two one.* "I may have missed an item or two without that helpful list."

"That's what mothers are for," she says, crossing to sit at her vanity. "Nagging, inducing guilt and putting their daughters on the defensive."

I curl my fingers into my palm, my nails biting into my skin.

"I'm not defensive," I say and yes, it comes out rather defensive-ish. "Mothers are also responsible for making sure their children are well fed. Yet here I am, starving with no dinner to be seen."

She gives me the raised-eyebrow look in the mirror. "Mothers are responsible for that? Not fathers?"

"Let's not make this a discussion on feminism and gender roles in society. Let's focus on the fact that I'm hungry."

"Or we could focus on the fact that you're more than capable of feeding yourself. Order takeout and put it on the credit card."

Well, of course I'm capable of feeding myself. It's just that for most of my life, I didn't have to and I guess being hangry has made me resent the fact that's no longer the case.

I cross my arms. "I'm sick of takeout."

Great. I've gone from defensive to whiny.

I blame it on low blood sugar.

"Then cook something," Mom says as if that's a perfectly reasonable solution to this little situation. I mean, it is, but she doesn't have to be right all the time. "There are boneless chicken breasts in the freezer."

I scoot to the end of the bed and stand. "Fine."

"Wait," she says before I can reach the door. "I need an opinion."

I lean against the doorframe while she ducks into her huge, walk-in closet. When she comes out, she's holding a strappy, red shoe in one hand, a black, peep-toe bootie in the other.

I point to the shoe. "And leave your hair down."

"Are you sure?" she asks, dropping both shoes to scoop her hair back with her hands and studying herself this way and that in the mirror. "You don't think wearing it down looks unprofessional?"

"You run an art gallery-slash-store. You're not a school marm on the prairie."

She lets her hair go and it falls in soft waves past her shoulders. "Is *marm* really a word?"

"If it's not," I say, stepping into the hall, "it should be."

I go down the stairs slowly, counting each step as I go. I read that habits have triggers, a reason for why the person does them in the first place. Replace the trigger and you can break the habit. But I can't figure out what triggers my need to count or to make lists. I just like doing it.

And it's not hurting anyone, least of all me. So there's no reason to change it.

Humming softly, I cross the foyer doing a series of moves from my solo. The doorbell rings, scaring the crap out of me and I stumble and whirl around.

Owen is early.

And I haven't even eaten yet.

I open the door and though I know darn well he'll be standing there on our front porch, though I'm expecting him, coming face-to-face with him leaves me feeling antsy and amped up, shot full of nervous energy that has nowhere to go. When I meet his eyes, a jolt goes through me. No, really, it's like a true shot of electricity skimming through my veins, warming my blood before shooting out my fingertips, leaving my skin tingling. My stomach tumbling.

My heart racing.

"Hi," I say, but instead of sounding pleasant and cheery and so-nice-seeing-you, I'm breathless. I open my mouth to try again but I can't seem to speak past the sudden lump in my throat so I stand there, hand gripping the door handle, and stare at him wordlessly like a freaking idiot.

He, of course, has no problem with my lack of manners, just holds my gaze steadily. "You change your mind?"

I blink. Blink again. "What? I mean…excuse me?"

One side of his mouth kicks up and that only makes the tingling worse, damn him. "Did you change your mind about helping me?"

"Of course not. My word is my bond and all that."

A heaping dose of guilt takes that moment to remind me how I gave my word to Philip that I wouldn't keep anything from him. That I'd always tell him the truth.

And yet he doesn't know Owen is here, with me, tonight.

He doesn't know about Owen changing my flat.

Or that Owen and I had a quiet, late-night phone conversation.

He doesn't know, and I don't want him to know. Ever.

"Do you want me to leave?"

Owen's deep voice pulls me back to the moment at hand. The moment where I need to make a choice. The right choice is to say yes. To send him on his way. To tell him we can only meet during eighth period, twice a week. That our friendship—as it were—can't extend beyond school property.

But that seems so silly. And as if I'm scared of something. As if I'm doing something wrong by helping him. By being his friend in the first place.

"No," I say. "I don't want you to leave."

He's quiet for a moment. Then two. Finally, he asks, "Would you rather we do this on the porch?"

I wrinkle my nose. "It's cold out there. Why would I want to do that?"

"Because you haven't let me in."

Oh. That.

"Sorry," I blurt, my face heating. "I just...I guess I have a lot on my mind. Please—" moving aside, I make a grand sweeping gesture "—come in."

He brushes past me and I shut the door.

And hope I'm not making a huge mistake.

Again.

"We'll work in the kitchen," I say as he takes his shoes off and leaves them on the mat. When he straightens, I head in that direction. I'm almost to the hallway when I realize he's not following me. I look back to find him standing in the foyer staring up at the staircase.

And my mom descending the stairs like a modern-day goddess in a designer dress and a pair of Jimmy Choos.

I edge closer to Owen but since I'm barefoot, I have to rise onto my toes to reach his ear and whisper, "You can blink. I promise she won't disappear."

A flush creeps up his neck and into his face. He's embarrassed, self-conscious about being caught gazing at my mom like some lovelorn puppy.

It's sweet.

I touch his arm and when he slides his glance my way, I smile to let him know I was teasing.

Mom reaches the bottom of the stairs, her heels clicking on the tile as she approaches us, her gaze taking in my hand and the fact that it's still on Owen's arm.

I pull it away and step back.

"Owen," Mom says with what Chase and I have dubbed her beauty queen smile—wide and toothy and totally fake. Hey, it helped her nab that coveted second runner up spot in the Miss Western Pennsylvania pageant back in '88. "Hello."

"Hi, Mrs. Hewitt."

"Is there something I can do for you?" she asks and though she's talking to him, she's shooting me a questioning glance so I go ahead and answer her.

"I told you a friend was coming over." I hold out my hands to indicate Owen—ta da!—like a magician's assistant minus the skimpy outfit. "And here he is."

"You said a *friend*," Mom reminds me, still smiling though now it's more like she's gritting her teeth. "What you failed to mention was your friend's name. Or that your friend is a boy."

I shrug. "You didn't ask."

She opens her mouth. Shuts it when she realizes I'm right.

"If this is a problem," Owen says while Mom's still trying to find her voice, "I can leave."

"It's not," I assure him quickly.

Only to have Mom speak at the same time. "I think that would be for the best."

"Mom! That is like, so rude. I told Owen I'd help him study for the SATs tonight. I already told you this. You said it was okay."

I mean, not in so many words. But she didn't say *no* which is technically the same as saying *yes*.

"Owen," she says instead of reminding me that she gave the all clear before she realized my friend was of the male persuasion, "could you please excuse us a minute?"

He starts edging toward the door. "I should probably just go…"

"Don't be silly," I say, taking his arm and guiding him toward the hall. "We'll have this straightened out in a minute. Until then, you can wait for me in the kitchen."

As soon as he's out of sight—and, please God, hearing range—Mom puts her hands on her hips. "Natalie Jane Hewitt. What on earth is going on?"

"First and middle names? Seems a bit much for this situation." She gives me a look that could cut glass. I frown. "I don't understand why you're upset."

"I'm upset because now I have to cancel my dinner plans and Belinda and her husband are flying to Philadelphia tomorrow, which means I won't have another chance to convince her to show her art at Kaleidoscope."

"Why do you have to cancel?"

"Why? Why?" she repeats, yanking her phone from her purse. She waves it at me like a lunatic and I step back, fearing for my life. Or at least my nose. "Because I can't leave my teenage daughter alone in the house with a teenage boy."

"Owen's not a boy. I mean, yes, he's a boy but he's just a friend. I'm going to help him with SAT prep work and then he'll go on his way. It's not like we're going to have wild sex on the kitchen table. And not just because that's completely gross and unsanitary."

"This isn't a joke, Natalie. We have rules—"

"Rules for when Philip—my *boyfriend*—is over. I can't believe you think I'm so slutty I'm going to hook up with any random guy who just happens to be in the house with me."

"That is *not* what this is about."

"It seems that way," I mutter. "You do realize I'm old enough to be left alone with a guy and not actually have sex with him, right? And that in less than a year I'll be at college where I could, possibly, spend every night—alone—with any number of boys?"

"I'll worry about that in a year," she says.

"You don't have to worry about it tonight, either."

"Does Philip know Owen is here?"

"Of course."

Which isn't exactly a complete lie. I'm not speaking to Philip at the moment but if I were, I'd totally tell him Owen was coming to my house and that we were going to hang out for a little bit. Alone.

Okay, yeah, that *is* a complete lie.

Mom's wavering but she's not there yet.

"I'm with Philip," I tell Mom. "I love Philip."

That isn't a lie. I do love him.

I just don't like him very much right now.

"Fine," Mom says with a sigh. "Owen can stay. But only for as long as it takes to help him study and not a minute more. Understood?"

I nod. "Thanks."

We walk together into the kitchen. Owen's standing by the table looking big and broad and out of place in his faded jeans and Pittsburgh Penguins' T-shirt, hands in his pockets. Or maybe it's not that he's out of place so much as that he looks really, really uncomfortable. As if he'd rather be pretty much anywhere (including, it seems, the bowels of hell) other than our tidy, gourmet kitchen.

"Owen," Mom asks, all smiley as she crosses to the fridge, "can I get you something to drink?" She opens the door. "We have diet soda or iced tea?"

"No, thank you, Mrs. Hewitt."

She shuts the door but holds on to the handle. Smiles some more. "Well, then, I guess I'll be going."

She doesn't move, just glances between us as if trying to figure something out. Like if we're going to jump each other's bones the moment she steps out the door.

"Don't you have reservations for seven?" I ask.

"Hmm? Oh, yes." Straightening, she checks her phone and tosses it into her purse. "Nice seeing you again, Owen."

"You, too," he says and it's like he really means it.

Then again, plenty of teenage boys, males of all ages, really, love seeing my mom.

"Don't forget," she says to me, loud enough that if a low flying plane just happened to be going by, the passengers inside could hear her, "your father will be home any minute."

She glances at Owen, making sure he gets her message.

"I'll remember," I tell her solemnly though the chances of Dad coming home before midnight are slim to none, which we both know. I hug her. "Don't worry," I whisper in her ear. "I'll be good."

Her hold tightens on me for a moment. "I know you will. Just...be careful."

But she doesn't have to worry about that, either.

I'm always careful.

33

Owen is staring at the door that Mom went through as if he wants to make a run for it.

Or chase after my mother.

"I should go," he says, still looking at that door.

"After I finally convinced her to let you stay?" I shake my head. "I don't think so. I won a major battle tonight and if you leave, it'll really sour the sweet taste of my victory. You're staying—if only for the principle of it."

He finally looks at me. "I don't want your mom to be pissed at me."

"It never seems to bother you when *I'm* pissed at you."

His answer? A shrug.

"Ugh. Please don't tell me you're one of those guys."

"What guys?" he asks, that old familiar scowl back on his face.

"The kind harboring MILF fantasies about my mom."

He blinks, color once again staining his neck. "You get a lot of those guys around here?"

I sit at the table, one leg bent underneath me, the other foot swinging. "Not so much lately but when Chase was in high school it was like an epidemic of smitten, hopeful, horny and completely delusional boys invading our space. And let me tell you, there's nothing quite as disturbing as witnessing a teenage boy trying to flirt with a grown woman—especially one who's as beautiful as my mom. If they stepped even one toe over the line, Mom shut them down quick. It was painful."

"So no guys like that come around now?" Owen asks as he bends the SAT prep book in his hand. "Not even Panos?"

My eyes narrow. "Are you insinuating Philip is with me so he can get closer to my mom?"

Owen switches the book from one hand to the other. Then back again. Folds it the other way. "I didn't say that."

"Maybe not in so many words—"

"Not in any words."

"—but your meaning was clear."

"Is Panos an idiot?"

"That feels like a trick question," I say, "because to be honest, he's had some idiotic tendencies this weekend." Owen's gaze sharpens, and I immediately feel disloyal to Philip. "But," I continue quickly, "I'm sure that's just a guy thing and will no doubt be resolved soon. So, no. Philip is definitely not an idiot."

"Then he's not using you to get to your mom."

"I don't see the connection."

His mouth thins and he drops his gaze a moment before meeting mine again. "Only an idiot would want someone else when they could have you."

The soft words float around me, swirling inside my head, and I stare at the table. I swing my leg harder. Faster. *One, two, three, four, five. Five, four, three, two, one.*

"We should..." I stop. Work some moisture into my throat before continuing. "We should get started. If we're lucky, you might have time to do two practice tests instead of just one."

"Yay," he says, so deadpanned I can't help but smile.

"I know. Exciting stuff, right?" Feeling less wound up, I indicate the chair opposite me. Hold out my hand for his prep book and resolve to make the rest of our time together as normal as possible.

He was just being nice, saying that about a boy not wanting anyone else if he was with me. Boosting my ego and all that, like a friend would.

Nothing more.

"What is it with you and books?" I ask. The pages of the prep book are curled, which drives me nuts. "Let me guess. You're part of a secret society of literary loathers who have huge, book-burning bonfires every other Saturday night."

"Every other Tuesday night. Too hard to get members to come on Saturdays."

"Look at you, all jokey and just so much fun." I open the book to the first practice test and give him a number two pencil. "Keep that sense of humor. You'll need it." I pull my phone out and set the timer for sixty-five minutes. "Ready?"

But he's already started.

Guess he is ready.

I press the start button.

I work on my own homework while Owen takes the practice test but it's tough to focus on Chem with him across from me. I keep checking on his progress. He's not moving through the test very fast.

He really is a very slow reader.

I notice other things, too. Like that when he reads, he mouths the words and skims his finger over the lines on the page. How his eyelashes are lighter at the tips then the base and so long, they curl up at the ends. And how he gets this little crease between his eyebrows when he's concentrating.

It's endearing, that little frown, and I find myself staring at it.

Staring at him.

Not exactly great for my own concentration.

"I can't read with you watching me," he says, his words a low rumble.

My face heats and I jerk my gaze to a point above his shoulder. "I'll just..." Sit here, embarrassed and out of sorts for the next—I check the timer—twenty-six minutes. I jump to my feet. "I'm hungry. Are you hungry? I'm hungry."

"You said that already."

"So I did." I can't seem to stand still so I cross to the fridge. Take out two blocks of cheese—cheddar and Monterey—and a half a brick of cream cheese. I turn to look at Owen over my shoulder. "Have you eaten dinner?"

He shakes his head.

"I'll make some macaroni and cheese while you finish up."

When the timer goes off twenty-six minutes later, I have a box of macaroni boiling away on the stove, a smaller pan with butter melting in it on the next burner, the cheddar and Monterey shredded and all the ingredients I need for the sauce neatly lined up in the order I'll be using them.

"Good job," I say, picking up his paper. But perhaps I spoke too soon. He didn't finish the test—which isn't all that big of a deal. Plenty of people don't finish in the allotted time. Except they usually get through three quarters of it.

Owen made it just over halfway.

I set it down. "I'll finish up the mac and cheese then go over this while we eat."

I'm surprised when, instead of staying at the table, maybe checking his phone or just doing that thing guys do where they sit and stare and think about nothing, Owen follows me to the center island.

"I didn't know you knew how to cook," he says.

"Don't sound so suspicious. Yes, I can cook. I cook with my mom all the time. This isn't some grand plan to knock you off with poisoned mac and cheese."

"You sure?" he asks when I add flour to the melted butter and whisk it together. "Because that looks like poison."

Tipping my head to the side, I study the gloppy mixture as I stir, stir, stir. "Looks more like paste to me. But once I'm done, it won't taste like it. You'll love it. Trust me."

"Need help?"

It's what he asked me that day in my driveway. Oh, how far we've come from that awkward encounter. And now look at us. Standing side-by-side next to the stove, cooking together.

Life sure is funny sometimes.

"Sure," I say, handing over the whisk. "You can stir while I add the milk." I pour the milk in slowly. "Keeping stirring until it thickens."

The microwave timer buzzes and I turn off the heat under the macaroni then carry it to the sink where I have the colander waiting. I pour it in, getting a pasta-scented steam facial in the process.

I go back to Owen's side, leaning against him a bit to look into the pan. "That's good." I turn off the heat and dump all three cheeses in. "I'll take it from here. Thanks."

Holding the handle of the pot, I stir the sauce until the cheese melts then add seasonings and the macaroni and stir some more. A chunk of hair sticks to my damp cheek and I try to brush it aside with my shoulder but can't quite reach it...

"Here," Owen says, stepping close.

And he hooks his finger around the hair and gently pulls it aside, his fingertips trailing against my skin.

"I...thanks," I manage to say, my cheek tingling. I stare at the macaroni, my heart racing.

"You look different."

I let go of the spoon to smooth my hair. Maybe I should have done more than put it in a messy bun after my shower. Should have put on some makeup and worn real clothes instead of yoga pants, an over-size Penn sweatshirt and thick socks. "What do you mean?"

"Not bad," he says, as if reading my mind, my worries that I'm less than presentable. Less than perfect. "Just different."

If it's not bad, does that mean it's good?

No way I'm asking that. No. Freaking. Way.

I fill a bowl with mac and cheese and practically shove it into his stomach. "Here."

While he sits at the table, I get two bottles of iced tea from the fridge and offer him one.

"No, thanks. I don't like tea."

"You drank it before. That day you carried the groceries in for me?"

Another shrug. "You offered it to me."

I don't bother pointing out that I'm offering him some now, too, and he's declining it. "Why didn't you just say *no thanks*, then?"

"Because you offered it to me," he repeats and I'm thinking that's all he has to say on the subject but then he wipes his palms down the front of his jeans. "And drinking it gave me an excuse to stay here longer."

"Oh," I breathe, unable to hold his gaze. "That's...you..." But there are no words to convey what I'm feeling (which is mostly panic with the tiniest dash of pleasure) and my brain is currently too scrambled to make sense of my thoughts, so I swipe up his practice test. "I should...this is..."

I wave it, as if that alone conveys my message then hold it up—all the better to hide my blush while pretending to read over his answers.

And though I can't see him, I can tell Owen finds my current stuttering and stumbling amusing.

So glad my anxiety tickles his funny bone.

We eat in silence—me going through his test, marking the wrong answers with my handy, dandy red pen, making notes in the margins and adding up his score.

It's not good.

When I'm done, I turn the paper face down on the table. My bowl is empty and Owen is plowing through his third helping.

I smirk at him. "Told you you'd love it."

"It's good." When I grin, he narrows his eyes. "You really love being right, don't you?"

"Who doesn't?"

He shakes his head but he's almost smiling at me.

Until he nods at his test. "How'd I do?" he asks, both hands on the table, shoulders tense as if he's bracing himself.

I have no idea how to answer that so I don't. I just hand over the book.

His face goes stony. Finally, he sets it aside. "What's an average score?"

"It's hard to say as there's no one SAT test, so the scores from each section can range in points. Besides, what is *average* anyway? I mean, it's just one way of measuring something." I stand and gather our bowls and spoons. "For instance, the average number of bowls of macaroni and cheese one eats. Yours is higher than mine. Does that mean I'm not as good at eating? Not as hungry?"

"I can just Google it," he says when I stop to take a much-needed breath. "So you might as well tell me."

He's got me there. I put the bowls in the sink, rinse them out then face him. "If I remember correctly, the average score is around eleven hundred."

Staring at his hand on the test, he flicks the bottom corner with his thumb. Flick...flick... flick... "What did you get?"

"That's not import—"

"Twelve hundred?" he asks, gaze still down, thumb still flicking. "Thirteen?"

I sigh, for the first time not that eager to talk about my score. "Fourteen ninety."

He flinches and slides down in his chair until his head is resting on the back. "Fuck me."

"But that was after taking an SAT prep course online, studying for them all last year and taking it more than once. This is your first time so you really can't expect to get, like, a perfect score or anything, right? This is just a base. So we know where you're at and what to focus on to bring up your score. We'll work on one area at a time and do a practice test just on that subject at the end of each week—"

"No."

"Well, I suppose we can try and fit two practice tests in a week. But with our other school work, that will be challenging."

"I'm not taking any practice tests." He stands and pushes the chair into the table, holds onto the back. "Because I'm not taking the SATs."

"Look, I know you might be a bit...discouraged—"

He laughs harshly, his knuckles going white. "I'm not discouraged. I'm being realistic. Christ, I barely got through half the test just now. There's no way I can do well enough to get into college. Even with an athletic scholarship."

"You don't know that. And even if that's true, there are a lot of different schools out there. Community college. Technical schools. Don't be so quick to give up because of one bad score."

"You say that because this kind of stuff—" he waves his hand over the book "—comes easy for you."

Pushing away from the counter, I begin to pace. "God, I hate when people say that."

"What?"

"How I have it so easy." I stop and whirl around to jab a finger in Owen's direction. "I'm smart but I still work hard to get good grades. I'm constantly pushing myself to do my best. It doesn't just—" I wave my hands in the air like a crazy person "—magically happen. Which is why I think you're limiting yourself by not even trying. Believe in yourself!" I say, like a walking, talking, hand-waving motivational poster. "Dream big! Reach for the stars and all that."

"I can't afford to dream big. I need to be realistic. Set goals I can actually meet."

"That's the thing," I say, crossing to stand before him. "You can achieve them. You just have to be brave enough to go after what you want."

He goes still then shifts ever so subtly closer to me. "What if what I want," he asks, the low rumble of his voice causing the nape of my neck to prickle, "is out of my reach?"

There's something about his soft tone, in the way he's looking at me, all intense and serious, that makes my heart thump heavily in my chest. Makes my palms sweat.

The kitchen seems to shrink around us and it's like we're in a cocoon, insulated from the rest of the world.

Just me and Owen.

"It's not," I whisper, not wanting to break the spell. I touch his forearm and his muscles twitch under my fingers. His warmth seeps into my palm. "I believe in you."

He opens his mouth but then looks over my head.

And steps back.

Hands shoved into his pockets, he jerks his head toward the patio. "I think your dad's home."

I turn to see the motion lights out back are, indeed, on. But Dad would come in through the garage.

"It might be a deer or something," I say crossing to look out the French doors only to stop halfway there and stare at the figure walking across the patio toward the door.

I go hot then cold all over. It's not my dad. It's not a deer.

It's Philip.

34

———

Frozen to my spot, all I can do is watch as Philip gets closer and closer and closer. I glance behind me. Yep, Owen is still here, big and broad and unsmiling as he, too, notices who is heading our way.

I look back to Philip. Then at Owen. Then to Philip again.

"Want me to hide in the closet?" Owen asks.

Ha ha. Great. Now he's a freaking comedian.

I glare at him—mainly because it's too late for him hide. Philip is knocking—hard—on the door.

I hurry over and open it. "Philip. What are you doing here?"

"I wanted to see you." He must have showered before coming here, his hair is damp and curling slightly and he smells like the cologne I bought him last Christmas. He jerks his head toward the driveway. "Whose truck is that?"

I sense movement behind me as does Philip obviously, as he glances over my shoulder. He stiffens. "What's going on?"

"Nothing," I say but it comes out a squeal that, even to me, sounds like a confession. Dear God. I swallow. Clear my throat and try again. "Nothing. Owen and I are just studying for the SATs."

Philip's eyes narrow. A muscle jumps in his jaw. "You going to let me in?"

I blink. And it occurs to me that for the second time today I am blocking a boy from entering my house.

It also occurs to me that if I'd listened to that little voice in my head telling me not to let Owen in, I wouldn't be standing here, right now, sick to my stomach with worry and something that feels suspiciously like guilt.

Though I have nothing to feel guilty about.

If I'd listened to that very wise voice, I wouldn't feel like I have a whole lot of explaining to do.

Since I can't exactly ask Philip to wait outside so I can shoo another boy out the front door in an attempt at making the next few minutes a little less awkward and uncomfortable, I step aside.

Philip comes in and I shut the door. When I turn back, he slips his arm around my waist and pulls me snug against his side, his hand slipping under the hem of my sweatshirt, his fingers pressing against my hipbone.

It seems I have been branded.

He gives Owen a cocky grin. "Radlowski."

Owen matches him smirk for smirk, the SAT prep book, the one with his practice test and his score written on top, in his hands, rolled into a fat tube. "Panos."

Had I worried that having these two in my kitchen at the same time would be awkward and uncomfortable? How silly of me. Awkward and uncomfortable would be an improvement. Because even though I'm standing next to my boyfriend, it feels like I'm smack dab in the middle.

Like I'm being pulled in two different directions.

Seeing them together like this only makes their differences that much more apparent. Tall, dark-haired Philip with his confidence and charm. Broad, blond Owen with his quiet intensity and pride.

The only thing they have in common is me.

"Do you want to take another practice test?" I ask Owen, the question sudden and loud in the thick silence.

"You're not done...studying?" Philip asks.

"We're done," Owen says before I can answer.

I step forward and Philip is right there with me, arm locked around my waist, hand glued to my hip.

"It's still early. If you don't want to take a practice test, we can go over some math problems." I turn to Philip. "You don't mind if we keep working, do you?"

He gives a soft, humorless laugh. "Yeah. Sure. You two just go ahead with what you were doing. Don't mind me."

But he says it in a way that clearly means *mind me. Mind me very much.*

"I have to go," Owen says.

Philip finally lifts his hand from my waist only to start playing with my hair.

"Oh. Well, okay," I say, fighting the strangest, strongest urge to swat Philip's hand away. "I'll walk you out."

Philip's hand once again drops to my waist, keeping me close. "The door's right there."

"Owen came in the front door."

"Doesn't mean he can't go out the back one."

"No, but his shoes are in the foyer."

For some reason, that makes Philip more upset. His fingers tighten, dig into my hip as he drops his gaze to Owen's feet. "I'm sure he can find his way to the foyer by himself. Can't you, Radlowski?"

Owen holds Philip's gaze. "It's a big house. I'd hate to get lost."

Their stare down continues, a silent dare in there somewhere about who is going to give in first.

That would be me.

"I'll walk you out," I say again to Owen before turning to Philip. "I'll be right back."

In other words, *stay here.*

"Hurry back," he says huskily as if he's going to miss me terribly in the two minutes I'll be out of his sight.

And then he kisses me.

Which would have been fine and nothing out of the ordinary. Certainly nothing for me to complain or get mad about. Except that he doesn't kiss me because he wants to, because he loves me or missed me like he said when he first arrived. He doesn't kiss me because he wants to apologize for missing my parents' anniversary dinner or for spending the day with Travis yesterday. He kisses me to make a point. A point that is oh-so-clear when he raises his head and doesn't look at me, but at Owen:

Mine.

"Later, Radlowski," Philip says, triumph in his tone, on his face.

My boyfriend, the caveman.

Owen nods and walks out. I send Philip a quick glare then stalk off after Owen. Philip was right; Owen does know the way. He's in the foyer at the door putting on his shoes by the time I catch up to him.

I stand in front of him, looking down at the back of his head, unsure what to say. What to do. The nape of his neck is tanned, the edge of his tattoo peeking out from the collar of his shirt and I flash back to seeing him bare chested at the gym that day.

Have the craziest urge to touch him there, to trace the sharp, black line with the tip of my finger.

Jerking my gaze away, I cross my arms, tucking my hands against my sides. I check behind me to make sure Philip didn't follow us out here. That he didn't see me staring at Owen.

Owen picks up the book and straightens, then opens the door.

And walks out.

And even though I know it's the absolute last thing I should do, I go after him.

Because I haven't made enough mistakes this weekend, obviously.

"I'm sorry," I call, pulling the door shut behind me as I step onto the porch.

I don't think he's going to stop, that he's going to go down the stairs and off into the night without a word. But he does stop, he stands at the edge of the porch and looks out over our dark, front lawn.

"For what?" he asks, not turning around.

For my boyfriend acting so weird. So possessive.

I cross my arms against the chill in the air. "For the interruption."

"We were done anyway."

We weren't. Not by a long shot. I hadn't convinced him not to give up on the idea of furthering his education. Of letting me help him.

"I'm still sorry. Philip showing up was..." A shock. A nightmare. Excruciatingly painful. "Unexpected." Owen is silent, and I can't spend any more time out here waiting for him to say something while my boyfriend waits for me inside. "Anyway, I'll see you at school tomorrow."

I turn and open the door.

"Are you going to tell him?"

I freeze, all the things I could tell Philip, all the confessions I could make, racing through my mind.

"Tell him what?"

Facing me, Owen slaps the rolled-up book against his thigh. "Are you going to tell Panos how stupid I am?"

My throat tightens. I hate to hear him call himself that. "You are *not* stupid. Some people don't test well, that's all."

Looking down, he snorts softly. "Right." Slaps the book against his thigh again. "You going to tell him that I don't test well?"

"No," I say, an adamant promise. "Never. What happens between us is just that. Between us." I realize what I've said. How it sounds. "Between us in the tutoring sense," I hurry on. My eyes widen and I bite back a groan. "Not that there's anything between us in any other sense. Just..." I stop. Inhale and hold it for the count of five. Exhale and try again. "What goes on during our tutoring sessions is strictly confidential. Like doctor/patient privilege. And I would never, ever break something that sacred."

"Not sure it's exactly like that."

"It is to me," I insist. I wish I could step closer, that I could reach out to him, make him see. "You can trust me, Owen."

"Promise?" he asks softly, and I'm reminded of our phone conversation Friday night. Of how I asked him for the very same thing.

There's no way I can do any less for him.

"I promise," I say, the words barely a breath of sound.

Another vow between us.

Another secret.

35

—————

I GO INSIDE, EXPECTING TO FIND PHILIP WAITING FOR ME IN THE FOYER, pacing out his frustration while he runs his hands through his hair, again and again and again, as if there's too much pressure building up in his brain and moving the strands around will help relieve some of it.

He's not.

Not pacing. Not messing with his hair. He's not even in the foyer.

He's in the kitchen, I find a moment later, glaring at the pot of left-over macaroni and cheese on the stove. His hair is sticking up, though, so there had definitely been some hair pulling and tugging going on.

He looks up when I come in. "Where are your parents?"

His voice is low and he asks the question slowly, as if the words are being pushed out of his mouth. As if he doesn't really want to know the answer.

I completely understand where he's coming from. I don't really want him to know the answer, either.

I stop at the end of the island, my stomach turning with nerves and guilt. "Dad's working."

His mouth thins. "But your mom's here, right?"

I shift. Rub my thumbnail along the smooth, rounded edge of the countertop. "She's...out."

Now his eyes narrow and his voice gets even softer. "Out? You mean she ran over to the guest house for something? But she's here. Was here with you and Radlowksi."

I drop my hand to my side. "Actually..." I stop. Clear my throat. "Actually, she wasn't. She's in Pittsburgh."

Philip's head snaps back as if I've punched him. "You and Radlowski were alone?"

"We were study—"

"How long?"

I frown. "What?"

"How long was he here?"

"Not long."

"Long enough for him to take an SAT practice test." Philip nods at the pot of leftover mac and cheese. "Long enough for you to cook him dinner."

"I didn't cook him dinner. I made myself dinner," I say, choosing my words carefully because I don't want to lie to Philip. Not more than I already have, anyway. "I was hungry and—"

"But he had some. You two ate together."

I'm jittery, unable to stand still and maintain eye contact, so I go to the sink to put the bowls and silverware into the dishwasher. "Well I couldn't very well eat in front of him and not offer him any, could I? That would be rude."

"Not answering your boyfriend's texts or calls is rude, too, but that doesn't seem to bother you. Jesus, Nat, I've been texting and calling you all day so we can work through our fight and the whole time you're hanging out with another guy!"

Facing him, I cross my arms, feeling a sick combination of guilt and defensiveness. "I wasn't hanging out with another guy. Not the whole time and not in the way you mean. I told you, I was helping Owen study for the SATs."

Philip's eyes narrow. "I thought you were tutoring him in English."

"I am but—"

"You're only supposed to tutor him twice a week. At school."

"I know, but he called—"

"Wait, wait," Philips says, holding his hands up. "He called you?"

I shift, the guilt now winning out over the defensiveness. "He needed my help."

Philip begins to pace, back and forth, back and forth, the length of the island. "Can't you see? He just wanted to spend time with you. He used the SATs as an excuse."

"He needed my help," I repeat. "He took a practice test. We went over it. That's it. It wasn't some—" I wave my hand in the air "—grand plan to get with me."

Except that wasn't all we did. Not really. We talked.

Only an idiot would want someone else when they could have you.

Drinking it gave me an excuse to stay here longer.

What if what I want is out of my reach?

And Owen touched me, that slight brush of his fingers against my cheek when he moved the hair out of my face.

We shared another secret, one more to add to our growing list.

Any remaining defensiveness rushes out of my body, the space it empties quickly filling with guilt, guilt and more guilt.

"You didn't answer my texts," Philip says, still pacing, his hair crazy, his voice a low growl, "so I come here to talk to you, to make things right so we can work through what happened this weekend and I find you, alone, with Radlowski." He stops and whirls around. "What is this? Payback for not going to your parents' anniversary dinner?"

"Of course not!" Though I can't help but remember that was part of the reason why I called Owen after that dinner, why I asked him to help me with my flat tire. Not something I want to think about. Not something I ever plan on admitting to. "If anyone is guilty of trying to get payback it's you."

"What the hell is that supposed to mean?"

"You ditched me and went to a party with Travis then spent the entire weekend with him to get back at me for not telling you about Owen's and my conversation—our innocent conversation—that night after dance class."

"Oh, no, you don't get to turn this around on me. I'm not the one who was alone with another girl."

"It wasn't like how you're making it sound," I say, my face hot, my heart racing. "Like I went down on him while the macaroni cooked."

He goes completely still. "Not. Funny."

"You want to know what else isn't funny? This whole jealousy thing you've got going on right now."

"I am not jealous of Radlowski," Philip says through clenched teeth. "Unless..."

"Unless what?"

He drops his gaze to the floor before meeting my eyes. "Unless there's a reason I should be?"

"There's not," I say quickly. Though I can understand why some girl might find Owen attractive—and not just for his looks. I get how she could like his intensity and quiet nature, those subtle hints of humor and his work ethic.

Some other girl. Not me.

Definitely not me.

"Why don't you admit what this is really about?" I ask. "You don't trust me."

"I don't trust *him*."

"You don't even know him."

"I know his type," Philip insists.

"Is that why you were acting like some Neanderthal, wanting to drag me back to your cave by my hair. How about I just get a tattoo?" I run the tip of my finger across my forehead. "*Property of Philip Panos. Would that make you happy?*"

"Quit trying to turn this around. You're the one who was alone with another guy." He runs his hand through his hair and sits at the table. Exhales heavily, his head down, his hands between his knees. "I see how he looks at you, Nat," he continues softly, his tone worried. He looks up. "I don't want to lose you. Not ever."

My heart trips with love and affection, but there's something else, something lurking around the edges of those safe, familiar feelings.

Doubt.

I try to ignore it, try to brush it aside, but it remains, strong and persistent, like chains I can't break.

A promise I can't keep.

Because for the first time, thinking about being with Philip forever doesn't fill me with peace, doesn't seem like it's meant to be. It seems daunting.

And that scares me more than anything.

"You won't lose me," I say, and I hope he can't hear the unsteadiness in my voice, can't read something on my face I don't want him to see. I step closer so that our knees touch. Lay my hands on his shoulders and look into his eyes. "I'm right here. I'm not going anywhere."

I kiss him, to prove I mean what I say. To show him how much I love him. How much I need him.

He sets his hands on my waist and tugs me onto his lap then wraps his arms around me. His mouth is hot and hungry on mine, his hold on me tight, as if he's afraid of that if he loosens it for even a moment, I'll slip away.

I want to tell him I won't, to repeat what I just told him.

I'm right here. I'm not going anywhere. I love you, I love you, I love you. I'll always love you.

But always is a very long time. And always loving Philip isn't the same as loving *only* him.

I rear back, the thought jolting me.

"What's wrong?" he asks.

I shake my head. "Nothing."

He doesn't believe me so I kiss him again before he can question me some more. Before he can see what I'm trying so hard to hide.

I concentrate on his kiss, the softness of his hair under my fingers, the way it feels when he slides his hands under my shirt and touches my back, then my sides. This is how it's supposed to be. The two of us together. Safe and familiar and right.

Nothing will ever come between us.

We get carried away, kissing and touching and breathing hard. We forget where we're at. Forget that Philip isn't allowed to be here. We forget to be safe. To be cautious. To be good.

And don't realize my dad is home until he walks into the kitchen.

36

AN HOUR LATER, I'M SITTING ON MY BED, WAITING FOR MOM TO
get home.

I've been restricted to my room until she returns at which time
Dad will discuss what happened with her and they will come up with
an appropriate punishment for my behavior. He wouldn't even listen
to me when I tried to explain that what he saw wasn't what he
thought he saw.

Though I'll admit it was pretty close.

He was so angry he could barely look at me.

So obviously stunned and disappointed, it gutted me.

All he said was that Philip needed to leave then he proclaimed my
banishment.

I flop onto my back and stare sightlessly at the ceiling. I'm not
sure which is worse. The fact that Dad walked in on me and Philip in
a rated PG-13 lip-lock. Or that I was, for the first time ever mind you,
sent to my room like a five-year-old who refuses to eat her broccoli.

Okay, so I know the first one is worse. But the second is almost as
humiliating.

I can't even text Philip to see if he's okay because Dad made me
leave my phone on the table. I've spent the time alternately counting

the flowers on my wall, listing every Leo DiCaprio movie I can think of, and reliving the nightmare of my dad seeing me straddling my boyfriend.

With a groan I put my arm over my eyes. It's official.

Worst. Weekend. Ever.

A few minutes later I hear footsteps coming up the stairs then someone knocks on my door.

I sit up. "Come in."

Mom and Dad come in like a unit, a team wearing equally grave expressions and holding hands.

"Nothing happened," I blurt out to Mom as I slide off the bed to stand. "We weren't doing anything."

"Not doing anything?" Dad asks and there's this bulging vein in his neck that's worrisome as it's never been there before. Then again, I've never seen him look like his head is about to pop off before, either. "You were on that boy's lap. His hand was up your shirt."

I wince, my face heating with renewed embarrassment. When Dad slammed the kitchen door—a not-so-subtle announcement of his arrival and his anger—I'd yelped in surprise and jumped off Philip's lap.

Well, I'd tried to jump off. I'd ended up sprawled across his legs, tangled up because *that boy's* hand was, indeed, up my shirt.

Dad turns to Mom. "His hand was up her shirt."

She pats his shoulder. "I know."

"I can't unsee it," he tells her in a hoarse whisper, as if he's reliving some traumatic event. He hits the side of his head with the heel of his hand—several times. "It's lodged in there. Forever."

Okay, that seems a bit overly dramatic.

"We were just kissing."

Mom sends me her raised-eyebrow look. "You sure that's the tone you want to adopt in this particular situation?"

My shoulders droop. "No."

Though to be fair, I'm not sure what tone or attitude is appropriate as I've never been in this particular situation before.

"You're grounded for a week," Mom says.

My eyes widen. "For one little comment?"

"No. For having your boyfriend over when neither of us was home."

"But Friday is Homecoming!"

They exchange a look and some form of silent communication then Mom says, "You can still be in the parade, attend the game and the dance, but you'll come home right after."

"We weren't doing anything! And I didn't even know he was coming over. He just showed up."

"Then you should have told him to leave," Mom says while Dad nods along, the horrendous ordeal of seeing me and Philip rendering him mute now.

"That's not fair," I say, starting to cry because...because...well, I'm not sure why exactly. I mean, I did get caught doing something I know is wrong and honestly, being grounded for a week seems a fitting punishment—and so much better than my worst fear which is that they're going to forbid me and Philip from seeing each other.

And they're still letting me go to Homecoming.

It's just...it's been a really long weekend what with my fights with Philip and the flat tire and everything with Owen and now this...

I'm feeling very overwhelmed.

And ill-equipped to deal with it.

"We think it's extremely fair," Mom says. "No hanging out with your friends, no TV or phone—"

"That's just mean. And cruel and unusual punishment!"

No phone for a week? I'll die. I. Will. Die.

"For a week," Mom continues, all calm, cool and collected. As if punishing her wayward daughter is something she does every other day and not a once-in-a-lifetime thing. "You can attend tennis practice and matches, and dance classes, but you will go directly to and from them. Do you understand?"

"Yeah." I sniff.

I understand that being good my entire life has been for nothing. I've tried so hard to be honest and trustworthy and responsible and now, one teeny, tiny screw-up and a lifetime of really excellent behavior is just...Bam!...blown to bits.

"Okay then." Mom sighs and shakes her head. "We love you, but right now, we're very, very disappointed in you."

That's it. Forget my not having my phone for a week, that, right there, is the true death knell.

"I'm sorry." I'm sobbing now, unable to stop long enough to even catch my breath. Sitting on the edge of my bed, I cover my face with my hands, my words muffled. "I'm...real...really...sor...sorry."

"What's happening?" Dad whispers to Mom. "Did we break her?"

"She's not broken. She's remorseful."

"That's good." He pauses. "Isn't it?"

"Well, it means we're not raising a sociopath," Mom says dryly. "So, yes. I'd say that's very good."

I cry even harder. "This isn't funny!"

Mom sits next to me and wraps her arm around me. "You're right. This isn't funny. It's okay. We know you're sorry," she murmurs, rubbing my back. "And we appreciate it and we forgive you—"

"Dad doesn't," I cry, my shoulders shaking. "He hates me."

"Hey," Dad says, sitting on my other side. "I could never hate you."

Wiping my cheeks, I raise my head to look at him. "Never?"

"Never." He pulls me into a hug and kisses the top of my head. "Although I'm not saying the same about that boy."

I whirl around to Mom. "Mom!"

She pats my knee. "He's kidding."

"Not even a little," Dad says.

Mom just shakes her head, as if my father hating my boyfriend is the least of her worries when it's the greatest of mine. "I think this conversation is going down a road no one wants it to. Why don't we call it a night?"

They both hug me then stand. Dad walks out but Mom hangs back.

"You're still mad," I say, stretching across the bed to grab a tissue from my nightstand. I blow my nose. "I can tell."

"I'm not mad so much as confused."

"Dad's making it sound worse than it was. We really were just kissing."

"That's not it. Well, not all of it." She shuts my door and lowers her voice. "This isn't like you. First you invite Owen over to study putting me in a very difficult position then you invite Philip over—"

"I didn't invite him! He just showed up."

"—when you know that's against our rules. I just...I'm worried about you." Her expression softens. "Is there something going on you're not telling me? Something happening with you and Philip?"

"No! Philip and I are fine. I mean, yeah, we had a fight. Two, actually, but they're over now."

She makes a humming sound. "I don't suppose one of those fights was about Owen being here?"

I narrow my eyes. "Don't use your psychic mom powers on me. Not tonight. I'm not strong enough to resist."

She crosses the room and once more sits next to me. "I don't have to be psychic to know your boyfriend might be less than pleased to find you spending time with another boy." She's silent a beat. "A good-looking boy."

I go hot all over. "Mom! God."

"All I'm saying is that it might not be in your best interest—or the best interest of your relationship with Philip—for you to continue to tutor Owen."

I push to my feet. Begin to pace. "I don't see why I should have to give up helping someone just because Philip is acting jealous."

"That's the thing about relationships. Sometimes one of you has to give up something for the other. That is if you still want to be with Philip?"

I freeze. "Of course I do. I love Philip."

"I know you do. But, you're still so young. You have your whole life ahead of you and plenty of time to figure things out. And it's okay if you change your mind about things. What college you want to go to, what you want to study. Who you spend time with. Who you want to be with."

"I want to be with Philip," I say, but something about my tone is off. How it feels to say it. Like I'm repeating a long-ago memorized phrase. One that has no real meaning. "And I don't need to rethink my future."

I'm going to Penn. Philip and I are going to stay together. Astrid and I will remain best friends.

I have a plan. And sticking to it is the one thing I can control.

"I just want you to be careful," Mom says, standing. "What we think we want at seventeen isn't always what's best for us. Sometimes, it's not even what we really want."

She kisses my cheek and leaves. I stare at the door. That makes no sense. Of course what I want is what I really want.

Why else would I want it?

I'm definitely not going to change my mind. Not about Penn. Not about Philip. Not about anything.

Change one thing and everything changes.

And is out of your control.

That's a risk I'm not about to take.

37

———

THE NEXT MORNING, PHILIP AND ASTRID TAKE THEIR MOM'S CAR TO school so Astrid can go to a dentist appointment later. I get to school early, hoping to catch Philip before homeroom so I can tell him what happened after he left, but he's already there and waiting for me in the parking lot.

Relief sweeps through me. Last night, unable to sleep and without my phone to distract me, I had a lot of time to ponder what's been happening between us. And I realized that, as we're both to blame for the problems we're having, we'll both have to be responsible for fixing them.

That's where the worry came in.

Philip isn't all that good at admitting when he's wrong. He's much better at charming people into seeing things his way.

But he's here. He's waiting. He's willing to put in the time, effort and work to make things right between us. Everything between us is going to be okay. Because it's what we both want.

We're choosing each other.

I pull in a few spaces away but he's by my side as soon as I step out of the Jeep.

"Hey," I say, smiling. "Good morn—"

"I texted and called you all night. Where were you?"

My smile fades at his question, at the accusation in his tone, and I'm torn between wanting to offer an apology and wanting to snap back at him.

I take great pride in doing neither.

Instead I count to five then back to one as I turn and grab my bags from the Jeep. When I face him again, I keep my own tone mild. No hint of sorry or snap to be found. "I was home. Dad took my phone."

His mouth flattens. "Are you in trouble?"

I stare at him. We were caught, alone in my kitchen, making out. I was straddling him. His hand was up my shirt.

Am I in trouble?

God. Has he not met my dad?

I heft the strap of my backpack over my shoulder. Nod. "I'm grounded for a week."

"Shit."

"And phoneless during that time."

He stabs a hand through his hair and paces away. I take the opportunity to quickly lock and shut the door, tug on the handle three times then push the lock button on my key.

The lights flash.

For the first time, though, I don't feel any better. Something feels...unfinished. Like there's something I know I need to do but can't remember what it is, and the twitchy sensation in my stomach remains.

"I'll talk to your dad tonight," Philip says when he strides toward me. "Apologize again."

"That's sweet of you to offer..." Sweet and slightly delusional if he thinks he can sway my father. "But the best thing to do is let it go. I really, really don't think my dad wants to be reminded of it. Ever."

Philip tips his head back. Blows out a heavy breath. "Great. Now your dad hates me."

"He doesn't."

But then I remember what Dad said last night. How he kept calling Philip *that boy*.

Okay, maybe Dad does hate him. But only a little. I'm sure it'll pass.

Eventually.

To be honest, I'm more concerned about my parents being mad at me. But Mom and Dad don't hold grudges. They were both fine this morning at breakfast, treating me the same way they always do, as if I'm all things special and wonderful and not a huge disappointment because I broke a rule and traumatized my father.

It was all very normal. Almost as if last night had never happened.

Until Mom reminded me to come straight home after tennis practice.

"Let's just get through the week," I continue, "and let it all die a natural death."

"You sure?"

"Positive."

"What about Homecoming?"

My hair blows in my face and I tuck it behind my ear. "I can still go to the game and dance, but I have to come home right after."

"Travis is having a party after," he says, as if being grounded has caused amnesia and I no longer remember the plans we made for Friday night.

"I can't go."

Now it's his turn to tell me that if I'm not going, neither is he. I wait. And wait. And wait.

He stays silent.

And the twitchiness increases.

A car drives past with a friendly beep. Philip and I both wave though I have no idea who it was. I swing my backpack around to get my phone out of the outer pocket before I remember it's been confiscated.

"What time is it?" I ask Philip. I got here early and we've only been talking a few minutes, but the parking lot is filling up rather quickly. It might be almost time for the first bell.

But Philip doesn't give me the time. He doesn't even bother reaching for his own phone.

"Look," he says, "I've been thinking and...I don't want you to see Radlowski anymore."

A swooping sensation comes over me and I sway but steady myself before he can notice. "What?"

"I don't trust him. And I don't want him around you."

"You mean you don't trust me."

Philip's jaw tightens. "I bet he doesn't even really need help with English or the SATs. He's on scholarship to play hockey. That's all the administration cares about. They don't give a shit if he gets As or Fs and any college that accepts him will be the same way."

I'm shaking my head but I can hardly tell Philip about Owen's struggles getting through

The Catcher in the Rye. Would never tell him or anyone about the score Owen got on the practice SATs.

That's our secret.

"It's not up to you to decide whether or not someone feels they need extra help," I say.

Philip throws up his hands. "He's trying to get with you and you're too naïve to even see it."

"I am not naïve and Owen is not trying to get with me!"

Except...oh, God...the things he's said, the way he looks at me...

Philip's not the only one who's noticed.

My heart pounds and there's the metallic taste of panic in my mouth.

Not at the idea of Owen wanting to be with me. Not at Philip knowing that.

But at the horrible, awful idea of not seeing Owen anymore. Not talking to him again.

Oh, no. No, no, no, no, no.

I swallow. "I..."

"Maybe I am being stupid. Maybe I'm way off base," Philip says, his snide tone making it clear he doesn't believe that. "Even if I am, shouldn't the fact that I'm asking you not to see some other guy be enough of a reason not to?"

This...this is what Mom is always talking about. This is really what it means to choose someone. It's not always about compromise and working things out.

Sometimes, it means giving something up.

Even when you don't want to.

And I don't want to. Not at all.

Everything inside of me is rebelling against it. Telling me to stand my ground. To not give in.

That I'm going to regret it if I don't.

But that can't be right. I can't insist on remaining friends with Owen.

I can't choose him over Philip.

"I'll talk to Miss Marchand," I say, my voice barely a whisper. "Tell her I can't be a tutor anymore."

The relief on Philip's face assures me I made the right choice.

The choice to choose him and our relationship. To show him how much he means to me. How much I love him.

So why does it feel so wrong?

"Thanks, babe." He reaches out and touches my cheek. "Hey, I *do* trust you. You know that, right?"

I nod and do my best to smile and Philip pulls me close, his strong arms around me warm and familiar.

I cling to him. To him and what we've been and what I want us to be in the future.

Except, that feels wrong, too.

So I hold on tighter. Convince myself that I made the right decision. Philip and I may not be okay right now, but we will be. I haven't broken his trust. Not really.

And by agreeing not to see Owen again, I'm making sure I never do.

* * *

I know the only way I'm going to be able to break things off with Owen is if I do it right away. But I couldn't very well leave Philip standing in the parking lot so I could search the campus for another boy. And I don't see Owen, not once, all day.

So after school I hurry out to the back parking lot to wait for him. Not that I'm afraid to be seen speaking with him, but there is a greater chance of someone spying us together inside the school than outside.

And of that someone telling Philip they saw us together.

I'm just being prudent. No sense stirring up trouble with Philip by...say...waiting at Owen's locker and chatting with him there. Not after everything that's happened between me and Philip.

Not when I'm trying so hard to make things right between us.

Owen's truck is at a spot near the ice rink and I cross to it, then do my best to look nonchalant as I wait which, can I say, would be a lot easier if my parents hadn't taken my phone. Instead I'm left pretending to search through my purse as if I just oh-so-coinciden- tally needed to check for my keys right next to Owen's truck.

The keys to my Jeep which is parked on the other side of the school.

As an SUV pulls out, I raise my head to see Owen heading toward me from the side entrance, his eyes on me. My heart races. My pulse jumps.

Putting some distance between us and keeping that distance is definitely the best decision I've ever made.

Not to mention the smartest.

"Hey," I say when he's a few feet from me.

"No boyfriend?"

Well, that was a bit confrontational.

Even for Owen.

Since this might be...could be...probably is...our very last conver- sation, I decide to let it slide.

"If you're so against using the word hello after someone greets you politely," I tell him, "you could give me one of those nods guys use. You know, like this—"

I demonstrate by jerking my head in a *what's up?* sort of way.

He edges forward and I take a quick step back, my shoulders banging into his truck's door. He keeps coming, closer and closer and closer until I have to tip my head back to maintain eye contact.

"Hello, Natalie," he says, the soft words scraping against my already raw nerves.

I really need to learn to keep my freaking mouth shut.

"Hi," I squeak then blush because I've already *hey-ed* the boy. No reason to repeat it in a chipmunk voice.

He makes a show of looking all around the parking lot. "Where's Panos?"

I shrug my backpack up higher. "Soccer practice I imagine."

"And yet you're here. Talking to me."

"I'm here," I agree. "Talking to you. Is there a reason you're narrating for me?"

"Figured the only way you'd be allowed to talk to me was if Panos was by your side. Or better yet, standing in front of you, blocking you from my view."

Because that's a little too close to the truth, I glare at him.

He's not intimidated in the least.

"Philip doesn't allow me to do anything..." But, wait. That doesn't sound right. "I mean, he allows me to do things..." Nope. Not what I meant, either. I inhale and hold it for the count of five. Exhale back to one.

"Philip," I say slowly and concisely, "is not the boss of me. And I mean that in the most mature way possible."

"You two break up?"

"What? No! Of course not. Why would we break up?"

Owen shrugs but his eyes remain on mine, intense and searching. "He seemed pretty pissed last night."

No sense denying that. Owen was there. He saw Philip's reaction.

Pretty pissed is putting it mildly.

Then again, I hadn't exactly loved how Philip had acted, either.

I shove that thought away. This isn't about last night or being upset with Philip.

This is about doing what's best for my relationship with my boyfriend.

Doing what's right.

"We worked it out," I tell Owen. "He's not upset anymore."

"That why you're here?" Owen asks as he opens his truck door. "So you can tell me everything with you and Panos is all roses and rainbows?"

"No," I tell his back because he's staring at his truck's interior, his shoulders rigid, "but I appreciate the imagery." I hug my purse to my chest. "Actually, I wanted to talk to you about tutoring…"

Owen turns. "What about it?"

He knows. It's in his tone, the expression on his face. He knows I'm about to back out of tutoring him. That I'm doing it for Philip, to keep the peace between us.

He knows, and he could opt out first, tell me he's changed his mind (again) about the whole tutoring thing. Or that he's going to find someone else to help him.

He could make it seem like us not working together anymore is his choice. What he wants. He could save some of his pride. He could make it easier for me.

But he won't.

I fidget, searching for what to say, how to say it while he watches me. While he waits.

And I can't help but hate him for it, just a little. For making me be the one to say it. To end things between us.

Except there is no *us*. There's nothing to end.

But I'm afraid there could be. Terrified I want there to be.

"I can't tutor you anymore," I say, but I can't get the rest out. The part about not seeing him anymore period. Not talking to him again.

I should. I'm supposed to—that's what Philip asked for. That's what I promised him.

But I can't.

Owen stares at the ground. "Guess things between you and Panos aren't as good as you say."

"Philip has nothing to do with this."

He lifts his head. "No? He didn't tell you to stop tutoring me? That he doesn't want you talking to me?"

I open my mouth to deny it but Owen's watching me, studying me in that way that makes me feel he's peering inside my head. Dissecting every one of my thoughts.

Seeing every one of my lies.

He smirks. "I thought so."

He grabs his duffel from his truck and slams the door shut.

I hurry over to block him before he can leave. "Look, this isn't about Philip. I'm dropping out of the tutoring program completely. With tennis and dance and college apps coming up and me helping my mom at her new gallery, I just don't have time to devote to it right now."

He stares over my head, his hand curled around the strap of his duffel, his knuckles white. I expect him to call me on it, to remind me how he told me not to lie. Not to him.

I'm holding my breath waiting, torn between hoping he'll let me off the hook.

And demanding the truth from me.

If only so I could demand the same from him.

But I should know better than to give so much power to something as out of my control as hope. Because Owen does neither.

Instead, he finally meets my eyes, the blue of his gaze cool, his voice even colder. "You're in my way."

My eyes sting. He wants to leave. He's through with this conversation.

He's through with me.

I can't blame him.

I reach out to touch his forearm only to pull back when he stiffens. Curling my fingers into my palm I step away. "I'm sorry."

And because I can't be the one to watch him walk away, not this time, I turn.

But before I leave, I hear him say, soft and gruff, "Me, too."

38

———

My feet are killing me, my tiara is digging into my skull, the techno dance music is so loud it's making my teeth ache, and I haven't eaten since I gulped down a protein bar over six hours ago.

Homecoming isn't anything close to everything I thought it'd be cracked up to be.

Don't get me wrong. I really am grateful and happy that Philip and I won King and Queen. And it was super sweet of Mary Alice and Hailey to come to the parade and the football game to cheer me on. Mom and Dad made it to both, too, and Chase sent flowers wishing me good luck and Leah texted me while I was getting my hair done.

But Astrid didn't even come to the dance. She said Sean didn't want her going with any other guy, even one who is just a friend, so she decided to skip it even though I told her, like, a hundred times she could go with me and Philip and our group.

My guess is Sean didn't want her going at all.

And since I have my own boyfriend issues—or should I say, my boyfriend has his own issues—I could hardly say anything about hers.

One of my boyfriend's issues is that he insisted we take pictures beforehand at his house and not mine. He *said* it was because he was afraid of upsetting my dad, though I think he's just afraid, period.

Whatever.

And when I walked into the Panoses' living room, he looked up from his phone long enough to send me a quick, distracted grin and murmured, *you look pretty*, then went back to texting Travis, making plans for Travis's party later.

Pretty. Okay, it's not exactly an insult but I am killing it tonight. My hair is loose and wavy, captured in a sparkly barrette on one side, my eye makeup subtle, my lips a bold, glossy red. And my black sequined dress is long, strapless and fits me like a glove.

A very tight glove.

Pretty.

God.

But I just thanked him, then smiled brightly for all the millions of pictures his parents insisted we take standing in front of the cold fireplace then out on the back deck then in front of the large maple tree.

Now, hours later, here we are, at the dance in the colorfully decorated gym, the music thump, thump, thumping, strobe lights flashing.

And my boyfriend wants to leave.

"It's not even ten o'clock," I say, pitching my voice to be heard over the music.

But Philip must not hear me, or else he wants privacy, because he takes my hand and tugs me away from our swaying, bouncing, jostling, sweating classmates on the makeshift dance floor and into the cool, brightly lit hallway. He keeps his fingers intertwined with mine as we reach the third set of windows from the double doors.

The same exact spot where I'd stood and looked for Owen almost a month ago.

Except, I'm not supposed to be thinking about Owen. Not now, with my boyfriend's hand in mine. Not ever again. I'm not supposed to look for him during the school day. Not supposed to wonder what he's doing after school. If he found someone else to help him with English. If he's changed his mind about taking the SATs.

I'm not supposed to be disappointed he wasn't at the parade. That I didn't see him at the football game. That he's not here tonight.

That was the whole point of telling him I couldn't tutor him anymore. Cutting any and all ties between us.

But there must be a thread or two left because I do think of him. A lot. More than I should considering we'd only really known each other a couple weeks and were just friends. Barely even that.

Way more than I should considering I have a boyfriend.

A boyfriend who is giving me a charming, lopsided grin. It works on him, that's for sure, goes with his dark suit and tie, his slicked back hair and the plastic crown on his head.

If anyone was born to be king, it's Philip.

"Travis wants to get a fire started before people get there," he's telling me. "So we thought we'd cut out early."

Early. Well, it's certainly that. We've only been at the dance half an hour and already Philip wants to leave so he and Travis can build a bonfire to keep all our friends nice and toasty warm while they get wasted.

Thoughtful of them.

"But what if Mrs. Melvin wants us to do something?" I ask. Mrs. Melvin is this year's Homecoming advisor. "In our official capacities of King and Queen, I mean?"

More importantly, what about me?

He laughs. "I think we covered all the royal duties, babe."

True. We had our picture taken on the football field after being newly crowned, then again after they announced the entire court to everyone at the dance in case they'd skipped the game.

Not sure what else being Homecoming Queen entails.

Seems like one of those puppet regimes to me.

Philip looks around. "Things are dying down here anyway."

Yes. Things are mighty dead...

Out here in the empty hall!

But the dance is still going on.

"If you leave," I say, hating myself for it, hating how whiny I sound, how pathetic, "I won't have anyone to hang out with."

He grins some more. "Sure you will. You're the queen, babe. Everyone wants to hang out with the queen."

Yeah. Everyone except the king.

"Aw, come on," he says, obviously reading something on my face —like the fact that I want to kick him. "Don't be that way."

I narrow my eyes. "Don't be what way?"

He backtracks. Fast. "Hey, why don't you come with us? Your mom's not picking you up until midnight, right?"

"Right," I say slowly, drawing the word out. Part of being grounded means being unable to drive yourself to Homecoming or letting your boyfriend bring you home after.

Who knew?

"You could come to the party for a little bit then," Philip says, like this is the best idea he's ever had. "We'll make sure you're back here by 11:45. She'll never know."

Great idea. You know, except for the part where I'd have to disobey my parents—again, this time purposely and premeditatedly.

Not to mention the fact that I'm finding myself in a less and less celebratory mood and don't even want to go to a party tonight.

"I'd better not," I tell Philip as the sound of footsteps—many, many footsteps—echo from down the hall. "If I get caught, I'll be grounded until Christmas."

Which he should know. Which should worry him.

That it doesn't only worries *me*.

"Hey, Panos!" Travis calls from the end of the hall. "You coming?"

Behind Travis is a sizable group of semi-formally dressed friends and classmates. Jessica steps forward in her spiked heels and super short, super low-cut, red dress and presses against his side to whisper something to him.

But her eyes are on Philip.

"Hang on," Philip tells him then turns to me. "You sure you don't want to come?"

That's what he has to say to me? Not, *hey, if it means that much to you I'll stick around. I won't abandon you. I won't walk away.*

"I'm sure," I say.

Travis calls Philip's name again and Philip holds up his finger in the *one-minute* sign. "Are you going to be pissed if I go?"

I glance over at the group. Most of them have taken off, but Travis is still there.

So is Jessica.

And while I could answer Philip's question with a big, old resounding *duh!*, it won't do any good. It won't change anything. He didn't ask because he's concerned about my feelings.

He's trying to figure out what he's going to have to deal with.

Sure, I could get him to stay with me, but he'll just spend the rest of the night moody and quiet. And the first chance he gets, he'll head out to the party. He'll stay there, drinking and having fun.

Without me.

My stomach is twitchy, my breathing getting shallow.

"I won't be mad," I say, but it comes out shaky.

He doesn't notice.

And that's why I don't say anything about him ditching me—again. What would be the point?

Plus, to be honest, I no longer want him to stay.

I don't want to be around him right now. I want to be alone so I can catch my breath. Concentrate on slowing my racing heart.

"You sure?" he asks but he's already taken a step—consciously or subconsciously—toward Travis. And Jessica.

Not trusting myself to speak, afraid if I do, I'll start yelling or sobbing, I nod.

"Cool!" He's all smiling and relieved. And totally, one-hundred-percent oblivious. He leans in but his kiss barely brushes my cheek and I'm not sure it's his hurry or if I lean away.

Then he's walking backward, still smiling, happy with the world in general, his life in particular and me letting him go so easily. "I'll text you later."

He turns away before I can remind him I won't have my phone until Sunday.

Slinging one arm around Travis' shoulders, he and his best buddy nudge and jostle each other the way boys do as they lope down the hall, Jessica doing her best to slink after them in her too-high heels.

She's the only one who turns back.

Even from this distance, it's hard to miss her gloating expression, like she's the one with the win tonight—if not the actual tiara on her head.

I stand there for a minute. Then two. The music from the dance is a muted thud of too-heavy bass that reverberates through the walls, vibrates the floor. My breathing is still shallow but now it's fast. Too fast. My fingers are tingling and curling of their own accord, like my hands are turning into claws and I can't control it. Just stare down at them, watch them tremble.

I'm terrified I'm going to pass out, right here where anybody could see me so I rush down the hall, away from the gym, and duck into the girls' room in the marching band wing. Turning on the cold water, I dip my head and drink deeply, water dripping off my chin. When I'm done, I straighten, the back of my unsteady hand pressed against my mouth.

My reflection stares back, eyes wide and panicked, chin wet, lipstick smeared.

Oh, God.

I yank two paper towels out of the dispenser, blot them over my chin, carefully wipe away the errant lipstick.

I can do this. I can do this. I can do this.

I inhale. Hold it for five. Exhale. Hold it for another five. Repeat the process. Again. And again.

Finally, thankfully, my breathing calms. My heartrate settles. My hands relax enough that I'm able to get my lipstick from my purse and apply a fresh coat without looking like a clown. I use my fingertips to carefully wipe away any traces of smudged eyeliner or mascara from under my eyes then reach up and reset the tiara on my head.

Better. Much, much better.

I look perfectly normal.

The new role I play.

Pretending to be normal. To be okay.

Not feeling either until I've walked up and down the hall three times, staying in the third row from the right, counting the colored tiles as I go.

Hoping I'll look up and see Owen heading my way.

39

———

Sunday night, Philip and I are celebrating my official first day of freedom by watching a movie at his house. We're on his huge sofa in the family room, sitting hip-to-hip, his arm around my shoulders while Dwayne Johnson saves the day on the huge, flat screen TV on the wall.

I don't ask him about the party.

I don't ask him what time he got home or if he drank.

I don't ask if he talked to Jessica or any other girls while he was there.

I don't tell him how, after he left me, alone, at the Homecoming dance I borrowed Miss Ashby's phone and called my mom to come get me early.

I don't tell him that I told both Miss Ashby and Mom I wasn't feeling well, or that while Miss Ashby bought it, Mom wasn't fooled in the least.

But she didn't call me on it. Instead, we swung by Chef's 771, Mom's favorite burger joint and ate cheeseburgers, fries and onion rings and drank chocolate milkshakes, Mom in her yoga pants and a Penn State sweatshirt, me in my tiara and gown.

I don't mention how that was the best part of my night.

I don't ask and I don't tell.

Because things finally feel normal between us. Comfortable.

And I don't want to do or say anything to ruin it.

We're at the car chase part of the action movie he chose, some rock and roll song from the seventies playing over the sound of revving engines and screeching tires. Philip pulls me closer and I tense, my shoulders rigid, my back straight.

Okay, maybe things aren't completely normal.

Guess I have to work a bit harder.

Forcing myself to relax, I tuck my legs underneath me and snuggle against him the way I used to. The way I'm supposed to.

We usually hang out at my house since his dad has to get up super early to do prep work at the restaurant every morning. But Philip talked his mom into letting me stay until my curfew at ten instead of their usually strictly enforced lights-out-at-nine-p.m. policy.

That woman hates telling any of her sons no or denying them anything.

Though she has no problem doing so with Astrid.

It didn't hurt that Philip played the *we haven't seen each other for a week* card (conveniently forgetting Homecoming, which I'm trying to do as well) then threw in the bit about my parents being out to dinner and that I get nervous staying home alone.

It's a lie. Well, partly. My parents aren't out to dinner or anywhere else. As far as I know, they're home, probably snuggled up on our sofa in front of the television like Philip and I are but watching something way more interesting.

The part about me being nervous to be home alone? Totally true.

But Philip doesn't know that.

He just doesn't want to face my dad. Still.

I hope he gets over it soon.

If only so I don't freeze to death.

Mr. Panos refuses to turn on the heat in their huge, drafty Victorian until Thanksgiving. He's super frugal. He won't even buy Philip and Astrid a car to share—not even a used one—even though he could totally afford it.

Normally I don't mind Mr. Panos's penny-pinching ways, but it's a cold one tonight. I literally cannot feel my toes.

I move closer to Philip, hoping our combined body heat will stave off frostbite.

"You good?" he murmurs, rubbing his hand up and down my arm.

Resting my head on his shoulder, I look at him and remind myself how lucky I am to have him. How I don't want to lose him.

So I smile. "Never better."

My tone is cheery and bright, and I want to mean what I say. I want it to be true down to the very depths of my bones. But it's not. Not completely.

But I can make it true. I just need to try harder. I kiss Philip, a long, lingering kiss. One that proves how much I care about him. How much I want to be with him and no one else.

He kisses me back, the feel of his mouth against mine, the taste of him familiar. But when he deepens the kiss, when he touches the tip of his tongue to mine, I tense once again, cold prickling the nape of my neck.

No. No, that's not right. That's just the lingering anger from Homecoming rearing its ugly head. Pushing me to start a fight, to make waves.

I won't. I'll keep us steady. No matter what.

I kiss him and kiss him, my fingers in his hair, our bodies pressed against each other. He starts to tug me onto his lap when my phone buzzes.

I break the kiss and Philip presses his forehead against mine, his breathing ragged. "Shit," he mutters. "Did your dad put some sort of tracking device on you?"

Rolling my eyes, I clamber off his lap, not about to admit to myself how relieved I am at the interruption. "It might not even be him."

Not sure who else it could be. I'm with Philip and Astrid is up in her room.

She didn't even come down when I got here.

But my dad's been more than eager to communicate with me. He's texted me three times tonight and I've only been here an hour. The first message simply said *I love you* complete with several heart emojis (Dad loves emojis. Loves. Them.).

The second: *Make good choices* and a thumbs up emoji.

The third: *Just say no* along with praying hands (which is hilarious as Dad is not the least bit religious) and the smiley-face-with-a-halo.

Subtle, my dad isn't.

My phone buzzes again and I shift forward to get it from the coffee table in front of us. Apollo, the Panoses's ancient black lab, lying at Philip's feet, lifts his head, his tail thump, thump, thumping against the wood floor. I give him a quick scratch behind his ears then grab my phone and settle back on the couch.

"It's not him," I say.

Guess that HELP text I sent Mom, along with forwarding Dad's messages, worked.

Philip frowns and looks over my shoulder, trying to read the message.

Dad isn't the only non-subtle guy in my life.

"Who is it?"

I bristle. He never used to ask who was texting me. Probably because the only people who did were my parents, Chase, him and Astrid and occasionally Leah. But now he's become very curious.

And very suspicious.

"Mary Alice."

"Yeah?"

Funny how one word can convey so much meaning. In this case *I don't believe you.*

"Yeah," I say, turning the phone so he can clearly see the screen. And read Mary Alice's message. "See?"

God. It's like I'm on trial. He doesn't even have the grace to be embarrassed. Just shrugs, as if it's his right to monitor my text messages.

Picking up on the tension in the room, or just my irritation in general, Apollo whines and struggles to his feet. Puts his head on Philip's lap.

Philip pats Apollo's head while reading Mary Alice's message. "You're hanging out with her again?"

I make a sound of agreement as I respond to the text then lower my phone. "We're working our choreography for the performance."

Miss Laurie offered to stay after dance class tomorrow night and see what we've come up with. We'll probably go out and grab a bite to eat after now that I've been paroled.

Ah, sweet, sweet freedom!

"Weren't you with her today doing that?" Philip asks.

"Yes," I say slowly because he knows full well I was. He texted me at least a dozen times this afternoon while Mary Alice and I worked. "It's probably going to take us months to get it perfected."

"That long?"

"Is that a problem?" I ask.

"You've just been hanging out with her a lot."

"So? We're friends."

Before he can respond, I get another text from Mary Alice.

"Is that still her?" he asks.

Seriously?

"Yes," I say through gritted teeth. "It's still her."

"What does she want now?"

"Nothing. She invited me to a party one of her friend's is having Saturday night."

He sits up so fast, Apollo yelps in surprise then pads off in search of a quiet spot. "You're not going, are you?"

"Why wouldn't I?"

"What about Astrid?"

"I'm sure she already has plans with Sean." Astrid always has plans with Sean. "But if not, I'll ask Mary Alice to ask her friend if Astrid can come, too."

"That's not what I mean."

"What do you mean then?"

He shifts, turning to face me and our knees bump. He keeps his pressed against mine. "Promise you won't tell Astrid I said anything, okay? She'll kill me if she finds out."

"You *haven't* said anything," I point out.

"Nat," he says, drawing my name.

"Yes, yes. I promise I won't say anything."

Leaning forward, he lowers his voice. "She feels like you two are drifting apart."

"She said that?"

He nods. "She says you two haven't been hanging out or talking much lately."

And who's fault is that?

"We just talked this afternoon," I say, defensive and hurt that Astrid would try and lay the blame on the distance between us all on me.

That Philip would take her side over mine.

"I called her to see if she wanted to do something after her meet Wednesday," I continue. "She said Sean might want to do something so she'd have to let me know later. I'm not the one who's spending all her time with her boyfriend."

Philip holds up his hands. "Don't blame me. I'm just the messenger. And Sean is her first real boyfriend. Of course she wants to spend all her time with him. Cut her some slack."

That's exactly, exactly what I've been telling myself.

But hearing Philip say it? Having him lecture me about it?

Nope.

"I've done nothing but cut her some slack," I say, uncurling my legs and scooting forward so I'm sitting like a statue on the edge of the cushions. "Here's an idea. Why don't the two of you try cutting me some?"

"Hey, hey," Philip says in this soothing tone, like I'm some wild animal he's trying to calm down. I want to bite his hand off. "Look, I think Astrid is just worried you're going to replace her with Mary Alice."

"No one is getting replaced. Yes, I'm friends with Mary Alice but

Astrid will always be my best friend. And if she goes to the party with me, maybe she and Mary Alice will become friends, too."

His mouth thins. "I don't want you to go to a party without me."

There's a weird rushing sound in my ears. I shake my head but it just gets louder. "Are you serious right now?"

He nods once. "You know I have a tournament in Toledo next weekend."

"Please tell me you don't really think I should sit at home by myself, counting the minutes until you return."

"We agreed we wouldn't party without each other, remember?"

I lurch to my feet. "Oh, my God. You are unbelievable. You've gone to parties without me two weekends in a row!"

Expression hardening, he stands. "I told you. The only reason I went to Carlson's was because of Travis."

"Yeah? And Friday night when you left me alone at the Homecoming dance? What was your excuse then?"

"You told me I could go!"

"Because I didn't want to fight about it!"

"You could've come with me," he says, like this is a logical, reasonable response and not about the dumbest thing he could say.

"I was grounded. I didn't want to get into any more trouble. *You* could've stayed at the dance with me, but you didn't. And it's completely unfair that you get to do what you want but you expect me to sit at home, alone, all weekend while you're off having fun with your friends."

My voice cracks on the last word and I clear my throat. I want to cry. And not just because we're arguing—again. But because everything feels so different between us. So out of my control.

"I don't expect that," he insists. "I just don't see why you have to go to a party. If you want to hang out with Mary Alice, can't you do something else?"

"She invited me out," I say. "I'm not going to ask her to change her plans because my boyfriend doesn't trust me."

Philip stabs a hand through his hair, leaving the dark strands sticking up every which way. "I'm not getting into that again," he mutters, grabbing his phone from the coffee table and flopping back onto the couch. "Look, I don't want to fight. Do what you want."

As if I need his permission!

I stand there, silently fuming, arms crossed, toe tapping, glaring at him...the whole bit.

He doesn't even look up, just types something into his phone.

But I don't want to fight, either. I'm tired of fighting—which was why I didn't say anything to him at Homecoming.

It's why I don't say any more now.

Instead I sigh and roll my eyes then sit on the edge of the cushion, back ramrod straight. I sit even though I'm still mad. I stay, even though he didn't never apologized for ditching me. Twice. I pretend to watch a stupid movie while he ignores me.

I give in.

It's just easier. Safer.

And when I get home, I sit cross-legged on my bed, staring at the flowers on my wall, and think about how Philip barely said two words to me the rest of the night. How he didn't walk me to my car, just to the door and watched me get into my Jeep.

How relieved I was that he didn't lean in for a kiss.

How happy I was to leave.

I think about all of that and I count the flowers. Once. Twice. Three times.

It's not enough. I want to count them again. And again.

But I can't. I won't let myself. I have to have some control. Some willpower.

Before my harmless, little quirk turns into something bigger.

I deliberately turn and face my headboard. Pick up my phone and open my contacts. Scroll down to the *Os*.

Hover my finger over Owen's name.

Yet another habit that's threatening to become too big and out of control. Too dangerous.

Wanting to text him. To talk to him.

Missing him.

I hit Edit then Delete Contact before I can change my mind.

One unpleasant task done. One to go.

I open Mary Alice's last text, the one inviting me to the party.

Hey! Sorry I didn't get back to you sooner. Thanks for inviting me, but my mom wants me to help her at her store/gallery Saturday night. Maybe we can do something Sunday?

Biting my lower lip, I stare at what I typed. Think about Philip again. But this time I think about how I felt when he went to Justin's party. When he left me at the dance. How he changes the rules to suit him.

I don't want him to feel the way I did these past two weekends. Don't want to be the cause of it. Don't want to play some petty game of revenge.

But I'm tired of worrying about him. If he'll be upset. If he'll get mad.

If he'll stop loving me.

I'm so very tired of being the one who compromises. Who gives in.

Haven't I done both of those enough?

Do what you want to do.

I snort. Right. What he meant was, *do what I want you to do.*

I almost do. Because...again...easier. Safer.

Except the easy route hasn't gotten me anywhere. The safe choice hasn't made me feel any more in control.

Maybe it's time for something different.

I erase the text and type up new one.

Sorry I didn't get back to you sooner. The party sounds like fun—thanks for inviting me! I can drive. What time should I pick you up?

And I push Send.

40

THE PARTY AT DARCY MCCORMICK'S—A TINY, RANCH-STYLE HOUSE outside of town—is, for the most part, like any other party I'd been to. The people may be different (though there are a few I recognize from school) but there's still the same varied assortment of booze (including a bottle of peppermint schnapps Mary Alice said someone brought as a joke to a bonfire last spring that keeps popping up every weekend, still half-full) the air hazy with the familiar scents of cigarette and pot smoke.

A typical, small-town Saturday night.

"You're sure her parents won't be home tonight?" I ask Mary Alice whose hair is currently a shade of orange I wasn't sure existed until she showed up to ballet class with it the other night.

She owns it, of course and to be honest, it looks great on her (though I preferred the purple). But even if it looked like crap, she'd keep it that color. If only because her mom hates it.

Mary Alice loves anything her mom hates.

Just one of the interesting tidbits I've discovered about her over the past few weeks.

"They went to Virginia for the weekend," Mary Alice says of Darcy's parents. "They won't be home until tomorrow night."

Another typical aspect of me at a party. Nerves. I get paranoid. Worried we're too loud and someone is going to call the cops. Or worse, the party-thrower's parents arrive home unexpectedly. I'm afraid of what an underage citation will do to my chances of getting into Penn.

Not to mention how upset my parents would be.

Which is why I've been sipping diet soda since I got here over two hours ago.

That and because of the long-ago promise I made Philip that I wouldn't drink when we weren't together.

A promise, I'd like to point out, he didn't keep but, whatever.

"What if they come home early?" I ask because I have a hard time letting things go.

Another of my fun, quirky personality traits that drives my brother, my boyfriend and my best friend nuts.

One Mary Alice doesn't seem to mind. She smiles. "They won't. They're visiting her stepdad's parents for some big birthday party tonight. Darcy begged off, saying she needed to study for a Bio exam."

"They bought that?"

My parents wouldn't. Then again, I like my grandparents—both sets—so they'd definitely know something was up if I didn't go.

"From what I've heard about the stepdad, he's more than happy to rid himself of Darcy whenever possible. He's an asshole."

I raise my eyebrows. "Uh, are you sure you should swear? If your mom finds out, you'll be saying *Our Fathers* the rest of the weekend."

Mrs. Gibson is one of those extremely religious types—daily mass, weekly confession and lots of Bible quoting.

I've only met her once but I can honestly say if she was my mom, she'd have scared any and all sin right out of me by this point.

Luckily, Mary Alice is made of tougher stuff.

Sipping her beer, she shrugs. "Mom isn't the one who doles out the *Our Fathers* and *Hail Marys*. The priest does. But first you have to confess. Catholicism is a very guilt-based religion and on this subject, I have absolutely none. If anyone deserves to be labeled an asshole, it's Darcy's stepdad. He keeps dropping hints that she'd be happier living with her dad in Erie but he really just wants to get rid of her."

"Ugh. That sucks. She seems really nice."

Darcy, a pretty brunette with dimples and dark eyes, was very friendly to me when Mary Alice introduced us. And she had no problem with my being invited to her party, even though she doesn't know me.

"Yeah, Darcy's great. Hey, you should come with us tomorrow. A bunch of us are going thrift shopping to look for Halloween costume ideas."

"I'd like that," I say but then I remember what Philip said about Astrid feeling left out. As if she's losing me. "Do you think it would be okay if I brought Astrid, too?"

Once Astrid spends time with Mary Alice, she'll realize how great she is and that she has nothing to be worried about.

It'll be one of those; *she's not losing an old friend, she's gaining a new one* scenarios. We'll all be buddy-buddy by the end of the year.

"Sure," Mary Alice says. "I'll text you more details when I get them."

"Sounds good."

Someone calls Mary Alice's name. She turns and holds up a finger for them to wait. "I'll be right back. You want anything?"

Holding up my soda can, I shake my head. "I'm good, thanks."

She walks over to a group of girls in the corner leaving me standing by myself in the living room. I'm about to head to the restroom when the nape of my neck prickles with awareness. Not so much that feeling you get when someone is watching you, more like a premonition. And I have the very real, very frightening sense that something is about to happen. Something big.

Something possibly life altering.

I give an inner eye roll at my dramatics. An uneasy feeling does not a catastrophe make.

God. You'd think I'd learn that by now.

But though I try to brush off the sensation, that feeling of impending doom lingers. Grows stronger until it feels like a dozen spiders are crawling up my spine, making me itchy. Antsy.

I lift my gaze.

And lock eyes with Owen as he comes through the front door.

My breath catches. He's been hurt. His left eye is black and almost swollen shut, his cheek scraped and bruised. A bandage covers a row of stitches above his left eyebrow.

Emotions rush through me, conflicting and oh, so confusing. Excitement and fear. Joy and sadness. He hesitates, standing in the doorway for two long heartbeats, his hand on the doorknob, indecision in his expression. His expression hardens, and he turns as if to leave.

I take half a step forward, to go to him. To stop him and ask him to stay.

To ask if he's all right.

Something is wrong, something other than his face getting broken. I can sense it. There's an energy about him, something dark and dangerous circling him.

But going to him now and asking him what's going on would be a colossal mistake. What if it sparks some reconnection between us? What if Owen takes it as an overture for us to resume our friendship?

Oh, God, what if he blows me off?

No. None of the outcomes are worth the risk. I'm working so hard to make things right with Philip and having an innocent conversation with Owen will only put a huge wrinkle in my once again smooth life.

I need to stay as far away from him as possible.

With that resolve firmly in hand, I watch Owen close the door.

He, too, it seems, has made up his mind. He's staying.

Which means I need to leave. Now.

And I totally will. In a minute.

He steps into the room, eyes on mine, and does the unthinkable.

He walks toward me, closer and closer and closer, intent evident in his stride, his expression determined.

Only to pass me by without a word.

A wave of heat engulfs me, and I try to tell myself the sick feeling in my stomach is from too much soda. Or relief.

Not disappointment or, God forbid, longing.

Owen heads to the kitchen and everyone gives him a wide berth —a bruised and battered Moses, parting the red sea to lead his people to alcohol.

I'm not the only one smart enough to keep her distance from him.

But I watch him. I can't help it. He takes a plastic cup from the stack on the counter and fills it at the keg. My unease grows. I try to shake it off. It's silly, really, to worry about him. Owen is one of the most self-assured people I know. And he's smart. Smarter than he gives himself credit for.

He has too much control to let anything bad happen. Too much pride to do anything dumb or self-destructive.

Owen straightens, lifts the cup to his mouth and chugs his beer in what seems like two swallows.

Then Mr. Self-Assured and Controlled bends over and refills it.

Crap.

"Sorry about that," Mary Alice says when she rejoins me. She frowns. Edges closer and lowers her voice. "You okay?"

My throat is tight and I'm afraid if I open my mouth, what comes out won't be an assurance that I'm fine and dandy but a shout for Owen to put his cup down and step away from the keg, so I nod and even try a smile.

Doesn't work. Mary Alice looks even more concerned.

"You're pale. If you're not feeling well, I can find someone to drive you home." Looking around at her friends, she wrinkles her nose. "Probably. I can probably find someone sober enough to drive you home."

She's giving me the perfect excuse to slip away without too many questions or her thinking I wasn't having fun or that I don't like her friends. All I have to do is say she's right, that I'm not feeling well—a headache or stomachache or, God, I don't know, cramps—but that I'm okay to drive myself home.

I plan on doing just that. Until I glance at Owen who is in the middle of downing beer number two.

And I know I'm not going anywhere.

41

Mistake number one.

Mistake number two was pretending I needed another soda so I had an excuse to go into the kitchen.

Mistake number three was being hurt when, as soon as I stepped foot into the room, Owen turned on his heel and walked away.

To talk to another girl.

But my biggest mistake is staying for another hour during which I spend way too much time being way too aware of what he's doing, which is basically flirting hardcore with some girl named Cora Richards.

Yeah. I asked Mary Alice who she was. Pathetic, right?

Thank God Mary Alice didn't question why I wanted to know.

Probably because she'd already figured it out.

She didn't call me on it, though.

Cora is a junior who plays volleyball, works summers as a lifeguard at the public pool and has an on-again, off-again boyfriend named Ryan Goode.

A sometimes boyfriend who is nowhere to be found tonight.

From my spot next to the microwave, I have the perfect view of

Owen and Cora. Owen, now well into his fifth beer, leans in close to Cora and says something so hilarious, she tips her head back and laughs. Loudly.

Yes, because we all know what a freaking jokester Owen Radlowski is. Such fun! Such wacky wit! Always with the jokes and light-heartedness!

Blech.

Shaking back her long, blond hair, the motion which serves absolutely no purpose other than to set her boobs a-jiggling, she continues to chuckle as if he's just the. Funniest. Thing. Ever.

It's like I've walked into some weird dream. Up is down, the sky is pink, the grass is purple and Owen is charming. What has happened to the world?

Finally settling down, Cora lays her hand on Owen's shoulder and rises to her toes, pressing her entire upper body against his as she whispers something into his ear.

I jerk my gaze away.

It's either that or gouge my eyes out with a spoon.

There's an odd ache in my chest and I rub a hand over it. My fingers are tingling and I'm having a hard time catching my breath. What if I'm having a heart attack? Or stroking out? Yes, okay, so both of those seem improbable, but either could, technically, happen.

Well, they could.

Pretending I'm reading a text, I stare blindly at my phone and concentrate on taking in a deep, slow breath, then letting it out. I do it again. And again. Then I inhale and hold it for three counts of five—one to five then five to one then one to five again—tapping my finger against my phone with each second. I exhale and hold it again, three counts of five.

The roaring in my head subsides. The tightness in my chest eases.

But the ache stays.

I turn and tap Mary Alice's shoulder, drawing her attention away from one of her school friends.

"I'm heading home," I say.

She checks her phone. "Already? It's not even midnight."

"I know," I say in faux disappointment, as if the last thing I want is to tear myself away from all this fun and frivolity, "but I promised my mom I'd help her at her shop first thing in the morning. I'll talk to you tomorrow." I hug her as Trent joins us. "You're not planning on driving, are you?" I ask him.

Trent grins and shakes his head. He's the poster boy for cute with his floppy brown hair and easy smile. "Andy's DD tonight."

Mary Alice pouts. "But if you go, who will I talk to?"

"Uh...everyone else here? These people are your friends," I remind her. "I'm the outsider."

She waves that away. "Exactly. I talk to them all the time. I want to talk to you."

"You can talk to me." Nuzzling her neck, Trent slides his arm around her waist, pulling her close. "I love talking. But it's so noisy in here. Let's go to one of the bedrooms, where it's quieter. So I can hear you better."

Mary Alice and I exchange a look. Boys. So obvious.

"Talking? Is that what you're calling it now?" Mary Alice asks, lifting her shoulder to dislodge him. "Because my mom calls it fornication."

Straightening, Trent winces. "Could you not bring up your mom? It kills my mood."

"Nothing kills your mood."

He brightens. "True. Lucky you. But if it'll make you feel better, I'll talk the entire time."

"I hadn't realized you were so good at multitasking."

"Let's go see," he suggests with an eyebrow wiggle.

I laugh. "Yeah. I'm definitely leaving." I hug her again. "Don't forget to text me about the thrift store shopping."

"I won't."

Since I have a good twenty-minute drive back into town, alone, in the dark, that I'm in no hurry to get started, I head to the bathroom first. When I come out, Owen and Cora are in the hallway.

Coincidence?

I have my doubts.

Cora, her back against the wall, smiles up at Owen, her hand on his forearm while he leans over her in that way guys do—crowding just a little, the stance protective and possessive and predatory all in one—his hand pressed to the wall near her head.

My stomach turns. No way to avoid it. I have to go around them.

I keep my eyes straight ahead, my stride easy and expression clear. I manage the whole happy, content and carefree vibe pretty well, if I do say so myself. No one watching would ever get the wrong idea.

Like that it bothers me that Owen ignored me all night. Or that I'm angry about how he invaded my personal space and my thoughts by showing up here, drawing my attention to him time and time again.

That I care, even a little, that he's flirting with another girl.

As much as I want to walk past them without a word, I can't. Owen is taking up too much room, leaving barely a foot between him and the opposite wall. I clear my throat and he oh-so-slowly turns his head to look at me, his broad shoulders blocking Cora from view.

I wince. His bruise looks even worse up close.

And more painful.

One side of his mouth kicks up but it isn't his real smile—a rare occurrence on its own. No, this one is a self-satisfied, cocky, none-too-sober grin. One that says he knows, exactly, how I feel about him being here, like this with Cora. How upset it makes me.

And that he's glad.

Which is when I realize that he needs saving from himself.

Because the Owen I've come to know wouldn't hurt me. Not purposely.

Not even though I'd hurt him first.

He needs me.

"There you are," I say, adding a light laugh, as if I'd been searching for him for hours and only now just noticed him smack dab in front of me. "I've been looking for you."

"That right?" he murmurs, taking a sip of the beer in his hand.

I nod. Blink in faux surprise when he shifts to reveal Cora still plastered against the wall like some not-so-virginal sacrifice in high waisted jeggings and a crop top. "Oh, hi. Sorry. I didn't notice you there."

Her gaze narrows. "Really? That's funny because I could have sworn you've been watching me plenty tonight."

My face flames. She'd noticed? Does that mean other people had as well?

I slide a glance at Owen. Had he?

"That *is* funny that you'd think that," I say, smiling meanly.

Her eyes narrow and she drops her hands from Owen's body. "Did you want something?"

"Yes. Owen." The moment the words are out of my mouth I wish them back. Hope neither Cora nor Owen misinterpret my meaning.

Pray they can't hear the truth in it.

"My Jeep won't start," I rush on, holding up my keys and giving a shrug. "I think it's the battery."

"So have someone give you a jump," he says, turning back to Cora.

Dismissing me.

"Trent doesn't have jumper cables." It could be true. I have no idea what Trent carries in his car. Plus, he's not driving tonight. Taking a huge risk, I brush my fingertips over Owen's shoulder, but he stiffens and I yank my hand back. "Please, Owen."

His jaw tightens. Oh, God, he's going to refuse me. Reject me in front of this girl he's hitting on. But then he mutters something under his breath I can't make out.

Not that I want to know.

"I'll be back," he tells Cora.

Her mouth a thin line, her arms crossed, she shifts her gaze from him to me then back again. "Yeah? Maybe I'll be here. And maybe I won't."

She sashays down the hall toward the kitchen, in full butt-swinging, hips-swaying beg-for-it mode.

And Owen can't take his eyes off her.

"Owen?" I ask, and his back goes rigid. "Are you ready?"

Chugging the rest of his beer, he crushes the empty cup in his hand and nods toward the door. "Lead on, princess."

Princess.

Ouch.

Though Owen follows me, I have the strangest sensation I'm the one trailing after him. Any triumph I felt at achieving my goal of getting him alone, of getting him away from Cora, disappears as soon as we step onto the small front porch.

I quickly shut the door.

Oh, God, what have I done?

Okay, I know what I've done. I left the party. Not exactly a crime. Except I left with a guy.

A guy who is not my boyfriend.

And at least a dozen people saw me do it.

Not to mention the teeny, tiny fact that Philip doesn't know I'm here. He never asked if I was going.

So I never told him.

I haven't done anything wrong. Certainly nothing that would live up to the guilt twisting inside of me. I have every right to be here. And I'm helping Owen. Being a good person, giving to others and all that.

Certainly Philip will understand.

"Where're you parked?" Owen asks, already brushing past me to descend the steps.

The wind picks up, whipping my hair into my face. I gather it over my shoulder and hold it in one hand. "What?"

"Your Jeep? Where is it?"

"Out back."

He heads around the side of the house and I chase after him, jogging to catch up to his hurried strides, checking over my shoulder to make sure no one is watching. Darcy lives on a hill, the second to last house on a rarely used, dead-end street surrounded by woods. A good spot for an underage party.

The backyard is dark, the night broken up by a few stars in the inky sky and the lights coming from the house. But the glow only reaches a few feet out, leaving the rest of the yard in shadows.

Owen passes my Jeep.

"Where are you going?"

"Jumper cables won't reach across the yard," he says, not slowing.

"Yes...I mean, I know but..." I reach him. Hurry around to block him from going any farther. "It's just...you've been drinking. You shouldn't drive..."

"It's fifty feet. Not the highway."

"You could still crash into something. Or someone."

He makes a show of looking around. "No one out here but us."

"For now," I insist, shoving my hair out of my face, my eyes adjusting enough to the dark to make out his features. "Someone could come out. Plus, you only have one good eye which cuts your ability to see clearly in half. What if you don't notice someone stepping into the yard until it's too late? What if you're too impaired to even drive across the yard? What if—"

"Okay, okay. Jesus." He holds his keys out to me. "You do it then."

I take the keys, my fingers trailing against his palm.

"Problem?" he asks when I just stand there shivering like an idiot because I didn't bring a coat.

I clear my throat. "More like there's *not* a problem. There's nothing wrong with my Jeep."

"You said it wouldn't start."

"I lied."

He stills. "You lied?"

I hope he can see my nod because there is no way I'm admitting it again out loud.

"Why?"

I open my mouth. Shut it. Squeeze his keys until they bite into my palm.

He steps closer. "Why, Natalie?" he asks, beer on his breath, voice low and husky. "Why'd you lie?"

Because I'm stupid enough to think you're hurting. Reckless enough to want to help you. Hopeful enough to think you need me.

Selfish enough to hate seeing you with another girl, to have you turning to her instead of me.

A guy with bright red hair stumbles out the back door, rights himself and unzips his pants.

Shoving Owen's keys into my front pocket, I take his hand and drag him toward the edge of the yard. Away from the house, the windows and the people inside.

Not to mention the redhead, currently taking a leak off the back steps.

Owen stops behind a double-cab, pickup truck, making me realize the only reason I could pull him as far as I did was because he let me.

"What're you doing?" he asks.

"I..." Realizing I'm still holding his hand, that his fingers are curled around mine in a way that feels entirely too intimate, I tug my hand free. "I lied because I wanted to talk to you. Alone." My face heats, but I barrel on, confident he can't see my blush. Can't see how nervous, how unsettled being this close to him in the dark makes me. "I wanted to see if you're all right."

"Why wouldn't I be?"

"Uh, maybe because you look like you've been kicked in the face a few times?"

"We had a scrimmage today and a high stick caught me under my face mask," he says, a shrug in his tone as if a black eye and stitches are nothing compared to the glory of skating around and trying to get some stupid, small puck into a tiny net. "Bruises happen."

"A scrimmage you won?"

"Can't win them all," he says, but there's something in his tone, an acceptance of defeat that makes me wonder if we're still talking about hockey.

"Is that why you're so upset?" I ask. "And don't try and tell me you're not because I can tell you are." He doesn't answer, and I step closer. "You're not acting like yourself."

"And you know this how?"

"Because I know *you*."

"That so?"

I hesitate at the silky, dangerous note in his voice. The way he leans forward, invading my space. "I..." I swallow. Nod once. "Yes. That's so."

"Then you know there are only two things I want to do tonight," he whispers to me in the dark, confiding in me. Sharing his secrets once again. "Get drunk. And get laid."

I flinch. "She has a boyfriend. Cora, I mean. Cora has a boyfriend."

"Not tonight she doesn't."

"But she will. They'll probably be back together by tomorrow."

According to Mary Alice that's their usual M.O.

Owen's mouth curves, as if I amuse him to no end.

As if he knows I have no idea what I'm talking about.

As if he knows I'm lying through my teeth.

"Then I'd better get back inside. Make the most of her currently being single." But he doesn't move. "Unless..."

"Unless what?"

Shaking his head, he grabs the back of his neck.

"Unless what?" I repeat, ignoring the little voice inside of me urging me to let it go. To let *him* go.

Mesmerized, breath locked in my lungs, I watch as he slowly reaches out and touches the ends of my hair.

"Unless you want to take her place."

42

———————

Owen's gruff words may have been flirtatious but his meaning is beyond crude. I should be insulted. Tell myself I am insulted. But mostly I'm hurt. And desperate for him not to know how much.

I bat his hand away. "We're not interchangeable. Just because we're both blondes and girls does not mean I am a stand-in for Cora Richards."

He hangs his head for a moment and when he looks at me again, his gaze is stark. "No," he says quietly. "You're not a stand-in for her."

My heartbeat echoes in my ears. My mouth dries.

You're not a stand-in for her.

Oh God. Oh God, oh God, oh God.

Does that mean...is he saying she's the stand-in?

A stand-in for...for me?

I try and push the thought aside. If I don't rid myself of it as quickly as possible, a few of the crazy ideas floating around in my head will get free. I might tell him he doesn't need a stand-in, that whatever he's looking for from Cora—release or comfort—he can get from me.

Whatever he needs. Whatever he wants.

I take an involuntary step back. Then another. We're too close, out here in the dark. Owen is too good-looking. Too intense.

Too tempting.

He smirks, as if reading my mind. "You'd better go, princess. Wouldn't want you to miss curfew." He hesitates a beat. "Or get into trouble with Panos."

He's right. I need to leave. But not because I'm worried about being late or getting into trouble with Philip. For the first time in my life, I don't trust myself. Don't trust that I'll make the right decision.

I'm turning away when a car pulls in the driveway, the headlights blinding me. It barely screeches to a stop when a figure jumps out of the driver's side and storms toward us, the lights casting him in shadow.

"Radlowski!" a male voice growls and for one terrifying moment I think it's Philip, that he somehow found out I'm out here with Owen. That he knows how close I'd come to saying something, doing something I couldn't take back.

But as he gets closer, I realize he's too tall. Too thin.

I realize it's someone else's boyfriend.

"What the fuck, man?" the boy I'm guessing is Ryan Goode growls, not stopping until he and Owen are toe-to-toe. "You trying to get with my girl?"

Ryan, a few inches over six feet, looms over Owen, long and lean but muscular. Owen doesn't seem fazed in the least to be facing down an irate boyfriend. Which, if you think about it, is pretty stupid. For God's sake a hockey stick got the better of him today. How's he going to fare against an actual person?

Plus, he's been drinking. All those beers can't be good for his reflexes.

They're obviously not good for his decision-making skills either because while I hold my breath and silently will Owen to back up and proclaim his innocence, maybe even apologize for trying to horn in on another guy's territory, he smirks.

And things only get worse when that smirk turns into a confident, shit-eating smile. "Working on it."

I suck in a sharp breath. For a few seconds, nothing happens. The lull before the storm. Time slows as Ryan frowns, digesting Owen's admission as if unsure whether to believe it or not. From the corner of my eye, I notice the back door opening. People rush out, a few of the more eager souls running.

And then Ryan punches Owen in the nose.

There's a sickening crack that turns my stomach. Owen takes a step to regain his balance, his face turned to the side. He wipes his forearm across his nose, blood streaking on his arm, and lifts his head, a look of eagerness in his eyes, satisfaction on his face.

His stupid, already-bruised-and-now-currently-bloody face.

He comes up swinging, his fist connecting with the side of Ryan's head. A crowd gathers, some calling encouragement, more than a few people recording the fight on their phones. No one tries to stop it.

I've never seen a fight like it, one taken that far. I stand off to the side, wanting to run, to get away from the sight of blood and them pounding on each other. Want to cover my ears so I can't hear the sounds—grunts of pain, of the punches connecting. I want to scream at them to stop. I want to jump on Ryan's back and tear him away from Owen who, though holding his own, is obviously not in top fighting form this evening.

"Ryan!" Cora screeches, pushing people out of her way. "Stop!" She wades into the fray, grabbing Ryan's arm and yanking him back two steps. "What is wrong with you?"

"Me?" he asks incredulous, his shirt ripped and bloody.

"Yes. You. You broke up with me, remember?" She tosses up her hands. "God!"

She stomps off toward the house, hair flouncing.

Ryan hesitates, glancing back at Owen then at Cora's retreating figure before doing a limping jog after her. "Cora! Babe, hold on…"

The rest of the party eventually follows, eager for another, if less physical and bloody, fight.

Everyone that is except for me.

And Owen.

Deliberately not looking at him, I spin on my heel and cross to my

Jeep. My hands are shaking so badly, I drop my keys and I have to crouch and pat the damp, cold grass to find them. Finally finding them, I unlock the door as I straighten, then slide in behind the steering wheel. I turn on the ignition and sit there, head down, heart racing, stomach turning. I gulp in air, but I can't escape the memory of Owen getting hit. Of him getting hurt.

I am in so much trouble here.

When I'm fairly certain the urge to throw up has passed, I lift my head. And about jump out of my skin when someone knocks on my window.

Owen. Of course.

I glare at him. He raises his eyebrows.

Well, one eyebrow. The one with the stitches stays down.

Finally, grudgingly, I roll my window down a crack. "What?"

He peers at me. "You have my keys."

His keys. My hand flies to my pocket. Right.

I almost do it. I almost dig them out and throw them at him, but then I take a better look at his face. His nose is still bleeding as are his stitches, not to mention getting into that fight did not help the bruising around his left eye.

He sways slightly, either due to the beer catching up to him or the blows he took.

It doesn't matter. The results are the same. He's in no shape to drive.

"Get in," I tell him.

"Just give me—"

"Get. In." When he doesn't move, I shrug. Put the Jeep into Reverse. "Or don't. But I'm leaving. You can get your keys in the morning. I'll leave them in our mailbox."

I start to back up very slowly because, even though I'm so angry and upset and confused I can barely see straight, I don't want to accidentally run over his foot.

I move so slowly in fact that he easily rounds the front of the Jeep and walks to the passenger side door. I stop and unlock it. He gets in, the interior light showing the extent of his bruises, his bloody and scraped his knuckles.

I open the glove box, take out a handful of napkins and shove them at him. "Don't even think about bleeding in my Jeep."

"Yes, princess."

Again with the princess.

I send him a flinty look, but he's already shut the door and the light has dimmed. I back out of my spot and head home. At the stop sign a half mile down the road, I glance at Owen. He's packed his nose with napkins, has his head back against the seat, his mouth open.

Sound asleep.

My hands tighten on the steering wheel. I grind my teeth together.

And I wish I'd run over his foot after all.

43

I TURN ONTO THE MAIN ROAD, DRIVING SLOWLY, CAREFULLY, LEANING forward as I scan the road ahead of me, looking for deer.

No matter how hard I try to calm my spinning thoughts, to control them, they continue to whirl around like a tornado, picking up speed, flashes of what just happened bursting free like lightning.

Owen and Cora in the hallway, his body close to hers, her fingers on his arm. The feel of Owen's hand in mine, warm and strong and somehow right despite my knowing damn well it's wrong. The look in his eyes—mean and violent and so lost it broke my heart—after Ryan punched him.

The things I said. The things he said.

Everything I shouldn't remember, shouldn't be thinking about at all.

Everything I'm afraid I'll never forget.

Anxiety fills me. I need to focus on something else, anything else, so I drive landmark to landmark to landmark, reciting my short list over and over in my head and adding one once I pass the first on the list.

Crawford's Bait shop. The Elm Tree Restaurant. Elliott Quick's camp. Over and over and over.

The Elm Tree Restaurant. Elliott Quick's camp. The township's volunteer fire station. Over and over and over.

Elliott Quick's camp. The township's volunteer fire station. The reservoir. Over and over and over.

The township's volunteer fire station. The reservoir. The town limits. Over and over and over.

Lights blaze at the fire station, cars and trucks parked out front. I'm halfway to town, ten...thirteen minutes, top...and I'll be able to drop Owen off and get back to my life. Pretend this night never happ—

My phone rings through the Bluetooth, loud and shrill in the silence.

I jump. Check the screen on the dash.

Philip.

It rings again.

I promised I'd call him at eleven.

I check the clock. 11:58.

Crap.

Another ring.

I glance at Owen. Still asleep. Or passed out.

I clear my throat, my eyes on the road. And push the Answer button on the steering wheel. "Hello?"

I sense more than see Owen tense beside me but when I check, he's still motionless, eyes closed.

"Hey, babe," Philip says, his voice low and gravely. "You forgot to call me."

I open my mouth but nothing comes out. Tears sting my eyes, swift and sharp. Hearing his voice should help me. Should center me and remind me of how good I have it. How lucky I am.

So lucky I have absolutely no right to be wishing things could be different, if only for one night. I have no right to want more.

To want someone else.

The reservoir. The town limits. Willowdale cemetery.

"Nat?" Philip asks. "You there?"

"Hi," I choke out. "I mean, yes, I'm here. I...I'm sorry I didn't call earlier. I guess I lost track of time."

He's silent for a moment. "Where are you?"

My hands tighten on the wheel. Of course he can tell I'm in my car. That I'm not home, where he wanted me to be.

Where I should be.

"I went to Darcy's party," I say. "The one Mary Alice invited me to?"

More silence.

"But I'm almost home," I add quickly. "I'm passing the reservoir now."

I hear a rustling sound, like he's sitting up in bed. I can imagine him running his hand through his hair, leaning against the wall or getting up to go into the bathroom so he won't wake up the other guys in his hotel room. "You went to the party?"

"Yeah. It was fun." You know, minus all the parts relating to Owen. "Mary Alice's friends are really nice. But, like I said, I'm on my way home now."

"Text me when you get home. So I know you're okay."

"Sure but it...uh...might be another fifteen minutes."

"You just said you were at the reservoir."

"I am. I mean, I was. I passed it, yes." Houses come into view, getting closer together. I wipe my palms down the front of my jeans— first one, then the other. "But...I'm...uh...dropping Owen off first. At his house."

I wince because of course I'm dropping him off at his house. Where else would I take him? Church? Not that both of us couldn't use a good dose of prayer, but still...

This silence is the worst one yet. Longer. Tenser. My pulse pounds in my ears.

The town limits. Willowdale cemetery. Grover's Pond.

"He had too much to drink," I continue quickly. "I didn't think he should be driving."

I brake, slowing down as I approach the sign welcoming me to town, the posted speed limit dropping to thirty-five. More silence on Philip's end.

Willowdale cemetery. Grover's Pond. YMCA.

Willowdale cemetery. Grover's Pond. YMCA.

Willowdale cemetery. Grover's Pond. YMCA.

"You went to a party," Philip says in this weird, flat tone, "without me. Without telling me you were going and Radlowski was there. And now you're driving him home because he had too much to drink?"

I slow even more as I round a curve before the cemetery. "Yes. Are you…" I lower my voice. "Are you mad I'm helping Owen out?"

Grover's Pond. YMCA. Owen's house.

"You said he's there, with you, right now?" Philip asks in a harsh whisper. "And I'm on speaker?"

"Yes."

More silence.

I never should have answered his call.

How many mistakes can a girl make in one freaking night?

"Philip?"

"Call me when you get home," he says.

This isn't a question or even a request. It's a demand, one given in a rough, angry tone.

I signal then turn right onto Owen's street. "I thought you had get up early for your first game?"

"Just call me. I don't want to talk about this anymore in front of him."

Definitely mad.

"Okay," I whisper.

I'm about to hang up when he curses. "Nat?"

"Yeah?"

"I love you," he says quietly. "You know that, right?"

I pull to a stop in front of Owen's house, my throat tight. "I know."

It's not until after I hang up that I realize I didn't tell him that I love him, too.

Sighing, I rest my forehead on the steering wheel.

"Was that for my benefit?"

I sigh again. Of course, Owen is awake. I'm sure he's been awake the entire time. I roll my head to the side to look at him. "Did you get hit harder than I thought? Scramble your brains a bit? Yes. This ride home was for your benefit."

It sure isn't doing me any good.

Owen unhooks his seatbelt. "No, I meant that little talk with Panos. You reminding me you have a boyfriend, Natalie? Or are you reminding yourself?"

I refuse to dignify that with an answer.

Mainly because I'm not sure what that answer would be.

I sit up and dig his keys from my pocket but don't hand them over. "Can I trust you not to go back to the party and try to drive your truck home?"

He takes the napkins out of his nose and I avert my eyes because that is just disgusting. "I'm not in the mood for a ten-mile hike."

"No, you were just in the mood to hit on a girl with a jealous boyfriend."

He snorts softly and when he speaks, his tone is resigned. "What can I say? I have a bad habit of wanting things that don't belong to me."

I run my free hand back and forth across the steering wheel. Back and forth. Back and forth. Keep my eyes on the movement of my fingers. "You mean Cora?"

"You and me both know I don't mean Cora," he says, his quiet words like a bomb—explosive and dangerous.

One strong enough to implode my life as I know it.

"You and I," I blurt out, trying to diffuse the tension. To pretend he didn't just say what he just said.

He looks at me as if I'm the one who's had a few too many recent blows to the head. "What?"

"It's *you and I* both know. Not *you and me.*"

He shakes his head. "Christ, but you drive me nuts."

"What?" I ask, offended and—as much as I don't want to be—hurt that he obviously still considers me a pain-in-the-ass. "Proper grammar is important."

He faces me, the bridge of his nose swollen, turning purple to match his eye. "You schooling me on how to talk isn't why you drive me crazy."

"Oh."

I stare out my window at his house. It's completely dark, as if no one's home, but two cars are in the driveway. If someone is there, they didn't wait up for him. Didn't leave a light on.

"Don't you want to know why you drive me crazy?" he asks.

Of course I do. But there's no way I'm going any farther down this road with him. I've gone way too far as it is.

But not so far that I can't still turn around.

Not so far I can't get back to where I'm supposed to be.

"I don't think that'd be a very smart idea. My asking," I clarify. "Or my knowing."

He gives a slow nod. "And you're always smart, aren't you, Natalie?"

"Yes." Smart and careful and honest.

Except dragging Owen from that party was stupid. Driving him home, being alone with him now is reckless.

Pretending I feel only friendship for him is nothing but a lie.

One I plan on clinging to for as long as possible.

Easier said than done when Owen is looking at me the way he is now, all intense and searching, as if he's trying to find that truth.

"You are so fucking beautiful," he says, and the soft words make me dizzy, the raw scrape of his voice causes me to tremble. "When I'm with you…"

Frowning, he trails off.

"When you're with me what?" I whisper.

But he shakes his head and opens the door. "You're not the only one who can be smart."

I stare out the windshield as he climbs out of my Jeep, refusing to look at him as he walks to his house. Refusing to admit how badly I want to know what he was about to say.

Wanting nothing more than to pretend that absolutely nothing in my life has changed.

44

———

That was the text Philip sent me twenty minutes ago, the one that had my stomach quivering with nerves. I always thought guys were the only ones who hated those four little words. Seems they have the power to make us girls break out into a cold sweat, too.

Who knew?

It took me a good five minutes to respond. We're not fighting—not exactly. Mainly because we haven't really spoken since our conversation in my Jeep last night. I ended up skipping the shopping trip with Mary Alice and her friends, opting instead to help Mom at Kaleidoscope to keep my mind off everything that's happened. And Philip's been at his soccer tournament in Toledo and didn't get home until an hour ago.

Yes, I called him when I got home after dropping Owen off, but Philip barely said two words while I babbled on and on and on about every topic under the sun including the recent weather, homework assignments and what I had for lunch that day.

Every topic except the one I—and I suspect Philip as well—couldn't stop thinking about.

Owen Radlowski.

I did respond to his text—eventually—and now I'm in my kitchen, staring out the window looking for his headlights. My dad was less than thrilled when I told him and Mom Philip was on his way. I'm not sure if that's because it's so late (past ten-thirty on a school night) or because he's holding a grudge about catching Philip with his hand up my shirt. Luckily, cooler heads (namely Mom) prevailed and she gave me permission to have Philip stay until eleven.

His headlights flash through the darkness and I hurry out to meet him on the patio. The cold night air cuts through my thin pajama pants and heavy socks and I tug the sleeves of my sweatshirt over my hands.

"Hey," I say softly when he reaches the edge of the patio. His hands are in his jacket pockets and his face is drawn. He looks tired. Sad.

And it's all my fault.

He stops near the patio table. "Hey."

This is so weird and I hate it. But I'm not sure what to do. I want to go to him, to wrap my arms around him, to pretend everything is okay between us, that nothing has changed. But even I'm not that good at pretending.

"Do you…" I have to stop and clear my throat. "Do you want to come in? My parents are upstairs," I add quickly, knowing he's still hesitant about facing my dad.

"Can we stay out here?"

I try to smile but it's wobbly. I wonder if he notices. "Sure."

But he doesn't sit, just stands there, studying me in this way like he's trying to figure me out. Like he doesn't know me anymore.

I shift the weight from my left let to my right. "How was the soccer tournament?" I ask, unable to handle the silence. The waiting.

"We came in second."

"That's great," I say, my voice unsteady. "Congratulations."

"Nat," he asks, looking down at the patio, "are we okay?"

"What do you mean?"

"You're pulling away from me," he says so quietly, it's as if he's speaking to himself. He lifts his head. "I'm losing you."

"I'm right here."

"Are you?"

My scalp prickles and I shiver. "Yes."

"You're cold," he says. "We should go in—"

"I'm scared." I wave my hand between us. "This is wrong. Whatever's going on, it's not how we're supposed to be, but I don't know how to fix it."

"Is that what you want?" he asks softly. "To fix it?"

I can't answer. The truth is, I don't know what I want.

Or else I do, but I'm too afraid to admit it.

Too afraid of what fixing it will cost me.

"Because that's what I want," he continues when I keep silent. "I want that more than anything."

I believe him. And I don't want to hurt him. Not when I can see he's scared, too.

But I can't tell him what he wants to hear. No matter how badly I want to.

"I want things between us to go back to how they used to be," I say slowly and while that's the truth, it's not nearly the whole truth.

Not nearly enough of it.

Nodding, he takes a step toward me. "Me, too." He swallows visibly. "Did you know Radlowski was going to be at that party? Is that why you went? Because of him?"

"I had no idea he was going to be there." It's a relief, being honest for once. Even if it's only for a moment. "I swear."

He rubs his palm up and down the side of his leg. Up and down. Up and down. "Did...did anything...happen between you two?"

"No. Nothing happened."

Nothing like what Philip's asking about.

But I held Owen's hand.

He touched my hair.

He told me I was beautiful.

"Nothing happened," I repeat firmly. "Owen was drunk and I didn't think he should be driving. I would have done the same for any of our friends—Travis or Stuart. Any of them." I'm talking too quickly, wanting too desperately for him to believe me. Am too desperate to believe it myself. "He wasn't even awake during the drive. He passed out two minutes after we left the party. I dropped him off at his house then went home and called you. End of story."

But it's not the whole story. Not even close.

"Do you like him?" Philip asks hoarsely and the air whooshes out of my lungs. "Do you...do you have...feelings...for him?"

A denial rises in my throat, fast and furious, but it's another lie. One that stays there, hard and aching. One I can't get out no matter how hard I try. No matter how much I want to.

"I don't know," I whisper.

Philp goes white, his expression stricken. He ducks his head, gulps in deep breaths of air, his hands cupped behind his neck.

Tears sting my eyes, the tip of my nose. I want to reach out for him. Want to touch him. Wrap my arms around him and take his pain away.

I had that right only moments ago. Now I'm not so sure.

I hug my arms around myself. "Philip, I—"

"I love you, you know," he says, lifting his head to meet my eyes, voice raw. "That hasn't changed for me."

I didn't want it to change for me, either.

But I'm afraid it's already too late.

I'm terrified *I've* changed. And that I'll never be able to go back to how I was.

To who I was.

I brush the tears from my cheeks. "What are we going to do?"

He shakes his head. "I guess that," he says quietly, "is up to you."

* * *

Though Philip leaves where we go next up to me, I have no idea what to do, say or even think. In the end, I once again revert to what's easy and safe.

I do nothing.

For four days I go through the motions: school, tennis, dance class, homework, repeat. Repeat. Repeat. Repeat.

It's all very…normal.

Well, normal-ish.

Everything except the Philip and Astrid parts. Those are definitely against the norm.

I drive to school by myself as Astrid, who stayed home sick for three days, texted me early this morning that Sean will be taking her to school from now on.

And the last thing Philip said to me before he left my house—and the fate of our relationship in my hands—Sunday night (actually, the last thing he's said to me period) was that he'd find another ride to school for a little while.

Every day since, I make sure to get to school fifteen minutes early. Just in case he finds that ride with Jessica or another member of his fan club. Not something I need to see right now.

If only because I don't need anything else messing with my mind or with how I feel about Philip.

I eat lunch in Miss Marchand's room and pretend to work on my college apps so no one in the cafeteria can see how weird things are between us.

So no one can ask about it.

He hasn't texted me. Hasn't called.

And while part of me likes to think he's giving me space to get my head on straight, another part, a small, secret, cynical part, wonders if his silence is his way of punishing me for being honest.

For not playing the part I've always played.

For changing things between us.

It's only been four days but it's the longest we've gone without talking in years. It's weird. And sad.

I miss him.

But not as much as I thought I would.

Not as much as I should.

Which only brings more doubts to my mind. More guilt.

In other words, it's been a completely sucky week so far. And it's only Thursday.

It gets worse when I show up at the courts for what will be my very last high school tennis match, the one where all of us seniors will individually be honored by our coach.

It's an ending.

And I hate when things end.

My parents aren't here yet even though I reminded them both of the match, and the importance of it to me, every morning this week.

Chase didn't text or call me, wishing me good luck.

Neither did Leah.

I'm grabbing my stuff from my Jeep when someone calls my name. I turn, but it takes me a minute to realize it's Astrid walking toward me. She started straightening her hair last week and I'm still not used to it.

I miss her curls.

I miss *her*.

And I'm so happy to see her, so glad someone came to support me, that I'm smiling and waving before I realize that walking isn't quite the right word for what she's doing. More like stalking. Or stomping.

And then she's close enough I can see her expression, fierce and hard and ticked-off.

Definitely stomping. Maybe even storming.

Smile fading, I slowly lower my arm. "What's the matter?" I ask as soon as she reaches me.

"What's the matter?" she repeats, albeit much, much louder than I'd been. "Are you kidding?"

I glance around. The other team has filed off the bus and is making their way toward the courts in groups of twos and threes. Parents and friends are passing us, carrying blankets and lawn chairs or cushions for the bleachers.

No one has noticed my very irate, very red-faced, very loud best friend.

Yet.

"No," I say. "I'm not kidding. Is something wrong?"

"Oh, let's see…" She taps her forefinger against her lower lip as if in deep thought. "You dumped my brother, ground his heart underneath one of your high heels and shredded his pride." She drops her hand. Glares. "Yeah. I'd say something is wrong."

My stomach sinks. "What are you talking about? I didn't break up with Philip. Did…did he say I did? Did he say I broke his heart?"

Because, yeah, he was upset when he left my house Sunday night. Hurt and disappointed and even angry. But heartbroken?

I didn't think so.

But what if I was wrong? Again.

"What did he say?" I ask, grabbing her arm.

She shakes me off. "He didn't *say* anything. It's pretty clear you two aren't together anymore."

A wave of heat and nausea washes over me. I swallow carefully. "That's not true."

Philip and I are very much still together.

Aren't we?

What if…what if his silence all week isn't him giving me space or punishing me?

What if we really are over?

"Not true, huh?" She starts ticking items off on her fingers as she lists them. "You don't drive him to school anymore. You don't eat lunch with him. No one's seen you so much as say hello to him all week and he's been moping around the house since he got back from Toledo."

"That doesn't…" I stop. Clear my throat. "That doesn't mean we broke up."

She sneers. "Please. Everyone knows you hooked up with Owen Radlowski Saturday night. That you broke up with Philip to be with that loser. Though, if you ask me, Philip should've been the one to dump your ass."

The sick feeling spreads and my hands start to tingle. I look around again and yes, we're attracting some interest. "I didn't hook up with Owen. He had too much to drink and I gave him a ride home. That's it. We didn't...we're not together. I'm with Philip."

Her eyes narrow and she nods her head at something behind me. "You sure about that?"

Don't look. Don't look. Don't look.

Of course I look.

It's that stupid curiosity again. Always getting me in trouble.

There, at the edge of the grass, way, way, way back from everyone else, standing alone, hands in his jeans pockets, blond hair turning gold in the sun, is Owen. He's in another hooded sweatshirt, a dark blue pullover that I'm sure, should I venture close enough to see, brings out the color of his eyes.

I'm not. Going to venture close enough, that is. Or even closer. Nope. And I'm not going to think about how I never returned his other sweatshirt, the gray one I borrowed the night he fixed my flat. The one I keep hidden in the back corner of my closet.

The one I've worn to bed. Twice.

My first initial reaction upon seeing him, unsmiling and stand-offish and *here,* is joy. Pure, unadulterated happiness, the bright, shining kind that lights you from the inside and can't be dimmed by guilt, doubt or glowering best friends.

My second, more reasonable reaction is fear.

Followed swiftly by that oldie, but goody; denial.

I turn to Astrid. "He's not here for me."

She sneers and, to be honest, I give myself a little mental sneer as well because...ugh. Who else would he be here for? Next thing I know I'm going to try and tell her he's only here because he just loves the game of tennis.

God.

"I didn't know he'd be here," I clarify, which only reminds me that I'd told her brother pretty much the same thing, but about Owen being at Darcy's party Saturday night.

That damn party. I should have stayed home.

"I didn't ask him to come here," I try again because, hey, third time's a charm and all that. "I'm not going to talk to him."

That's been my strategy ever since I dropped him off at his house Saturday night: Avoid Owen at all costs.

Too bad I can't stop thinking about him.

But that's what this little...break...with Philip is about. Time for me to get past my confusing feelings for another boy. To get back to who I used to be.

"Do what you want," Astrid says, all snotty tone and curled upper lip, a fair imitation of her twin when he'd said something similar to me last week. "You always do."

That part is new.

"What's that supposed to mean?" I ask.

"It means you're a spoiled little bitch who doesn't care about anyone but yourself."

My head snaps back like I've been slapped. I *feel* like I've been slapped.

Or sucker punched.

"You know that's not true," I whisper hoarsely.

"I know that whatever you want, you get. I know that you wanted Philip so you went after him. It didn't matter to you how I felt about it or how it would affect our friendship. And this," she continues, "this is why I didn't want you with my brother. I knew...God...I knew you'd hurt him. That you'd get bored and go looking for something else or that he wouldn't be able to live up to your exacting standards of perfection. I knew it, but it didn't matter because once again, Princess Natalie gets her way."

I shake my head, a denial of her words, a demand that she stop saying these horrible things or maybe just a plea to myself to stop listening.

Doesn't work on any of those areas.

"Philip doesn't deserve to be treated this way," Astrid tells me, harsh and unyielding. A shark smelling blood in the water. "What he deserves is someone so much better than *you*."

She whirls on one heel and takes off the way she came; stomping, ticked-off and righteous.

Leaving me shaking and on the verge of tears.

I duck my head and gulp in huge breaths of air. Pray no one noticed our fight, that no one heard the things she said to me. That no one knows.

But a quick glance behind me confirms that's a wasted prayer.

Owen is looking right at me.

And though he's too far away to have heard anything Astrid or I said, I'm sure our body language spoke loud and clear.

No amount of praying, wishing or hoping is going to work. Is going to save me from this.

It's not going to fix this.

Once again, that's going to be up to me.

45

For obvious and myriad reasons, I lost my match.

No, more like I was annihilated. I mean, if you want to get technical about it. My opponent beat me in three straight sets. I only won four games the entire match.

Four. Out of what turned out to be twenty-two games.

You don't have to get an A in Calc to figure out that percentage equals suckage.

To cap off my very last match in high school, I completely blew it in our doubles match and even served into the back of my partner's head.

Twice.

I've never, not ever, been so glad to get home in my entire life.

If only so I can lay into my parents.

They didn't come. Neither one of them. Yeah, sure, Dad probably got stuck at the hospital; last-minute emergency, life-saving surgery, blah, blah, blah. But Mom has no excuse. No good one, anyway. Though I'm sure she'll try. Will probably say she got wrapped up painting at Kaleidoscope or had to take a very important phone call that had her losing track of time or that she totally forgot about my match or even the fact that she still has a daughter.

Whatever it is, I'm not buying it.

Except, my sucky week and horrible day continue when I get home.

They're not here, either.

Why can't people be where I want them to be?

Better yet, why can't they act the way I want them to act? Why do I always have to be the one doing the acting?

I grab my stuff from my Jeep—tennis gear, backpack, purse and my large ice caramel macchiato—lean my racket against the front tire, swing my backpack onto my shoulder, slide my purse strap over my head crosswise, and lock and shut the door.

Then tug on the handle three times and press the lock button on my key.

The lights flash.

I grab my racket, start heading toward the garage when I notice the distant whine of what sounds like a vacuum.

I whirl around, do a complete three-sixty but there's no one here, vacuuming the pavement or grass. Then I notice the lawn is a deep, lush, green. Freshly cut.

The sound seems to get louder the longer I stand there, a signal calling me. But I won't heed it. I'm pretty sure I know where it's coming from just as I'm positive I know what I need to do.

Be smart. Be careful. Do what's right.

And the only way to do all those things is to go inside.

But I'm not smart. Not careful. And I'm not sure I care anymore about doing what's right.

Because I once again lean my racket against my front tire, set my coffee on the hood, take off my purse and put it there as well then slide off my backpack and drop it to the pavement.

And go around the house to the backyard, cross that deep, lush, freshly cut grass and head down the path to the guest house.

My heart pounds with each step I take, the sound echoing in my ears. The farther I go, the louder the whining sound gets, pulling me closer and closer until I'm standing in the clearing. The house is small, cottage style with a porch and windows on either side of the front door. Dad had it built for his parents to live in when they retired except Papa and Mimi only made it through one Western Pennsylvania winter before hightailing it to Florida. Now it mostly sits empty though Mom makes sure it gets a top-to-bottom cleaning once a month and, of course, the small yard is tended to weekly.

This week, as it's been for the past two years, it's being tended by Owen.

He's in the side yard under the huge maple tree, a leaf blower strapped to his back.

Owen is here. At my house. Sort of.

I turn around to walk away while I still can.

Owen is here and I'm here.

And that's the whole problem because in no situation does the two of us being alone together add up to a good thing.

Yeah. I should definitely, *definitely* leave.

But as tempted as I am to go, I have to admit, I'm more tempted to stay.

So I turn back around. He hasn't noticed me yet and I can't help but watch him. He moves in slow, steady steps, adding more and more leaves to the pile. He took off his sweatshirt and his white T-shirt clings to his back and shoulders, the muscles in his arms flexing and contracting as he sweeps the leaf blower side to side.

My mouth goes dry. Who knew yard work could be so enticing?

It shouldn't be. Damn it, he has no right to make it be that way. To make me feel this way, nervous and excited and scared.

Owen goes still, his shoulders tensing. Turning by slow degrees, he faces me and when our eyes meet, I wish I'd' left when I had the chance.

Hindsight. Such a fun way to rub your nose in your mistakes.

And suddenly, I'm furious. Seeing red, blood boiling, kicking and screaming furious. I'm so freaking tired of feeling guilty. Of being the one to make concessions. The one who compromises.

I'm mad at Astrid for the things she said, for not taking my side, for not being a better friend.

I'm hurt and disappointed in my parents for not showing up at my match. At my mom for not being who she used to be. At Chase for ignoring me.

I'm angry with Philip for having separate rules for what he can do and what I can do. For putting the entire responsibility of fixing what's wrong between us on me.

But mostly, I am totally and completely pissed off at Owen.

He turns the machine off as I storm up to him.

"What are you doing here?" I demand.

"Working," he says, sliding the motor thingie off his back. There's a slight bump on the bridge of his nose, but his bruises have faded to a mottled purple, his stitches not so red and angry looking.

No, the only thing angry here is me.

"You came here on purpose!" I snap.

He frowns. Gives me a look like I've lost my mind.

Could be, Blondie Boy. Could just be.

"This is where I work."

"You came to my tennis match."

Okay, I do sort of sound like a crazy person, narrating the things he's done, but I can't help it.

I'm feeling a bit crazy. Or at least, out of control.

His response?

A shrug.

And then he walks away.

"Oh, no, you don't," I say, chasing after him.

He doesn't stop until he reaches the porch. His sweatshirt is draped over the railing next to a full sports drink bottle. He reaches for the drink and I grab his arm, yanking him around to face me.

"You don't get to just—" I mimic his shrug and his stupid, stoic expression "—and walk away." I slam my hands on my hips. "Why did you come to my tennis match?"

He hesitates. Drops his gaze for a moment. "I wanted to see you play."

"You left after the first set."

"I had to get to work." He hesitates. Rubs a hand over his head, causing his hair to stick up. "And you were struggling. I thought you'd do better if I wasn't there."

Struggling. Yes, I'm struggling. Struggling to figure out how to get back to who I used to be. Struggling to decide whether or not I even want to be that person anymore.

"You left," I repeat, shakily. I'm trembling and would love nothing more than to blame it on the cool breeze and the fact that I'm still in my tennis uniform. "You were the only person who was there for me and you left."

"You were upset. I thought I was making it worse." He hesitates. "I saw you and Panos' sister."

"She's mad at me. Everyone's mad at me," I say, tears clogging my throat. "Astrid. Philip." I swallow. "You."

He stares at the ground. "What do you want from me, Natalie?"

I hug my arms around myself. "I...I..."

He lifts his head. Softens his voice. "The truth."

The truth. God. I'm not even sure I know what that is anymore.

"I don't know."

It's the same thing I told Philip Sunday night when he asked if I had feelings for Owen.

It is the truth.

And it's a lie.

"Tell me," Owen says, a quiet demand. A plea. "Why did you come out here? Why did you drive me home Saturday night?"

I can't answer the first so I focus on the second. "I was worried you'd get into an accident if you drove. I helped you," I say, latching on to that fact, riding it for all it's worth. "And you didn't even thank me."

"I didn't ask for your help."

"No, but you needed it."

"You have no idea what I need," he says in this low, husky tone that reverberates in my chest. "No idea what I want."

But we both know that's a lie. I do know.

I'm just not strong enough, not nearly brave enough to admit I want it, too.

The truth of it, finally set free, is like a kick in the stomach. The air whooshes from my lungs and I bend over, trying to breathe, arms wrapped around my waist as if holding myself together.

What is wrong with me? This isn't me. I'm not the type of person who likes some other guy. I have a boyfriend. The only boy I've ever loved.

But what if...what if Philip is not, as I'd once thought, the *only* boy I'll ever love?

"What's the matter?" Owen asks, tone concerned, hand on my back gentle. "Are you sick?"

A bubble of hysterical laughter rises in my throat but I swallow it down, down, down. Yes, that must be it, I'm sick.

Or just crazy.

I straighten. "You said I was beautiful."

He goes completely still and I wonder if he was too drunk to even remember what he said to me that night I drove him home from Darcy's.

I don't think I'll ever forget it.

"You know you're beautiful," he says.

"I didn't know you think so," I whisper then lick my lips. "How do you...how do you feel when you're with me?"

Shaking his head, he takes a step back. "Don't."

But I can't stop. It's as if something inside of me has busted loose. Has burst free.

I don't want to have these feelings for him but since I do, since I can no longer ignore them or pretend they don't exist, I need to know that it's not just me.

I need to know it's him, too.

"I see how you look at me," I say, my voice soft. Unsteady.

His mouth flattens and when he speaks, it's through clenched teeth. "I'm not doing this."

"Not doing what?"

"I'm not going to make your choice for you."

But I want him to! I want him to say something, do something that will take the choice out of my hands. So I can claim I was swept away.

That it wasn't my fault.

But he won't do it.

One more decision that's up to me.

Another choice that's mine to make.

I don't think. I don't weigh the pros and cons. Don't make a mental list of all the ways it's right or wrong. I don't play it safe or take the easy way.

I don't do what's right.

For once, I do what I really want.

I throw my arms around his neck, press against him and pull his head down.

And I kiss him.

He jerks, as if he's been shocked, but then he groans, wraps his arms around me, fists one hand in my shirt, pulls me even closer and kisses me back.

His other hand goes to the back of my neck, his palm cradling my head, fingers in my hair. He turns us around so that I'm pressed back against the railing. The spindles dig into my back but I don't care. I just keep kissing Owen. Touching him, my hands sweeping across his shoulders and down his arms then back up. My fingers diving into his short, soft hair, tracing the hard line of his jaw.

We kiss and kiss and kiss and it's...God...it's wonderful. Perfect.

And so very, very wrong.

I slide my hands between us and press gently on his chest and he immediately lets me go. Covering my mouth with my trembling hand, I stare at him, horrified by what just happened.

By what I'd just done.

Miserable and sick because I want to do it again.

My eyes well with tears and I push past him, feeling Owen's fingers brush against my arm as he tries to reach for me. "Natalie, wait..."

But I don't wait.

I run.

<h1 style="text-align:center">46</h1>

I RUN, FAST AND HARD, DOWN THE DIRT PATH, THROUGH THE WOODS, spurred on by my panic and the fact that if Owen really wanted to catch me, he could. My sneakers slap against the ground, my lungs burn. Ahead of me, the sun is setting behind the rolling hills behind my house, casting everything in shadows. I pick up speed, getting closer and closer to the edge of our lawn when my toe catches on something and I pitch forward, landing on my hands and knees.

I scramble to my feet, keep running, ignoring the sharp sting in my knees. I run and run and run; across the thick grass, around the side of the house, past my Jeep and my tennis racket and backpack and purse and coffee. Through the garage and into the kitchen.

I slam the door shut. Lock it.

Then lean against it, shut my eyes and slide to the floor, legs bent and curled into my chest. I wrap my arms around my knees, press my forehead against them. I'm shaking. My teeth chattering, my skin covered in goosebumps.

I am a horrible, horrible person.

I've done the unthinkable. The unforgivable. I've broken Philip's trust.

Someone knocks on the door and I yelp and jump, my elbow hitting the door with a thud.

"Natalie?" Owen calls through the door. "You in there?"

Pressing my lips together I shut my eyes. Stay absolutely still.

I didn't close the garage door.

It's yet one more mistake and I've already made too many. I didn't close the garage door and now Owen is in my garage. He's knocking on my door.

Oh, God. What if he asks more of those questions I can't answer? More of those questions he has no right to ask?

"Natalie?" He knocks again. "I just want to make sure you're okay."

And him being thoughtful is the last thing I need right now.

I stay silent, stare at my legs. That's when I notice my knees are scraped and scratched, dirt and pebbles mixing with blood. The heels of my palms are red and abraded.

"Just tell me you're okay," Owen says, still in that same quiet, soothing tone.

I cover my ears. Start rocking, back and forth. Back and forth. Back and forth. I count the seconds. One minute. Then two. Then three.

Heart racing, I pull my hands away from my ears. Wait another minute.

"Please, Natalie."

At his gruff plea, I shoot to my feet. Run out of the kitchen before I give in and open the door.

I go into my bathroom, turn on the shower as hot as it will go. Steam fills the room and I toe off my sneakers, strip off my clothes and get under the spray.

It's like I'm cleansing myself of my sin, ridding my skin of any and all lingering residue of what happened. I wash away the scent of Owen, the feel of his fist pressed against my back, of his hand in my hair. The way his mouth moved over mine, the light touch of his tongue. The taste of him.

I scrub and scrub and scrub with brisk, rough strokes, taking the sharp sting in my knees and palms, the burn of the water as my penance. Doing the full body lathering and rinse cycle three times.

And then I leave my head under the spray of hot water and cry until the water cools. Until I have nothing left and I'm completely empty inside.

After I dry off, I put on a pair of flannel, pajama pants and one of Philip's old sweatshirts. It's full on dark now but my house is eerily quiet.

Too quiet.

My parents still aren't home.

I want to cry all over again.

I really, really want my mom.

Leaving the lights off, hair dripping down my back, I make my way downstairs. Tiptoe across the kitchen and press my ear against the door.

Nothing.

I hold my breath and slowly turn the lock, wincing at the sound of it unclicking. Wait a moment then open the door. My stuff is on the floor; my tennis racket and backpack and purse and ice coffee.

Owen is gone.

The garage door is still open so I push the button on the wall. Grab my purse and backpack as it steadily lowers to the ground. I carry them inside, turn to get my racket and cup when I hear the faint sound of my phone buzzing from inside my purse.

Biting my lower lip, I stare at my purse on the table. What if it's Owen?

Or worse. What if it's Philip?

Because that would be my luck lately, having my boyfriend decide to end his almost week-long silent treatment an hour after I kissed another boy.

It stops buzzing and I quickly bring in the rest of my stuff. Set it down and dig my phone out of my purse. It wasn't Owen. Or Philip.

It was my mom.

And she's called four times in the past two hours. Has texted me three times.

Where are you?

Answer your phone!

CALL ME!!

I go cold all over, my feet turning to ice. She wouldn't call me that many times to tell me she's at Kaleidoscope and will be home late. Wouldn't text me that unless something was wrong.

I press the button for her number and she answers after the first ring. "Natalie. Thank God. Where have you been?"

"My tennis match," I manage to say, fear threatening to choke my vocal chords. "What's wrong?"

I clutch the phone, wait for her to say nothing's wrong. For her to laugh and gently chide me about worrying so much. To warn me not to borrow trouble when everything's perfect. Like it always is.

I wait. But her denial doesn't come.

"It's your brother," she says and though her tone starts calm, her voice wobbles on the last word. As if she's trying to be strong for my benefit but is close to breaking down. "There's been an...accident."

My grip tightens on the phone. My hands go clammy. An accident? Chase?

"Is he...is he okay?" She doesn't answer, and I hear the soft sound of crying. My own tears return as my fear spikes. "Mom?"

There's murmuring on the other end of the line as Mom talks to someone then my dad's familiar voice as he responds.

"Daddy?" I cry, hoping he can hear me. "Daddy, what's going on? Is Chase okay?"

Oh, please...please, please, please...let him be okay.

"Natalie," Dad says in his doctor voice, equal parts professional briskness and personal compassion, "your brother is in the Critical Care Unit at UPMC Altoona."

Critical Care Unit? *Oh, God, oh, God, oh, God...*

"I'm on my way," I say, already running upstairs. "I'm leaving now."

I half-expect him to tell me not come. That Chase is going to be just fine and that he doesn't want me driving by myself in the dark the almost three hours it'll take me to get to Altoona.

I half-expect him to say all that. Hope and pray he does.

Instead he softly says, "Hurry."

So I do.

47

———

It happens as I'm driving across the Fourth Avenue Bridge over the river.

It didn't start there. It started the moment I pulled out of my driveway after getting dressed and packing an overnight bag. My usual nervousness about driving alone, driving alone at night, was stronger than usual. But I pushed myself to just keep going.

Until I came to this stupid bridge.

I tried holding my breath but there's so much anxiety inside of me, ballooning in my chest, there's no room for air. I inch along, keep my gaze straight ahead but I know…I just know if I keep driving, I'm going to veer off the side and plunge into the murky river. It plays in my head like a movie—my Jeep hitting the water, me sitting frozen as I sink, lower and lower. Screaming for help. Trapped as the water pours in, cold and lethal, filling the interior.

It covers my feet then my legs. My hips and my chest. Rising and rising to my shoulders and chin—

Someone lays on their horn and I blink. Force myself to inhale past the tightness in my chest. Oh, God. I've stopped in the middle of the bridge, my hands strangling the steering wheel, my head tipped back as if trying to avoid that rising water.

326

The rising water that's a complete figment of my imagination.

But I feel like I'm drowning anyway.

The person behind me beeps again, angry and impatient, in a hurry to pick up some dinner or get home after a long day at work. Heat suffuses me. My eyes water. I'm blocking the vehicles behind me and since it's only a two-lane bridge and steady with evening traffic, no one can drive around me.

I have to move.

But I'm not sure I can.

When the person behind me beeps for a third time, I gently press the gas pedal. I crawl forward, slowly, carefully, then press the gas harder, increasing my speed to around fifteen miles per hour. It's slow and painful but eventually, finally, I get all the way across without stopping again.

Or, you know, plunging to my death, so...yay.

I go at a crawl, palms sweaty, my grip on the wheel so tight, my knuckles are white, my hands aching. I signal and slow even more to turn into the Methodist Church's parking lot, but it's half-full, not empty like I'd hoped.

There's that hope again. Always coming back to bite a girl in the butt.

Still, I can't drive any farther. I have to stop. Get my bearings. Catch my breath. I pull into the lot and, spying an empty spot in the far corner, head that way. I'm halfway there when someone starts backing out of their spot in front of me. Even though I'm barely moving, I stomp on my brakes so hard, I'm jerked forward, my seatbelt digging into the side of my neck. Breathing fast, leg aching from pressing the brake so hard, I wait for the car to back up.

It takes me a good fifteen seconds before I realize they're waiting for me to go.

Which is super polite and all—whoopee for good manners—but now I have to drive past them and I'm scared they're going to change their mind or else they stopped to check their phone or read a quick Bible passage because this is a church after all, or else they don't really want me to go or possibly didn't even see me in the first place.

And as soon as I pull forward, they're going to back up into me.

I consider giving my horn a light tap, letting them know I want them to go first, but if they do, there won't be much room for them to get past me and I have visions of me sideswiping them. Or hitting them head-on.

Plus, I'm not sure I can let go of the steering wheel long enough to beep the horn so that idea is out.

I creep forward, holding my breath until I'm past them. Keep my eyes on that empty spot in the corner. Almost there...almost there...

I pull into the spot and, with unsteady hands, put the Jeep into Park. Roll down all four windows and take in huge, grateful gulps of the cool, night air. I try all my tricks; counting to five and back again but I go too fast and my breathing goes quick and shallow. Listing the states in alphabetical order but I only get to Idaho before my mind blanks, which only causes me to feel more anxious that I can't remember what comes next.

I picture the wall of flowers in my bedroom, the one thing, the only thing that always, always works, but it's not the same, imagining it, and the image is fuzzy and blurred, like some impressionist painting.

There's a loud, buzzing sound in my head. I'm sweating and nauseous and shaking.

I sit there for five minutes. Then ten. My sweat cools. My stomach and breathing both settle.

Only the shaking remains.

Still, I have to go. I told Dad I was leaving and I don't want him to worry if I arrive late.

He and Mom have enough on their minds.

I sit up straight, press the brake and put the Jeep into Reverse. Check behind me, left then right. Check my mirrors. No cars pulling in or out, no one driving past.

But I have to check again.

And again.

And again.

I check and I recheck.

But I don't move.

I can't.

Oh, God. I can't do it. I can't drive all the way to Altoona.

I can't even back out of this parking spot.

Makes sense. If ever there was a day destined for my complete and utter mental breakdown, this would be it.

Except I don't have time for a breakdown. Can't do that to my parents. They need me. Chase needs me.

I have to be strong.

I have to be strong and smart and careful.

Most of all, I have to keep playing my part.

And to do that, I have to keep pretending everything is fine.

Especially me.

* * *

It's past midnight when I get to the hospital.

I texted Dad from the church parking lot and told him something was wrong with my Jeep and he bought me a plane ticket out of Pittsburgh. But I missed the last, nonstop flight to Altoona and had to get one to State College instead, which had a layover in D.C.

Why is nothing easy?

God.

I get an Uber from the State College airport to the hospital in Altoona—just like I got one from the parking lot to the Pittsburgh airport—and find Mom, Dad and Leah in a small waiting room outside the CCU.

And once again, I'm crying.

"Mom," I say, and she looks up, her face drawn and tired.

And scared. So very, very scared.

Her own eyes fill, and she lifts a hand to her wobbling mouth as she stands. "Oh, honey..."

Then she holds out her arms.

I drop my bag and run to her. We hug, and Dad comes over and wraps his arms around both of us. Kisses me on the top of my head.

It helps. It helps a lot.

I can finally breathe.

Just not fully. Not until I know Chase is okay.

After a moment we break apart, Mom and I both sniffling. Mom presses a tissue into my hand, and I wipe my eyes and nose. Turn to Leah. Her dark red hair is pulled back, her face pale, her eyeliner and mascara smudged.

"Hey," I say, giving her a hug.

She squeezes me hard. "He's going to be okay," she whispers to me. "He's going to be fine."

Nodding, I let go. Step back. "I know."

But, of course, that's a lie.

One I desperately want to be true.

Mom and Dad are standing with their arms around each other's waist, Mom's head on Dad's shoulder.

"What happened?" I ask. "You said there was an accident? A car accident?"

They exchange a look. Behind me, Leah makes a sound of distress.

No one answers me.

Anxiety spikes through me and there's a sick taste in my mouth. I swallow it down.

"Was Chase driving?" I ask as image after image of Chase and his frat buddies flick through my mind, like I'm scrolling through his Instagram account. Image after image of him with a beer bottle or mixed drink or red plastic cup in his hand. I wipe my palms down the front of my yoga pants. "Was he...was he drinking and driving?"

"No," Mom says. "Nothing like that."

Thank God.

But something's not right. Their hesitancy doesn't add up.

Whatever happened is even worse than I thought.

"What aren't you telling me?"

Dad sighs, looking older than I've ever seen him. "Your brother overdosed."

Mom starts crying again. Leah comes up beside me and takes my hand.

I hold on tight.

"Over—" I stop. Swallow. "Overdosed? But you...you said there'd been an accident."

"It *was* an accident," Mom says, quick and firm. She looks at Dad, wet eyes wide and beseeching. "It was."

But he just shuts his eyes.

My mind blanks for a moment, but then understanding washes over me and I rear back, wanting to get as far away from their meaning as possible.

"You..." I trail off. My voice is barely a whisper. My throat aches, like there's a peach pit lodged there, wedged in so tight, I can't clear it away. But I have to ask. I have to know. "You think he did it on...on purpose?"

"No," Mom says, crying harder, at the same time Dad says, "We won't know that until Chase wakes up."

No. No. That's not possible. Chase is clean. He's clean and honest and has everything under control. He told me so just a few weeks ago. He doesn't take drugs. Doesn't lie to us.

Doesn't keep secrets.

Not anymore.

And he'd never, ever, try to hurt himself.

Except, he obviously does take drugs. He took so many he wound up in the CCU. He's been lying to us all for weeks...maybe even months.

What if...what if that's not his only secret? For all we know, he could've been hiding something else, too. Emotional or psychological pain.

Something so far out of his control, the only way he could stop it was to get high.

Or worse.

"He will wake up, though," I say, looking at Dad, needing his reassurance. Needing a small bit of hope I can hold onto. "Right?"

"He's stable," Dad says slowly, not giving me anything at all, "which is the most we can ask for at this point. All we can do now is wait."

"Excuse me," Mom says, her voice breaking, then she hurries out of the room.

I should go after her, should try and comfort her, but I can't move. It feels as if my lungs are being squeezed in a vise, and I'm fighting for every breath, each inhale sharp. Each exhale shaky.

I watch her go, feeling helpless. Useless.

And so very, very weak.

"Why don't you and Leah get your mother a coffee?" Dad says, pulling out his wallet. He hands me some cash. "Get us all something to eat."

I blink at the money, but I don't move and it's Leah who takes the cash.

"We'll be right back," she tells my dad as she lets go of my hand. "Come on," she says to me. "I know where there are some vending machines."

Wrapping her arm around my waist, she guides me out into the hall.

We don't speak as we make our way toward the elevators and I try to get my thoughts centered. To calm down before someone notices there's something wrong.

There is something so very wrong with me. Something I need to fix. Now. Right now.

I count doors as we pass—one, two, three, four, five, six, seven...

But my mind won't settle.

When we reach the elevator, Leah pushes the button with her free hand. The doors open and she steps forward, but when I start to take a step as well, I suddenly freeze, my heart racing. Everything inside of me balks at getting into the elevator, at being shut in that small space, but Leah's arm is still around my waist and I can't do anything, can't say anything that will make her think something's wrong.

You know, other than my brother being unconscious and possibly dying from a drug overdose, that is.

I can't do or say anything that will make her think something's wrong with *me*.

So I get on the elevator, leaning against the far wall as Leah lets go of me and presses the floor button.

I watch the doors slowly shut, my breathing shallow. Ragged. It's stupid. There's plenty of room in here, more than enough space—and oxygen—for me, Leah and at least twenty more people, but it feels as if the walls are inching closer and closer to me. As if the air itself is thick and unbreathable.

The elevator moves and my stomach drops. Prickles of heat engulf me, and I start sweating.

"Are you okay?" Leah asks, frowning at me in concern.

Nodding, I lay my hand on my stomach. Swallow the sick taste rising in my throat. "Just a little nauseous. I haven't eaten since lunch. How about you?" I ask, needing to get the focus off me. "How are you holding up?"

"Best I can. It just...it doesn't even seem real, you know?"

My throat clogs. "Yeah. I know."

Reaching up, Leah takes the band from her hair and puts it on her wrist then combs her fingers through her hair. She drops her hands and her hair falls, straight and silky, the blunt ends barely grazing her shoulders.

"You cut your hair," I blurt then wince. It's a dumb thing to say, telling someone something they already know.

Dumb and inane and, at a time like this, completely unimportant.

"Oh. Yes." She tucks one side behind her ear. "A few months ago."

A few months ago?

I try to remember the last time I saw her. She rarely posts on social media and when she does, it's usually scenery shots of campus or Philadelphia. And she only comes home during the longer breaks —Christmas and Spring Break.

Has it really been months?

How did that happen?

"It looks great," I say belatedly, because when you bring up someone's new look, the least you can do is compliment them on it. Plus, it's the truth. "I bet Chase loves it."

Flushing, Leah drops her gaze and shrugs.

Before I can ask if my brother said something completely idiotic —like how much he loved her long hair, how he wished she hadn't cut it—the elevator finally stops and the doors open, releasing us from the death box.

I follow Leah down the quiet hall and around the corner where there are several vending machines. Leah gives me the money and I get Mom's coffee, adding sugar to her regular cream-only brew.

We could all use a little extra dose of sweetness right now.

"Did you suspect?" I ask Leah softly as I stare at our reflections in the glass of the vending machine. "That Chase was using again?"

Leah was the only one of us who knew before. The only reason Chase got help in the first place.

"No. Not using. I...I know he's been drinking a lot lately, though. When I tried to talk to him about it, he blew me off."

"Me, too."

The stupid, stubborn idiot.

Oh, please, please, let him be all right.

I get Mom's coffee. Hand it to Leah to hold while I pick out food items. There's fresh fruit so I get a couple bananas and oranges. Leah gets a granola bar and I pick a bag of mixed nuts for Dad and a nonfat, sugar-free yogurt for Mom.

And a king-size Snicker's bar for me.

We're heading toward the elevators, our hands full, when I spy the door leading to the stairwell.

"Do you mind if we take the stairs?" I ask as casually as possible, as if it's a simple request and not one born out of my desire to not lose my freaking mind on the return trip to the CCU. "I did so much sitting on the planes...I'd like to stretch my legs a bit."

"That's fine."

"I'm really glad you're here," I tell her, our footsteps echoing in the empty stairway. "I know Mom and Dad are, too. I mean, I know you're not a part of our family officially—at least not yet—"

She stops suddenly, looking stricken, her eyes welling with tears.

"What?" I ask. "Did I say something wrong?"

"No. No, it's not you." She licks her lips. "There's something I need to tell you, but you have to promise me you won't say anything to your parents."

My eyes widen and I flick a glance at her belly. "Oh, my God. Are you pregnant?"

She goes beet-red, the curse of having such a fair complexion, I guess. "No. Nothing like that." Shifting her feet, she inhales deeply. "The reason I didn't know, or even suspect Chase was using again is because we...we broke up."

I shake my head, my scalp prickling painfully. "I don't...I don't understand."

"We broke up," she repeats gently. "I thought Chase told you after you texted me last month about not hearing from him, but when your parents called me this afternoon, I realized he didn't and I just... I can't bear to tell your mom and dad. Not now. But I hate lying to them. Hate all this pretending."

Pretending. Ha. The Hewitt family motto.

I can't even process what she's telling me. It can't be right. "Wait a minute. You were broken up when I texted you last month?"

"We broke up at the end of August."

August. I'm stunned. That's over two months ago.

But...but...I asked Chase about Leah the night of Mom and Dad's anniversary party and he said everything was fine between them.

Didn't he?

"I'm really sorry to put this on you," Leah continues, "but I had to tell someone. Just promise me you won't tell your parents. Not until Chase is doing better."

I shake my head, my mind whirling. "I won't. I promise. But...this is just temporary, right? I mean, whatever happened, you two can work through it."

She smiles, but it's sad. Almost pitying because I am just so darn sweet and naïve with my silly, hopeful, fantasies. "I don't think so."

And I know, with sudden clarity, their breakup wasn't some mutual decision, discussed and debated calmly and rationally.

"You broke up with him."

It comes out a cross between disbelief and accusing, but Leah holds my gaze, strong and steady and, it seems, guilt-free.

"Yes."

"He was using," I say. "Whatever he did or said...that wasn't him. Not really. And once he gets clean again, things will be different. Better."

"I hope so. For his sake. For all your sakes. But it won't change my decision." Her tone softens. "I love Chase. I'll always love him, but I just...I can't do it anymore. I can't put up with the lies and the secrets. I can't keep coming in second in his life. It's not fair. I deserve more. I deserve better."

I want to argue with her. I want plead Chase's case, remind Leah of how much they love each other, all the plans they had. I want to beg her not to give up on him. But I can't. I can't pick his side over hers, even though he is my brother. Because she's right. She does deserve better than to come in second in her boyfriend's life, behind his secrets and lies and addictions.

She deserves better.

Just like Astrid said Philip deserves better than me.

48

───────

It's the longest night of my life.

Around 2:00 a.m., Mom and Dad tried to get Leah and me to go to a hotel to get some rest but we both refused.

We want to be here when Chase wakes up.

We spend the long, dragging minutes in silence, Mom staring at the walls, Leah looking at her phone. Dad's on his phone, rescheduling surgeries, getting other doctors to cover for him for a few days.

Me? I just sit, but I don't stay still. I fidget, curling my leg under me then straightening it. Crossing my ankle over my knee then putting my foot back on the floor. And I jiggle my leg. Tap my forefinger and middle finger against the arm of the chair.

Jiggle jiggle, tap tap.

Jiggle jiggle, tap tap.

I can't stop. There's this pressure inside of me, like water boiling, steam building and building and I'm afraid if I don't do something to relieve it, I'm going to start screaming like a tea kettle.

My phone sits, heavy and silent, in the waistband of my yoga pants. I turned it off once I got to the hospital. I don't want to look at it. Can't imagine scrolling through Instagram or seeing what people are doing on Snapchat.

337

But mostly, I'm afraid to turn it on. Worried I'll have missed calls and waiting text messages.

Calls and texts from Owen.

Scared I'll respond.

Great. Now I'm thinking about Owen.

Again.

But instead of only thinking about the things he's said, the way he looks at me, how I feel when I'm with him, I have that kiss to replay over and over and over in my mind.

I squeeze my eyes shut. Ugh.

The pressure is still inside of me so I blow out a heavy breath, but it's not enough and I keep exhaling and exhaling until I'm forced to breathe in a wheezing, desperate breath. I need a distraction. I count the number of chairs in the waiting room—there are nine which, as a big fan of the number three, I can truly appreciate, but it seems as if there should be an even number of them. Then I count the magazines which takes a bit more time as they're spread out on a table in the center, piled up on smaller tables next to two of the chairs and lined up on a hanging magazine rack.

Which means I have to oh-so-casually walk around the room and rifle through them all, pretending I'm looking for something to read. When I'm done—there are thirty-one—I take a five-year-old copy of *People* back to my chair and blindly flip through it as I mentally list all the characters I can think of in the *Toy Story* movies, leg once more jiggling away.

I sit and count and list and jiggle and think and think and think some more.

And when a nurse walks in at 4:15 a.m., I jump to my feet along with Mom and Dad and hope and pray that this time, they'll tell us Chase's condition has improved.

She doesn't. Just gives my parents an update.

If you consider *no change* being an update, that is.

I glance at Leah. She's curled up in her chair, one of the blankets the nurse brought us a few hours ago covering her. Her head is back, her eyes closed. Her mouth open slightly.

I still can't believe she and Chase broke up. They've always been so solid. So strong.

They were supposed to last forever. Like Mom and Dad.

Like me and Philip.

Except, I'm no longer certain forever is in Philip's and my future.

Not after everything I've done.

I messed up. I messed up so badly.

Just like Chase did with Leah.

God. I can't believe I bought all that crap he spouted the night of Mom and Dad's anniversary.

No need to worry. I have everything under control.

If you want you and Philip together, forever, choose it. And make it happen.

What. A. Crock.

Chase obviously had nothing under control or we wouldn't be here, half out of our minds with fear. As far as choosing to be with someone, yes, that's important, but it's not everything. If it was, Chase would've chosen Leah.

And she would have continued choosing him.

End of story.

No, there's so much more to being with someone. It's like what Mom said the night Dad caught Philip and me in the kitchen. A relationship takes work. Compromise.

Any kind of relationship.

All kinds of relationships.

Yes, yes, she also said I was young and could change my mind about what I wanted, but that hasn't gotten me anywhere.

At least, nowhere I want to be.

Change one thing and everything changes.

Truer words have never floated through my head.

I don't want this. I don't want to be this person. The type of girl who cheats on her boyfriend. Who plays games and keeps a guy hanging by a thread. Chase lost Leah because of his secrets and lies. Because he didn't put her first.

I did the same thing to Philip.

I made a mistake. A huge one.

Now I just want everything to be how it used to be. How it was before I started tutoring Owen. Before doubts and fears crept in and had me second guessing myself. My feelings.

I want everything to go back to normal.

Before I can change my mind, I stand. "I'll be right back," I whisper to my mom. She nods and I head out into the hall, keep walking, my shoes squeaking on the shiny floor, and duck into the Ladies' restroom.

It's empty, the toilet seats all up from a recent scrubbing, and I go into the last stall. Shut and lock the door, pull out my phone and turn it on.

And call Philip.

It rings six times then goes to voicemail. I hang up. Check the time.

4:27.

He gets up at 5:30 for his shift at the restaurant. Still has an hour left to sleep. I should let him. But now that I've made my decision, I need to follow through with it. Now. Right now. I need to apologize for the distance between us. I need to tell him that I love him. That I'll always love him.

And I need to confess what happened with Owen at the guest house.

So Philip can forgive me.

Then we can move on. Go back to how we should be.

I call again and this time he answers, his voice low and rumbly and sleep-laden. "'Lo?"

"Hi." I have to clear my throat. "Hi," I say again. "It's me. Sorry to wake you."

There's a pause and I can't help but think he's trying to decide whether or not to hang up on me.

"Nat?" he asks, sounding more awake. "You okay? Did something happen?"

Yes. Oh, God, yes, but even though I know I have to tell him I kissed Owen, even though it's the right thing to do and Philip needs to know...I can't. Not like this. Not over the phone. He deserves to be told face-to-face, to have me look him in the eyes when I admit what I've done. To apologize for it.

All very good, very sound reasons for keeping one last secret, but the truth is, I don't tell him because I'm a coward. Because I'm afraid he won't forgive me, no matter how sorry I am.

That if he finds out I kissed Owen, we'll never be able to go back to how we were.

We'll end.

I'm not ready for that. Don't want that. I know that now.

"It's Chase," I say. "He's...there's been an accident."

"He okay?"

"We're not sure. He's in the CCU. In Altoona. That's where I am. I just..." I squeeze my phone harder. "I'm scared," I admit softly. "He's still unconscious and I'm scared he won't wake up." I take a deep, careful inhale. "And I'm scared I've lost you."

He sighs. "You haven't lost me, Nat."

"I'm sorry," I say, quick and fierce. "I'm so sorry about everything. And I was hoping that when I get back to town, maybe we could talk. Figure out a way to move on. Together."

"I'd like that," he says gruffly.

I shut my eyes in relief. "I'll text you later. Let you know how Chase is and when I'm coming home."

"Okay," he says around a yawn.

"I'll let you get back to sleep. Philip, I..." There's a lump in my throat but I speak around it, forcing out what I should've said to him last weekend on my patio. "I love you."

But the words feel foreign on my tongue, heavy and acidic, and I'm desperate to believe it's because I haven't said them enough lately. Haven't told him nearly enough.

Haven't told him it first in a very long time.

"Love you, too, babe," he says huskily.

I end the call and press my forehead against the cool, metal door.

And don't feel one bit better.

* * *

Chase wakes up Saturday afternoon.

He won't let me see him.

Mom and Dad go in. So does Leah. One at a time they take turns sitting next to his bed. Holding his hand. Talking to him. Telling him how much they care about him. How happy they are he pulled through. Offering their support and encouragement that he can get clean for good.

I sit in the waiting room.

It guts me. But I don't let on. I act like it's fine. That my brother refusing to let me into his room, refusing to talk to me, doesn't bother me one teeny, tiny bit. I do it because I don't want to cause any problems. Because Mom isn't crying so much and Dad doesn't look so haggard.

I do it because I know my part.

And I need to go back to playing it well.

I'm not the only one playing a part.

Leah pretends she and Chase are still together. She told me he asked her to keep up the charade until he's stronger, but promised he'd tell them soon.

I'm pretty sure he's hoping if they pretend to be together long enough, he can convince her to take him back for real.

Another Hewitt family trait—ever-hopeful delusions.

Leah went along with it. Guess it's hard to say no to someone who literally almost died.

Sunday night, she leaves to go back to school and Dad goes home Monday night. I convince him to let me stay a few more days so I can be here for Mom, but really, I'm hoping Chase will change his mind and let me see him.

He doesn't.

By Wednesday evening, Chase is doing well enough to be moved to a regular room, and Dad insists I need to get back to school.

He's right, of course. It's time. Past time for me to get back to my old life.

Past time for things to go back to normal.

49

When Dad and I get into town Thursday afternoon, he takes me
to the garage to pick up my Jeep. They couldn't find anything wrong
with it, so I had the all-clear to drive myself to school to collect the
work I missed.

Lucky me.

It wasn't so bad, not nearly as awful as I thought it was going to
be. Yes, I was a bit shaky, and okay, maybe I drove even slower than
normal, but I did it.

I did it because I'm determined.

I did it because I am in control.

Hey, if I say it enough times, it's bound to come true eventually.

It's the middle of fifth period when I'm heading up the empty
stairwell to my locker, my arms laden with books and papers and all
the many, many things I need to do and catch up on when I hear footsteps above me. I lift my head.

And see Owen heading straight toward me.

Because of course he is the first person I see when I
get back.

What is with my luck?

My toe catches on the tread and I stumble but manage to catch my balance before taking a faceplant on the step. Breathing hard, I turn away from him slightly.

Stepping onto the landing, he raises his eyebrows as if he can read my mind. "Going to run away from me again, Natalie?"

That's the plan.

I start down the stairs when his next quiet words stop me cold.

"I'll come after you."

It's not a threat, exactly. More like a promise.

One I don't believe.

Yes, he came after me after our kiss but he didn't text me. Hasn't called.

It's his pride that's bruised, I tell myself. Nothing more.

I glance around. Lick my lips. We're still alone but that could change at any moment and the last thing I need is someone seeing us here, together, like some clandestine meeting.

Not when I'm trying to get my old life back.

Not when I'm trying to fix things with Philip.

No, the last thing I need is for Owen to *come after me.*

Not when I'm so weak around him.

Lifting my chin, I know I only have one option here.

Brazen it out.

"I'm not running anywhere," I say, continuing my slow climb.

When I reach the landing, he blocks my path even though there's plenty of room for the both of us, along with a half dozen more people should the need arise.

I move left. He moves right. I move right. He moves left.

It's a dance. One I'd prefer to sit out, especially when he edges closer, forcing me to retreat a step. Then another. And another until my back is pressed against the cold, concrete wall.

He's not touching me but I still feel trapped, caught between him and the wall. If someone comes by now, if they see us like this, standing too close, they could get the wrong idea.

Or worse. They could get the right one.

"Excuse me," I say.

"Always so polite," he murmurs, his voice scraping against my nerve endings. His gaze travels over my face. "How long are you going to ignore me?"

"I'm not ignoring you."

"Liar."

The word drifts between us, soft and smoky, an accusation that hits me in the chest. Steals my breath. I am a liar. I'm such a liar and I need to stop. I won't be like Chase, lying and keeping secrets.

I won't lose everything like he did.

"You skipped school for a week," Owen continues, "just so you wouldn't have to see me."

I roll my eyes. "Wow. And you say I have a big ego. I didn't *skip* school and it had nothing to do with you. My brother's in the hospital and I was there with my family."

"He okay?" he asks, frowning in concern.

"Yes." If you consider Chase now has to go back to rehab, will miss all his finals for his classes this semester and will possibly have to skip next semester as well so he can get sober and healthy, then yeah. He's doing just great. "Thank you for asking," I say, because it's the polite thing to do and because I'm trying to put us back to where we were two months ago.

Strangers.

"I have to go," I say, the tone of my voice desperate and nervous. I take a step sideways, edging along the wall. He follows. "I have to get something from my locker..."

"We need to talk," he says.

And that is not the course of action I need to take. "I'd rather not."

"I know." His tone is so gentle, so understanding, it makes me want to bawl. "But we have to. Please, Natalie."

I'm tempted. I'm so freaking tempted and he sees it, can sense it because he leans in even closer. "Meet me at your guest house tonight at six."

The guest house. That sounds perfect. Us returning to the scene of the crime. What could go wrong?

The door below us opens with a clang and Owen turns. I take

advantage of his distraction to push past him and jog up the stairs. I feel him watching me.

I don't look back.

* * *

I don't go the guest house that night at six.

I go to Philip's soccer match.

It's a chilly, but still sunny evening, the breeze whipping the flags at the soccer field. The team is warming up off to the side and I spy Philip in his burgundy and gray uniform, his dark hair blowing in the wind.

I cross the track and step onto the grass, walking up behind him to tap him on the shoulder. "Good luck."

He whirls around and smiles. "Nat. I didn't think you'd make it."

Because I have ballet class at 6:30.

Yet one more thing I'll have to catch up on.

But it's worth it, having to make up the class—along with the ones I missed while I was in Altoona—at some point because Philip is so excited I'm here, at his first playoff game. That I'm home.

We've been talking regularly since I texted him Friday morning, about school and soccer and our friends and his family and Chase.

But not about what happened. Not about our fight or that week of silence. Not about where we go from here.

Not about Owen.

It's a streak I'm hoping to continue for...oh...forever would be good.

"I didn't want to miss this," I tell Philip.

Couldn't take the chance of NOT being here. Didn't trust that I'd have the willpower not to go to the guest house.

My stomach turns. Is Owen there now? Is he waiting for me?

I push all those thoughts away.

Philip tugs me aside so we can talk privately. "How's Chase?"

"Better," I say. "They're hoping he can be discharged in a few days."

347

"That's great." His grin widens and he links his hand with mine. "I still can't believe you're here. You never skip ballet."

True. Though he's asked me to before.

But while ballet is important to me, he's more important. It's time I started remembering that.

"I wanted to be here for you," I tell him. "And I...I wanted to apologize, again, face-to-face, for being so..." I wave my hand. "Distant. For acting weird and different lately. I haven't been myself but that's over."

He touches my hair. "I know things have been weird between us and part of it's my fault. It may seem like maybe I didn't trust you, but I do, Nat. I just...I want us to go back to how we used to be."

I want that, too, but I can't get the words out so I just nod then hug him. His arms wrap around me, strong and familiar and I tuck my head under his chin, just like I used to do.

It should feel comfortable, being back in his arms, breathing in his scent. Should feel right.

Instead it feels...off. Cold touches the back of my neck and my skin feels itchy, like ants are crawling over it.

Like I'm trapped.

But that's just my guilt for all the lies I've told. The secrets I've kept.

It's my penance for kissing Owen. For thinking I have feelings for another boy.

So I hold on tighter and make an inner promise to be worthy of Philip's trust from now on. To do whatever I have to do to make this up to him.

No matter what.

* * *

I'm in your driveway. Come out.

That's the text I get while I'm in my bedroom studying late that night.

Even though it only lists the number it's from, not a name, I know it's Owen.

I'd gone to Philip's game, cheered and supported him like a good girlfriend should. Sitting with Astrid and her family wasn't quite as comfortable as it used to be, but her attitude toward me was much less hostile than our last encounter. And she did text me while I was in Altoona, telling me she hopes Chase is okay.

I mean, yeah, she barely said two words to me the entire game but at least she wasn't yelling at or insulting me.

Big improvement over our last face-to-face encounter.

I'll take it.

Rebuilding our friendship, strengthening it to where it used to be is something for me to work on later.

For now, my focus is on Philip.

I need to do whatever it takes to get things between me and Philip back to how they were. And the first step in doing that is to avoid temptation at all costs.

Easier said than done when it keeps testing me.

Oh, and is parked in my driveway.

I don't respond soon enough—okay, I really didn't plan on responding at all—and Owen sends another message.

Come out. Or I'm knocking on your front door.

Crap.

I'm coming, I type back. *Do not—I repeat, DO NOT—knock on my door.*

I kick the covers off and slide out of bed. Tossing on a sweatshirt, I tiptoe into the hallway. It's past midnight and the light under my parents' room is off but Dad is a super light sleeper due to being on call several nights a week and having to wake up at a moment's notice to save a life, so it takes me forever to descend the stairs, stepping carefully to avoid the creak in the fifth step.

In the foyer, I turn off the alarm then hold my breath as I ease the door open. I think I hear something and I freeze, listening so hard it hurts my head, but when Dad fails to materialize and ask me what I'm doing sneaking out of the house at midnight, I step outside.

And realize I'm such an idiot.

And not just because I didn't bother putting on shoes.

But because there's no way Owen is going to knock on my front door at this hour. What would he possibly say? *Your daughter kissed me and I'd like to discuss that with her, in depth, and thought this was the best time to do so?*

No way he would do anything to make my dad upset.

No way he would do anything to get me into trouble.

But even knowing I fell for an idle threat, I still carefully make my way toward his pickup, parked at the end of our driveway out of sight of the house, the pavement damp and cold under my feet.

Worse? When I reach his truck, I open the door and climb in.

He doesn't look at me. "Where were you?"

Though his voice is soft, I startle. Have to swallow before speaking. "In my bedroom."

"No. Earlier. You didn't come to the guest house."

"I...I had something to do."

He stares out the windshield and I know I should leave, that coming out here isn't going to end well but I can't make myself move.

"What did you have to do?" he asks.

"Wha—what?"

He grips the steering wheel, making a back-and-forth motion, like he's strangling it. Back and forth. Back and forth. "What did you have to do? Tonight at six. Instead of being with me?"

The way he says it, *being with me* instead of *meeting me* or *talking to me*, makes my mouth dry. "I went to the soccer game."

His hands still. "You went to Panos."

"He's my boyfriend."

"Is that what you want?"

"What?"

He faces me. "Do you want him to be your boyfriend?"

I open my mouth, expecting a *yes* to come out, a confident and sure sounding, unequivocal assurance that, of course, that's what I want. It's what I've always wanted.

It's what I've decided.

But I can't say anything.

"Why did you kiss me?" Owen asks, and the question has that moment flashing in my mind. The touch of his lips, how it felt to be in his arms.

As if I don't already think about it way too often as it is.

I link my fingers together in my lap. Stare down at my hands. "That was a mistake."

"That's not an answer."

Maybe not, but it's all I have.

He unbuckles his seat belt and slides across the seat and gently turns my face toward him, his fingers warm on my cheek. "Why, Natalie?"

I want to lean into his touch, want to cover his hand with my own.

Instead, I pull away.

It's too easy to forget myself when he touches me, when he's close. When he says my name. "I...I don't know."

"Bullshit. You drove me home from that party because you couldn't stand the thought of me being with another girl."

"No. You were drunk," I say, desperate for him to believe me. For it to be the truth. "I was trying to help you. We're friends—"

"We aren't friends. And that isn't why you lied to get me away from Cora."

I reach for the door handle. "I have to go—"

"Why did you kiss me?" he asks again.

"I don't know," I cry, my voice a wail. "All I know is that it was a mistake. It never should have happened, and it will never happen again. I'm with Philip."

Owen flinches and drops his gaze. "What if..." He inhales and meets my eyes. "What if I told you I didn't want you to be with him? What if I told you I want you to be with me?"

His words, the longing in his gaze rips through me.

The idea of being with him tears me apart.

"It wouldn't matter," I say, but my voice shakes and I have to stop and steady myself. Firm my tone. "It doesn't matter."

I've hurt him. I can see I've hurt him so much, and I hate it. Hate myself.

But I can't change it.

"So that's how it's going to be?" he asks. "You're just going to pretend there's nothing between us?"

"There is nothing between us."

He shakes his head. "What are you so afraid of?"

"Nothing! I just...I don't know why you're doing this."

"Don't you?"

I drop my gaze, my hand still on the door handle.

"When I'm with you," Owen says quietly, "I feel like I can do anything."

My head whips up, my mouth parting. I'm shaking my head, silently begging him not to say anything else. Not to make this harder than it already is, but he continues, relentless and brutal and honest.

"When I'm with you, when you smile at me, I feel like I'm worth something. Like I'm worthy of you."

Tears clog my throat, sting the backs of my eyes but I won't let them fall.

If I do, I may never stop.

"You are worth something," I whisper.

You're worth everything.

He snorts. "Just not worth giving up your safety net."

"Philip's not my safety net."

"He is. He's safe. Familiar. If you break up with him, it'll be a big change. You'll risk your friendships, your social standing, your popularity."

"I'm not..." I swallow. "I'm not with Philip so I can be popular."

"No, you're with him because it's easy. I like you, Natalie," Owen says and my heart leaps with a painful tug. "I like you a lot. And I know it won't be easy for you to pick me. I know that and maybe I'm an asshole for asking you to. But I am asking. Pick me. Please," he says, low and gruff, "please, pick me."

The ache in my throat grows, expands into every cell in my body until I'm filled with pain, each breath a struggle, each beat of my heart agonizing.

Please pick me.

"I can't," I whisper, my voice catching. "I'm sorry. I'm so, so sorry."

Owen is once again staring through the windshield, keeps his gaze there as I finally open the door and lurch out of the truck. It's not until I'm about to shut the door when he speaks again.

"You asked me once if I've ever done anything without thinking through the consequences first." He glances at me. "Remember?"

I don't nod, but of course I remember. It was during our first tutoring session and I was trying to find common ground between him and fictional Holden.

I remember.

I remember everything.

"I lied," he continues, his tone flat and cold. "I told you I hadn't. But with you…" His mouth thins. "With you, I didn't think through the consequences." Now he looks at me straight on and it's with so much hurt and anger, I wish he hadn't. "That was a mistake. One I won't make again."

He shifts into Reverse and slowly starts to back up. I quickly shut the door and step away.

And I watch as he turns around, continue watching until his taillights disappear into the dark night. I stand there and stare at nothing until my feet are numb, my teeth chattering, my entire body shivering violently. From the cold. From Owen's words.

From having to let him go.

Only then do I hurry up the driveway and slip inside my house, lock the door, re-engage the alarm and tiptoe up to my room.

I sit at the end of my bed, sweatshirt pulled down over my feet, arms wrapped around my bent knees.

I rock. Back and forth. Back and forth.

Everything is okay. Everything is how it's supposed to be.

Everything is just fine.

I count the flowers on my wall, like always. Top left corner to right, like reading a book. Then reverse. Then by color, blue, purple, red, pink, yellow and orange. Orange, yellow, pink, red, purple and blue.

But it doesn't help. I'm still shivering uncontrollably. Still numb with cold. Still rocking back and forth. Back and forth.

I'm still out of control.

So I start from the beginning and do it again...

And when that doesn't work, I do it again...

And again...

And again...

50

Over the next four weeks, my life goes back to how it used to be.

Well, for the most part, anyway.

Some things aren't quite the same.

Chase is in rehab—again. This time in Vermont, some place Dad researched that he thinks will be better for Chase's long-term recovery.

And driving has been slightly…problematic.

At first it was fine. Well, maybe not *fine*, but at least I was still able do it.

Lately, though, it's been harder and harder to get behind the wheel.

I still do it, though. I drive Philip to and from school every day, am the designated DD on the weekends for him and his friends. Run errands for Mom and Dad so they don't have to worry about things like getting groceries and picking up Dad's dry-cleaning and bringing home takeout for dinner.

But, unlike the good old days of just a few weeks ago, I don't do it to prove anything.

I do it because I have to.

I do it so no one knows I'm growing more and more afraid of driving. So they'll never suspect that when I'm behind the wheel I have horrible, terrifying delusions of ramming into a tree or running over someone.

I do it so no one will ever be able to tell there's something very, very wrong with me.

My parents don't need that extra worry in their lives right now. And things between me and Philip are finally smooth once again.

No way I'm going to do anything to make waves.

Besides, I've got it under control. The fear. The anxiety. I still do the whole breath-holding thing, but I've also come up with a routine that helps settle my nerves, helps calm me, before I start driving.

Each time I get behind the wheel, I re-adjust my seat and all three mirrors then turn on the ignition. With my foot on the brake, my hands on the wheel, I check the mirrors—left side, rearview, right side, rearview again—then look over my right shoulder. Repeat. Repeat again. Then, and only then, am I able to shift into gear and tootle away.

Not that it works all the time. The few times Philip's beat me to my car after school, I've had to condense the routine and skip the whole re-adjust-the-already-adjusted-seat-and-mirrors steps and ended up white-knuckling the entire drive.

And the other night when I was leaving my house for dance class it was snowing and I panicked. Just sat there, in the garage, the Jeep running, my routine successfully completed, for a good fifteen minutes. Finally, I gave in, turned off the car, grabbed my bag and spent the night in my room.

But other than those two tiny, insignificant changes, everything has gone back to normal.

Dad still works crazy long hours, tells the corniest, groan-worthy jokes and looks at Mom like she's his sun, stars and moon all wrapped up in one beautiful, sparkling package. After spending ten days at the hospital with Chase then helping him get settled at the rehab center, Mom is home, once again working furiously on getting Kaleidoscope up and running before Christmas.

Astrid and I are slowly working on mending our friendship. She still spends most of her time with Sean but I've managed to talk her into spending the night with me once and we've hung out a few times after school. I've stopped spending time with Mary Alice outside of dance class, which wasn't an easy decision, but I need to focus on making things right with Astrid. Need to keep focused on my relationship with Philip.

As for me and Philip, we're as strong as ever.

I don't talk to Owen. Not even when I pass him in the hallway. No cheery, polite hello. No smile. I lower my head, count the colored tiles and walk right on past him.

And when I start to think about him—which still happens way more often than it should—I count or list items instead.

About time my quirks came in handy.

Even if some of them are getting just a little bit out of hand. Like having to turn the light off three times when I leave a room or go to bed. Or how I wash my hair, my body and my hands three times before moving on with my life.

Or how I stay awake until after I'm sure my parents are both asleep, slip downstairs and re-set the alarm. Three times. Just to make sure.

Yeah, those things aren't great. But for the most part, the most important things are back to how they used to be.

Just how I wanted them to be.

* * *

The morning after Thanksgiving, Mom and Dad leave to visit Chase in rehab.

He didn't want me to come.

I haven't seen him at all, haven't spoken to him. During his weekly calls home, he refuses to talk to me, even though both Mom and Dad have tried to get him to change his mind. I've written him letters, two every week, sent on Monday and Thursday mornings—but he's yet to respond.

I don't know what I did wrong. Why he won't talk to me.

I don't know how to fix it and it kills me.

So when Philip suggested we have a party at my house Saturday night, I agreed.

I didn't want to be alone.

I'm rethinking that. Big time.

My house is packed with people, most of whom I don't even know. That's what happens when your boyfriend issues an open invitation to his friends—of which there are many. But it's fine. I mean, it's great that so many people showed up. That they're having fun drinking in my kitchen and living room. Hooking up in the basement. It's awesome that they're smoking on the porch. Getting high on the patio.

It's fan-freaking-tabulous.

The best part? Jessica is here. At my house. Leaning heavily against Philip's side as she whispers something in his ear.

I down the rest of my strawberry margarita and go in search of my third.

But, someone must've tilted the house because I seem to be tipping to the side. I right myself. Keep walking, focusing on slow, steady footsteps.

I'm pouring the pink, icy concoction that Hannah Greer whipped up in my mom's blender into my cup when Astrid joins me.

"You'd better take it easy on those," she says, frowning at the amount I'm pouring. "Hannah's got a heavy hand with the tequila."

I shrug. "I'm fine."

Yes, indeed, fine is exactly what I am. I'm fine with the way my life is going. I'm fine with my brother's relapse. With him not answering my letters. With him not wanting to see me. I'm fine with my best friend still treating me with barely hidden disdain. I'm fine that I basically ghosted Mary Alice, one of the nicest people I know.

And I'm fine that my boyfriend is drinking and laughing it up with a girl I can't stand.

In. My. Living. Room.

I take a drink and motion with it to Philip, almost dumping it on Astrid—which would just be a crying shame as it is delicious. Sweet and tart without the slightest horrible taste of tequila to be found.

"Why is she even here?" I ask of Jessica. "Did he invite her?"

Astrid follows my gaze then looks back at me. "Who knows? But don't make a big deal about it."

I frown at her. "What do you mean don't make a big deal? She's flirting with him right in front of me."

And he's not stopping her.

"Look," Astrid says, "you and Philip are just now getting back to normal. Don't ruin it by acting all jealous."

I gape at her which, okay, could be due to the two and a half drinks I've had, but still...

"I'm not jealous."

Sad part? That's true. Or maybe I'm a little bit jealous but mostly I'm irritated that he'd disrespect me like that. That he'd invite her to this party when he knows she wants to get with him. That he'd let her flirt with him, that he'd smile and laugh and flirt back, right in front of me.

I'm pissed that I gave up so much—Mary Alice and Owen and what I wanted—and Philip gave up nothing. Nothing.

I down the rest of my drink in three, long, brain-freeze inducing gulps, slam my plastic cup on my cluttered kitchen counter.

And head his way.

Astrid grabs my arm, stopping me. "Don't make a scene. It's not something to get upset about. Philip loves you."

"I'm not going to make a scene," I say with as much dignity as I can considering the buzz I've got going. "I'm just going to gently extricate him from her presence."

Astrid lets go and I make my way through the throng. These people...they're animals. Rude, disrespectful, *loud* animals. My house is a mess—empty bottles and abandoned plastic cups litter every available flat surface, chip crumbs are scattered over the sofa and the no matter what room I'm in, the floor is sticky with spilled alcohol.

They have no respect. Not for me or my parents or our home.

I can't help but think they're not the only ones. Not when I'm reminded that when this party is over—which can't come soon enough—I'm going to be the one tasked with cleaning up.

Not Astrid, my supposed best friend.

Not Philip, the brilliant mastermind behind this shindig.

Me.

My eyes sting but I blink rapidly. I will not be one of those girls who starts blubbering like a baby after a few drinks.

I will be strong.

In control.

I pass a group of idiots playing Beer Pong on my mom's antique coffee table—the only thing she has of her grandmother's—the bottoms of the cups leaving rings, beer sloshing out whenever the ball bounces into a cup. And I just...stop. My stomach turning, my fingers curling like claws.

I stop and I stand there but I don't say anything.

I'm afraid if I open my mouth I'll start screaming.

And I won't stop.

Forcing myself to move, I continue on, my stomach still twitchy. I blow out a heavy breath and walk up to Philip.

Force myself to smile because Astrid is right. It's taken weeks for Philip and me to get to this point, to get back to normal. I don't want to ruin it now.

Not when I've worked so hard, given up so much, to get to this point.

"Hey," I say, pressing against his side.

But when he wraps his arm around my waist and pulls me even closer, it takes all I have not to step away.

He smiles down at me. "Hey, babe."

I lean over to give Jessica a bright grin. "Hi, Jessica! Having fun?"

She gives me that old, familiar evil eye then looks at Philip. "I'll talk to you later."

"She's a very rude person," I tell Philip.

"Don't let her get to you," he says, playing with my hair.

Unease pricks the base of my spine and I want to swat his hand away.

I fight both.

"I wonder who told her about the party," I say, which isn't exactly accusing him of doing it.

It's fishing for information.

He doesn't bite. "Could've been anyone." He slides his hand lower on my hip. Leans down to whisper. "Let's go upstairs."

I stiffen. Look around. "And leave these people unsupervised? God only knows what kind of damage they'll do."

Filthy animals.

He laughs even though I wasn't trying to be funny. "Come on. It'll be fine. Astrid's down here. She'll keep everyone in line."

Well, he's right about one thing. Astrid is down here, but she's sitting on Sean's lap, the only time she's left his side when she came into the kitchen to tell me how to act and what I should and shouldn't say to my boyfriend.

"Come on," Philip repeats, gently steering me toward the stairs. "It'll be fine. Trust me."

I have to bite my tongue so I don't snap back something I shouldn't. Like, *the way you trusted me?*

Then again, I did kiss another guy so maybe his mistrust was accurate.

But I am not thinking about Owen. Not now. I gave all that up. It's in the past. He has no place in my here and now, my perfect life.

And if I think about him, I might just slip up and say something to Philip about that kiss.

So I let Philip lead me upstairs. Of course, it takes a while as we're stopped every few feet with someone else wanting to talk to my boyfriend.

We get to my room—at least Philip made it clear at the beginning of the party that no one was allowed upstairs—and he flips on the lamp next to the bed then walks toward me.

"Come here," he says, all husky.

Used to be that tone sent a shiver of anticipation through me. A thrill. Pleasure.

Tonight all that's there is dread.

I push it aside. Let him pull me into his arms. His hands immediately go to my ass, cupping me through my jeans, pulling me against him. My heart starts pounding but it's not in a good way, not in the way it should so I wrap my arms around his neck, meet his mouth for a hot, heavy kiss.

We haven't been alone like this in weeks. Not since that night in the kitchen when my dad walked in on us. Haven't been together like this since the night at the guest house.

We could have, we've had several opportunities, but I've made excuses every time. Worry about Chase. Needing to get home before curfew. A case of the oncoming sniffles I didn't want him to catch.

I've run out of them.

He's kissing me and kissing me and I'm doing my best to keep up, to quiet my mind, to kiss him back when I hear a noise, a loud thump. I lift my head. Look behind me. "The door…"

"No one's coming up here," he says, moving his mouth to my neck. "We told them not to."

Yes, but now that we've broken that rule, they might think they can, too.

"Philip…"

He gives me a quick peck on the nose. "I'll lock it."

He crosses the room and I stand there, arms wrapped around my waist, shoulders hunched, skin chilled though it's warm in here.

When he comes back, he takes me by the hand and sits on the bed. Tugs me down beside him. Plays with my fingers. Strokes my wrist and my palm, his gaze on what he's doing.

Then he tugs my hand over and places it on his zipper.

I try to pull it back but he holds it there. "What if someone comes up here looking for us?"

"They won't," he says, voice husky, eyes heavy-lidded. He trails the fingers of his free hand down the side of my neck. "Astrid won't let them. And if they do, we'll hear them coming up the stairs."

That creaky fifth step.

But I'm undecided for too long and he takes my silence as permission, presses my hand harder against him and leans over to kiss me.

I don't stop him.

I don't stop him when he slides his hand under the hem of my sweater, his fingers cool against my stomach. Or when he pulls my sweater up and off, tossing it to the floor.

I don't stop him when he drags me closer.

I don't stop him when he leans me back.

I don't stop him when he lays on top of me.

I don't stop him. I just lay there, heart pounding, eyes wide open. He's kissing my throat and neck, hands smoothing over me, body pressing against mine.

It's what we've done before. What I used to love. What I was desperate for only two months ago when I dragged him into the guest house. A few weeks ago when we were alone in my kitchen.

But it's not what I want now. Not tonight.

Except I don't know how to tell him. Don't want him to get upset. Don't know how to explain. Don't want to ruin what I've worked so hard to make right between us.

So I don't say anything.

And I don't stop him.

I stare at the flowers on my wall, eyes burning. Try to count them but the lamp isn't bright enough and the edges between them are all blurry and I keep losing count. My stomach roils and I begin to sweat.

Philip's hand covers my breast over my bra and I squeeze my eyes shut. Start listing the states in alphabetical order.

Alabama...Alaska...Arizona...Arkansas...

He grinds against me and I swallow. Swallow again. My hands shake. My fingers curl.

California...Colorado...Connecticut...Delaware...

He reaches between us, for his zipper or mine, and I can't fight the sick feeling inside of me any longer, can't hold it back.

"Get off!" I gasp, shoving at him, bile rising in my throat. "Off!"

He bolts upright, face a mask of confusion. "Nat, what—"

I shove harder, legs kicking, body twisting and he leaps back, freeing me. I scramble to my feet and run into my bathroom. Slam the door shut and lock it. Then fall to my knees in front of the toilet and throw up again and again, until I'm empty. Until I'm numb.

51

I cover my mouth, trying to hold back the hysterical sob rising in my throat.

No, I'm not okay. Leaning against the wall behind me, I hug my knees to my chest and lay my head on them, watering eyes squeezed shut. I rock. Back and forth. Back and forth. I'm shivering with cold and exhausted, my throat is raw from throwing up, my stomach still churning.

This wasn't supposed to happen. I was supposed to be getting better.

It's not fair. I did everything right. Everything.

But the harder I try to pretend I'm fine, the more I try to control, the tighter I hold on to who I used to be, the further from okay I get.

Philip jiggles the handle then pounds on the door again. "Babe," he says, his tone urgent. Worried. "Let me in." More jiggling. More pounding. More urgency when he repeats, "Let me in."

And I have a sudden vision of him getting help from a few of his burlier friends and busting into my bathroom, only to find me rocking back and forth on the floor, half-naked and in the throes of some sort of mental breakdown.

I roll onto my hands and knees then push myself to standing. "One minute," I say, but it's little more than a croak.

Luckily, it's enough. The jiggling and pounding stop.

I shakily cross to the sink and turn on the water then lift my head. My reflection stares back at me. I look haunted. Wide-eyed and pale, eye makeup smeared, trails of mascara running down my cheeks. Bending, I splash water on my face. Realize there's puke in my hair and do my best to rinse it out.

I want to shower. I want to scrub myself clean but I can't. Philip's waiting for me. And my house is full of people. So I put my hair up in a sloppy bun. Wash my hands—three times—then brush my teeth. And when I finally unlock the door, the handle turns beneath my hand and Philip pulls the door open.

"Hey," he says softly, watching me closely. "Feeling better?"

I open my mouth to tell him yes but the lie won't come out. I swallow. "Sorry. I..." But there's too much going on in my head, too many things I can't explain. Too many things I can never tell him. "Sorry," I say again.

Wrapping his arm around my shoulder, he kisses my forehead. Guides me to the bed. "How much did you drink tonight?"

As soon as we reach the bed, I shrug out of his hold and grab my sweater and pull it on. Keep my back to him, my arms crossed.

He thinks I'm drunk. That I got sick because of my three margaritas. And maybe he's right. Maybe that's exactly what happened.

But it's not all that happened.

No matter how much I want it to be.

"Come on," he says, trailing his hand down the back of my arm. "Let's go downstairs. Get you some ginger ale."

He's being sweet. Considerate. Like he used to be when we first started going out. He really does care about me. And I care about him. I do.

Maybe that's all it takes. Us caring about each other. Wanting to make it work. Maybe it's enough.

But then I think about all those mornings when I show up at The Fat Greek and find him surrounded by girls. How Jessica was flirting with him downstairs, right in front of me. How he ditched me to go to parties with his buddies.

I think about all the mistakes I've made. My secrets and lies.

And suddenly I know, without a doubt, that wanting something to work, caring about someone, even loving them, isn't enough. Not always.

Sometimes, it just keeps you stuck.

"Philip," I say, sitting on the edge of the bed, but tears clog my throat and I have to stop. Clear them away. "Philip, I—I can't do this."

One corner of his mouth lifts. "Yeah. I figured that out when you shoved me off and locked yourself in the bathroom."

He thinks I'm talking about sex. That I'm telling him I can't have sex with him right now.

I shake my head. "No. That's not what I meant. I can't...I can't do *this*. I can't...I can't be with you anymore."

He frowns in confusion. Disbelief. "What?"

I'm trembling, my legs jiggling. I can't stop. Can't stay still. I'm afraid if I do, everything inside of me, my doubts and fears and all the wrong choices I've made, will build and build and I'll explode.

I force myself to meet his eyes. "I can't be with you anymore."

His head goes back. "You're breaking up with me?"

"I'm sorry," I whisper.

"You're *sorry*? What the fuck, Nat?" He stabs both hands into his hair. Tugs on it. "Why are you doing this? Is it because of Radlowski?"

"No. It's because of me." My eyes well. "I thought if I tried hard enough, I could make this work."

He crouches in front of me. Lays his hands on my knees. "It is working. We're working. Just like we used to."

"That's just it. I don't want us to be like we used to."

His expression hardens. "I don't believe this. After everything we've gone through..." He stands and paces to the door. Whirls around and jabs a finger in my direction. "You came back to me! You told me you wanted a second chance. And now you're just going to walk away?"

"I have to," I whisper.

For me.

"If you do this," he says, "it's sticking. I mean it, Nat. I'm not going to keep going back and forth."

I nod. "I know."

"Fuck this," he snarls and opens the door.

"I'm sorry," I say again but he's already gone.

I follow him slowly and when I reach the first floor, he's obviously upset and is telling Astrid about it. She looks up and sees me standing at the bottom of the stairs. I don't move even as she storms up to me.

Don't do more than blink when she tosses her drink in my face.

"Bitch," she says, her expression daring me to respond.

To retaliate.

I just wipe the wetness from my face with my sleeve. "Make sure he gets home okay," I tell her quietly. Then I brush past her. We've gathered a crowd and it's quiet as no one wants to miss the excitement.

Jessica is eagerly gobbling it up from her spot in the doorway.

"I want everyone out," I say. They don't move. Just look to each other, look to Philip as if for permission and something inside of me...it just snaps.

"Out!" I scream and several of them jump, more scurry out of my way as I plunge into the crowd, start shoving people toward the door.

But it doesn't matter. Doesn't matter what they think about me. Doesn't matter how out of control I am. Doesn't matter that I'm yelling and crying in front of them all, that there's puke in my hair and strawberry margarita dripping down my neck.

Let them see.

For once, I don't care.

"Out, out, out!" I hold up my phone. "If anyone is still here five minutes from now, I'm calling the cops."

It's that threat, that promise, that finally gets them moving. Grumbling, pissed off and shooting me dirty looks or calling me names under their breath but moving.

Philip walks out without a backward glance, a bottle of whiskey in his hand.

Jessica calls his name and runs after him.

Astrid is still at the bottom of the stairs but I no longer care what she thinks. I've put in so much work, so much time and effort and both she and Philip took it for granted.

No more.

"You said Philip deserves better than me," I remind her softly as people pass us, shooting us curious looks. "And maybe you're right. Or maybe..." I step closer and lower my voice. "Maybe I'm the one who deserves better than either of you."

She goes white, her mouth open in shock or denial. Doesn't matter.

Our friendship is over. Has been over for a long time.

Finally she turns on her heel and stomps over to Sean who's waiting by the door. Tugs him out.

In less than three minutes my house is empty once again.

Everything in my life has changed and I can't tell if I'm terrified.

Or elated.

Probably equal parts of both.

I lock all the doors, set and reset the alarm (three times) then spend the next twenty minutes going room to room, checking closets and under the beds to make sure I really am alone.

Then I do what I should've done weeks ago.

I make a phone call.

"It's me," I say as soon as it's picked up. "I know you probably don't ever want to talk to me again but I could really use a friend right now."

52

"You okay?" Mary Alice asks the next morning as we sit in her car.

I nod. "Yeah. Thanks again. For everything."

I broke down on the phone with her last night—complete and utter meltdown, sobbing and gasping for breath, a freak-out for the ages.

And instead of hanging up on, instead of giving up on me, she showed up at my house half an hour later with a bag of double stuff Oreos, two pints of Ben & Jerry's and a gallon of chocolate milk.

I don't deserve her but I'm so, so grateful to have her as a friend.

I'm even more grateful that she forgave me for being such a crappy one these past few weeks.

Last night, I was too scared to shower while I was alone in the house and as soon as Mary Alice took one look at me, she slipped her arm around my waist and led me upstairs. While I showered—a twenty-minute ordeal, what with the repetitive lathering and rinsing —she cleaned the kitchen, helped me clean the rest of the house when I came down. Then we ordered pizza to offset the sweet of our snacks. And we talked. A lot. I told her about the party. That I broke up with Philip. That Astrid and I are no longer friends.

But I didn't tell her everything. I didn't tell her the most important things.

There's someone else I need to tell first.

Last night was the first time in weeks that my life finally felt really, truly normal.

That I felt like me.

"You can do this," Mary Alice tells me now.

She's right. I can do this.

No more hiding. No more pretending.

I get out and check for cars then tempt the traffic Gods by jogging across the middle of the street. There's a dusting of snow on the ground, covering the grass with white.

No Barbies, naked or otherwise, are in sight.

I quickly climb the porch steps and knock on the door.

Please be home. Please, please, be home.

A woman a few inches shorter than I am opens the door. He looks like her, Owen does. He looks like his mom.

And for some reason, that makes me want to smile.

She's pretty with glasses and a slightly round face, her hair two shades darker than Owen's, her eyes the same blue as his. "Can I help you?" she asks.

"Is...is Owen home?"

Her eyes narrow, her mouth pinches. I see where Piper gets that suspicious streak. "And you are?"

Except I'm pretty sure she already knows who I am.

She knows and she's not the least bit happy I'm here.

I switch the sweatshirt I'm holding from my left hand to my right and wish I had on something nicer than yoga pants and my puffy winter coat. That I'd done more to my hair than pull it back. That I'd put on some mascara and lip gloss.

First impressions are important.

"I'm Natalie. Natalie Hewitt."

Her frown deepens, her lips all but disappear.

Yikes. What did Owen tell her about me?

Nothing good it seems.

Now I really wish I was more presentable.

Looking good is great armor.

"I'll see if he's home," she says.

And shuts the door.

I purse my lips. Okay. That hadn't gone exactly as I'd hoped but I'm not going to be discouraged.

At least she didn't shove me off her porch.

I wait, shivering despite my coat and gloves, the thin material of my yoga pants no match for the cold breeze. A minute passes. Then two.

Then I hear the fall of heavy footsteps inside just before the door opens.

And Owen's there, in front of me wearing a pair of gray sweatpants and that blue sweatshirt he wore to my tennis match.

I was right. It does bring out his eyes.

His hair is sticking up and there's a sleep mark on his cheek.

It's ridiculously cute.

What's not cute? Me dragging him out of bed first thing Sunday morning.

"Did your mom wake you up? I'm so sorry!"

"What are you doing here?" he asks.

Okay, that whole not being discouraged thing is getting harder and harder to do. "I wanted to give this back to you," I say, holding out his sweatshirt. "I'm sorry I kept it so long."

He stares at it, reminding me of that moment in his truck when he handed me his T-shirt to dry my face and I wonder if he's going to refuse accepting it. If he's going to let me keep it.

I really, really hope he lets me keep it.

But then he reaches out, taking it from me, careful, I notice, not to touch me.

Not to look at me.

Behind him, we're gathering quite the audience. His mom. Piper.

Piper waves. I wave back then focus on Owen again.

"Could you..." I tip my head to the right. He doesn't move. I sigh.

"We went over this before, remember? This—" I tip my head again. "—means, could you please come outside?"

Before Gus and his mom's creepster boyfriend join us, too.

Mouth a grim line, he steps out onto the porch, pulling the door shut behind him.

His feet are bare.

His feet are bare and it's freezing out, snow dusting the porch, and I've asked him to stand outside while I stare at him and try to find the courage to tell him what I came here to tell him.

Good God.

"What, Natalie?" he asks and while he's not exactly snapping at me, he's not all that patient, either.

Not like he normally is.

"My brother's in rehab," I blurt.

He frowns. "What?"

That wasn't where I'd planned to start when I went over—and over and over—my speech in my head, but maybe that's what I need to do. Less planning. More doing.

"My brother. Chase. Everyone thinks he was hurt in wreck because we only tell them there was an accident, but he overdosed."

I'm talking fast, the words rushing together but I can't slow down. Can't stop. It's the first truth, the first full truth, I've told in what seems like years and the more I speak, the lighter I feel, that constant pressure inside of me lessening. Just a little.

"He's an addict. He got addicted in high school but was sober for a few years. I don't know what happened because he won't talk to me. He won't answer my letters—he can't have a phone in rehab and when he calls home Sunday nights he'll only talk to Mom or Dad. He wouldn't let me see him in the hospital or visit him at the facility... and I..." I take a much-needed breath. "I don't know what I did to make him mad at me."

Unlike the boy in front of me.

I know very well why he's mad.

"He's embarrassed," Owen says.

I blink. "What? I mean...excuse me?"

"Your brother. He's probably embarrassed. Or he just doesn't want you to see him that way. Doesn't want you to think of him as weak. That's what I'd do. If it was me. I wouldn't want Piper or Gus to see me in rehab."

"I never thought of it like that," I say softly. "Thank you."

But my gratitude only seems to irritate him further.

And believe me, he was plenty irritated to begin with.

"Mary Alice drove me here," I tell him, the next truth I need to say. "I've been having some...problems...driving. A month ago, the night of Chase's overdose, I...I had a...a breakdown or panic attack on the Fourth Avenue Bridge and somedays I can't drive. So I asked her to bring me here. So I could return your sweatshirt and so...so I could talk to you."

"We said everything we have to say to each other."

"I broke up with Philip last night."

That gets his attention. He goes rigid, his shoulders tense, his jaw tight.

But he doesn't speak. Doesn't make this easier on me.

That's okay. I don't need easy. Not anymore.

"Things...things have been different between us for a while now," I continue, "and I just...I couldn't. I couldn't keep pretending it wasn't."

"Why are you telling me this?"

"Because..." I inhale deeply. "Because I like you. I like you so much."

He drops his gaze, his grip on the sweatshirt so tight, his knuckles are white. "Nata—"

"I like you," I repeat. "But I didn't break up with Philip for you. I...just...I can't be with him right now. I can't be with anyone. Not until... not until I get my life straightened out. But I'm going to. I'm going to straighten it out and when I do, I hope...I hope you'll give me another chance."

He hesitates, his gaze still on the ground, his hands now twisting the sweatshirt and I hold my breath, that hope I told him about filling me.

But then he shakes his head once. Takes a half step back. And says the words that scare me the most. "It's too late."

I promised myself I wouldn't cry. I've done enough of that already. Too much. But the tears come unbidden. "It doesn't have to be."

"Maybe not but…" He shrugs. And finally meets my eyes. "It'd never work between us anyway."

It hurts. It hurts so much, and I can't help but think this is what I deserve. For hurting him first. For being such a coward. For not being brave enough to tell him how I felt last month when we sat in his truck in my driveway.

For all my lies.

"You're wrong," I whisper.

There's no softening in his expression. No regret.

Just determination.

"Guess we'll never know," he says then turns and opens the door.

Walking away from me for the last time.

"The last time we talked," I say, and he stops just inside the door-way, keeping his back to me, "you asked me what I was afraid of. I lied. I told you nothing but the truth is, I'm afraid of everything. I was afraid of staying with Philip and afraid of not being with him. I'm afraid my brother isn't going to get better. I'm afraid of the future and of making a mistake and taking a risk. I'm afraid of failing and not being good enough. I'm just…I'm terrified. All the time. About every-thing. But when I'm with you…"

My voice breaks and I stop. Inhale and hold it for the count of five then exhale slowly. "When I'm with you," I repeat quietly, "I'm not so scared. When I'm with you, I can breathe. And I just…I wanted you to know that."

I wait, breath held, and count the seconds.

One two three four five.

Five four three two one.

One two three four five.

Five four three two one.

There's nothing more I can say, no more truths I can share, so I turn and hurry down the steps, but as I walk toward Mary Alice's car, I keep hoping Owen will stop me. That he'll stop me. That he'll come after me. Give me that second chance I asked for.

He doesn't.

And I have to learn to live with that.

53

After we leave Owen's house, I ask Mary Alice to stop by Kaleidoscope. While she waits in the car, I run inside and gather what I need then put it in the trunk.

As she drives me home, I tell her the truth about Chase. About my issues with driving.

About my feelings for Owen.

Though I'm guessing she already figured that part out.

She offers to stay with me until my parents get home tonight but there's something I need to do and I need to do it alone. So after she drops me off, I lock all the doors, check them all three times then set and re-set the alarm.

I go to my room and lay everything I'll need on the floor then spread out the drop cloth I brought from Kaleidoscope over the carpet.

The paint is called Iron Mountain. Mom used it on the shelves where she's going to use to display jewelry from local artisans.

It's a dark gray with a purple undertone I figured would sort of go with the three lavender walls.

Plus, it was the fullest can there and I'm guessing I'm going to need more than one coat.

I set everything out on the drop cloth: paint can, roller tray, roller, stir stick, tape, and two paint brushes—a regular one and an angled one for the corners.

It's time I took control of my life. Real control.

Every habit has a trigger. Replace the trigger and you can break the habit.

Change one thing, and everything changes.

And the easiest, the fastest way to stop counting the flowers on my wall, is to erase them.

But first, I count them one more time.

One last time.

Top left to bottom right—like a book. Bottom right to top left. Blue, purple, red and pink, yellow and orange. Orange, yellow, pink and red, purple and blue.

I count them again.

And again.

Then I dip the brush into the paint. It'd be easier, faster, to use the roller, but I can't. I have to do it this way. With the brush. One at a time.

I climb onto my desk chair and paint over the light blue tulip in the top left corner, covering it in Iron Mountain. Then I move to the right, like reading a book, and paint over the next one. Then the next. And the next.

One, by one, by one...subtracting from eighty-three as I go.

The End

* * *

If you enjoyed Counting Flowers, I hope you'll considering leaving a review.

* * *

Thank you so much for reading Counting Flowers! Natalie's story—and her quirks—are near and dear to my heart. I, too, wish I had more control over many aspects of my life and often feel anxious when that control is hard to find. Since my husband read the book, he often points out ways that Natalie and are alike. Counting Flowers was actually meant to be a different book. I started out writing about Natalie's life AFTER dealing with all the changes that take place for her in Counting Flowers, but the more I wrote, the more I wanted to experience those changes with her. What began as a way to explore Natalie's backstory, grew into an entire book. And while Counting Flowers concludes certain aspects, Natalie's story will continue in book 2, coming early 2020!

* * *

Want all the updates, sneak peeks of upcoming releases, cover reveals, exclusive excerpts, giveaways and more? Sign up for my newsletter at www.bethandrews.net/contact

* * *

Check out my website - www.bethandrews.net

Sign up for my newsletter - www.bethandrews.net/contact

Find me on:

Facebook - www.facebook.com/bethandrewsauthor
Instagram - www.instagram.com/bethandrewsauthor

If you're interested in my small-town, contemporary adult romances, or my shorter, sexier stories, written as Bebe Marks, please check my website at www.bethandrews.net/books for a complete list of all my available books.

ACKNOWLEDGMENTS

This book is a dream come true for me and it wouldn't have been possible without help from some amazing people.

Special thanks to my wonderful editor Wanda Ottewell for her hard work and enthusiasm.

Thank you to Su at Earthy Charms for designing the cover and Kayla Johnson for proofreading.

Love and gratitude to my family for always believing in me.

ABOUT THE AUTHOR

Beth Andrews is the award-winning author of over 20 contemporary romance novels. She lives in Northwestern Pennsylvania and loves coffee, hockey and '80s teen movies. This is her first young adult novel.

Visit Beth at her website - www.bethandrews.net
Sing up for her newsletter - www.bethandrews.net/contact
Email her at: beth@bethandrews.net